Love, loneliness, adventure, crime, humor, and ghosts, all the ingredients of great short stories appear in this collection. Here are gems from the writing of Maugham, Conrad, Mansfield, Kipling, Plomer, Wells, Pritchett, Chesterton, Forster, Lawrence, Graves, Mayne, and Moore—men and women who have brought the art of the English short story to a brilliant peak. With a general Foreword and individual introductions to each of the thirteen stories, by Christopher Isherwood, this volume is guaranteed to provide pleasure when it is read for instruction, instruction when it is read for pleasure.

ABOUT THE EDITOR

Born in England, Christopher Bradshaw-Isherwood has lived in Santa Monica since 1939. After his first novel, *All the Conspirators,* appeared in 1928, Isherwood went to Berlin, where he lived for the better part of four years. During the 'thirties he traveled in Europe as a correspondent, and made a trip to China. In collaboration with W. H. Auden, he wrote three plays. *Goodbye to Berlin* (1939), a collection of short stories, includes "Sally Bowles," the basis for the movie *I Am a Camera. Prater Violet* (1945) and a fictional biography, *Lions and Shadows* (1947), have been followed by several works on Indian religion, and by screenplays including, currently, *Jean Christophe.*

Great English Short Stories

Edited, and with a Foreword
and Introductions
by Christopher Isherwood

Published by
DELL PUBLISHING COMPANY, INC.
261 Fifth Avenue
New York 16, N. Y.

Library of Congress Catalog Card No. 57-8264

Designed and produced by
Western Printing & Lithographing Company

Cover design by John Alcorn

Dedicated to: DON BACHARDY

Printed in U.S.A.

ACKNOWLEDGMENTS The following selections in this anthology are reproduced by permission of the authors, their publishers, or their agents:

"The Secret Sharer" by Joseph Conrad, from 'TWIXT LAND AND SEA by Joseph Conrad. Reprinted by permission of J. M. Dent & Sons Ltd.

"The Invisible Man" by G. K. Chesterton, from THE INNOCENCE OF FATHER BROWN by G. K. Chesterton, Copyright © 1910, 1938, by Frances Chesterton. Reprinted by permission of Dodd, Mead & Company, Inc.

"Albert Nobbs" by George Moore, from CELIBATE LIVES by George Moore, Copyright © 1954, by C. D. Medley. Reprinted by permission of Liveright Publishers, New York.

First printing—May, 1957

CONTENTS

Foreword

If I had called this anthology "Thirteen Worlds" some people might have bought it by mistake as science fiction and then complained that they had been cheated. Nevertheless, the title would have been accurately descriptive. Each one of these stories represents—for me, at least—a part of a world; a world that I can share with its author.

There are plenty of excellent stories which are just stories; they express nothing beyond themselves. When they have been told to you, you say "that was exciting" or "that was funny" or "I certainly never expected *that* ending!" You can retell such a story in your own words to your friends and it will lose little in the retelling, provided that you remember all the important details and get them in the right order. But you can never adequately retell in other words a story which is part of a world, because, in such a story, every sentence does something to help create the sound of the characters' voices, the smell of the atmosphere, the feel of the setting. This kind of story is larger than itself; it also serves as an entrance-gate to its author's world—and by "world" I mean not only the rest of his works but also the kind of people and places he may be expected to write about in the future or about which he might have written if he had lived longer: his entire artistic potentiality. Such a story, in fact, sets the responsive reader storytelling for himself; inventing characters and situations in the manner of its author. (The world of Ernest Hemingway, for example, is nowadays as crowded as a national park; and I remember nostalgically how I used to visit it before the season opened.) A story which is just a story—an anecdote merely designed to amaze you or thrill you or make you laugh—can never produce this effect upon the reader. It is not an entrance-gate. It leads nowhere.

I have made no attempt here to be definitive, as they call it—to trace the development of the Short Story in the British Isles and select the best examples of its most important types. That is one kind of anthology; valuable for students, perhaps, but a weary and dreary job for the anthologist, since there is nothing in Life or Art so depressing as that which one admires but does not love—and how can one love what is utterly and unquestionably The Best? The other kind of anthology—the kind I have tried to make—is, or should be, autobiographical. I, the anthologist, must not waste time guessing what the reader's taste may be; I must boldly confess my own. The reader may not approve of it or of me, but at least my book will have a certain individuality.

The worst of short stories is that they are short. That very economy in the telling which is imposed by the medium of the short story is liable to stunt its characters and thin its atmosphere by denying them enough space to develop in. This does not matter so much if you read a whole volume of stories by the same author, for they will lend each other substance. But in an anthology, where each author is represented by a single specimen only, the experience of reading any one story is over much too soon. Also, there is a curious "seepage" between authors, like the mingling of flavors among foods placed too close together in an icebox; it is nearly impossible to appreciate Kipling while you have the taste of Forster still in your mouth. To avoid the first of these disadvantages, I have preferred the longer of any two possible choices. To avoid the second, I can only advise you not to read more than one story at a sitting.

I began by arranging these stories according to their authors' birth-dates; but this didn't seem to make sense because the story itself may belong to the author's early, middle or late period. For example, Maugham comes sixth on the list in order of birth and Lawrence ninth, but Maugham's contribution to this book was written after Lawrence's. Finally, I decided to arrange the stories more or less according to the period in which they are set—pre-1914, World-War One, the Twenties, the Thirties.

Five of my authors are still alive as I write this. But the youngest of them is over fifty. The reader may well ask: Why is there no representative of the younger generation? Why is there no story set in the period of World-War Two or after?

I am sorry for this. But, as I have said above, this book reflects my own taste; it is not the work of a literary historian. I could politely blame myself by saying that I am past fifty and therefore, no doubt, subconsciously envious of the young and prejudiced against their products. But that would be insincere. If this were an anthology of American authors, I should have no difficulty in finding at least half a dozen stories to include, all of them written since 1939 by men and women who are still young or youngish today. I can certainly praise without any reservations several novels produced by young English writers during this same period, but I cannot say as much about any short stories. What does this prove? I leave the reader to decide.

Two of the stories I wished to include—Conan Doyle's *The Speckled Band* and Dylan Thomas' *One Warm Saturday*—had to be dropped from the anthology. It was not possible to obtain permission to reprint the Dylon Thomas story. The Trustee of the Conan Doyle Estate made it a condition of his agreement that my comments on the story should be submitted to him and subjected to his editing. This condition I rejected on principle, believing it to be an unallowable kind of censorship.

CHRISTOPHER ISHERWOOD
March, 1957

JOSEPH CONRAD

The Secret Sharer

Joseph Conrad was born in Poland in 1857, his full baptismal name being Jozef Teodor Konrad Nalecz Korzeniowski. However, he spent fifteen years at sea in English ships, first as a seaman and later as an officer, was naturalized a British subject and eventually settled down to live in England until his death in 1924. During his last twenty years, he became an acknowledged master of English fiction.

Yet he remained essentially an alien. And this was to his advantage as a writer. It gave him a critical distance from his subject-matter and his style is enhanced by the attractive strangeness of his foreign accent. Take this sentence from *The Nigger of the Narcissus:*

> A big, foaming sea came out of the mist; it made for the ship, roaring wildly, and in its rush it looked as mischievous and discomposing as a madman with an axe.

There is the characteristic tone of Conrad—the tone of a man who is acccustomed to confront danger with coolly observant detachment. The adjective "discomposing" sounds oddly prim and foreign, even if it was deliberately chosen for the humor of the understatement. And then we have a touch of Conrad's greatness, in the simple and appalling power of the simile.

This theme of being alien is doubly woven into *The Secret Sharer*. The young Captain who narrates the story is new to his ship, his first command, and a stranger to her crew. And beyond him, at a further remove from human society, stands the outcast and fugitive Sharer, who seems to embody the fundamental loneliness of any and every individual man upon the earth. Conrad tells us in a foreword that the story is based on a true-life anecdote of the sailing-ships of the mid-'eighties. It is told with an epic lack of sentiment, the way sailors and airmen talk about each other's misadventures, with hardly so much as a "poor bastard!" thrown in for sympathy.

The works of Conrad that I most admire are among his longer ones—novelettes such as *The End of the Tether,* full-length novels such as *Chance.* This story is the shortest of them, the only one that will fit into a small anthology; but it is also one of the best. And I think it conveys many of Conrad's personal qualities—his admirably independent moral sense (the Captain never for an instant considers handing the Sharer over to legal injustice), his stiff but charming courtesy, his devotion to his command ("my hand resting lightly on my ship's rail as if on the shoulder of a trusted friend") and his never-failing awe and wonder on finding himself alone in the presence of Nature. It is common to say of a man that he loves the sea. But Conrad was beyond loving or hating, he had dedicated himself to it absolutely. He writes about his sea-life with the unquestioning matter-of-factness of a monk speaking of his vocation. He did not marry until he had left it for good.

ON MY RIGHT HAND THERE WERE LINES OF FISHING-STAKES resembling a mysterious system of half-submerged bamboo fences, incomprehensible in its division of the domain of tropical fishes, and crazy of aspect as if abandoned for ever by some nomad tribe of fishermen now gone to the other end of the ocean; for there was no sign of human habitation as far as the eye could reach. To the left a group of barren islets, suggesting ruins of stone walls, towers, and blockhouses, had its foundation set in a blue sea that itself looked solid, so still and stable did it lie below my feet; even the track of light from the westering sun shone smoothly, without that animated glitter which tells of an imperceptible ripple. And when I turned my head to take a parting glance at the tug which had just left us anchored outside the bar, I saw the straight line of the flat shore joined to the stable sea, edge to edge, with a perfect and unmarked closeness, in one levelled floor half brown, half blue under the enormous dome of the sky. Corresponding in their insignificance to the islets of the sea, two small clumps of trees, one on each side of the only fault in the impeccable joint, marked the mouth of the river Meinam we had just left on the first preparatory stage of our homeward journey; and, far back on the inland level, a larger and loftier mass, the grove surrounding the great Paknam pagoda, was the only thing on which the eye could rest from the vain task of exploring the monotonous sweep of the horizon. Here and there gleams as of a few scattered pieces of silver marked the windings of the great river; and on the nearest of them, just within the bar, the tug steaming right into the land became lost to my sight, hull and funnel and masts, as though the impassive earth had swallowed her up without an effort, without a tremor. My eye followed the light cloud of her smoke, now here, now there, above the plain, according to the devious curves of the stream, but always fainter and farther away, till I lost it at last behind the mitre-shaped hill of the great pagoda. And then I was left alone with my ship, anchored at the head of the Gulf of Siam.

She floated at the starting-point of a long journey, very still in an immense stillness, the shadows of her spars flung far to the eastward by the setting sun. At that moment I was alone on her decks. There was not a sound in her—and around us nothing moved, nothing lived, not a canoe on the water, not a bird in the air, not a cloud in the sky. In this breathless pause at the threshold of a long passage we seemed to be measuring our fitness for a long and arduous enterprise, the appointed task of both our existences to be carried out, far from all human eyes, with only sky and sea for spectators and for judges.

There must have been some glare in the air to interfere with one's sight, because it was only just before the sun left us that my roaming eyes made out beyond the highest ridge of the principal islet of the group something which did away with the solemnity of perfect solitude. The tide of darkness flowed on swiftly; and with tropical suddenness a swarm of stars came out above the shadowy earth, while I lingered yet, my hand resting lightly on my ship's rail as if on the shoulder of a trusted friend. But, with all that multitude of celestial bodies staring down at once, the comfort of quiet communion with her was gone for good. And there were also disturbing sounds by this time—voices, footsteps forward; the steward flitted along the maindeck, a busily ministering spirit; a hand-bell tinkled urgently under the poop-deck. . . .

I found my two officers waiting for me near the supper table, in the lighted cuddy. We sat down at once, and as I helped the chief mate, I said:

"Are you aware that there is a ship anchored inside the islands? I saw her mastheads above the ridge as the sun went down."

He raised sharply his simple face, overcharged by a terrible growth of whisker, and emitted his usual ejaculations: "Bless my soul, sir! You don't say so!"

My second mate was a round-cheeked, silent young man, grave beyond his years, I thought; but as our eyes happened to meet I detected a slight quiver on his lips. I looked down at once. It was not my part to encourage sneering on board my ship. It must be said, too, that I knew very little of my officers. In consequence of certain events of no particular significance, except to myself, I had been appointed to the command only a fortnight before. Neither did I know much of the hands forward. All these people had been together for eighteen months or so, and my position was that of the only stranger on board. I mention this because it has some bearing on what is to follow. But what I felt most was my being a stranger to the ship; and if all the truth must be told, I was somewhat of a stranger to myself. The youngest man on board (barring the second mate), and untried as yet by a position of the fullest responsibility, I was willing to take the adequacy of the others for granted. They had simply to be equal to their tasks; but I wondered how far I should turn out faithful to that ideal conception of one's own personality every man sets up for himself secretly.

Meantime the chief mate, with an almost visible effect of collaboration on the part of his round eyes and frightful whiskers, was trying to evolve a theory of the anchored ship. His dominant trait was to take all things into earnest consideration. He was of a painstaking turn of mind. As he used to say, he "liked to account to himself" for practically everything that came in his way, down to a miserable scorpion he had found in his cabin a week before. The why and the wherefore of that scorpion—how it got on board and came to select his room rather than the pantry (which was a dark place and more what a scorpion would be partial to), and how on earth it managed to drown itself in the inkwell of his writing desk—had exercised him infinitely. The ship within the islands was much more easily accounted for; and just as we were about to rise from table he made his pronouncement. She was, he doubted not, a ship from home lately arrived. Probably she drew too much water to cross the bar except at the top of spring tides. Therefore she went into that natural harbour to wait for a few days in preference to remaining in an open roadstead.

"That's so," confirmed the second mate, suddenly, in his slightly hoarse voice. "She draws over twenty feet. She's the Liverpool ship *Sephora* with a cargo of coal. Hundred and twenty-three days from Cardiff."

We looked at him in surprise.

"The tugboat skipper told me when he came on board for your letters, sir," explained the young man. "He expects to take her up the river the day after tomorrow."

After thus overwhelming us with the extent of his information he slipped out of the cabin. The mate observed regretfully that he "could not account for that young fellow's whims." What prevented him telling us all about it at once, he wanted to know.

I detained him as he was making a move. For the last two days the crew had had plenty of hard work, and the night before they had very little sleep. I felt painfully that I—a stranger—was doing something unusual when I directed him to let all hands turn in without setting an anchor-watch. I proposed to keep on deck myself till one o'clock or thereabouts. I would get the second mate to relieve me at that hour.

"He will turn out the cook and the steward at four," I concluded, "and then give you a call. Of course at the slightest sign of any sort of wind we'll have the hands up and make a start at once."

He concealed his astonishment. "Very well, sir." Outside the cuddy he put his head in the second mate's door to inform him of my unheard-of caprice to take a five hours' anchor-watch on myself. I heard the other raise his voice incredulously—"What? The Captain himself?" Then a few more murmurs, a door closed, then another. A few moments later I went on deck.

My strangeness, which had made me sleepless, had prompted that unconventional arrangement, as if I had expected in those solitary hours of the night to get on terms with the ship of which I knew nothing, manned by men of whom I knew very little more. Fast alongside a wharf, littered like any ship in port with a tangle of unrelated things, invaded by unrelated shore people, I had hardly seen her yet properly. Now, as she lay cleared for sea, the stretch of her main-deck seemed to me very fine under the stars. Very fine, very roomy for her size, and very inviting. I descended the poop and paced the waist, my mind picturing to myself the coming passage through the Malay Archipelago, down the Indian Ocean, and up the Atlantic. All its phases were familiar enough to me, every characteristic, all the alternatives which were likely to face me on the high seas—everything! . . . except the novel responsibility of command. But I took heart from the reasonable thought that the ship was like other ships, the men like other men, and that the sea was not likely to keep any special surprises for my discomfiture.

Arrived at that comforting conclusion, I bethought myself of a cigar and went below to get it. All was still down there. Everybody at the after end of the ship was sleeping profoundly. I came out again on the quarter-deck, agreeably at ease in my sleeping-suit on that warm breathless night, barefooted, a glowing cigar in my teeth, and, going forward, I was met by the profound silence of the fore end of the ship. Only as I passed the door of the forecastle I heard a deep, quiet, trustful sigh of some sleeper inside. And suddenly I rejoiced in the great security of the sea as compared with the unrest of the land, in my choice of that untempted life presenting no disquieting problems, invested with an elementary moral beauty by the absolute straightforwardness of its appeal and by the singleness of its purpose.

The riding-light in the fore-rigging burned with a clear, untroubled, as if symbolic, flame, confident and bright in the mysterious shades of the night. Passing on my way aft along the other side of the ship, I observed that the rope side-ladder, put over, no doubt, for the master of the tug when he came to fetch away our letters, had not been hauled in as it should have been. I became annoyed at this, for exactitude in small matters is the very soul of discipline. Then I reflected that I had myself peremptorily dismissed my officers from duty, and by my own act had prevented the anchor-watch being formally set and things properly attended to. I asked myself whether it was wise ever to interfere with the established routine of duties even from the kindest of motives. My action might have made me appear eccentric. Goodness only knew how that absurdly whiskered mate would "account" for my conduct, and what the whole ship thought of that informality of their new captain. I was vexed with myself.

Not from compunction certainly, but, as it were mechanically, I proceeded to get the ladder in myself. Now a side-ladder of that sort is a light affair and comes in easily, yet my vigorous tug, which should have brought it flying on board, merely recoiled upon my body in a totally unexpected jerk. What the devil! . . . I was so astounded by the immovableness of that ladder that I remained stock-still, trying to account for it to myself like that imbecile mate of mine. In the end, of course, I put my head over the rail.

The side of the ship made an opaque belt of shadow on the darkling glassy shimmer of the sea. But I saw at once something elongated and pale floating very close to the ladder. Before I could form a guess a faint flash of phosphorescent light, which seemed to issue suddenly from the naked body of a man, flickered in the sleeping water with the elusive, silent play of summer lightning in a night sky. With a gasp I saw revealed to my stare a pair of feet, the long legs, a broad livid back immersed right up to the neck in a greenish cadaverous glow. One hand, awash, clutched the bottom rung of the ladder. He was complete but for the head. A headless corpse! The cigar dropped out of my gaping mouth with a tiny plop and a short hiss quite audible in the absolute stillness of all things under heaven. At that I suppose he raised up his face, a dimly pale oval in the shadow of the ship's side. But even then I could only barely make out down there the shape of his black-haired head. However, it was enough for the horrid, frost-bound sensation which had gripped me about the chest to pass off. The moment of vain exclamations was past, too. I only climbed on the spare spar and leaned over the rail as far as I could, to bring my eyes nearer to that mystery floating alongside.

As he hung by the ladder, like a resting swimmer, the sea-lightning played about his limbs at every stir; and he appeared in it ghastly, silvery, fish-like. He remained as mute as a fish too. He made no motion to get out of the water, either. It was inconceivable that he should not attempt to come on board, and strangely troubling to suspect that perhaps he did not want to. And my first words were prompted by just that troubled incertitude.

"What's the matter?" I asked in my ordinary tone, speaking down to the face upturned exactly under mine.

"Cramp," it answered, no louder. Then slightly anxious, "I say, no need to call any one."

"I was not going to," I said.

"Are you alone on deck?"

"Yes."

I had somehow the impression that he was on the point of letting go the ladder to swim away beyond my ken—mysterious as he came. But, for the moment, this being appearing as if he had risen from the bottom of the sea (it was certainly the nearest land to the ship) wanted only to know the time. I told him. And he, down there, tentatively:

"I suppose your captain's turned in?"

"I am sure he isn't," I said.

He seemed to struggle with himself, for I heard something like the low, bitter murmur of doubt. "What's the good?" His next words came out with a hesitating effort.

"Look here, my man. Could you call him out quietly?"

I thought the time had come to declare myself.

"*I* am the captain."

I heard a "By Jove!" whispered at the level of the water. The phosphorescence flashed in the swirl of the water all about his limbs, his other hand seized the ladder.

"My name's Leggatt."

The voice was calm and resolute. A good voice. The self-possession of that man had somehow induced a corresponding state in myself. It was very quietly that I remarked:

"You must be a good swimmer."

"Yes. I've been in the water practically since nine o'clock. The question for me now is whether I am to let go this ladder and go on swimming till I sink from exhaustion, or—to come on board here."

I felt this was no mere formula of desperate speech, but a real alternative in the view of a strong soul. I should have gathered from this that he was young; indeed, it is only the young who are ever confronted by such clear issues. But at the time it was pure intuition on my part. A mysterious communication was established already between us two—in the face of that silent, darkened tropical sea. I was young, too; young enough to make no comment. The man in the water began suddenly to climb up the ladder, and I hastened away from the rail to fetch some clothes.

Before entering the cabin I stood still, listening in the lobby at the foot of the stairs. A faint snore came through the closed door of the chief mate's room. The second mate's door was on the hook, but the darkness in there was absolutely soundless. He, too, was young and could sleep like a stone. Remained the steward, but he was not likely to wake up before he was called. I got a sleeping-suit out of my room and, coming back on deck, saw the naked man from the sea sitting on the main-hatch, glimmering white in the darkness, his elbows on his knees and his head in his hands. In a moment he had concealed his damp body in a sleeping-suit of the same grey-stripe pattern as the one I was wearing and followed me like my double on the poop. Together we moved right aft, barefooted, silent.

"What is it?" I asked in a deadened voice, taking the lighted lamp out of the binnacle, and raising it to his face.

"An ugly business."

He had rather regular features; a good mouth; light eyes under somewhat heavy, dark eyebrows; a smooth, square forehead; no growth on his cheeks; a small, brown moustache, and a well-shaped, round chin. His expression was concentrated, meditative, under the inspecting light of the lamp I held up to his face; such as a man thinking hard in solitude might wear. My sleeping-suit was just right for his size. A well-knit young fellow of twenty-five at most. He caught his lower lip with the edge of white, even teeth.

"Yes," I said, replacing the lamp in the binnacle. The warm, heavy tropical night closed upon his head again.

"There's a ship over there," he murmured.

"Yes, I know. The *Sephora*. Did you know of us?"

"Hadn't the slightest idea. I am the mate of her—" He paused and corrected himself. "I should say I *was*."

"Aha! Something wrong?"

"Yes. Very wrong indeed. I've killed a man."

"What do you mean? Just now?"

"No, on the passage. Weeks ago. Thirty-nine south. When I say a man—"

"Fit of temper," I suggested, confidently.

The shadowy, dark head, like mine, seemed to nod imperceptibly above the ghostly grey of my sleeping-suit. It was, in the night, as though I had been faced by my own reflection in the depths of a sombre and immense mirror.

"A pretty thing to have to own up to for a Conway boy," murmured my double, distinctly.

"You're a Conway boy?"

"I am," he said, as if startled. Then, slowly . . . "Perhaps you too—"

It was so; but being a couple of years older I had left before he joined. After a quick interchange of dates a silence fell; and I thought suddenly of my absurd mate with his terrific whiskers and the "Bless my soul—you don't say so" type of intellect. My double gave me an inkling of his thoughts by saying: "My father's a parson in Norfolk. Do you see me before a judge and jury on that charge? For myself I can't see the necessity. There are fellows that an angel from heaven— And I am not that. He was one of those creatures that are just simmering all the time with a silly sort of wickedness. Miserable devils that have no business to live at all. He wouldn't do his duty and wouldn't let anybody else do theirs. But what's the good of talking! You know well enough the sort of ill-conditioned snarling cur—"

He appealed to me as if our experiences had been as identical as our clothes. And I knew well enough the pestiferous danger of such a character where there are no means of legal repression. And I knew well enough also that my double there was no homicidal ruffian. I did not think of asking him for details, and he told me the story roughly in brusque, disconnected sentences. I needed no more. I saw it all going on as though I were myself inside that other sleeping-suit.

"It happened while we were setting a reefed foresail, at dusk. Reefed foresail! You understand the sort of weather. The only sail we had left to keep the ship running; so you may guess what it had been like for days. Anxious sort of job, that. He gave me some of his cursed insolence at the sheet. I tell you I was overdone with this terrific weather that seemed to have no end to it. Terrific, I tell you—and a deep ship. I believe the fellow himself was half crazed with funk. It was not time for gentlemanly reproof, so I turned round and felled him like an ox. He up and at me. We closed just as an awful sea made for the ship. All hands saw it coming and took to the rigging, but I had him by the throat, and went on shaking him like a rat, the men above us yelling, 'Look out! look out!' Then a crash as if the sky had fallen on my head. They say that for over ten minutes hardly anything was to be seen of the ship—just the three masts and a bit of the forecastle head and of the poop all awash driving along in a smother of foam. It was a miracle that they found us, jammed together behind the forebits. It's clear that I meant business, because I was holding him by the throat still when they picked us up. He was black in the face. It was too much for them. It seems they rushed us aft together, gripped as we were, screaming 'Murder!' like a lot of lunatics, and broke into the cuddy. And the ship running for her life, touch and go all the time, any minute her last in a sea fit to turn your hair grey only a-looking at it. I understand that the skipper, too, started raving like the rest of them. The man had been deprived of sleep for more than a week, and to have this sprung on him at the height of a furious gale nearly drove him out of his mind. I wonder they didn't fling me overboard after getting the carcass of their precious ship-mate out of my fingers. They had rather a job to separate us, I've been told. A sufficiently fierce story to make an old judge and a respectable jury sit up a bit. The first thing I heard when I came to myself was the maddening howling of that endless gale, and on that the voice of the old man. He was hanging on to my bunk, staring into my face out of his sou'wester.

" 'Mr. Leggatt, you have killed a man. You can act no longer as chief mate of this ship.' "

His care to subdue his voice made it sound monotonous. He rested a hand on the end of the skylight to steady himself with, and all that time did not stir a limb, so far as I could see. "Nice little tale for a quiet tea-party," he concluded in the same tone.

One of my hands, too, rested on the end of the skylight; neither did I stir a limb, so far as I knew. We stood less than a foot from each other. It occurred to me that if old "Bless my soul—you don't say so" were to put his head up the companion and catch sight of us, he would think he was seeing double, or imagine himself come upon a scene of weird witchcraft; the strange captain having a quiet confabulation by the wheel with his own grey ghost. I became very much concerned to prevent anything of the sort. I heard the other's soothing undertone.

"My father's a parson in Norfolk," it said. Evidently he had forgotten he had told me this important fact before. Truly a nice little tale.

"You had better slip down into my stateroom now," I said, moving off stealthily. My double followed my movements; our bare feet made no sound; I let him in, closed the door with care, and, after giving a call to the second mate, returned on deck for my relief.

"Not much sign of any wind yet," I remarked when he approached.

"No, sir. Not much," he assented, sleepily, in his

hoarse voice, with just enough deference, no more, and barely suppressing a yawn.

"Well, that's all you have to look out for. You have got your orders."

"Yes, sir."

I paced a turn or two on the poop and saw him take up his position face forward with his elbow in the ratlines of the mizzen-rigging before I went below. The mate's faint snoring was still going on peacefully. The cuddy lamp was burning over the table on which stood a vase with flowers, a polite attention from the ship's provision merchant—the last flowers we should see for the next three months at the very least. Two bunches of bananas hung from the beam symmetrically, one on each side of the rudder-casing. Everything was as before in the ship—except that two of her captain's sleeping-suits were simultaneously in use, one motionless in the cuddy, the other keeping very still in the captain's stateroom.

It must be explained here that my cabin had the form of the capital letter L, the door being within the angle and opening into the short part of the letter. A couch was to the left, the bed-place to the right; my writing-desk and the chronometers' table faced the door. But any one opening it, unless he stepped right inside, had no view of what I call the long (or vertical) part of the letter. It contained some lockers surmounted by a bookcase; and a few clothes, a thick jacket or two, caps, oilskin coat, and such like, hung on hooks. There was at the bottom of that part a door opening into my bathroom, which could be entered also directly from the saloon. But that way was never used.

The mysterious arrival had discovered the advantage of this particular shape. Entering my room, lighted strongly by a big bulkhead lamp swung on gimbals above my writing-desk, I did not see him anywhere till he stepped out quietly from behind the coats hung in the recessed part.

"I heard somebody moving about, and went in there at once," he whispered.

I, too, spoke under my breath.

"Nobody is likely to come in here without knocking and getting permission."

He nodded. His face was thin and the sunburn faded, as though he had been ill. And no wonder. He had been, I heard presently, kept under arrest in his cabin for nearly seven weeks. But there was nothing sickly in his eyes or in his expression. He was not a bit like me really; yet, as we stood leaning over my bed-place, whispering side by side, with our dark heads together and our backs to the door, anybody bold enough to open it stealthily would have been treated to the uncanny sight of a double captain busy talking in whispers with his other self.

"But all this doesn't tell me how you came to hang on to our side-ladder," I inquired, in the hardly audible murmurs we used, after he had told me something more of the proceedings on board the *Sephora* once the bad weather was over.

"When we sighted Java Head I had had time to think all those matters out several times over. I had six weeks of doing nothing else, and with only an hour or so every evening for a tramp on the quarter-deck."

He whispered, his arms folded on the side of my bed-place, staring through the open port. And I could imagine perfectly the manner of this thinking out—a stubborn if not a steadfast operation; something of which I should have been perfectly incapable.

"I reckoned it would be dark before we closed with the land," he continued, so low that I had to strain my hearing, near as we were to each other, shoulder touching shoulder almost. "So I asked to speak to the old man. He always seemed very sick when he came to see me—as if he could not look me in the face. You know, that foresail saved the ship. She was too deep to have run long under bare poles. And it was I that managed to set it for him. Anyway, he came. When I had him in my cabin—he stood by the door looking at me as if I had the halter round my neck already—I asked him right away to leave my cabin door unlocked at night while the ship was going through Sunda Straits. There would be the Java coast within two or three miles, off Angier Point. I wanted nothing more. I've had a prize for swimming my second year in the Conway."

"I can believe it," I breathed out.

"God only knows why they locked me in every night. To see some of their faces you'd have thought they were afraid I'd go about at night strangling people. Am I a murdering brute? Do I look it? By Jove! If I had been he wouldn't have trusted himself like that into my room. You'll say I might have chucked him aside and bolted out, there and then—it was dark already. Well, no. And for the same reason I wouldn't think of trying to smash the door. There would have been a rush to stop me at the noise, and I did not mean to get into a confounded scrimmage. Somebody else might have got killed—for I would not have broken out only to get chucked back, and I did not want any more of that work. He refused, looking more sick than ever. He was afraid of the men, and also of that old second mate of his who had been sailing with him for years—a grey-headed old humbug; and his steward, too, had been with him devil knows how long—seventeen years or more—a dogmatic sort of loafer who hated me like poison, just because I was the chief mate. No chief mate ever made more than one voyage in the *Sephora,* you know. Those two old chaps ran the ship. Devil only knows what the skipper wasn't afraid of (all his nerve went to pieces altogether in that hellish spell of bad weather we had)—of what the law would do to him—of his wife, perhaps. Oh, yes! she's on board. Though I don't think she would have meddled. She would have been only too glad to have me out of the ship in any way. The 'brand of Cain' business, don't you see. That's all right. I was ready enough to go off wandering on the face of the earth—and that was price enough to pay for an Abel of that sort. Anyhow, he wouldn't listen to me. 'This thing must take its course. I represent the law here.' He was shaking like a leaf. 'So you won't?' 'No!' 'Then I hope you will be able to sleep on that,' I said, and turned my back on him. 'I wonder that *you* can,' cries he, and locks the door.

"Well, after that, I couldn't. Not very well. That was three weeks ago. We have had a slow passage through the Java Sea; drifted about Carimata for ten days. When we anchored here they thought, I suppose, it was all right. The nearest land (and that's five miles) is the ship's destination; the consul would soon set about catching me; and there would have been no object in bolting to these islets there. I don't suppose there's a drop of water on them. I don't know how it was, but tonight that steward, after bringing me my supper, went out to let me eat it, and left the door unlocked. And I ate it—all there was, too. After I had finished I strolled out on the quarter-deck. I don't know that I meant to do anything. A breath of fresh air was all I wanted, I believe. Then a sudden temptation came over me. I kicked off my slippers and was in the water before I had made up my mind fairly. Somebody heard the splash and they raised an awful hullabaloo. 'He's gone! Lower the boats! He's committed suicide! No, he's swimming.' Certainly I was swimming. It's not so easy for a swimmer like me to commit suicide by drowning. I landed on the nearest islet before the boat left the ship's side. I heard them pulling about in the dark, hailing, and so on, but after a bit they gave up. Everything quieted down and the anchorage became as still as death. I sat down on a stone and began to think. I felt certain they would start searching for me at daylight. There was no place to hide on those stony things—and if there had been, what would have been the good? But now I was clear of that ship, I was not going back. So after a while I took off all my clothes, tied them up in a bundle with a stone inside, and dropped them in the deep water on the outer side of that islet. That was suicide enough for me. Let them think what they liked, but I didn't mean to drown myself. I meant to swim till I sank—but that's not the same thing. I struck out for another of these little islands, and it was from that one that I first saw your riding-light. Something to swim for. I went on easily, and on the way I came upon a flat rock a foot or two above water. In the daytime, I dare say, you might make it out with a glass from your poop. I scrambled up on it and rested myself for a bit. Then I made another start. That last spell must have been over a mile."

His whisper was getting fainter and fainter, and all the time he stared straight out through the port-hole, in which there was not even a star to be seen. I had not interrupted him. There was something that made comment impossible in his narrative, or perhaps in himself;

a sort of feeling, a quality, which I can't find a name for. And when he ceased, all I found was a futile whisper: "So you swam for our light?"

"Yes—straight for it. It was something to swim for. I couldn't see any stars low down because the coast was in the way, and I couldn't see the land, either. The water was like glass. One might have been swimming in a confounded thousand-feet deep cistern with no place for scrambling out anywhere; but what I didn't like was the notion of swimming round and round like a crazed bullock before I gave out; and as I didn't mean to go back . . . No. Do you see me being hauled back, stark naked, off one of these little islands by the scruff of the neck and fighting like a wild beast? Somebody would have got killed for certain, and I did not want any of that. So I went on. Then your ladder—"

"Why didn't you hail the ship?" I asked, a little louder.

He touched my shoulder lightly. Lazy footsteps came right over our heads and stopped. The second mate had crossed from the other side of the poop and might have been hanging over the rail, for all we knew.

"He couldn't hear us talking—could he?" My double breathed into my very ear, anxiously.

His anxiety was an answer, a sufficient answer, to the question I had put to him. An answer containing all the difficulty of that situation. I closed the port-hole quietly, to make sure. A louder word might have been overheard.

"Who's that?" he whispered then.

"My second mate. But I don't know much more of the fellow than you do."

And I told him a little about myself. I had been appointed to take charge while I least expected anything of the sort, not quite a fortnight ago. I didn't know either the ship or the people. Hadn't had the time in port to look about me or size anybody up. And as to the crew, all they knew was that I was appointed to take the ship home. For the rest, I was almost as much of a stranger on board as himself, I said. And at the moment I felt it most acutely. I felt that it would take very little to make me a suspect person in the eyes of the ship's company.

He had turned about meantime; and we, the two strangers in the ship, faced each other in identical attitudes.

"Your ladder–" he murmured, after a silence. "Who'd have thought of finding a ladder hanging over at night in a ship anchored out here! I felt just then a very unpleasant faintness. After the life I've been leading for nine weeks, anybody would have got out of condition. I wasn't capable of swimming round as far as your rudder-chains. And, lo and behold! there was a ladder to get hold of. After I gripped it I said to myself, 'What's the good?' When I saw a man's head looking over I thought I would swim away presently and leave him shouting–in whatever language it was. I didn't mind being looked at. I–I liked it. And then you speaking to me so quietly–as if you had expected me–made me hold on a little longer. It had been a confounded lonely time–I don't mean while swimming. I was glad to talk a little to somebody that didn't belong to the *Sephora*. As to asking for the captain, that was a mere impulse. It could have been no use, with all the ship knowing about me and the other people pretty certain to be round here in the morning. I don't know–I wanted to be seen, to talk with somebody, before I went on. I don't know what I would have said. . . . 'Fine night, isn't it?' or something of the sort."

"Do you think they will be round here presently?" I asked with some incredulity.

"Quite likely," he said, faintly.

He looked extremely haggard all of a sudden. His head rolled on his shoulders.

"H'm. We shall see then. Meantime get into that bed," I whispered. "Want help? There."

It was a rather high bed-place with a set of drawers underneath. This amazing swimmer really needed the lift I gave him by seizing his leg. He tumbled in, rolled over on his back, and flung one arm across his eyes. And then, with his face nearly hidden, he must have looked exactly as I used to look in that bed. I gazed upon my other self for a while before drawing across carefully the two green serge curtains which ran on a brass rod. I thought for a moment of pinning them together for greater safety, but I sat down on the couch, and once there I felt unwilling to rise and hunt for a pin. I would do it in a moment. I was extremely tired, in a peculiarly intimate way, by the strain of stealthiness, by the effort of whispering and the general secrecy of this excitement. It was three o'clock by now and I had been on my feet since nine, but I was not sleepy; I could not have gone to sleep. I sat there, fagged out, looking at the curtains, trying to clear my mind of the confused sensation of being in two places at once, and greatly bothered by an exasperating knocking in my head. It was a relief to discover suddenly that it was not in my head at all, but on the outside of the door. Before I could collect myself, the words "Come in" were out of my mouth, and the steward entered with a tray, bringing in my morning coffee. I had slept, after all, and I was so frightened that I shouted, "This way! I am here, steward," as though he had been miles away. He put down the tray on the table next the couch and only then said, very quietly, "I can see you are here, sir." I felt him give me a keen look, but I dared not meet his eyes just then. He must have wondered why I had drawn the curtains of my bed before going to sleep on the couch. He went out, hooking the door open as usual.

I heard the crew washing decks above me. I knew I would have been told at once if there had been any wind. Calm, I thought, and I was doubly vexed. Indeed, I felt dual more than ever. The steward reappeared suddenly in the doorway. I jumped up from the couch so quickly that he gave a start.

"What do you want here?"

"Close your port, sir—they are washing decks."

"It is closed," I said, reddening.

"Very well, sir." But he did not move from the doorway and returned my stare in an extraordinary, equivocal manner for a time. Then his eyes wavered, all his expression changed, and in a voice unusually gentle, almost coaxingly:

"May I come in to take the empty cup away, sir?"

"Of course!" I turned my back on him while he popped in and out. Then I unhooked and closed the door and even pushed the bolt. This sort of thing could not go on very long. The cabin was as hot as an oven, too. I took a peep at my double, and discovered that he had not moved, his arm was still over his eyes; but his chest heaved; his hair was wet; his chin glistened with perspiration. I reached over him and opened the port.

"I must show myself on deck," I reflected.

Of course, theoretically, I could do what I liked, with

no one to say nay to me within the whole circle of the horizon; but to lock my cabin door and take the key away I did not dare. Directly I put my head out of the companion I saw the group of my two officers, the second mate barefooted, the chief mate in long india-rubber boots, near the break of the poop, and the steward half-way down the poop-ladder talking to them eagerly. He happened to catch sight of me and dived, the second ran down on the main-deck shouting some order or other, and the chief mate came to meet me, touching his cap.

There was a sort of curiosity in his eye that I did not like. I don't know whether the steward had told them that I was "queer" only, or downright drunk, but I know the man meant to have a good look at me. I watched him coming with a smile which, as he got into point-blank range, took effect and froze his very whiskers. I did not give him time to open his lips.

"Square the yards by lifts and braces before the hands go to breakfast."

It was the first particular order I had given on board that ship; and I stayed on deck to see it executed, too. I had felt the need of asserting myself without loss of time. That sneering young cub got taken down a peg or two on that occasion, and I also seized the opportunity of having a good look at the face of every foremast man as they filed past me to go to the after braces. At breakfast time, eating nothing myself, I presided with such frigid dignity that the two mates were only too glad to escape from the cabin as soon as decency permitted; and all the time the dual working of my mind distracted me almost to the point of insanity. I was constantly watching myself, my secret self, as dependent on my actions as my own personality, sleeping in that bed, behind that door which faced me as I sat at the head of the table. It was very much like being mad, only it was worse because one was aware of it.

I had to shake him for a solid minute, but when at last he opened his eyes it was in the full possession of his senses, with an inquiring look.

"All's well so far," I whispered. "Now you must vanish into the bath-room."

He did so, as noiseless as a ghost, and then I rang for the steward, and facing him boldly, directed him to tidy up my stateroom while I was having my bath—"and be quick about it." As my tone admitted of no excuses, he said, "Yes, sir," and ran off to fetch his dust-pan and brushes. I took a bath and did most of my dressing, splashing, and whistling softly for the steward's edification, while the secret sharer of my life stood drawn up bolt upright in that little space, his face looking very sunken in daylight, his eyelids lowered under the stern, dark line of his eyebrows drawn together by a slight frown.

When I left him there to go back to my room the steward was finishing dusting. I sent for the mate and engaged him in some insignificant conversation. It was, as it were, trifling with the terrific character of his whiskers; but my object was to give him an opportunity for a good look at my cabin. And then I could at last shut, with a clear conscience, the door of my stateroom and get my double back into the recessed part. There was nothing else for it. He had to sit still on a small folding stool, half smothered by the heavy coats hanging there. We listened to the steward going into the bath-room out of the saloon, filling the water-bottles there, scrubbing the bath, setting things to rights, whisk, bang, clatter—out again into the saloon—turn the key—click. Such was my scheme for keeping my second self invisible. Nothing better could be contrived under the circumstances. And there we sat; I at my writing-desk ready to appear busy with some papers, he behind me out of sight of the door. It would not have been prudent to talk in daytime; and I could not have stood the excitement of that queer sense of whispering to myself. Now and then, glancing over my shoulder, I saw him far back there, sitting rigidly on the low stool, his bare feet close together, his arms folded, his head hanging on his breast—and perfectly still. Anybody would have taken him for me.

I was fascinated by it myself. Every moment I had to glance over my shoulder. I was looking at him when a voice outside the door said:

"Beg pardon, sir."

"Well!" . . . I kept my eyes on him, and so when the voice outside the door announced, "There's a ship's boat coming our way, sir," I saw him give a start—the first movement he had made for hours. But he did not raise his bowed head.

"All right. Get the ladder over."

I hesitated. Should I whisper something to him? But what? His immobility seemed to have been never disturbed. What could I tell him he did not know already? . . . Finally I went on deck.

2

The skipper of the *Sephora* had a thin red whisker all round his face, and the sort of complexion that goes with hair of that colour; also the particular, rather smeary shade of blue in the eyes. He was not exactly a showy figure; his shoulders were high, his stature but middling—one leg slightly more bandy than the other. He shook hands, looking vaguely around. A spiritless tenacity was his main characteristic, I judged. I behaved with a politeness which seemed to disconcert him. Perhaps he was shy. He mumbled to me as if he were ashamed of what he was saying; gave his name (it was something like Archbold—but at this distance of years I hardly am sure), his ship's name, and a few other particulars of that sort, in the manner of a criminal making a reluctant and doleful confession. He had had terrible weather on the passage out—terrible—terrible—wife aboard, too.

By this time we were seated in the cabin and the steward brought in a tray with a bottle and glasses. "Thanks! No." Never took liquor. Would have some water, though. He drank two tumblerfuls. Terrible thirsty work. Ever since daylight had been exploring the islands round his ship.

"What was that for—fun?" I asked, with an appearance of polite interest.

"No!" He sighed. "Painful duty."

As he persisted in his mumbling and I wanted my double to hear every word, I hit upon the notion of informing him that I regretted to say I was hard of hearing.

"Such a young man, too!" he nodded, keeping his smeary blue, unintelligent eyes fastened upon me. "What was the cause of it—some disease?" he inquired, without the least sympathy and as if he thought that, if so, I'd got no more than I deserved.

"Yes; disease," I admitted in a cheerful tone which seemed to shock him. But my point was gained, because he had to raise his voice to give me his tale. It is not worth while to record that version. It was just over two months since all this had happened, and he had thought so much about it that he seemed completely muddled as to its bearings, but still immensely impressed.

"What would you think of such a thing happening on board your own ship? I've had the *Sephora* for these fifteen years. I am a well-known shipmaster."

He was densely distressed—and perhaps I should have sympathized with him if I had been able to detach my mental vision from the unsuspected sharer of my cabin as though he were my second self. There he was on the other side of the bulkhead, four or five feet from us, no more, as we sat in the saloon. I looked politely at Captain Archbold (if that was his name), but it was the other I saw, in a grey sleeping-suit, seated on a low stool, his bare feet close together, his arms folded, and every word said between us falling into the ears of his dark head bowed on his chest.

"I have been at sea now, man and boy, for seven-and-thirty years, and I've never heard of such a thing happening in an English ship. And that it should be my ship. Wife on board, too."

I was hardly listening to him.

"Don't you think," I said, "that the heavy sea which, you told me, came aboard just then might have killed the man? I have seen the sheer weight of a sea kill a man very neatly, by simply breaking his neck."

"Good God!" he uttered, impressively, fixing his smeary blue eyes on me. "The sea! No man killed by the sea ever looked like that." He seemed positively scandalized at my suggestion. And as I gazed at him, certainly not prepared for anything original on his part, he advanced his head close to mine and thrust his tongue out at me so suddenly that I couldn't help starting back.

After scoring over my calmness in this graphic way he nodded wisely. If I had seen the sight, he assured me, I would never forget it as long as I lived. The weather was too bad to give the corpse a proper sea burial. So next day at dawn they took it up on the poop, covering its face with a bit of bunting; he read a short prayer, and then, just as it was, in its oilskins and long boots, they launched it amongst those mountainous seas that seemed ready every moment to swallow up the ship herself and the terrified lives on board of her.

"That reefed foresail saved you," I threw in.

"Under God—it did," he exclaimed fervently. "It was by a special mercy, I firmly believe, that it stood some of those hurricane squalls."

"It was the setting of that sail which—" I began.

"God's own hand in it," he interrupted me. "Nothing less could have done it. I don't mind telling you that I hardly dared give the order. It seemed impossible that we could touch anything without losing it, and then our last hope would have been gone."

The terror of that gale was on him yet. I let him go on for a bit, then said, casually—as if returning to a minor subject:

"You were very anxious to give up your mate to the shore people, I believe?"

He was. To the law. His obscure tenacity on that point had in it something incomprehensible and a little awful; something, as it were, mystical, quite apart from his anxiety that he should not be suspected of "countenancing any doings of that sort." Seven-and-thirty virtuous years at sea, of which over twenty of immaculate command, and the last fifteen in the *Sephora,* seemed to have laid him under some pitiless obligation.

"And you know," he went on, groping shamefacedly

amongst his feelings, "I did not engage that young fellow. His people had some interest with my owners. I was in a way forced to take him on. He looked very smart, very gentlemanly, and all that. But do you know —I never liked him, somehow. I am a plain man. You see, he wasn't exactly the sort for the chief mate of a ship like the *Sephora.*"

I had become so connected in thoughts and impressions with the secret sharer of my cabin that I felt as if I, personally, were being given to understand that I, too, was not the sort that would have done for the chief mate of a ship like the *Sephora.* I had no doubt of it in my mind.

"Not at all the style of man. You understand," he insisted, superfluously, looking at me.

I smiled urbanely. He seemed at a loss for a while.

"I suppose I must report a suicide."

"Beg pardon?"

"Sui-cide! That's what I'll have to write to my owners directly I get in."

"Unless you manage to recover him before tomorrow," I assented, dispassionately. . . . "I mean, alive."

He mumbled something which I really did not catch, and I turned my ear to him in a puzzled manner. He fairly bawled:

"The land—I say, the mainland is at least seven miles off my anchorage."

"About that."

My lack of excitement, of curiosity, of surprise, of any sort of pronounced interest, began to arouse his distrust. But except for the felicitous pretense of deafness I had not tried to pretend anything. I had felt utterly incapable of playing the part of ignorance properly, and therefore was afraid to try. It is also certain that he had brought some ready-made suspicions with him, and that he viewed my politeness as a strange and unnatural phenomenon. And yet how else could I have received him? Not heartily! That was impossible for psychological reasons, which I need not state here. My only object was to keep off his inquiries. Surlily? Yes, but surliness might have provoked a point-blank question. From its novelty to him and from its nature, punctilious courtesy was the manner best calculated to restrain the man. But there was the danger of his breaking through my defense bluntly. I could not, I think, have met him by a direct lie, also for psychological (not moral) reasons. If he had only known how afraid I was of his putting my feeling of identity with the other to the test! But, strangely enough—(I thought of it only afterwards)—I believe that he was not a little disconcerted by the reverse side of that weird situation, by something in me that reminded him of the man he was seeking—suggested a mysterious similitude to the young fellow he had distrusted and disliked from the first.

However that might have been, the silence was not very prolonged. He took another oblique step.

"I reckon I had no more than a two-mile pull to your ship. Not a bit more."

"And quite enough, too, in this awful heat," I said.

Another pause full of mistrust followed. Necessity, they say, is mother of invention, but fear, too, is not barren of ingenious suggestions. And I was afraid he would ask me point-blank for news of my other self.

"Nice little saloon, isn't it?" I remarked, as if noticing for the first time the way his eyes roamed from one closed door to the other. "And very well fitted out, too. Here, for instance," I continued, reaching over the back of my seat negligently and flinging the door open, "is my bath-room."

He made an eager movement, but hardly gave it a glance. I got up, shut the door of the bath-room, and invited him to have a look round, as if I were very proud of my accommodation. He had to rise and be shown round, but he went through the business without any raptures whatever.

"And now we'll have a look at my stateroom," I declared, in a voice as loud as I dared to make it, crossing the cabin to the starboard side with purposely heavy steps.

He followed me in and gazed around. My intelligent double had vanished. I played my part.

"Very convenient—isn't it?"

"Very nice. Very comf . . ." He didn't finish and went out brusquely as if to escape from some unrighteous wiles of mine. But it was not to be. I had been too frightened not to feel vengeful; I felt I had him on the run, and I meant to keep him on the run. My polite insistence must have had something menacing in it, because he gave in suddenly. And I did not let him off a single item; mate's room, pantry, storerooms, the very sail-locker which was also under the poop—he had to look into them all. When at last I showed him out on the quarter-deck he drew a long, spiritless sigh, and mumbled dismally that he must really be going back to his ship now. I desired my mate, who had joined us, to see to the captain's boat.

The man of whiskers gave a blast on the whistle which he used to wear hanging round his neck, and yelled, "*Sephora's* away!" My double down there in my cabin must have heard, and certainly could not feel more relieved than I. Four fellows came running out from somewhere forward and went over the side, while my own men, appearing on deck too, lined the rail. I escorted my visitor to the gangway ceremoniously, and nearly overdid it. He was a tenacious beast. On the very ladder he lingered, and in that unique, guiltily conscientious manner of sticking to the point:

"I say . . . you . . . you don't think that–"

I covered his voice loudly:

"Certainly not. . . . I am delighted. Goodbye."

I had an idea of what he meant to say, and just saved myself by the privilege of defective hearing. He was too shaken generally to insist, but my mate, close witness of that parting, looked mystified and his face took on a thoughtful cast. As I did not want to appear as if I wished to avoid all communication with my officers, he had the opportunity to address me.

"Seems a very nice man. His boat's crew told our chaps a very extraordinary story, if what I am told by the steward is true. I suppose you had it from the captain, sir?"

"Yes. I had a story from the captain."

"A very horrible affair–isn't it, sir?"

"It is."

"Beats all these tales we hear about murders in Yankee ships."

"I don't think it beats them. I don't think it resembles them in the least."

"Bless my soul–you don't say so! But of course I've no acquaintance whatever with American ships, not I, so I couldn't go against your knowledge. It's horrible enough for me. . . . But the queerest part is that those fellows seemed to have some idea the man was hidden aboard here. They had really. Did you ever hear of such a thing?"

"Preposterous—isn't it?"

We were walking to and fro athwart the quarter-deck. No one of the crew forward could be seen (the day was Sunday), and the mate pursued:

"There was some little dispute about it. Our chaps took offense. 'As if we would harbour a thing like that,' they said. 'Wouldn't you like to look for him in our coalhole?' Quite a tiff. But they made it up in the end. I suppose he did drown himself. Don't you, sir?"

"I don't suppose anything."

"You have no doubt in the matter, sir?"

"None whatever."

I left him suddenly. I felt I was producing a bad impression, but with my double down there it was most trying to be on deck. And it was almost as trying to be below. Altogether a nerve-trying situation. But on the whole I felt less torn in two when I was with him. There was no one in the whole ship whom I dared take into my confidence. Since the hands had got to know his story, it would have been impossible to pass him off for any one else, and an accidental discovery was to be dreaded now more than ever. . . .

The steward being engaged in laying the table for dinner, we could talk only with our eyes when I first went down. Later in the afternoon we had a cautious try at whispering. The Sunday quietness of the ship was against us; the elements, the men were against us—everything was against us in our secret partnership; time itself—for this could not go on forever. The very trust in Providence was, I suppose, denied to his guilt. Shall I confess that this thought cast me down very much? And as to the chapter of accidents which counts for so much in the book of success, I could only hope that it was closed. For what favourable accident could be expected?

"Did you hear everything?" were my first words as soon as we took up our position side by side, leaning over my bed-place.

He had. And the proof of it was his earnest whisper, "The man told you he hardly dared to give the order."

I understood the reference to be to that saving foresail.

"Yes. He was afraid of it being lost in the setting."

"I assure you he never gave the order. He may think he did, but he never gave it. He stood there with me on the break of the poop after the maintopsail blew away, and whimpered about our last hope—positively whimpered about it and nothing else—and the night coming on! To hear one's skipper go on like that in such weather was enough to drive any fellow out of his mind. It worked me up into a sort of desperation. I just took it into my own hands and went away from him, boiling, and— But what's the use telling you? *You* know! . . . Do you think that if I had not been pretty fierce with them I should have got the men to do anything? Not I! The bo's'n perhaps? Perhaps! It wasn't a heavy sea—it was a sea gone mad! I suppose the end of the world will be something like that; and a man may have the heart to see it coming once and be done with it—but to have to face it day after day— I don't blame anybody. I was precious little better than the rest. Only—I was an officer of that old coal-wagon, anyhow—"

"I quite understand," I conveyed that sincere assurance into his ear. He was out of breath with whispering; I could hear him pant slightly. It was all very simple. The same strung-up force which had given twenty-four men a chance, at least, for their lives, had, in a sort of recoil, crushed an unworthy mutinous existence.

But I had no leisure to weigh the merits of the matter —footsteps in the saloon, a heavy knock. "There's enough wind to get under way with, sir." Here was the call of a new claim upon my thoughts and even upon my feelings.

"Turn the hands up," I cried through the door. "I'll be on deck directly."

I was going out to make the acquaintance of my ship. Before I left the cabin our eyes met—the eyes of the only two strangers on board. I pointed to the recessed part where the little camp-stool awaited him and laid my fingers on my lips. He made a gesture—somewhat vague—a little mysterious, accompanied by a faint smile, as if of regret.

This is not the place to enlarge upon the sensations of a man who feels for the first time a ship move under his feet to his own independent word. In my case they were not unalloyed. I was not wholly alone with my command; for there was that stranger in my cabin. Or rather, I was not completely and wholly with her. Part of me was absent. That mental feeling of being in two places at once affected me physically as if the mood of secrecy had penetrated my very soul. Before an hour had elapsed since the ship had begun to move, having occasion to ask the mate (he stood by my side) to take a compass bearing of the Pagoda, I caught myself reaching up to his ear in whispers. I say I caught myself, but enough had escaped to startle the man. I can't describe it otherwise than by saying that he shied. A grave, preoccupied manner, as though he were in possession of some perplexing intelligence, did not leave him henceforth. A little later I moved away from the rail to look at the compass with such a stealthy gait that the helmsman noticed it—and I could not help noticing the unusual roundness of his eyes. These are trifling instances, though it's to no commander's advantage to be suspected of ludicrous eccentricities. But I was also more seriously affected. There are to a seaman certain words, gestures, that should in given conditions come as naturally, as instinctively as the winking of a menaced eye. A certain order should spring on to his lips without thinking; a certain sign should get itself made, so to speak, without reflection. But all unconscious alertness had abandoned me. I had to make an effort of will to recall myself back (from the cabin) to the conditions of the moment. I felt that I was appearing an irresolute commander to those people who were watching me more or less critically.

And, besides, there were the scares. On the second day out, for instance, coming off the deck in the afternoon (I had straw slippers on my bare feet) I stopped at the open pantry door and spoke to the steward. He was doing something there with his back to me. At the sound of my voice he nearly jumped out of his skin, as the saying is, and incidentally broke a cup.

"What on earth's the matter with you?" I asked, astonished.

He was extremely confused. "Beg your pardon, sir. I made sure you were in your cabin."

"You see I wasn't."

"No, sir. I could have sworn I had heard you moving in there not a moment ago. It's most extraordinary . . . very sorry, sir."

I passed on with an inward shudder. I was so identified with my secret double that I did not even mention the fact in those scanty, fearful whispers we exchanged. I suppose he had made some slight noise of some kind or other. It would have been miraculous if he hadn't at one time or another. And yet, haggard as he appeared, he looked always perfectly self-controlled, more than calm—almost invulnerable. On my suggestion he remained almost entirely in the bath-room, which, upon the whole, was the safest place. There could be really no shadow of an excuse for any one ever wanting to go in there, once the steward had done with it. It was a very tiny place. Sometimes he reclined on the floor, his legs bent, his head sustained on one elbow. At others I would find him on the camp-stool, sitting in his grey sleeping-suit and with his cropped dark hair like a patient, unmoved convict. At night I would smuggle him into my bed-place, and we would whisper together with the regular footfalls of the officer of the watch passing and repassing over our heads. It was an infinitely miserable time. It was lucky that some tins of fine preserves were stowed in a locker in my stateroom; hard bread I could always get hold of; and so he lived on stewed chicken, paté de foie gras, asparagus, cooked oysters, sardines—on all sorts of abominable sham delicacies out of tins. My early morning coffee he always drank; and it was all I dared do for him in that respect.

Every day there was the horrible manoeuvring to go through so that my room and then the bath-room should be done in the usual way. I came to hate the sight of the steward, to abhor the voice of that harmless man. I felt that it was he who would bring on the disaster of discovery. It hung like a sword over our heads.

The fourth day out, I think (we were then working

down the east side of the Gulf of Siam, tack for tack, in light winds and smooth water)—the fourth day, I say, of this miserable juggling with the unavoidable, as we sat at our evening meal, that man, whose slightest movement I dreaded, after putting down the dishes ran up on deck busily. This could not be dangerous. Presently he came down again; and then it appeared that he had remembered a coat of mine which I had thrown over a rail to dry after having been wetted in a shower which had passed over the ship in the afternoon. Sitting stolidly at the head of the table I became terrified at the sight of the garment on his arm. Of course he made for my door. There was no time to lose.

"Steward," I thundered. My nerves were so shaken that I could not govern my voice and conceal my agitation. This was the sort of thing that made my terrifically whiskered mate tap his forehead with his forefinger. I had detected him using that gesture while talking on deck with a confidential air to the carpenter. It was too far to hear a word, but I had no doubt that this pantomime could only refer to the strange new captain.

"Yes, sir," the pale-faced steward turned resignedly to me. It was this maddening course of being shouted at, checked without rhyme or reason, arbitrarily chased out of my cabin, suddenly called into it, sent flying out of his pantry on incomprehensible errands, that accounted for the growing wretchedness of his expression.

"Where are you going with that coat?"

"To your room, sir."

"Is there another shower coming?"

"I'm sure I don't know, sir. Shall I go up again and see, sir?"

"No! never mind."

My object was attained, as of course my other self in

there would have heard everything that passed. During this interlude my two officers never raised their eyes off their respective plates; but the lip of that confounded cub, the second mate, quivered visibly.

I expected the steward to hook my coat on and come out at once. He was very slow about it; but I dominated my nervousness sufficiently not to shout after him. Suddenly I became aware (it could be heard plainly enough) that the fellow for some reason or other was opening the door of the bath-room. It was the end. The place was literally not big enough to swing a cat in. My voice died in my throat and I went stony all over. I expected to hear a yell of surprise and terror, and made a movement, but had not the strength to get on my legs. Everything remained still. Had my second self taken the poor wretch by the throat? I don't know what I could have done next moment if I had not seen the steward come out of my room, close the door, and then stand quietly by the sideboard.

"Saved," I thought. "But, no! Lost! Gone! He was gone!"

I laid my knife and fork down and leaned back in my chair. My head swam. After a while, when sufficiently recovered to speak in a steady voice, I instructed my mate to put the ship round at eight o'clock himself.

"I won't come on deck," I went on. "I think I'll turn in, and unless the wind shifts I don't want to be disturbed before midnight. I feel a bit seedy."

"You did look middling bad a little while ago," the chief mate remarked without showing any great concern.

They both went out, and I stared at the steward clearing the table. There was nothing to be read on that wretched man's face. But why did he avoid my eyes, I asked myself. Then I thought I should like to hear the sound of his voice.

"Steward!"

"Sir!" Startled as usual.

"Where did you hang up that coat?"

"In the bath-room, sir." The usual anxious tone. "It's not quite dry yet, sir."

For some time longer I sat in the cuddy. Had my double vanished as he had come? But of his coming there was an explanation, whereas his disappearance would be inexplicable. . . . I went slowly into my dark room, shut the door, lighted the lamp, and for a time dared not turn round. When at last I did I saw him standing bolt-upright in the narrow recessed part. It would not be true to say I had a shock, but an irresistible doubt of his bodily existence flitted through my mind. Can it be, I asked myself, that he is not visible to other eyes than mine? It was like being haunted. Motionless, with a grave face, he raised his hands slightly at me in a gesture which meant clearly, "Heavens! what a narrow escape!" Narrow indeed. I think I had come creeping quietly as near insanity as any man who has not actually gone over the border. That gesture restrained me, so to speak.

The mate with the terrific whiskers was now putting the ship on the other tack. In the moment of profound silence which follows upon the hands going to their stations I heard on the poop his raised voice: "Hard alee!" and the distant shout of the order repeated on the maindeck. The sails, in that light breeze, made but a faint fluttering noise. It ceased. The ship was coming round slowly; I held my breath in the renewed stillness of expectation; one wouldn't have thought that there was a single living soul on her decks. A sudden brisk shout, "Mainsail haul!" broke the spell, and in the noisy cries and rush overhead of the men running away with the main-brace we two, down in my cabin, came together in our usual position by the bed-place.

He did not wait for my question. "I heard him fumbling here and just managed to squat myself down in the bath," he whispered to me. "The fellow only opened the door and put his arm in to hang the coat up. All the same—"

"I never thought of that," I whispered back, even more appalled than before at the closeness of the shave, and marvelling at that something unyielding in his character which was carrying him through so finely. There was no agitation in his whisper. Whoever was being driven distracted, it was not he. He was sane. And the proof of his sanity was continued when he took up the whispering again.

"It would never do for me to come to life again."

It was something that a ghost might have said. But what he was alluding to was his old captain's reluctant admission of the theory of suicide. It would obviously serve his turn—if I had understood at all the view which seemed to govern the unalterable purpose of his action.

"You must maroon me as soon as ever you can get amongst these islands off the Cambodge shore," he went on.

"Maroon you! We are not living in a boy's adventure tale," I protested. His scornful whispering took me up.

"We aren't indeed! There's nothing of a boy's tale in this. But there's nothing else for it. I want no more. You don't suppose I am afraid of what can be done to me? Prison or gallows or whatever they may please. But you don't see me coming back to explain such things to an old fellow in a wig and twelve respectable tradesmen, do you? What can they know whether I am guilty or not—or of *what* I am guilty, either? That's my affair. What does the Bible say? 'Driven off the face of the earth.' Very well. I am off the face of the earth now. As I came at night so I shall go."

"Impossible!" I murmured. "You can't."

"Can't? . . . Not naked like a soul on the Day of Judgment, I shall freeze on to this sleeping-suit. The Last Day is not yet—and . . . you have understood thoroughly. Didn't you?"

I felt suddenly ashamed of myself. I may say truly that I understood—and my hesitation in letting that man swim away from my ship's side had been a mere sham sentiment, a sort of cowardice.

"It can't be done now till next night," I breathed out. "The ship is on the off-shore tack and the wind may fail us."

"As long as I know that you understand," he whispered. "But of course you do. It's a great satisfaction to have got somebody to understand. You seem to have been there on purpose." And in the same whisper, as if we two whenever we talked had to say things to each other which were not fit for the world to hear, he added, "It's very wonderful."

We remained side by side talking in our secret way—but sometimes silent or just exchanging a whispered word or two at long intervals. And as usual he stared through the port. A breath of wind came now and again into our faces. The ship might have been moored in dock, so gently and on an even keel she slipped through the water, that did not murmur even at our passage, shadowy and silent like a phantom sea.

At midnight I went on deck, and to my mate's great

surprise put the ship round on the other tack. His terrible whiskers flitted round me in silent criticism. I certainly should not have done it if it had been only a question of getting out of that sleepy gulf as quickly as possible. I believe he told the second mate, who relieved him, that it was a great want of judgment. The other only yawned. That intolerable cub shuffled about so sleepily and lolled against the rails in such a slack, improper fashion that I came down on him sharply.

"Aren't you properly awake yet?"

"Yes, sir! I am awake."

"Well, then, be good enough to hold yourself as if you were. And keep a look-out. If there's any current we'll be closing with some islands before daylight."

The east side of the gulf's fringed with islands, some solitary, others in groups. On the blue background of the high coast they seem to float on silvery patches of calm water, arid and grey, or dark green and rounded like clumps of evergreen bushes, with the larger ones, a mile or two long, showing the outlines of ridges, ribs of grey rock under the dank mantle of matted leafage. Unknown to trade, to travel, almost to geography, the manner of life they harbour is an unsolved secret. There must be villages—settlements of fishermen at least—on the largest of them, and some communication with the world is probably kept up by native craft. But all that forenoon, as we headed for them, fanned along by the faintest of breezes, I saw no sign of man or canoe in the field of the telescope I kept on pointing at the scattered group.

At noon I gave no orders for a change of course, and the mate's whiskers became much concerned and seemed to be offering themselves unduly to my notice. At last I said:

"I am going to stand right in. Quite in—as far as I can take her."

The stare of extreme surprise imparted an air of ferocity also to his eyes, and he looked truly terrific for a moment.

"We're not doing well in the middle of the gulf," I continued, casually. "I am going to look for the land breezes tonight."

"Bless my soul! Do you mean, sir, in the dark amongst the lot of all them islands and reefs and shoals?"

"Well—if there are any regular land breezes at all on this coast one must get close inshore to find them, mustn't one?"

"Bless my soul!" he exclaimed again under his breath. All that afternoon he wore a dreamy, contemplative appearance which in him was a mark of perplexity. After dinner I went into my stateroom as if I meant to take some rest. There we two bent our dark heads over a half-unrolled chart lying on my bed.

"There," I said. "It's got to be Koh-ring. I've been looking at it ever since sunrise. It has got two hills and a low point. It must be inhabited. And on the coast opposite there is what looks like the mouth of a biggish river—with some town, no doubt, not far up. It's the best chance for you that I can see."

"Anything. Koh-ring let it be."

He looked thoughtfully at the chart as if surveying chances and distances from a lofty height—and following with his eyes his own figure wandering on the blank land of Cochin-China, and then passing off that piece of paper clean out of sight into uncharted regions. And it was as if the ship had two captains to plan her course for her. I had been so worried and restless running up and down that I had not had the patience to dress that day. I had remained in my sleeping-suit, with straw slippers and a soft floppy hat. The closeness of the heat in the gulf had been most oppressive, and the crew were used to see me wandering in that airy attire.

"She will clear the south point as she heads now," I whispered into his ear. "Goodness only knows when, though, but certainly after dark. I'll edge her in to half a mile, as far as I may be able to judge in the dark—"

"Be careful," he murmured, warningly—and I realized suddenly that all my future, the only future for which I was fit, would perhaps go irretrievably to pieces in any mishap to my first command.

I could not stop a moment longer in the room. I motioned him to get out of sight and made my way on the poop. That unplayful cub had the watch. I walked up and down for a while thinking things out, then beckoned him over.

"Send a couple of hands to open the two quarter-deck ports," I said, mildly.

He actually had the impudence, or else so forgot himself in his wonder at such an incomprehensible order, as to repeat:

"Open the quarter-deck ports! What for, sir?"

"The only reason you need concern yourself about is because I tell you to do so. Have them opened wide and fastened properly."

He reddened and went off, but I believe made some jeering remark to the carpenter as to the sensible practice of ventilating a ship's quarter-deck. I know he popped into the mate's cabin to impart the fact to him because the whiskers came on deck, as it were by chance, and stole glances at me from below—for signs of lunacy or drunkenness, I suppose.

A little before supper, feeling more restless than ever, I rejoined, for a moment, my second self. And to find him sitting so quietly was surprising, like something against nature, inhuman.

I developed my plan in a hurried whisper.

"I shall stand in as close as I dare and then put her round. I will presently find means to smuggle you out of here into the sail-locker, which communicates with the lobby. But there is an opening, a sort of square for hauling the sails out, which gives straight on the quarter-deck and which is never closed in fine weather, so as to give air to the sails. When the ship's way is deadened in stays and all the hands are aft at the main-braces you will have a clear road to slip out and get overboard through the open quarter-deck port. I've had them both fastened up. Use a rope's end to lower yourself into the water so as to avoid a splash—you know. It could be heard and cause some beastly complication."

He kept silent for a while, then whispered, "I understand."

"I won't be there to see you go," I began with an effort. "The rest . . . I only hope I have understood, too."

"You have. From first to last"—and for the first time there seemed to be a faltering, something strained in his whisper. He caught hold of my arm, but the ringing of the supper bell made me start. He didn't, though; he only released his grip.

After supper I didn't come below again till well past eight o'clock. The faint, steady breeze was loaded with dew; and the wet, darkened sails held all there was of propelling power in it. The night, clear and starry, sparkled darkly, and the opaque, lightless patches shifting slowly against the low stars were the drifting islets.

On the port bow there was a big one more distant and shadowily imposing by the great space of sky it eclipsed.

On opening the door I had a back view of my very own self looking at a chart. He had come out of the recess and was standing near the table.

"Quite dark enough," I whispered.

He stepped back and leaned against my bed with a level, quiet glance. I sat on the couch. We had nothing to say to each other. Over our heads the officer of the watch moved here and there. Then I heard him move quickly. I knew what that meant. He was making for the companion; and presently his voice was outside my door.

"We are drawing in pretty fast, sir. Land looks rather close."

"Very well," I answered. "I am coming on deck directly."

I waited till he was gone out of the cuddy, then rose. My double moved too. The time had come to exchange our last whispers, for neither of us was ever to hear each other's natural voice.

"Look here!" I opened a drawer and took out three sovereigns. "Take this anyhow. I've got six and I'd give you the lot, only I must keep a little money to buy some fruit and vegetables for the crew from native boats as we go through Sunda Straits."

He shook his head.

"Take it," I urged him, whispering desperately. "No one can tell what—"

He smiled and slapped meaningly the only pocket of the sleeping-jacket. It was not safe, certainly. But I produced a large old silk handkerchief of mine, and tying the three pieces of gold in a corner, pressed it on him. He was touched, I suppose, because he took it at last and tied it quickly round his waist under the jacket, on his bare skin.

Our eyes met; several seconds elapsed, till, our glances still mingled, I extended my hand and turned the lamp out. Then I passed through the cuddy, leaving the door of my room wide open. . . . "Steward!"

He was still lingering in the pantry in the greatness of his zeal, giving a rub-up to a plated cruet stand the last thing before going to bed. Being careful not to wake up the mate, whose room was opposite, I spoke in an undertone.

He looked round anxiously. "Sir!"

"Can you get me a little hot water from the galley?"

"I am afraid, sir, the galley fire's been out for some time now."

"Go and see."

He flew up the stairs.

"Now," I whispered, loudly, into the saloon—too loudly, perhaps, but I was afraid I couldn't make a sound. He was by my side in an instant—the double captain slipped past the stairs—through a tiny dark passage . . . a sliding door. We were in the sail-locker, scrambling on our knees over the sails. A sudden thought struck me. I saw myself wandering barefooted, bareheaded, the sun beating on my dark poll. I snatched off my floppy hat and tried hurriedly in the dark to ram it on my other self. He dodged and fended off silently. I wonder what he thought had come to me before he understood and suddenly desisted. Our hands met gropingly, lingered united in a steady, motionless clasp for a second. . . . No word was breathed by either of us when they separated.

I was standing quietly by the pantry door when the steward returned.

"Sorry, sir. Kettle barely warm. Shall I light the spirit-lamp?"

"Never mind."

I came out on deck slowly. It was now a matter of conscience to shave the land as close as possible—for now he must go overboard whenever the ship was put in stays. Must! There could be no going back for him. After a moment I walked over to leeward and my heart flew into my mouth at the nearness of the land on the bow. Under any other circumstances I would not have held on a minute longer. The second mate had followed me anxiously.

I looked on till I felt I could command my voice.

"She will weather," I said then in a quiet tone.

"Are you going to try that, sir?" he stammered out incredulously.

I took no notice of him and raised my tone just enough to be heard by the helmsman.

"Keep her good full."

"Good full, sir."

The wind fanned my cheek, the sails slept, the world was silent. The strain of watching the dark loom of the land grow bigger and denser was too much for me. I had shut my eyes—because the ship must go closer. She must! The stillness was intolerable. Were we standing still?

When I opened my eyes the second view started my heart with a thump. The black southern hill of Koh-ring seemed to hang right over the ship like a towering fragment of the everlasting night. On that enormous mass of blackness there was not a gleam to be seen, not a sound to be heard. It was gliding irresistibly towards us and yet seemed already within reach of the hand. I saw the vague figures of the watch grouped in the waist, gazing in awed silence.

"Are you going on, sir?" inquired an unsteady voice at my elbow.

I ignored it. I had to go on.

"Keep her full. Don't check her way. That won't do now," I said, warningly.

"I can't see the sails very well," the helmsman answered me, in strange, quavering tones.

Was she close enough? Already she was, I won't say in the shadow of the land, but in the very blackness of it, already swallowed up as it were, gone too close to be recalled, gone from me altogether.

"Give the mate a call," I said to the young man who stood at my elbow as still as death. "And turn all hands up."

My tone had a borrowed loudness reverberated from the height of the land. Several voices cried out together: "We are all on deck, sir."

Then stillness again, with the great shadow gliding closer, towering higher, without a light, without a sound. Such a hush had fallen on the ship that she might have been a bark of the dead floating in slowly under the very gate of Erebus.

"My God! Where are we?"

It was the mate moaning at my elbow. He was thunderstruck, and as it were deprived of the moral support of his whiskers. He clapped his hands and absolutely cried out, "Lost!"

"Be quiet," I said, sternly.

He lowered his tone, but I saw the shadowy gesture of his despair. "What are we doing here?"

"Looking for the land wind."

He made as if to tear his hair, and addressed me recklessly.

"She will never get out. You have done it, sir. I knew it'd end in something like this. She will never weather, and you are too close now to stay. She'll drift ashore before she's round. O my God!"

I caught his arm as he was raising it to batter his poor devoted head, and shook it violently.

"She's ashore already," he wailed, trying to tear himself away.

"Is she? . . . Keep good full there!"

"Good full, sir," cried the helmsman in a frightened, thin, child-like voice.

I hadn't let go the mate's arm and went on shaking it. "Ready about, do you hear? You go forward"—shake—"and stop there"—shake—"and hold your noise"—shake—"and see these head-sheets properly overhauled"—shake, shake—shake.

And all the time I dared not look towards the land lest my heart should fail me. I released my grip at last and he ran forward as if fleeing for dear life.

I wondered what my double there in the sail-locker thought of this commotion. He was able to hear everything—and perhaps he was able to understand why, on my conscience, it had to be thus close—no less. My first order "Hard alee!" re-echoed ominously under the towering shadow of Koh-ring as if I had shouted in a mountain gorge. And then I watched the land intently. In that smooth water and light wind it was impossible to feel the ship coming-to. No! I could not feel her. And my second self was making now ready to slip out and lower himself overboard. Perhaps he was gone already . . . ?

The great black mass brooding over our very mastheads began to pivot away from the ship's side silently. And now I forgot the secret stranger ready to depart, and remembered only that I was a total stranger to the ship. I did not know her. Would she do it? How was she to be handled?

I swung the mainyard and waited helplessly. She was perhaps stopped, and her very fate hung in the balance, with the black mass of Koh-ring like the gate of the everlasting night towering over her taffrail. What would she do now? Had she way on her yet? I stepped to the side swiftly, and on the shadowy water I could see nothing except a faint phosphorescent flash revealing the glassy smoothness of the sleeping surface. It was impossible to tell—and I had not learned yet the feel of my ship. Was she moving? What I needed was something easily seen, a piece of paper, which I could throw overboard and watch. I had nothing on me. To run down for it I didn't dare. There was no time. All at once my strained, yearning stare distinguished a white object floating within a yard of the ship's side. White on the black water. A phosphorescent flash passed under it. What was that thing? . . . I recognized my own floppy hat. It must have fallen off his head . . . and he didn't bother. Now I had what I wanted—the saving mark for my eyes. But I hardly thought of my other self, now gone from the ship, to be hidden for ever from all friendly faces, to be a fugitive and a vagabond on the earth, with no brand of the curse on his sane forehead to stay a slaying hand . . . too proud to explain.

And I watched the hat—the expression of my sudden pity for his mere flesh. It had been meant to save his homeless head from the dangers of the sun. And now—

behold—it was saving the ship, by serving me for a mark to help out the ignorance of my strangeness. Ha! It was drifting forward, warning me just in time that the ship had gathered sternway.

"Shift the helm," I said in a low voice to the seaman standing still like a statue.

The man's eyes glistened wildly in the binnacle light as he jumped round to the other side and spun round the wheel.

I walked to the break of the poop. On the overshadowed deck all hands stood by the forebraces waiting for my order. The stars ahead seemed to be gliding from right to left. And all was so still in the world that I heard the quiet remark, "She's round," passed in a tone of intense relief between two seamen.

"Let go and haul."

The foreyards ran round with a great noise, amidst cheery cries. And now the frightful whiskers made themselves heard giving various orders. Already the ship was drawing ahead. And I was alone with her. Nothing! no one in the world should stand now between us, throwing a shadow on the way of silent knowledge and mute affection, the perfect communion of a seaman with his first command.

Walking to the taffrail, I was in time to make out, on the very edge of a darkness thrown by a towering black mass like the very gateway of Erebus—yes, I was in time to catch an evanescent glimpse of my white hat left behind to mark the spot where the secret sharer of my cabin and of my thoughts, as though he were my second self, had lowered himself into the water to take his punishment: a free man, a proud swimmer striking out for a new destiny.

G. K. CHESTERTON

The Invisible Man

The Invisible Man is taken from *The Innocence of Father Brown,* the first (1911) of three books of stories Chesterton wrote about his Catholic priest who solves crimes without the aid of criminology, by intuition and simple common sense.

It is hard to love the Amateur Detective, either in fiction or in real life. That a man should hound his fellow-men for pay is quite bad enough; and we, his paymasters, must all share in his guilt. But that an unpaid dilettante should do the same thing for his own amusement is infinitely worse. No amount of fine phrases about civic responsibility can alter that plain human truth. And the more the Amateur Detective tries to justify his hobby, the more contemptible he becomes.

Father Brown would deny the accusation that he is an amateur detective; and, indeed, he leaves most of the dirty work to his friend Flambeau, a French jewel-thief whom he has persuaded to move across on to the safe side of the Law. But he is one, just the same. Chesterton obviously loves Brown, whom he pictures as a round-faced little bundle of humor and humility, unspectacularly courageous, rich in the wisdom of true innocence; in fact, a near-saint. I dislike him greatly. I think him a smug creature, strong in the strength of his bigotry and astonishingly venomous when crossed.

And yet—how magical is the world that he inhabits! Robert Louis Stevenson and Arthur Conan Doyle had already created a romantic image of London at the turn of the century—a city of night, pea soup fogs, gaslight, hansom-cabs and opera-hats. Chesterton borrowed something from them, but his London is far more flamboyant than theirs; his sparkling alliterations and gaudy imagery light it up like a fairground:

> Against this one fiery glass were glued the noses of many gutter-snipes, for the chocolates were all wrapped in those red and gold and green metallic colours which are almost better than chocolate itself; and the huge white wedding-cake in the window was somehow at once remote and satisfying, just as if the whole North Pole were good to eat.

The setting of the Father Brown stories is nearly fantastic, nearly make-believe, but never quite. When Chesterton tried out-and-out fantasy, as he did in *The Napoleon of Notting Hill* for example, he was apt, in my opinion, to lose control of his medium. Here he plays fair, or fair enough—though some readers may be unable to accept the semantic trick upon which this story is based: namely, that the Invisible Man proves, after all, to be only "mentally invisible."

> "Who is this fellow?" (Flambeau asks) "What does he look like? What is the usual get-up of a mentally invisible man?"
>
> (And Father Brown answers) "He is dressed rather handsomely in red, blue and gold, and in

this striking and even showy, costume he entered Himylaya Mansions under eight human eyes; he killed Smythe in cold blood, and came down into the street again carrying the dead body in his arms. . . ."

This, as we later have to admit, is no dishonest exaggeration but a literally truthful reply to Flambeau's question. And, whether you like the style of it or not, it strikes the authentic Chestertonian note. It could have been written by nobody else.

Since this story is offered as an entrance gate to the rest of Chesterton's world, I would like to call the reader's attention to another area of it, his literary criticism. Even if you ordinarily dislike this kind of reading, try *The Victorian Age in Literature* —a formidable title for one of the funniest and most exciting books I know.

IN THE COOL BLUE TWILIGHT OF TWO STEEP STREETS IN Camden Town, the shop at the corner, a confectioner's, glowed like the butt of a cigar. One should rather say, perhaps, like the butt of a firework, for the light was of many colours and some complexity, broken up by many mirrors and dancing on many gilt and gaily-coloured cakes and sweetmeats. Against this one fiery glass were glued the noses of many gutter-snipes, for the chocolates were all wrapped in those red and gold and green metallic colours which are almost better than chocolate itself; and the huge white wedding-cake in the window was somehow at once remote and satisfying, just as if the whole North Pole were good to eat. Such rainbow provocations could naturally collect the youth of the neighbourhood up to the ages of ten or twelve. But this corner was also attractive to youth at a later stage; and a young man, not less than twenty-four, was staring into the same shop window. To him, also, the shop was of fiery charm, but this attraction was not wholly to be explained by chocolates; which, however, he was far from despising.

He was a tall, burly, red-haired young man, with a resolute face but a listless manner. He carried under his arm a flat, grey portfolio of black-and-white sketches, which he had sold with more or less success to publishers ever since his uncle (who was an admiral) had disinherited him for Socialism, because of a lecture which he had delivered against that economic theory. His name was John Turnbull Angus.

Entering at last, he walked through the confectioner's shop to the back room, which was a sort of pastry-cook restaurant, merely raising his hat to the young lady who was serving there. She was a dark, elegant, alert girl in black, with a high colour and very quick, dark eyes; and after the ordinary interval she followed him into the inner room to take his order.

His order was evidently a usual one. "I want, please," he said with precision, "one halfpenny bun and a small cup of black coffee." An instant before the girl could turn away he added, "Also, I want you to marry me."

The young lady of the shop stiffened suddenly and said, "Those are jokes I don't allow."

The red-haired young man lifted grey eyes of an unexpected gravity.

"Really and truly," he said, "it's as serious—as serious as the halfpenny bun. It is expensive, like the bun; one pays for it. It is indigestible, like the bun. It hurts."

The dark young lady had never taken her dark eyes

off him, but seemed to be studying him with almost tragic exactitude. At the end of her scrutiny she had something like the shadow of a smile, and she sat down in a chair.

"Don't you think," observed Angus, absently, "that it's rather cruel to eat these halfpenny buns? They might grow up into penny buns. I shall give up these brutal sports when we are married."

The dark young lady rose from her chair and walked to the window, evidently in a state of strong but not unsympathetic cogitation. When at last she swung round again with an air of resolution she was bewildered to observe that the young man was carefully laying out on the table various objects from the shop window. They included a pyramid of highly coloured sweets, several plates of sandwiches, and the two decanters containing that mysterious port and sherry which are peculiar to pastry-cooks. In the middle of this neat arrangement he had carefully let down the enormous load of white sugared cake which had been the huge ornament of the window.

"What on earth are you doing?" she asked.

"Duty, my dear Laura," he began.

"Oh, for the Lord's sake, stop a minute," she cried, "and don't talk to me in that way. I mean, what is all that?"

"A ceremonial meal, Miss Hope."

"And what is *that?*" she asked impatiently, pointing to the mountain of sugar.

"The wedding-cake, Mrs. Angus," he said.

The girl marched to that article, removed it with some clatter, and put it back in the shop window; she then returned, and, putting her elegant elbows on the table, regarded the young man not unfavourably but with considerable exasperation.

"You don't give me any time to think," she said.

"I'm not such a fool," he answered; "that's my Christian humility."

She was still looking at him; but she had grown considerably graver behind the smile.

"Mr. Angus," she said steadily, "before there is a minute more of this nonsense I must tell you something about myself as shortly as I can."

"Delighted," replied Angus gravely. "You might tell me something about myself, too, while you are about it."

"Oh, do hold your tongue and listen," she said. "It's nothing that I'm ashamed of, and it isn't even anything that I'm specially sorry about. But what would you say if there were something that is no business of mine and yet is my nightmare?"

"In that case," said the man seriously, "I should suggest that you bring back the cake."

"Well, you must listen to the story first," said Laura, persistently. "To begin with, I must tell you that my father owned the inn called the 'Red Fish' at Ludbury, and I used to serve people in the bar."

"I have often wondered," he said, "why there was a kind of a Christian air about this one confectioner's shop."

"Ludbury is a sleepy, grassy little hole in the Eastern Counties, and the only kind of people who ever came to the 'Red Fish' were occasional commercial travellers, and for the rest, the most awful people you can see, only you've never seen them. I mean little, loungy men, who had just enough to live on and had nothing to do but lean about in bar-rooms and bet on horses, in bad clothes that were just too good for them. Even these wretched young rotters were not very common at our house; but there were two of them that were a lot too common—common in every sort of way. They both lived on money of their own, and were wearisomely idle and over-dressed. But yet I was a bit sorry for them, because I half believe they slunk into our little empty bar because each of them had a slight deformity; the sort of thing that some yokels laugh at. It wasn't exactly a deformity either; it was more an oddity. One of them was a surprisingly small man, something like a dwarf, or at least like a jockey. He was not at all jockeyish to look at, though; he had a round black head and a well-trimmed black beard, bright eyes like a bird's; he jingled money in his pockets; he jangled a great gold watch chain; and he never turned up except dressed just too much like a gentleman to be one. He was no fool though, though a futile idler; he was curiously clever at all kinds of things that couldn't be the slightest use; a sort of impromptu conjuring; making fifteen matches set fire to each other like a regular firework; or cutting a banana or some such thing into a dancing doll. His name was Isidore Smythe; and I can see him still, with his little dark face, just coming up to the counter, making a jumping kangaroo out of five cigars.

"The other fellow was more silent and more ordinary; but somehow he alarmed me much more than poor little Smythe. He was very tall and slight, and light-haired; his nose had a high bridge, and he might almost have been handsome in a spectral sort of way; but he had one of the most appalling squints I have ever seen or heard of. When he looked straight at you, you didn't know where you were yourself, let alone what he was looking at. I fancy this sort of disfigurement embittered the poor chap a little; for while Smythe was ready to show off his monkey tricks anywhere, James Welkin (that was the squinting man's name) never did anything except soak in our bar parlour, and go for great walks by himself in the flat, grey country all round. All the same, I think Smythe, too, was a little sensitive about being so small, though he carried it off more smartly. And so it was that I was really puzzled, as well as startled, and very sorry, when they both offered to marry me in the same week.

"Well, I did what I've since thought was perhaps a silly thing. But, after all, these freaks were my friends in a way; and I had a horror of their thinking I refused them for the real reason, which was that they were so impossibly ugly. So I made up some gas of another sort, about never meaning to marry anyone who hadn't carved his way in the world. I said it was a point of principle with me not to live on money that was just inherited like theirs. Two days after I had talked in this well-meaning sort of way, the whole trouble began. The first thing I heard was that both of them had gone off to seek their fortunes, as if they were in some silly fairy tale.

"Well, I've never seen either of them from that day to this. But I've had two letters from the little man called Smythe, and really they were rather exciting."

"Ever heard of the other man?" asked Angus.

"No, he never wrote," said the girl, after an instant's hesitation. "Smythe's first letter was simply to say that he had started out walking with Welkin to London; but Welkin was such a good walker that the little man dropped out of it, and took a rest by the roadside. He happened to be picked up by some travelling show, and, partly because he was nearly a dwarf, and partly because he was really a clever little wretch, he got on quite well in the show business, and was soon sent up to the Aquarium, to do some tricks that I forget. That was his first letter. His second was much more of a startler, and I only got it last week."

The man called Angus emptied his coffee-cup and regarded her with mild and patient eyes. Her own mouth took a slight twist of laughter as she resumed, "I suppose you've seen on the hoardings all about this 'Smythe's Silent Service'? Or you must be the only person that hasn't. Oh, I don't know much about it, it's some clockwork invention for doing all the housework by machinery. You know the sort of thing: 'Press a Button—A Butler who Never Drinks.' 'Turn a Handle—Ten Housemaids who Never Flirt.' You must have seen the advertisements. Well, whatever these machines are, they are making pots of money; and they are making it all for that little imp whom I knew down in Ludbury. I can't help feeling pleased the poor little chap has fallen on his feet; but the plain fact is, I'm in terror of his turning up any minute and telling me he's carved his way in the world—as he certainly has."

"And the other man?" repeated Angus with a sort of obstinate quietude.

Laura Hope got to her feet suddenly. "My friend," she said, "I think you are a witch. Yes, you are quite right. I have not seen a line of the other man's writing; and I have no more notion than the dead of what or where he is. But it is of him that I am frightened. It is he who is all about my path. It is he who has half driven me mad. Indeed, I think he has driven me mad for I have felt him where he could not have been, and I have heard his voice when he could not have spoken."

"Well, my dear," said the young man, cheerfully, "if he were Satan himself, he is done for now you have told somebody. One goes mad all alone, old girl. But when was it you fancied you felt and heard our squinting friend?"

"I heard James Welkin laugh as plainly as I hear you speak," said the girl, steadily. "There was nobody there, for I stood just outside the shop at the corner, and could see down both streets at once. I had forgotten how he laughed, though his laugh was as odd as his squint. I had not thought of him for nearly a year. But it's a solemn truth that a few seconds later the first letter came from his rival."

"Did you ever make the spectre speak or squeak, or anything?" asked Angus, with some interest.

Laura suddenly shuddered, and then said, with an unshaken voice. "Yes. Just when I had finished reading the second letter from Isidore Smythe announcing his success, just then, I heard Welkin say, 'He shan't have you, though.' It was quite plain, as if he were in the room. It is awful, I think I must be mad."

"If you really were mad," said the young man, "you would think you must be sane. But certainly there seems to me to be something a little rum about this unseen gentleman. Two heads are better than one—I spare you allusions to any other organs—and really, if you would allow me, as a sturdy, practical man, to bring back the wedding-cake out of the window—"

Even as he spoke, there was a sort of steely shriek in the street outside, and a small motor, driven at devilish speed, shot up to the door of the shop and stuck there. In the same flash of time a small man in a shiny top hat stood stamping in the outer room.

Angus, who had hitherto maintained hilarious ease

from motives of mental hygiene, revealed the strain of his soul by striding abruptly out of the inner room and confronting the new-comer. A glance at him was quite sufficient to confirm the savage guesswork of a man in love. This very dapper but dwarfish figure, with the spike of black beard carried insolently forward, the clever unrestful eyes, the neat but very nervous fingers, could be none other than the man just described to him: Isidore Smythe, who made dolls out of banana skins and match-boxes; Isidore Smythe, who made millions out of undrinking butlers and unflirting housemaids of metal. For a moment the two men, instinctively understanding each other's air of possession, looked at each other with that curious cold generosity which is the soul of rivalry.

Mr. Smythe, however, made no allusion to the ultimate ground of their antagonism, but said simply and explosively, "Has Miss Hope seen that thing on the window?"

"On the window?" repeated the staring Angus.

"There's no time to explain other things," said the small millionaire shortly. "There's some tomfoolery going on here that has to be investigated."

He pointed his polished walking-stick at the window, recently depleted by the bridal preparations of Mr. Angus; and that gentleman was astonished to see along the front of the glass a long strip of paper pasted, which had certainly not been on the window when he looked through it some time before. Following the energetic Smythe outside into the street, he found that some yard and a half of stamp paper had been carefully gummed along the glass outside, and on this was written in straggly characters, "If you marry Smythe, he will die."

"Laura," said Angus, putting his big red head into the shop, "you're not mad."

"It's the writing of that fellow Welkin," said Smythe gruffly. "I haven't seen him for years, but he's always bothering me. Five times in the last fortnight he's had threatening letters left at my flat, and I can't even find out who leaves them, let alone if it is Welkin himself. The porter of the flats swears that no suspicious characters have been seen, and here he has pasted up a sort of dado on a public shop window, while the people in the shop—"

"Quite so," said Angus modestly, "while the people in the shop were having tea. Well, sir, I can assure you I appreciate your common sense in dealing so directly with the matter. We can talk about other things afterwards. The fellow cannot be very far off yet, for I swear there was no paper there when I went last to the window, ten or fifteen minutes ago. On the other hand, he's too far off to be chased, as we don't even know the direction. If you'll take my advice, Mr. Smythe, you'll put this at once in the hands of some energetic inquiry man, private rather than public. I know an extremely clever fellow, who has set up in business five minutes from here in your car. His name's Flambeau, and though his youth was a bit stormy, he's a strictly honest man now, and his brains are worth money. He lives in Lucknow Mansions, Hampstead."

"That is odd," said the little man, arching his black eyebrows. "I live, myself, in Himylaya Mansions, round the corner. Perhaps you might care to come with me; I can go to my rooms and sort out these queer Welkin documents, while you run round and get your friend the detective."

"You are very good," said Angus politely. "Well, the sooner we act the better."

Both men, with a queer kind of impromptu fairness, took the same sort of formal farewell of the lady, and both jumped into the brisk little car. As Smythe took the handles and they turned the great corner of the street, Angus was amused to see a gigantesque poster of "Smythe's Silent Service," with a picture of a huge headless iron doll, carrying a saucepan with the legend, "A Cook Who is Never Cross."

"I use them in my own flat," said the little black-bearded man, laughing, "partly for advertisements, and partly for real convenience. Honestly, and all above board, those big clockwork dolls of mine do bring your coals or claret or a timetable quicker than any live servants I've ever known, if you know which knob to press. But I'll never deny, between ourselves, that such servants have their disadvantages, too."

"Indeed?" said Angus; "is there something they can't do?"

"Yes," replied Smythe coolly; "they can't tell me who left those threatening letters at my flat."

The man's motor was small and swift like himself; in fact, like his domestic service, it was of his own invention. If he was an advertising quack, he was one who believed in his own wares. The sense of something tiny and flying was accentuated as they swept up long white curves of road in the dead but open daylight of evening. Soon the white curves came sharper and dizzier; they were upon ascending spirals, as they say in the modern religions. For, indeed, they were cresting a corner of London which is almost as precipitous as Edinburgh, if not quite so picturesque. Terrace rose above terrace, and the special tower of flats they sought, rose above them all to almost Egyptian height, gilt by the level sunset. The change, as they turned the corner and entered the crescent known as Himylaya Mansions, was as abrupt as the opening of a window; for they found that pile of flats sitting above London as above a green sea of slate. Opposite to the mansions, on the other side of the gravel crescent, was a bushy enclosure more like a steep hedge or dyke than a garden, and some way below that ran a strip of artificial water, a sort of canal, like the moat of that embowered fortress. As the car swept round the crescent it passed, at one corner, the stray stall of a man selling chestnuts; and right away at the other end of the curve, Angus could see a dim blue policeman walking slowly. These were the only human shapes in that high suburban solitude; but he had an irrational sense that they expressed the speechless poetry of London. He felt as if they were figures in a story.

The little car shot up to the right house like a bullet, and shot out its owner like a bomb shell. He was immediately inquiring of a tall commissionaire in shining braid, and a short porter in shirt sleeves, whether anybody or anything had been seeking his apartments. He was assured that nobody and nothing had passed these officials since his last inquiries; whereupon he and the slightly bewildered Angus were shot up in the lift like a rocket, till they reached the top floor.

"Just come in for a minute," said the breathless Smythe. "I want to show you those Welkin letters. Then you might run round the corner and fetch your friend." He pressed a button concealed in the wall, and the door opened of itself.

It opened on a long, commodious ante-room, of which the only arresting features, ordinarily speaking, were the rows of tall half-human mechanical figures that stood up on both sides like tailors' dummies. Like tailors' dummies they were headless; and like tailors' dummies they had a handsome unnecessary humpiness in the shoulders, and a pigeon-breasted protuberance of chest; but barring this, they were not much more like a human figure than any automatic machine at a station that is about the human height. They had two great hooks like arms, for carrying trays; and they were painted pea-green, or vermilion, or black for convenience of distinction; in every other way they were only automatic machines and nobody would have looked twice at them. On this occasion, at least, nobody did. For between the two rows of these domestic dummies lay something more interesting than most of the mechanics of the world. It was a white, tattered scrap of paper scrawled with red ink; and the agile inventor had snatched it up almost as soon as the door flew open. He handed it to Angus without a word. The red ink on it actually was not dry, and the message ran, "If you have been to see her today, I shall kill you."

There was a short silence, and then Isidore Smythe said quietly, "Would you like a little whiskey? I rather feel as if I should."

"Thank you; I should like a little Flambeau," said Angus, gloomily. "This business seems to me to be getting rather grave. I'm going round at once to fetch him."

"Right you are," said the other, with admirable cheerfulness. "Bring him round here as quick as you can."

But as Angus closed the front door behind him he saw Smythe push back a button, and one of the clockwork images glided from its place and slid along a groove in the floor carrying a tray with syphon and decanter. There did seem something a trifle weird about leaving the little man alone among those dead servants, who were coming to life as the door closed.

Six steps down from Smythe's landing the man in shirt sleeves was doing something with a pail. Angus stopped to extract a promise, fortified with a prospective bribe, that he would remain in that place until the return with the detective, and would keep count of any kind of stranger coming up those stairs. Dashing down to the front hall he then laid similar charges of vigilance on the commissionaire at the front door, from whom he learned the simplifying circumstances that there was no back door. Not content with this, he captured the floating policeman and induced him to stand opposite the entrance and watch it; and finally paused an instant for a pennyworth of chestnuts, and an inquiry as to the probable length of the merchant's stay in the neighbourhood.

The chestnut seller, turning up the collar of his coat, told him he should probably be moving shortly, as he thought it was going to snow. Indeed, the evening was growing grey and bitter, but Angus, with all his eloquence, proceeded to nail the chestnut man to his post.

"Keep yourself warm on your own chestnuts," he said earnestly. "Eat up your whole stock; I'll make it worth your while. I'll give you a sovereign if you'll wait here till I come back, and then tell me whether any man, woman, or child has gone into that house where the commissionaire is standing."

He then walked away smartly, with a last look at the besieged tower.

"I've made a ring round that room, anyhow," he said. "They can't all four of them be Mr. Welkin's accomplices."

Lucknow Mansions were, so to speak, on a lower platform of that hill of houses, of which Himylaya Mansions might be called the peak. Mr. Flambeau's semi-official flat was on the ground floor, and presented in every way a marked contrast to the American machinery and cold hotel-like luxury of the flat of the Silent Service. Flambeau, who was a friend of Angus, received him in a rococo artistic den behind his office, of which the ornaments were sabres, harquebuses, Eastern curiosities, flasks of Italian wine, savage cooking-pots, a plumy Persian cat, and a small dusty-looking Roman Catholic priest, who looked particularly out of place.

"This is my friend Father Brown," said Flambeau. "I've often wanted you to meet him. Splendid weather, this; a little cold for Southerners like me."

"Yes, I think it will keep clear," said Angus, sitting down on a violet-striped Eastern ottoman.

"No," said the priest quietly, "it has begun to snow."

And, indeed, as he spoke, the first few flakes, foreseen by the man of chestnuts, began to drift across the darkening windowpane.

"Well," said Angus heavily. "I'm afraid I've come on business, and rather jumpy business at that. The fact is, Flambeau, within a stone's throw of your house is a fellow who badly wants your help; he's perpetually being haunted and threatened by an invisibile enemy—a scoundrel whom nobody has even seen." As Angus proceeded to tell the whole tale of Smythe and Welkin, beginning with Laura's story, and going on with his own, the supernatural laugh at the corner of two empty streets, the strange distinct words spoken in an empty room, Flambeau grew more and more vividly concerned, and the little priest seemed to be left out of it, like a piece of furniture. When it came to the scribbled stamp-paper pasted on the window, Flambeau rose, seeming to fill the room with his huge shoulders.

"If you don't mind," he said, "I think you had better tell me the rest on the nearest road to this man's house. It strikes me, somehow, that there is no time to be lost."

"Delighted," said Angus, rising also, "though he's safe enough for the present, for I've set four men to watch the only hole to his burrow."

They turned out into the street, the small priest trundling after them with the docility of a small dog. He merely said, in a cheerful way, like one making conversation, "How quick the snow gets thick on the ground."

As they threaded the steep side streets already powdered with silver, Angus finished his story; and by the time they reached the crescent with the towering flats, he had leisure to turn his attention to the four sentinels. The chestnut seller, both before and after receiving a sovereign, swore stubbornly that he had watched the door and seen no visitor enter. The policeman was even more emphatic. He said he had had experience of crooks of all kinds, in top hats and in rags; he wasn't so green as to expect suspicious characters to look suspicious; he looked out for anybody, and, so help him, there had been nobody. And when all three men gathered round the gilded commissionaire, who still stood smiling astride of the porch, the verdict was more final still.

"I've got a right to ask any man, duke or dustman, what he wants in these flats," said the genial and gold-laced giant, "and I'll swear there's been nobody to ask since this gentleman went away."

The unimportant Father Brown, who stood back, looking modestly at the pavement, here ventured to say meekly, "Has nobody been up and down stairs, then, since the snow began to fall? It began while we were all round at Flambeau's."

"Nobody's been in here, sir, you can take it from me," said the official, with beaming authority.

"Then I wonder what that is?" said the priest, and stared at the ground blankly like a fish.

The others all looked down also; and Flambeau used a fierce exclamation and a French gesture. For it was unquestionably true that down the middle of the entrance guarded by the man in gold lace, actually between the arrogant, stretched legs of that colossus, ran a stringy pattern of grey footprints stamped upon the white snow.

"God!" cried Angus involuntarily, "the Invisible Man!"

Without another word he turned and dashed up the stairs, with Flambeau following; but Father Brown still stood looking about him in the snow-clad street as if he had lost interest in his query.

Flambeau was plainly in a mood to break down the door with his big shoulders; but the Scotchman, with more reason, if less intuition, fumbled about on the frame of the door till he found the invisible button; and the door swung slowly open.

It showed substantially the same serried interior; the hall had grown darker, though it was still struck here and there with the last crimson shafts of sunset, and one or two of the headless machines had been moved from their places for this or that purpose, and stood here and there about the twilit place. The green and red of their coats were all darkened in the dusk; and their likeness to human shapes slightly increased by their very shapelessness. But in the middle of them all, exactly where the paper with the red ink had lain, there lay something that looked like red ink spilt out of its bottle. But it was not red ink.

With a French combination of reason and violence Flambeau simply said "Murder!" and, plunging into the flat, had explored every corner and cupboard of it in five minutes. But if he expected to find a corpse he found none. Isidore Smythe was not in the place, either dead or alive. After the most tearing search the two men met each other in the outer hall, with streaming faces and staring eyes. "My friend," said Flambeau, talking French in his excitement, "not only is your murderer invisible, but he makes invisible also the murdered man."

Angus looked round at the dim room full of dummies, and in some Celtic corner of his Scotch soul a shudder started. One of the life-size dolls stood immediately overshadowing the blood stain, summoned, perhaps, by the slain man an instant before he fell. One of the high-shouldered hooks that served the thing for arms, was a little lifted, and Angus had suddenly the horrid fancy that poor Smythe's own iron child had struck him down. Matter had rebelled, and these machines had killed their master. But even so, what had they done with him?

"Eaten him?" said the nightmare at his ear; and he sickened for an instant at the idea of rent, human remains absorbed and crushed into all that acephalous clockwork.

He recovered his mental health by an emphatic effort,

and said to Flambeau, "Well, there it is. The poor fellow has evaporated like a cloud and left a red streak on the floor. The tale does not belong to this world."

"There is only one thing to be done," said Flambeau, "whether it belongs to this world or the other. I must go down and talk to my friend."

They descended, passing the man with the pail, who again asseverated that he had let no intruder pass, down to the commissionaire and the hovering chestnut man, who rigidly reasserted their own watchfulness. But when Angus looked round for his fourth confirmation he could not see it, and called out with some nervousness, "Where is the policeman?"

"I beg your pardon," said Father Brown; "that is my fault. I just sent him down the road to investigate something—that I just thought worth investigating."

"Well, we want him back pretty soon," said Angus abruptly, "for the wretched man upstairs has not only been murdered, but wiped out."

"How?" asked the priest.

"Father," said Flambeau, after a pause, "upon my soul I believe it is more in your department than mine. No friend or foe has entered the house, but Smythe is gone, as if stolen by the fairies. If that is not supernatural, I—"

As he spoke they were all checked by an unusual sight; the big blue policeman came round the corner of the crescent, running. He came straight up to Brown.

"You're right, sir," he panted, "they've just found poor Mr. Smythe's body in the canal down below."

Angus put his hand wildly to his head. "Did he run down and drown himself?" he asked.

"He never came down, I'll swear," said the constable,

"and he wasn't drowned either, for he died of a great stab over the heart."

"And yet you saw no one enter?" said Flambeau in a grave voice.

"Let us walk down the road a little," said the priest.

As they reached the other end of the crescent he observed abruptly, "Stupid of me! I forgot to ask the policeman something. I wonder if they found a light brown sack."

"Why a light brown sack?" asked Angus, astonished.

"Because if it was any other coloured sack, the case must begin over again," said Father Brown; "but if it was a light brown sack, why, the case is finished."

"I am pleased to hear it," said Angus with hearty irony. "It hasn't begun, so far as I am concerned."

"You must tell us all about it," said Flambeau with a strange heavy simplicity, like a child.

Unconsciously they were walking with quickening steps down the long sweep of road on the other side of the high crescent, Father Brown leading briskly, though in silence. At last he said with an almost touching vagueness, "Well, I'm afraid you'll think it so prosy. We always begin at the abstract end of things, and you can't begin this story anywhere else.

"Have you ever noticed this—that people never answer what you say? They answer what you mean—or what they think you mean. Suppose one lady says to another in a country house, 'Is anybody staying with you?' the lady doesn't answer 'Yes; the butler, the three footmen, the parlourmaid, and so on,' though the parlourmaid may be in the room, or the butler behind her chair. She says 'There is *nobody* staying with us,' meaning nobody of the sort you mean. But suppose a doctor inquiring into an epidemic asks, 'Who is staying in the house?' then the lady will remember the butler, the parlourmaid, and the rest. All language is used like that; you never get a question answered literally, even when you get it answered truly. When those four quite honest men said that no man had gone into the Mansions, they did not really mean that *no man* had gone into them. They meant no man whom they could suspect of being your man. A man did go into the house, and did come out of it, but they never noticed him."

"An invisible man?" inquired Angus, raising his red eyebrows.

"A mentally invisible man," said Father Brown.

A minute or two after he resumed in the same unassuming voice, like a man thinking his way. "Of course you can't think of such a man, until you do think of him. That's where his cleverness comes in. But I came to think of him through two or three little things in the tale Mr. Angus told us. First, there was the fact that this Welkin went for long walks. And then there was the vast lot of stamp paper on the window. And then, most of all, there were the two things the young lady said—things that couldn't be true. Don't get annoyed," he added hastily, noting a sudden movement of the Scotchman's head; "she thought they were true. A person *can't* be quite alone in a street a second before she receives a letter. She can't be quite alone in a street when she starts reading a letter just received. There must be somebody pretty near her; he must be mentally invisible."

"Why must there be somebody near her?" asked Angus.

"Because," said Father Brown, "barring carrier-pigeons, somebody must have brought her the letter."

"Do you really mean to say," asked Flambeau, with energy, "that Welkin carried his rival's letters to his lady?"

"Yes," said the priest. "Welkin carried his rival's letters to his lady. You see, he had to."

"Oh, I can't stand much more of this," exploded Flambeau. "Who is this fellow? What does he look like? What is the usual get-up of a mentally invisible man?"

"He is dressed rather handsomely in red, blue and gold," replied the priest promptly with precision, "and in this striking, and even showy, costume he entered Himylaya Mansions under eight human eyes; he killed Smythe in cold blood, and came down into the street again carrying the dead body in his arms—"

"Reverend sir," cried Angus, standing still, "are you raving mad, or am I?"

"You are not mad," said Brown, "only a little unobservant. You have not noticed such a man as this, for example."

He took three quick strides forward, and put his hand on the shoulder of an ordinary passing postman who had bustled by them unnoticed under the shade of the trees.

"Nobody ever notices postmen somehow," he said thoughtfully; "yet they have passions like other men, and even carry large bags where a small corpse can be stowed quite easily."

The postman, instead of turning naturally, had ducked and tumbled against the garden fence. He was a lean fair-bearded man of very ordinary appearance, but as he turned an alarmed face over his shoulder, all three men were fixed with an almost fiendish squint.

Flambeau went back to his sabres, purple rugs and Persian cat, having many things to attend to. John Turnbull Angus went back to the lady at the shop, with whom that imprudent young man contrives to be extremely comfortable. But Father Brown walked those snow-covered hills under the stars for many hours with a murderer, and what they said to each other will never be known.

GEORGE MOORE

Albert Nobbs

George Moore may be described as a Franco-Irish writer. Born in Ireland in 1852, he spent ten years of his early manhood in Paris, studying to become a painter. Paris did not make a great artist of him but it had much to do with his development into a major novelist. His English style evolved from French models, notably Flaubert and Zola; and the scenery of his stories suggests touches of Degas and Manet, whose friend and admirer he was. Moore has charmingly described his Paris days in his *Confessions of a Young Man.* Thirty years later, Moore's footsteps were followed by James Joyce. (*He* came to Paris to become a concert-singer.) Another thirty years passed, and a third Irish immigrant appeared: Samuel Beckett, author of *Waiting for Godot.* Beckett's immigration has been the most thoroughgoing of the three, for he now writes only in French!

George Moore wrote about ten novels—three of which, at least (*Esther Waters, Evelyn Innes* and its sequel *Sister Teresa*), can fairly be called masterpieces in the old and more exact sense of the word; they show the craftsmanship, the compassionate understanding and the critical taste of a true master. He also wrote autobiography, ranging from the admirable *Confessions* I have mentioned above to some less-than-admirable, less-than-reliable revelations about his love-affairs. A woman friend who had undeservedly figured in these used to say, with a forgiving smile: "Other men kiss and tell. George didn't kiss and told."

Why is Moore so little read today? Perhaps because his method of storytelling has gone out of fashion. One of the greatest writers of our time has compared himself to a boxer. And that, apparently, is what we want—punch. We want to be played with, feinted at, jabbed, hooked, driven into a corner, smashed and floored. Moore's method is altogether different. He works continually but unspectacularly, almost imperceptibly, with tiny strokes. Very delicately, with the utmost caution, he builds a tall pagoda out of toothpicks. Or, if you insist on a metaphor of aggression, he piles straws on the camel, one by one, until he breaks its back.

The action of *Albert Nobbs* is supposed to take place in the Dublin of the 'sixties, but it might just as well have been set fifty years later. The hotel Moore describes here is exactly like the one my parents and I used to stop at on our journeys between England and Limerick, where we lived from 1912 to the outbreak of the War. No doubt these places haven't changed much, even today.

Retelling this story in modern terms, we should, of course, bring out its sexual overtones, and thereby make it much less interesting. Moore was perfectly well aware of these overtones, but he chose another emphasis. To call "Albert Nobbs" a subconscious lesbian—as many of us would be apt to—is not only inaccurate, it is also miserably superficial. "Albert" dressed as a man for economic, not sexual reasons; she wanted a job. Then, having entered upon this masquerade, she had to make the best of its consequences. She had to seek companionship where she could find it. If you think this story is risqué, you are no reader of mine. But if it makes you laugh, I don't blame you. It is very funny, as well as heartbreaking.

WHEN WE WENT UP TO DUBLIN IN THE 'SIXTIES, ALEC, we always put up at Morrison's Hotel, a big family hotel at the corner of Dawson Street, one that was well patronised by the gentry from all over Ireland, my father paying his bill every six months when he was able, which wasn't very often, for what with racing stables and elections following one after the other, Moore Hall wasn't what you'd call overflowing with money. Now that I come to think of it, I can see Morrison's as clearly almost as I do Moore Hall: the front door opening into a short passage, with some half-dozen steps leading up into the house, the glass doors of the coffee-room showing through the dimness, and in front of the visitor a big staircase running up to the second landing. I remember long passages on the second landing, and half-way down these passages was the well. I don't know if it's right to speak of the well of a staircase, but I used to think of it as a well. It was always being drummed into me that I mustn't climb on to the banisters, a thing I wished to do, but was afraid to get astride of them, lest I should lose my head and fall all the way down to the ground floor. There was nothing to stop me from reaching it, if I lost my balance, except a few gas lamps. I think that both the long passages led to minor stairs, but I never followed either lest I should miss my way. A very big building was Morrison's Hotel, with passages running hither and thither, and little flights of stairs in all kinds of odd corners by which the visitors climbed to their apartments, and it needed all my attention to remember the way to our rooms on the second floor. We were always on the second floor in a big sitting-room overlooking College Green, and I remember the pair of windows, their lace curtains and their rep curtains, better than the passages, and better than the windows I can remember myself looking through the pane interested in the coal carts going by, the bell hitched on to the horse's collar jangling all the way down the street, the coalman himself sitting with his legs hanging over the shafts, driving from the wrong side and looking up at the windows to see if he could spy out an order. Fine horses were in these coal carts, stepping out as well as those in our own carriage.

I'm telling you these things for the pleasure of looking back and nothing else. I can see the sitting-room and myself as plainly as I can see the mountains beyond, in some ways plainer, and the waiter that used to attend on us, I can see him, though not as plainly as I see you, Alec; but I'm more knowledgeable of him, if you understand me rightly, and to this day I can recall the frights he gave me when he came behind me, awakening me from my dream of a coalman's life—what he said is forgotten, but his squeaky voice remains in my ears. He seemed to be always laughing at me, showing long, yellow teeth, and I used to be afraid to open the sitting-room door, for I'd be sure to find him waiting on the landing, his napkin thrown over his right shoulder. I think I was afraid he'd pick me up and kiss me. As the whole of my story is about him, perhaps I'd better describe him more fully, and to do that I will tell you that he was a tall, scraggy fellow, with big hips sticking out, and a long, thin throat. It was his throat that frightened me as much as anything about him, unless it was his nose, which was a great high one, or his melancholy eyes, which were pale blue and very small, deep in the head. He was old, but how old I cannot say, for everybody except children seems old to children. He was the ugliest thing I'd seen out of a fairy-book, and I'd beg not to be left alone in the sitting-room; and I'm sure I often asked my father and mother to take another set of rooms, which they never did, for they liked Albert Nobbs. And the guests liked him, and the proprietress liked him, as well she might, for he was the most dependable servant in the hotel; no running round to public-houses and coming back with the smell of whisky and tobacco upon him; no rank pipe in his pocket; and of all, no playing the fool with the maid-servants. Nobody had ever been heard to say he had seen Albert out with one of them—a queer, hobgoblin sort of fellow that they mightn't have cared to be seen with, but all the same it seemed to them funny that he should never propose to walk out with one of them. I've heard the hall-porter say it was hard to understand a man living without taking pleasure in something outside of his work. Holidays he never asked for, and when Mrs. Baker pressed him to go to the salt water for a week, he'd try to rake up an excuse for not going away, asking if it wasn't true that the Blakes, the Joyces, and the Ruttledges were coming up to town, saying that he didn't like to be away, so used were they to him and he to them. A strange life his was, and mysterious, though every hour of it was before them, saving the hours he was asleep, which weren't many, for he was no great sleeper. From the time he got up in the morning till he went to bed at night he was before their eyes, running up and down the staircase, his napkin over his arm, taking orders with cheerfulness, as if an order were as good as a half-crown tip to him, always good-humoured, and making amends for his lack of interest in other people by his willingness to oblige. No one had ever heard him object to doing anything he was asked to do, or even put forward an excuse for not being able to do it. In fact, his willingness to oblige was so notorious in the hotel that Mrs. Baker (the proprietress of Morrison's Hotel at the time) could hardly believe she was listening to him when he began to stumble from one excuse to another for not sharing his bed with Hubert Page, and this after she had told him that his bed was Page's only chance of getting a stretch that night. All the other waiters were married men and went home to their wives. You see, Alec, it was Punchestown week, and beds are as scarce in Dublin that week as diamonds are on the slopes of Croagh Patrick.

But you haven't told me yet who Page was, Alec interjected, and I thought reprovingly. I'm just coming to him, I answered. Hubert Page was a house-painter, well known and well liked by Mrs. Baker. He came over every season, and was always welcome at Morrison's Hotel, and so pleasant were his manners that one forgot the smell of his paint. It is hardly saying too much to say that when Hubert Page had finished his job everybody in the hotel, men and women alike, missed the pleasant sight of this young man going to and fro in his suit of hollands, the long coat buttoned loosely to his figure with large bone buttons, going to and fro about his work, up and down the passages, with a sort of lolling, idle gait that attracted and pleased the eye—a young man that would seem preferable to most men if a man had to choose a bed-fellow, yet seemingly the very one that Albert Nobbs couldn't abide lying down with, a dislike that Mrs. Baker could understand so little that she stood staring at her confused and embarrassed waiter, who was still seeking excuses for his dislike to share his bed with Hubert Page. I suppose you fully understand, she said, that Page is leaving for Belfast by the morning train, and has come over here to ask us for a bed, there not being one at the hotel in which he is working? Albert answered that he understood well enough, but was thinking– He began again to fumble with words. Now, what are you trying to say? Mrs. Baker asked, and rather sharply. My bed is full of lumps, Albert answered. Your mattress full of lumps! the proprietress rapped out; why, your mattress was re-picked and buttoned six months ago, and came back as good as any mattress in the hotel. What kind of story are you telling me? So it was, ma'am, so it was, Albert mumbled, and it was some time before he got out his next excuse: he was a very light sleeper and had never slept with anybody before and was sure he wouldn't close his eyes; not that that would matter much, but his sleeplessness might keep Mr. Page awake. Mr. Page would get a better stretch on one of the sofas in the coffee-room than in my bed, I'm thinking, Mrs. Baker. A better stretch on the sofa in the coffee-room? Mrs. Baker repeated angrily. I don't understand you, not a little bit; and she stood staring at the two men, so dissimilar. But, ma'am, I wouldn't be putting Mr. Nobbs to the inconvenience of my company, the house-painter began. The night is a fine one; I'll keep myself warm with a sharp walk, and the train starts early. You'll do nothing of the kind, Page, she answered; and seeing that Mrs. Baker was now very angry, Albert thought it time to give in, and without more ado he began to assure them both that he'd be glad of Mr. Page's company in his bed. I should think so indeed! interjected Mrs. Baker. But I'm a light sleeper, he added. We've heard that before, Albert! Of course, if Mr. Page is pleased to share my bed, Albert continued, I shall be very glad. If Mr. Nobbs doesn't like my company I should– Don't say another word, Albert whispered, you'll only set her against me. Come upstairs at once; it'll be all right. Come along.

Good-night, ma'am, and I hope– No inconvenience whatever, Page, Mrs. Baker answered. This way, Mr. Page, Albert cried; and as soon as they were in the room he said: I hope you aren't going to cut up rough at anything I've said; it isn't at all as Mrs. Baker put it. I'm glad enough of your company, but you see, as I've never slept with anybody in my life, it may be that I shall be tossing about all night, keeping you awake. Well, if it's to be like that, Page answered, I might as well have a doze on the chair until it's time to go, and not trouble you at all. You won't be giving me any trouble; what I'm afraid of is–but enough has been said; we have to lie down together, whether we like it or whether we don't, for if Mrs. Baker heard that we hadn't been in the same bed together all the fault would lie with me. I'd be sent out of the hotel in double-quick time. But how can she know? Page cried. It's been settled one way, so let us make no more fuss about it.

Albert began to undo his white neck-tie, saying he would try to lie quiet, and Page started pulling off his clothes, thinking he'd be well pleased to be out of the job of lying down with Albert. But he was so dog-tired that he couldn't think any more about whom he was to sleep with, only of the long days of twelve and thirteen hours he had been doing, with a walk to and from his work; only sleep mattered to him, and Albert saw him tumble into bed in the long shirt that he wore under his clothes, and lay himself down next to the wall. It would be better for him to lie on the outside, Albert said to himself, but he didn't like to say anything lest Page might get out of his bed in a fit of ill-humour; but Page, as I've said, was too tired to trouble himself which side of the bed he was to doss on. A moment after he was asleep, and Albert stood listening, his loosened tie dangling, till the heavy breathing from the bed told him that Page was sound asleep. To make full sure he approached the bed stealthily, and overlooking Page, said: Poor fellow, I'm glad he's in my bed, for he'll get a good sleep there and he wants it; and considering that things had fallen out better than he hoped for, he began to undress.

He must have fallen asleep at once, and soundly, for he awoke out of nothingness. Flea! he muttered, and a strong one, too. It must have come from the house-painter alongside of me; a flea will leave anyone to come to me. And turning round in bed he remembered the look of dismay that had appeared on the housemaids' faces yesterday on his telling them that no man would ever love their hides as much as a flea loved his, which was so true that he couldn't understand how it was that the same flea had taken so long to find him out. Fleas must be as partial to him, he said, as they are to me. There it is again, trying to make up for lost time! and out went Albert's leg. I'm afraid I've awakened him, he said, but Hubert only turned over in the bed to sleep more soundly. It's a mercy indeed that he is so tired, Albert said, for if he wasn't very tired that last jump I gave would have awakened him. A moment after Albert was nipped again by another flea, or by the same one, he couldn't tell; he thought it must be a second one, so vigorous was the bite, and he was hard put to it to keep his nails off the spots. I shall only make them worse if I scratch, he said, and he strove to lie quiet. But the torment was too great. I've got to get up, he muttered, and raising himself up quietly, he listened. The striking of a match won't awaken him out of that sleep! and remembering where he had put the match-box, his hand was on it at once. The match flared up; he lighted the candle, and stood a while overlooking his bed-fellow. I'm safe, he said, and set himself to the task of catching the flea. There he is on the tail of my shirt, hardly able to move with all the blood he's taken from me. Now for the soap; and as he was about to dab it upon the blood-filled insect the painter awoke with a great yawn, and turning round, he said: Lord amassy! what is the meaning of this? Why, you're a woman!

If Albert had had the presence of mind to drop her shirt over her shoulders and to answer: You're dreaming, my man, Page might have turned over and fallen asleep and in the morning forgotten all about it, or thought he had been dreaming. But Albert hadn't a word in her chops. At last she began to blub. You won't tell on me, and ruin a poor man, will you, Mr. Page? That is all I ask of you, and on my knees I beg it. Get up from your knees, my good woman, said Hubert. My good woman! Albert repeated, for she had been about so long as a man that she only remembered occasionally that she was a woman. My good woman, Hubert repeated, get up from your knees and tell me how long you have been playing this part. Ever since I was a girl, Albert answered. You won't tell upon me, will you, Mr. Page, and prevent a poor woman from getting her living? Not likely, I've no thought of telling on you, but I'd like to hear how it all came about. How I went out as a youth to get my living? Yes; tell me the story, Hubert answered, for though I was very sleepy just now, the sleep has left my eyes and I'd like to hear it. But before you begin, tell me what you were doing with your shirt off. A flea, Albert answered. I suffer terribly from fleas, you must have brought some in with you, Mr. Page. I shall be covered in blotches in the morning. I'm sorry for that, Hubert said; but tell me how long ago it was that you became a man. Before you came to Dublin, of course? Oh, yes, long before. It is very cold, she said, and shuddering, dropped her shirt over her shoulders and pulled on her trousers.

2

It was in London, soon after the death of my old nurse, she began. You know I'm not Irish, Mr. Page. My parents may have been, for all I know. The only one who knew who they were was my old nurse, and she never told me. Never told you! interjected Hubert. No, she never told me, though I often asked her, saying no good could come of holding it back from me. She might have told me before she died, but she died suddenly. Died suddenly, Hubert repeated, without telling you who you were! You'd better begin at the beginning.

I don't know how I'm to do that, for the story seems to me to be without a beginning; anyway I don't know the beginning. I was a bastard, and no one but my old nurse, who brought me up, knew who I was; she said she'd tell me some day, and she hinted more than once that my people were grand folk, and I know she had a big allowance from them for my education. Whoever they were, a hundred a year was paid to her for my keep and education, and all went well with us so long as my parents lived, but when they died the allowance was no longer paid, and my nurse and myself had to go out to work. It was all very sudden: one day the Reverend Mother (I got my education at a convent school) told me that Mrs. Nobbs, my old nurse, had sent for me, and the first news I had on coming home was that my parents were dead and that we'd have to get our own living henceforth. There was no time for picking and choosing. We hadn't what would keep us until the end of the month in the house, so out we had to go in search of work; and the first job that came our way was looking after chambers in the Temple. We had three gentlemen to look after, so there was eighteen shillings a week between my old nurse and myself; the omnibus fares had to come out of these wages, and to save sixpence a day we went to live in Temple Lane. My old nurse didn't mind the lane; she had been a working woman all her life; but with me it was different, and the change was so great from the convent that I often thought I would sooner die than continue to live amid rough people. There was nothing wrong with them; they were honest enough; but they were poor, and when you are very poor you live like the animals, indecently, and life without decency is hardly bearable, so I thought. I've been through a great deal since in different hotels, and have become used to hard work, but even now I can't think of Temple Lane without goose-flesh; and when Mrs. Nobbs's brother lost his berth (he'd been a bandmaster, a bugler, or something to do with music in the country), my old nurse was obliged to give him sixpence a day, and the drop from eighteen shillings to fourteen and sixpence is a big one. My old nurse worried about the food, but it was the rough men I worried about; the bandsman wouldn't leave me alone, and many's the time I've waited until the staircase was clear, afraid that if I met him or another that I'd be caught hold of and held and pulled about. I was different then from what I am now, and might have been tempted if one of them had been less rough than the rest, and if I hadn't known I was a bastard; it was that, I think, that kept me straight more than anything else, for I had just begun to feel what a great misfortune it is for a poor girl to find herself in the family way; no greater misfortune can befall anyone in this world, but it would have been worse in my case, for I should have known that I was only bringing another bastard into the world.

I escaped being seduced in the lane, and in the chambers the barristers had their own mistresses; pleasant and considerate men they all were—pleasant to work for; and it wasn't until four o'clock came and our work was over for the day that my heart sank, for after four o'clock till we went to bed at night there was nothing for us to do but to listen to the screams of drunken women; I don't know which was the worser, the laughter or the curses.

One of the barristers we worked for was Mr. Congreve; he had chambers in Temple Gardens overlooking the river, and it was a pleasure to us to keep his pretty things clean, never breaking one of them; it was a pleasure for my old nurse as well as myself, myself more than for her, for though I wasn't very sure of myself at the time, looking back now I can see that I must have loved Mr. Congreve very dearly; and it couldn't be else, for I had come out of a convent of nuns where I had been given a good education, where all was good, quiet, refined and gentle, and Mr. Congreve seemed in many ways to remind me of the convent, for he never missed Church; as rare for him to miss a service as for parson. There was plenty of books in his chambers and he'd lend them to me, and talk to me over his newspaper when I took in his breakfast, and ask about the convent and what the nuns were like, and I'd stand in front of him, my eyes fixed on him, not feeling the time going by. I can see him now as plainly as if he were before me—very thin and elegant, with long white hands, and beautifully dressed. Even in the old clothes that he wore of a morning there wasn't much fault to find; he wore old clothes more elegantly than any man in the Temple wore his new clothes. I used to know all his suits, as well I might, for it was my job to look after them, to brush them; and I used to spend a great deal more time than was needed taking out spots with benzine, arranging his neck-ties—he had fifty or sixty, all kinds—and seven or eight great-coats. A real toff—my word he was that, but not one of those haughty ones too proud to give one a nod. He always smiled and nodded if we met under the clock, he on his way to the library and I returning to Temple Lane. I used to look round after him saying: He's got on the striped trousers and the embroidered waistcoat. Mr. Congreve was a compensation for Temple Lane; he had promised to take me into his private service, and I was counting the days when I should leave Temple Lane, when one day I said to myself: Why, here's a letter from a woman. You see, Mr. Congreve wasn't like the other young men in the Temple; I never found a hair-pin in his bed, and if I had I shouldn't have thought as much of him as I did. Nice is in France, I said, and thought no more about the matter until another letter arrived from Nice. Now what can she be writing to him about? I asked, and thought no more about it until the third letter arrived. Yesterday is already more than half forgotten, but the morning I took in that last letter is always before me. And it was a few mornings afterwards that a box of flowers came for him. A parcel for you, sir, I said. He roused himself up in bed. For me? he cried, putting out his hand, and the moment he saw the writing, he said: Put the flowers in water. He knows all about it, I said to myself, and so overcome was I as I picked them up out of the box that a sudden faintness came over me, and my old nurse said: What is the matter with thee? She never guessed, and I couldn't have told her if I had wished to, for at the time it was no more than a feeling that so far as I was concerned all was over. Of course I never thought that Mr. Congreve would look at me, and I don't know that I wanted him to, but I didn't want another woman about the place, and I seemed to know from that moment what was going to happen. She isn't far away now, in the train maybe, I said, as I went about my work, and these rooms will be mine no longer. Of course they never were mine; but you know what I mean.

A week later he said to me: There's a lady coming to luncheon here, and I remember the piercing that the words caused me; I can feel them here still; and Albert put her hand to her heart. Well, I had to serve the luncheon, working round the table and they not minding me at all, but sitting looking at each other lost in a sense of delight; the luncheon was forgotten. They don't want me waiting about, I thought. I knew all this, and said to myself in the kitchen: It's disgraceful, it's wicked, to lead a man into sin—for all my anger went out against the woman, and not against Mr. Congreve; in my eyes he seemed to be nothing more than a victim of a designing woman; that is how I looked at it at the time, being but a youngster only just come from a convent school.

I don't think that anyone suffered more than I did in those days. It all seems very silly now when I look back upon it, but it was very real then. It does seem silly to tell that I used to lie awake all night thinking to myself that Mr. Congreve was an elegant gentleman and I but a poor serving girl that he'd never look twice at, thinking of her only as somebody to go to the cellar for coal or to the kitchen to fetch his breakfast. I don't think I ever hoped he'd fall in love with me. It wasn't as bad as that. It was the hopelessness of it that set the tears streaming down my cheeks over my pillow, and I used to stuff the sheet into my mouth to keep back the sobs lest my old nurse should hear me; it wouldn't do to keep her awake, for she was very ill at that time; and soon afterward she died, and then I was left alone, without a friend in the world. The only people I knew were the charwomen that lived in Temple Lane, and the bugler, who began to bully me, saying that I must continue to give him the same money he had had from my old nurse. He caught me on the stairs once and twisted my arm until I thought he'd broken it. The month after my old nurse's death till I went to earn my living as a waiter was the hardest time of all, and Mr. Congreve's kindness seemed to hurt me more than anything. If only he'd spared me his kind words, and not spoken about the extra money he was going to give me for my attendance on his lady, I shouldn't have felt so much that they had lain side by side in the bed that I was making. She brought a dressing-gown to the chambers and some slippers, and then more luggage came along; and I think she must have guessed I was in love with Mr. Congreve, for I heard them quarrelling—my name was mentioned; and I said: I can't put up with it any longer; whatever the next life may be like, it can't be worse than this one for me at least; and as I went to and fro between Temple Lane and the chambers in Temple Gardens I began to think how I might make away with myself. I don't know if you know London, Hubert? Yes, he said; I'm a Londoner, but I come here to work every year. Then if you know the Temple, you know that the windows of Temple Gardens overlook the river. I used to stand at those windows watching the big brown river flowing through its bridges, thinking all the while of the sea into which it went, and that I must plunge into the river and be carried away down to the sea, or be picked up before I got there. I could only think about making an end to my trouble and of the Frenchwoman. Her suspicions that I cared for him made her harder on me than she need have been; she was always coming the missis over me. Her airs and graces stiffened my back more than anything else, and I'm sure if I hadn't met Bessie Lawrence I should have done away with myself. She was the woman who used to look after the chambers under Mr. Congreve's. We stopped talking outside the gateway by King's Bench Walk—if you know the Temple, you know where I mean. Bessie kept talking, but I wasn't listening, only catching a word here and there, not waking up from the dream how to make away with myself till I heard the words: If I had a figure like yours. As no one had ever spoken about my figure before, I said: Now what has my figure got to do with it? You haven't been listening to me, she said, and I answered that I had only missed the last few words. Just missed the last few words, she said testily; you didn't hear me telling you that there is a big dinner at the Freemason's Tavern tonight, and they're short of waiters. But what has that got to do with my figure? I asked. That shows, she rapped out, that you haven't been listening to me. Didn't I say that if it wasn't for my hips and bosom I'd very soon be into a suit of evening clothes and getting ten shillings for the job. But what has that got to do with my figure? I repeated. Your figure is just the one for a waiter's. Oh, I'd never thought of that, says I, and we said no more. But the words: Your figure is just the one for a waiter's, kept on in my head till my eyes caught sight of a bundle of old clothes that Mr. Congreve had given me to sell. A suit of evening clothes was in it. You see, Mr. Congreve and myself were about the same height and build. The trousers will want a bit of shortening, I said to myself, and I set to work; and at six o'clock I was in them and down at the Freemason's Tavern answering questions, saying that I had been accustomed to waiting at table. All the waiting I had done was bringing in Mr. Congreve's dinner from the kitchen to the sitting-room: a roast chicken or a chop, and in my fancy it seemed to me that the waiting at the Freemason's Tavern would be much the same. The head waiter looked me over a bit doubtfully and asked if I had had experience with public dinners. I thought he was going to turn me down, but they were short-handed, so I was taken on, and it was a mess that I made of it, getting in everybody's way; but my awkwardness was taken in good part and I received ten shillings, which was good money for the sort of work I did that night. But what stood to me was not so much the ten shillings that I earned as the bit I had learned. It was only a bit, not much bigger than a threepenny bit; but I had worked round a table at a big dinner, and feeling certain that I could learn what I didn't know, I asked for another job. I suppose the head waiter could see that there was the making of a waiter in me, for on coming out of the Freemason's Tavern he stopped me to ask if I was going back to private service as soon as I could get a place. The food I'd had and the excitement of the dinner, the guests, the lights, the talk, stood to me, and things seemed clearer than they had ever seemed before. My feet were of the same mind, for they wouldn't walk towards the Temple, and I answered the head waiter that I'd be glad of another job. Well, said he, you don't much know about the work, but you're an honest lad, I think, so I'll see what I can do for you; and at the moment a thought struck him. Just take this letter, said he, to the Holborn Restaurant. There's a dinner there and I've had word that they're short of a waiter or two. Be off as fast as you can. And away I went as fast as my legs could carry me, and they took me there in good time, in front, by a few seconds, of two other fellows who were after the job. I got it. Another job came along, and another and another. Each of them jobs was worth ten shillings to me, to say nothing of the learning of the trade; and having, as I've said, the making of a waiter in me, it didn't take more than about three months for me to be as quick and as smart and as watchful as the best of them, and without them qualities no one will succeed in waiting. I have worked round the tables in the biggest places in London and all over England in all the big towns, in Manchester, in Liverpool, and Birmingham; I am well known at the old Hen and Chickens, at the Queen's, and the Plough and Harrow in Birmingham. It was seven years ago that I came here, and here it would seem that I've come to be looked on as a fixture, for the Bakers are good people to work for and I didn't like to leave them when, three years ago, a good place was offered to me, so kind were they to me in my illness. I suppose one never remains always in the same place, but I may as well be here as elsewhere.

Seven years working in Morrison's Hotel, Page said, and on the second floor? Yes, the second floor is the best in the hotel; the money is better than in the coffee-room, and that is why the Bakers have put me here, Albert replied. I wouldn't care to leave them; they've often said they don't know what they'd do without me. Seven years, Hubert repeated, the same work up the stairs and down the stairs, banging into the kitchen and out again. There's more variety in the work than you think for, Hubert, Albert answered. Every family is different, and so you're always learning. Seven years, Page repeated, neither man nor woman, just a perhapser. He spoke these words more to himself than to Nobbs, but feeling he had expressed himself incautiously he raised his eyes and read on Albert's face that the words had gone home, and that this outcast from both sexes felt her loneliness perhaps more keenly than before. As Hubert was thinking what words he might use to conciliate Albert with her lot, Albert repeated the words: Neither man nor woman; yet nobody ever suspected, she muttered, and never would have suspected me till the day of my death if it hadn't been for that flea that you brought in with you. But what harm did the flea do? I'm bitten all over, said Albert, scratching her thighs. Never mind the bites, said Hubert; we wouldn't have had this talk if it hadn't been for the flea, and I shouldn't have heard your story.

Tears trembled on Albert's eyelids; she tried to keep them back, but they overflowed the lids and were soon running quickly down her cheeks. You've heard my story, she said. I thought nobody would ever hear it, and I thought I should never cry again; and Hubert watched the gaunt woman shaking with sobs under a coarse nightshirt. It's all much sadder than I thought it was, and if I'd known how sad it was I shouldn't have been able to live through it. But I've jostled along somehow, she added, always merry and bright, with never anyone to speak to, not really to speak to, only to ask for plates and dishes, for knives and forks and such like, tablecloths and napkins, cursing betimes the life you've been through; for the feeling cannot help coming over us, perhaps over the biggest as over the smallest, that all our trouble is for nothing and can end in nothing. It might have been better if I had taken the plunge. But why am I thinking these things? It's you that has set me thinking, Hubert. I'm sorry if– Oh, it's no use being sorry, and I'm a great silly to cry like this. I thought that regrets had passed away with the petticoats. But you've awakened the woman in me. You've brought it all up again. But I mustn't let on like this; it's very foolish of an old perhapser like me, neither man nor woman! But I can't help it. She began to sob again, and in the midst of her grief the word loneliness was uttered, and when the paroxysm was over, Hubert said: Lonely, yes, I suppose it is lonely; and he put his hand out towards Albert. You're very good, Mr. Page, and I'm sure you'll keep my secret, though indeed I don't care very much whether you do or not. Now, don't let on like that again, Hubert said. Let us have a little chat and try to understand each other. I'm sure it's lonely for you to live without man or without woman, thinking like a man and feeling like a woman. You seem to know all about it, Hubert. I hadn't thought of it like that before myself, but when you speak the words I feel you have spoken the truth. I suppose I was wrong to put off my petticoats and step into those trousers. I wouldn't go so far as to say that, Hubert answered, and the words were so unexpected that Albert forgot her grief for a moment and said: Why do you say that, Hubert? Well, because I was thinking, he replied, that you might marry. But I was never a success as a girl. Men didn't look at me then, so I'm sure they wouldn't now I'm a middle-aged woman. Marriage! whom should I marry? No, there's no marriage for me in the world; I must go on being a man. But you won't tell on me? You've promised, Hubert. Of course I won't tell, but I don't see why you shouldn't marry. What do you mean, Hubert? You aren't putting a joke upon me, are you? If you are it's very unkind. A joke upon you? no, Hubert answered. I didn't mean that you should marry a man, but you might marry a girl. Marry a girl? Albert repeated, her eyes wide open and staring. A girl? Well, anyway, that's what I've done, Hubert replied. But you're a young man and a very handsome young man too. Any girl would like to have you, and I dare say they were all after you before you met the right girl. I'm not a young man, I'm a woman, Hubert replied. Now I know for certain, cried Albert, you're putting a joke upon me. A woman! Yes, a woman; you can feel for yourself if you won't believe me. Put your hand under my shirt; you'll find nothing there. Albert moved away instinctively, her modesty having been shocked. You see I offered myself like that feeling you couldn't take my word for it. It isn't a thing there can be any doubt about. Oh, I believe you, Albert replied. And now that that matter is settled, Hubert began, perhaps you'd like to hear my story; and without waiting for an answer she related the story of her unhappy marriage: her husband, a house-painter, had changed towards her altogether after the birth of her second child, leaving her without money for food and selling up the home twice. At last I decided to have another cut at it, Hubert went on, and catching sight of my husband's working clothes one day I said to myself: He's often made me put these on and go out and help him with his job; why shouldn't I put them on for myself and go away for good? I didn't like leaving the children, but I couldn't remain with him. But the marriage? Albert asked. It was lonely going home to an empty room; I was as lonely as you, and one day, meeting a girl as lonely as myself, I said: Come along, and we arranged to live together, each paying our share. She had her work and I had mine, and between us we made a fair living; and this I can say with truth, that we haven't known an unhappy hour since we married. People began to talk, so we had to. I'd like you to see our home. I always return to my home after a job is finished with a light heart and leave it with a heavy one. But I don't understand, Albert said. What don't you understand? Hubert asked. Whatever Albert's thoughts were, they faded from her, and her eyelids dropped over her eyes. You're falling asleep, Hubert said, and I'm doing the same. It must be three o'clock in the morning and I've to catch the five o'clock train. I can't think now of what I was going to ask you, Albert muttered, but you'll tell me in the morning; and turning over, she made a place for Hubert.

3

What has become of him? Albert said, rousing herself, and then, remembering that Hubert's intention was to catch the early train, she began to remember. His train, she said, started from Amiens Street at—I must have slept heavily for him—for her not to have awakened me, or she must have stolen away very quietly. But, lord amassy, what time is it? And seeing she had overslept herself a full hour, she began to dress herself, muttering all the while: Such a thing never happened to me before. And the hotel as full as it can hold. Why didn't they send for me? The missis had a thought of my bed-fellow, mayhap, and let me sleep it out. I told her I shouldn't close an eye till she left me. But I mustn't fall into the habit of sheing him. Lord, if the missis knew everything! But I've overslept myself a full hour, and if nobody has been up before somebody soon will be. The greater haste the less speed. All the same, despite the difficulty of finding her clothes, Albert was at work on her landing some twenty minutes after, running up and down the stairs, preparing for the different breakfasts in the half-dozen sitting-rooms given to her charge, driving everybody before her, saying: We're late today, and the house full of visitors. How is it that 54 isn't turned out? Has 35 rung his bell? Lord, Albert, said a housemaid, I wouldn't worry my fat because I was down late; once in a way don't hurt. And sitting up half the night talking to Mr. Page, said another maid, and then rounding on us. Half the night talking, Albert repeated. My bed-fellow! Where is Mr. Page? I didn't hear him go away; he may have missed his train for aught I know. But do you be getting on with your work, and let me be getting on with mine. You're very cross this morning, Albert, the maid-servant muttered, and retired to chatter with two other maids who were looking over the banisters at the time.

Well, Mr. Nobbs, the head porter began, when Albert came running downstairs to see some visitors off, and to receive her tips—well, Mr. Nobbs, how did you find your bed-fellow? Oh, he was all right, but I'm not used to bed-fellows, and he brought a flea with him, and it kept me awake; and when I did fall asleep, I slept so heavily that I was an hour late. I hope he caught his train. But what is all this pother about bed-fellows? Albert asked herself, as she returned to her landing. Page hasn't said anything, no, she's said nothing, for we are both in the same boat, and to tell on me would be to tell on herself. I'd never have believed if—Albert's modesty prevented her from finishing the sentence. She's a woman right enough. But the cheek of it, to marry an innocent girl! Did she let the girl into the secret, or leave her to find it out when— The girl might have called in the police! This was a question one might ponder on, and by luncheon time Albert was inclined to believe that Hubert told his wife before— She couldn't have had the cheek to wed her, Albert said, without warning her that things might not turn out as she fancied. Mayhap, Albert continued, she didn't tell her before they wedded and mayhap she did, and being one of them like myself that isn't always hankering after a man she was glad to live with Hubert for companionship. Albert tried to remember the exact words that Hubert had used. It seemed to her that Hubert had said that she lived with a girl first and wedded her to put a stop to people's scandal. Of course they could hardly live together except as man and wife. She remembered Hubert saying that she always returned home with a light heart and never left it without a heavy one. So it would seem that this marriage was as successful as any and a great deal more than most.

At that moment 35 rang his bell. Albert hurried to answer it, and it was not till late in the evening, between nine and ten o'clock, when the guests were away at the theatres and concerts and nobody was about but two maids, that Albert, with her napkin over her shoulder, dozed and meditated on the advice that Hubert had given her. She should marry, Hubert had said; Hubert had married. Of course it wasn't a real marriage, it couldn't be that, but a very happy one it would seem. But the girl must have understood that she was not marrying a man. Did Hubert tell her before wedding her or after, and what were the words? She would have liked to know the words: For after all I've worked hard, she said, and her thoughts melted away into meditation of what her life had been for the last five-and-twenty years, a mere drifting, it seemed to her, from one hotel to another, without friends; meeting, it is true, sometimes men and women who seemed willing to be friendly. But her secret forced her to live apart from men as well as women; the clothes she wore smothered the woman in her; she no longer thought and felt as she used to when she wore petticoats, and she didn't think and feel like a man though she wore trousers. What was she? Nothing, neither man nor woman, so small wonder she was lonely. But Hubert had put off her sex, so she said. . . . Albert turned over in her mind the possibility that a joke had been put upon her, and fell to thinking what Hubert's home might be like, and was vexed with herself for not having asked if she had a clock and vases on the chimney-piece. One of the maids called from the end of the passage, and when Albert received 54's order and executed it, she returned to her seat in the passage, her napkin over her shoulder, and resumed her reverie. It seemed to her that Hubert once said that her wife was a milliner; Hubert may not have spoken the word milliner; but if she hadn't it was strange that the word should keep on coming up in her mind. There was no reason why the wife shouldn't be a milliner, and if that were so it was as likely as not that they owned a house in some quiet, insignificant street, letting the dining-room, back room and kitchen to a widow or to a pair of widows. The drawing-room was the workroom and showroom; Page and his wife slept in the room above. On second thoughts it seemed to Albert that if the business were millinery it might be that Mrs. Page would prefer the ground floor for her showroom. A third and fourth distribution of the "premises" presented itself to Albert's imagination. On thinking the matter over again it seemed to her that Hubert did not speak of a millinery business but of a seamstress, and if that were so, a small dressmaker's business in a quiet street would be in keeping with all Hubert had said about the home. Albert was not sure, however, that if she found a girl willing to share her life with her, it would be a seamstress's business she would be on the look-out for. She thought that a sweetmeat shop, newspapers and tobacco, would be her choice.

Why shouldn't she make a fresh start? Hubert had no difficulties. She had said—Albert could recall the very words—I didn't mean you should marry a man, but a girl. Albert had saved, oh! how she had tried to save, for she didn't wish to end her days in the workhouse. She had saved upwards of five hundred pounds, which was enough to purchase a little business, and her heart dilated as she thought of her two successful investments in house property. In six months' time she hoped to have six hundred pounds, and if it took her two years to find a partner and a business, she would have at least seventy or eighty pounds more, which would be a great help, for it would be a mistake to put one's money into a falling business. If she found a partner, she'd have to do like Hubert; for marriage would put a stop to all tittle-tattle; she'd be able to keep her place at Morrison's

Hotel, or perhaps leave Morrison's and rely on jobs; and with her connection it would be a case of picking and choosing the best: ten and sixpence a night, nothing under. She dreamed of a round. Belfast, Liverpool, Manchester, Bradford, rose up in her imagination, and after a month's absence, a couple of months maybe, she would return home, her heart anticipating a welcome—a real welcome, for though she would continue to be a man to the world, she would be a woman to the dear one at home. With a real partner, one whose heart was in the business, they might make as much as two hundred pounds a year—four pounds a week! And with four pounds a week their home would be as pretty and happy as any in the city of Dublin. Two rooms and a kitchen were what she foresaw. The furniture began to creep into her imagination little by little. A large sofa by the fireplace covered with a chintz! But chintz dirtied quickly in the city; a dark velvet sofa might be more suitable. It would cost a great deal of money, five or six pounds; and at that rate fifty pounds wouldn't go very far, for they must have a fine double-bed mattress; and if they were going to do things in that style, the home would cost them eighty pounds. With luck these eighty pounds could be earned within the next two years at Morrison's Hotel.

Albert ran over in her mind the tips she had received. The people in 34 were leaving tomorrow; they were always good for half a sovereign, and she decided then and there that tomorrow's half-sovereign must be put aside as a beginning of a sum of money for the purchase of a clock to stand on a marble chimney-piece or a mahogany chiffonier. A few days after she got a sovereign from a departing guest, and it revealed a pair of pretty candlesticks and a round mirror. Her tips were no longer mere white and yellow metal stamped with the effigy of a dead king or a living queen, but symbols of the future that awaited her. An unexpected crown set her pondering on the colour of the curtains in their sitting-room, and Albert became suddenly conscious that a change had come into her life: the show was the same—carrying plates and dishes upstairs and downstairs, and taking orders for drinks and cigars; but behind the show a new life was springing up—a life strangely personal and associated with the life without only in this much, that the life without was now a vassal state paying tribute to the life within. She wasn't as good a servant as heretofore. She knew it. Certain absences of mind, that was all; and the servants as they went by with their dusters began to wonder whatever Albert could be dreaming of.

It was about this time that the furnishing of the parlour at the back of the shop was completed, likewise that of the bedroom above the shop, and Albert had just entered on another dream—a dream of a shop with two counters, one at which cigars, tobacco, pipes and matches were sold, and at the other all kinds of sweetmeats, a shop with a door leading to her wife's parlour. A changing figure the wife was in Albert's imagination, turning from fair to dark, from plump to slender, but capturing her imagination equally in all her changes; sometimes she was accompanied by a child of three or four, a boy, the son of a dead man, for in one of her dreams Albert married a widow. In another and more frequent dream she married a woman who had transgressed the moral code and been deserted before the birth of her child. In this case it would be supposed that Albert had done the right thing, for after leading the girl astray he had made an honest woman of her. Albert would be the father in everybody's eyes except the mother's, and she hoped that the child's mother would outgrow all the memory of the accidental seed sown, as the saying runs, in a foolish five minutes. A child would be a pleasure to them both, and a girl in the family way appealed to her more than a widow; a girl that some soldier, the boot-boy, or the hotel porter, had gotten into trouble; and Albert kept her eyes and ears open, hoping to rescue from her precarious situation one of those unhappy girls that were always cropping up in Morrison's Hotel. Several had had to leave the hotel last year, but not one this year. But some revivalist meetings were going to be held in Dublin. Many of our girls attend them, and an unlucky girl will be in luck's way if we should run across one another. Her thought passed into a dream of the babe that would come into the world some three or four months after their marriage, her little soft hands and expressive eyes claiming their protection, asking for it. What matter whether she calls me father or mother? They are but mere words that the lips speak, but love is in the heart and only love matters.

Now whatever can Albert be brooding? an idle housemaid asked herself as she went by. Brooding a love-story? Not likely. A marriage with some girl outside? He isn't over-partial to any of us. That Albert was brooding something, that there was something on his mind, became the talk of the hotel, and soon after it came to be noticed that Albert was eager to avail himself of every excuse to absent himself from duty in the hotel. He had been seen in the smaller streets looking up at the houses. He had saved a good deal of money, and some of his savings were invested in house property, so it was possible that his presence in these streets might be explained by the supposition that he was investing new sums of money in house property, or, and it was the second suggestion that stimulated the imagination, that Albert was going to be married and was looking out for a house for his wife. He had been seen talking with Annie Watts; but she was not in the family way after all, and despite her wistful eyes and gentle voice she was not chosen. Her heart is not in her work, Albert said; she thinks only of when she can get out, and that isn't the sort for a shop, whereas Dorothy Keyes is a glutton for work; but Albert couldn't abide the tall, angular woman, built like a boy, with a neck like a swan's. Besides her unattractive appearance, her manner was abrupt. But Alice's small, neat figure and quick intelligence marked her out for the job. Alas! Alice was hot-tempered. We should quarrel, Albert said, and picking up her napkin, which had slipped from her knee to the floor, she considered the maids on the floor above. A certain stateliness of figure and also of gait put the thought into her mind that Mary O'Brien would make an attractive shopwoman. But her second thoughts were that Mary O'Brien was a Papist, and the experience of Irish Protestants shows that Papists and Protestants don't mix.

She had just begun to consider the next housemaid, when a voice interrupted her musing. That lazy girl, Annie Watts, on the look-out for an excuse to chatter the time away instead of being about her work, were the words that crossed Albert's mind as she raised her eyes, and so unwelcoming were they that Annie in her nervousness began to hesitate and stammer, unable for the moment to find a subject, plunging at last, and rather awkwardly, into the news of the arrival of the new kitchen-maid, Helen Dawes, but never dreaming that the news could have any interest for Albert. To her surprise, Albert's eyes lighted up. Do you know her? Annie asked. Know her? Albert answered. No, I don't know her, but– At that moment a bell rang. Oh, bother, Annie said, and while she moved away idling along the banisters, Albert hurried down the passage to enquire what No. 47 wanted, and to learn that he needed writing-paper and envelopes. He couldn't write with the pens the hotel furnished; would Albert be so kind as to ask the page-boy to fetch some J's? With pleasure, Albert said; with pleasure. Would you like to have the writing-paper and envelopes before the boy returns with the pens, sir? The visitor answered that the writing-paper and envelopes would be of no use to him till he had gotten the pens. With pleasure, sir; with pleasure; and whilst waiting for the page to return she passed through the swing doors and searched for a new face among the different young women passing to and fro between the white-aproned and white-capped chefs, bringing the dishes to the great zinc counter that divided the kitchen-maids and the scullions from the waiters. She must be here, she said, and returned again to the kitchen in the hope of meeting the new-comer, Helen Dawes, who, when she was found, proved to be very unlike the Helen Dawes of Albert's imagination. A thick-set, almost swarthy girl of three-and-twenty, rather under than above the medium height, with white, even teeth, but unfortunately protruding, giving her the appearance of a rabbit. Her eyes seemed to be dark brown, but on looking into them Albert discovered them to be grey-green, round eyes that dilated and flashed wonderfully while she talked. Her face lighted up; and there was a vindictiveness in her voice that appeared and disappeared; Albert suspected her, and was at once frightened and attracted. Vindictiveness in her voice! How could such a thing have come into my mind? she said a few days after. A more kindly girl it would be difficult to find. How could I have been so stupid? She is one of those, Albert continued, that will be a success in everything she undertakes; and dreams began soon after that the sweetstuff and tobacco shop could hardly fail to prosper under her direction. Nobody could befool Helen, and when I am away at work I shall feel certain that everything will be all right at home. It's a pity that she isn't in the family way, for it would be pleasant to have a little one running about the shop asking for lemon drops and to hear him calling us father and mother. At that moment a strange thought flitted across Albert's mind—after all, it wouldn't matter much to her if Helen were to get into the family way later; of course, there would be the expense of the lying-in. Her second thoughts were that women live happily enough till a man comes between them, and that it would be safer for her to forgo a child and choose an older woman. All the same, she could not keep herself from asking Helen to walk out with her, and the next time they met the words slipped out of her mouth: I shall be off duty at three today, and if you are not engaged— I am off duty at three, Helen answered. Are you engaged? Albert asked. Helen hesitated, it being the truth that she had been and was still walking out with one of the scullions, and was not sure he would look upon her going out with another, even though that one was such a harmless fellow as Albert Nobbs. Harmless in himself, she thought, and with a very good smell of money rising out of his pockets, very different from Joe, who seldom had a train fare upon him. But she hankered after Joe, and wouldn't give Albert a promise until she had asked him. Wants to walk out with you? Why, he has never been known to walk out with man, woman or child before. Well, that's a good one! I'd like to know what he's after, but I'm not jealous; you can go with him, there's no harm in Albert. I'm on duty: just go for a turn with him. Poke him up and see what he's after, and take him into a sweetshop and bring back a box of chocolates. Do you like chocolates? Helen asked, and her eyes flashing, she stood looking at Joe, who, thinking that her temper was rising, and wishing to quell it, asked hurriedly where she was going to meet him. At the corner, she answered. He is there already. Then be off, he said, and his tone grated. You wouldn't like me to keep him waiting? Helen said. Oh, dear no, not for Joe, not for Joseph, if he knows it, the scullion replied, lilting the song.

Helen turned away hoping that none of the maids would peach upon her, and Albert's heart rejoiced at seeing her on the other side of the street waiting for the tram to go by before she crossed it. Were you afraid I wasn't coming? she asked, and Albert, not being ready with words, answered shyly: Not very. A stupid answer this seemed to be to Helen, and it was in the hope of shuffling out of a tiresome silence that Albert asked her if she liked chocolates. Something under the tooth will help the time away, was the answer she got; and they went in search of a sweetmeat shop, Albert thinking that a shilling or one and sixpence would see her through it. But in a moment Helen's eyes were all over the shop, and spying out some large pictured boxes, she asked Albert if she might have one, and it being their first day out, Albert answered: Yes; but could not keep back the words: I'm afraid they'd cost a lot. For these words Albert got a contemptuous look, and Helen shook her shoulders so disdainfully that Albert pressed a second box on Helen—one to pass the time with, another to take home. To such a show of goodwill Helen felt she must respond, and her tongue rattled on pleasantly as she walked, crunching the chocolates, two between each lamp-post, Albert stinting herself to one, which she sucked slowly, hardly enjoying it at all, so worried was she by the loss of three and sixpence. As if Helen guessed the cause of Albert's disquiet, she called on her suitor to admire the damsel on the box, but Albert could not disengage her thoughts sufficiently from Helen's expensive tastes. If every walk were to cost three and sixpence there wouldn't be a lot left for the home in six months' time. And she fell to calculating how much it would cost her if they were to walk out once a week. Three fours are twelve and four sixpences are two shillings, fourteen shillings a month, twice that is twenty-eight; twenty-eight shillings a month, that is if Helen wanted two boxes a week. At this rate she'd be spending sixteen pounds sixteen shillings a year. Lord amassy! But perhaps Helen wouldn't want two boxes of chocolates every time they went out together— If she didn't, she'd want other things, and catching sight of a jeweller's shop, Albert called Helen's attention to a cyclist that had only just managed to escape a tram car by a sudden wriggle. But Albert was always unlucky. Helen had been wishing this long while for a bicycle, and if she did not ask Albert to buy her one it was because another jeweller's came into view. She stopped to gaze, and for a moment Albert's heart seemed to stand still, but Helen continued her chocolates, secure in her belief that the time had not yet come for substantial presents.

At Sackville Street bridge she would have liked to turn back, having little taste for the meaner parts of the city, but Albert wished to show her the north side, and she began to wonder what he could find to interest him in these streets, and why he should stand in admiration before all the small newspaper and tobacco shops, till she remembered suddenly that he had invested his savings in house property. Could these be his houses? All his own? and, moved by this consideration, she gave a more attentive ear to Albert's account of the daily takings of these shops, calculating that he was a richer man than anybody believed him to be, but a mean one. The idea of his thinking twice about a box of chocolates! I'll show him! and coming upon a big draper's shop in Sackville Street she asked him for a pair of six-button gloves. She needed a parasol and some shoes and stockings, and a silk kerchief would not be amiss, and at the end of the third month of their courtship it seemed to her that the time had come for her to speak of bangles, saying that for three pounds she could have a pretty one—one that would be a real pleasure to wear; it would always remind her of him. Albert coughed up with humility, and Helen felt that she had "got him," as she put it to herself, and afterwards to Joe Mackins. So he parted easily, Joe remarked, and pushing Helen aside he began to whip up the *rémoulade,* that had begun to show signs of turning, saying he'd have the chef after him. But I say, old girl, since he's coughing up so easily you might bring me something back; and a briar-wood pipe and a pound or two of tobacco seemed the least she might obtain for him. And Helen answered that to get these she would have to ask Albert for money. And why shouldn't you? Joe returned. Ask him for a thin 'un, and mayhap he'll give you a thick 'un. It's the first quid that's hard to get; every time after it's like shelling peas. Do you think he's that far gone on me? Helen asked. Well, don't you? Why should he give you these things if he wasn't?

Joe answered. Joe asked her of what she was thinking, and she replied that it was hard to say: she had walked out with many a man before but never with one like Albert Nobbs. In what way is he different? Joe asked. Helen was perplexed in her telling of Albert Nobbs's slackness. You mean that he doesn't pull you about, Joe rapped out; and she answered that there was something of that in it. All the same, she continued, that isn't the whole of it. I've been out before with men that didn't pull me about, but he seems to have something on his mind, and half the time he's thinking. Well, what does it matter, Joe asked, so long as there is coin in the pocket and so long as you have a hand to pull it out? Helen didn't like this description of Albert Nobbs's courtship, and the words rose to her lips to tell Joseph that she didn't want to go out any more with Albert, that she was tired of her job, but the words were quelled on her lips by a remark from Joe. Next time you go out with him work him up a bit and see what he is made of; just see if there's a sting in him or if he is no better than a capon. A capon! and what is a capon? she asked. A capon is a cut fowl. He may be like one. You think that, do you? she answered, and resolved to get the truth of the matter next time they went out together. It did seem odd that Albert should be willing to buy presents and not want to kiss her. In fact, it was more than odd. It might be as Joe had said. I might as well go out with my mother. Now what did it all mean? Was it a blind? Some other girl that he– Not being able to concoct a sufficiently reasonable story, Helen relinquished the attempt, without, however, regaining control of her temper, which had begun to rise, and which continued to boil up in her and overflow until her swarthy face was almost ugly. I'm beginning to feel ugly towards him, she said to herself. He is either in love with me or he's— And trying to discover his purpose, she descended the staircase, saying to herself: Now Albert must know that I'm partial to Joe Mackins. It can't be that he doesn't suspect. Well, I'm damned.

4

But Helen's perplexity on leaving the hotel was no greater than Albert's as she stood waiting by the kerb. She knew that Helen carried on with Joe Mackins, and she also knew that Joe Mackins had nothing to offer Helen but himself. She even suspected that some of the money she had given to Helen had gone to purchase pipes and tobacco for Joe: a certain shrewdness is not inconsistent with innocence, and it didn't trouble her much that Helen was perhaps having her fling with Joe Mackins. She didn't want Helen to fall into evil ways, but it was better for her to have her fling before than after marriage. On the other hand, a woman that had been bedded might be dissatisfied to settle down with another woman, though the home offered her was better than she could get from a man. She might hanker for children, which was only natural, and Albert felt that she would like a child as well as another. A child might be arranged for if Helen wanted one, but it would never do to have the father hanging about the shop: he would have to be got rid of as soon as Helen was in the family way. But could he be got rid of? Not very easily if Joe Mackins was the father; she foresaw trouble and would prefer another father, almost any other. But why trouble herself about the father of Helen's child before she knew whether Helen would send Joe packing? which she'd have to do clearly if they were to wed—she and Helen. Their wedding was what she had to look to, whether she should confide her sex to Helen tonight or wait. Why not tonight as well as tomorrow night? she asked herself. But how would she tell it to Helen? Blurt it out—I've something to tell you, Helen. I'm not a man, but a woman like yourself. No, that wouldn't do. How did Hubert tell her wife she was a woman? If she had only asked she'd have been spared all this trouble. After hearing Hubert's story she should have said: I've something to ask you; but sleep was so heavy on their eyelids that they couldn't think any more and both of them were falling asleep, which wasn't to be wondered at, for they had been talking for hours. It was on her mind to ask how her wife found out. Did Hubert tell her or did the wife— Albert's modesty prevented her from pursuing the subject; and she turned on herself, saying that she could not leave Helen to find out she was a woman; of that she was certain, and of that only. She'd have to tell Helen that. But should the confession come before they were married, or should she reserve it for the wedding night in the bridal chamber on the edge of the bed afterwards? If it were not for Helen's violent temper—I in my nightshirt, she in her nightgown. On the other hand, she might quieten down after an outburst and begin to see that it might be very much to her advantage to accept the situation, especially if a hope were held out to her of a child by Joe Mackins in two years' time; she'd have to agree to wait till then, and in two years Joe would probably be after another girl. But if she were to cut up rough and do me an injury! Helen might call the neighbours in, or the policeman, who'd take them both to the station. She'd have to return to Liverpool or to Manchester. She didn't know what the penalty would be for marrying one of her own sex. And her thoughts wandered on to the morning boat.

One of the advantages of Dublin is that one can get out of it as easily as any other city. Steamers were always leaving, morning and evening; she didn't know how many, but a great many. On the other hand, if she took the straight course and confided her sex to Helen before the marriage, Helen might promise not to tell; but she might break her promise; life in Morrison's Hotel would be unendurable, and she'd have to endure it. What a hue and cry! But one way was as bad as the other. If she had only asked Hubert Page! but she hadn't a thought at the time of going to do likewise. What's one man's meat is another man's poison, and she began to regret Hubert's confession to her. If it hadn't been for that flea she wouldn't be in this mess; and she was deep in it! Three month's company isn't a day, and everybody in Morrison's Hotel asking whether she or Joe Mackins would be the winner, urging her to make haste else Joe would come with a rush at the finish. A lot of racing talk that she didn't understand—or only half. If she could get out of this mess somehow— But it was too late. She must go through with it. But how? A different sort of girl altogether was needed, but she liked Helen. Her way of standing on a doorstep, her legs a little apart, jawing a tradesman, and she'd stand up to Mrs. Baker and to the chef himself. She liked the way Helen's eyes lighted up when a thought came into her mind; her cheery laugh warmed Albert's heart as nothing else did. Before she met Helen she often feared her heart was growing cold. She might try the world over and not find one that would run the shop she had in mind as well as Helen. But the shop wouldn't wait; the owners of the shop would withdraw their offer if it was not accepted before next Monday. And today is Friday, Albert said to herself. This evening or never. Tomorrow Helen'll be on duty all day; on Sunday she'll contrive some excuse to get out to meet Joe Mackins. After all, why not this evening? for what must be had better be faced bravely; and while the tram rattled down the long street, Rathmines Avenue, past the small houses atop of high steps, pretty boxes with ornamental trees in the garden, some with lawns, with here and there a more substantial house set in the middle of three or four fields at least, Albert meditated, plan after plan rising up in her mind; and when the car turned to the right and then to the left and proceeded at a steady pace up the long incline, Rathgar Avenue, Albert's courage was again at ebb. All the subterfuges she had woven—the long discussion in which she would maintain that marriage should not be considered as a sexual adventure, but a community of interests—seemed to have lost all significance; the points that had seemed so convincing in Rathmines Avenue were forgotten in Rathgar Avenue, and at Terenure she came to the conclusion that there was no use trying to think the story out beforehand; she would have to adapt her ideas to the chances that would arise as they talked under the trees in the dusk in a comfortable hollow, where they could lie at length out of hearing of the other lads and lasses whom they would find along the banks, resting after the labour of the day in dim contentment, vaguely conscious of each other, satisfied with a vague remark, a kick or a push.

It was the hope that the river's bank would tempt him into confidence that had suggested to Helen that they might spend the evening by the Dodder. Albert had welcomed the suggestion, feeling sure that if there was a place in the world that would make the telling of her secret easy it was the banks of the Dodder; and she was certain she would be able to speak it in the hollow under the ilex trees. But speech died from her lips, and the silence round them seemed sinister and foreboding. She seemed to dread the river flowing over its muddy bottom, without ripple or eddy; and she started when Helen asked her of what she was thinking. Albert answered: Of you, dear; and how pleasant it is to be sitting with you. On these words the silence fell again, and Albert tried to speak, but her tongue was too thick in her mouth; she felt like choking, and the silence was not broken for some seconds, each seeming a minute. At last a lad's voice was heard: I'll see if you have any lace on your drawers; and the lass answered: You shan't. There's a pair that's enjoying themselves, Helen said, and she looked upon the remark as fortunate, and hoped it would give Albert the courage to pursue his courtship. Albert, too, looked upon the remark as fortunate, and she tried to ask if there was lace on all women's drawers; and meditated a reply that would lead her into a confession of her sex. But the words: It's so long since I've worn any, died on her lips; and instead of speaking these words she spoke of the Dodder, saying: What a pity it isn't nearer Morrison's. Where would you have it? Helen replied—flowing down Sackville Street into the Liffey? We should be lying there as thick as herrings, without room to move, or we should be unable to speak to each other without being overheard. I dare say you are right, Albert answered, and she was so frightened that she added: But we have to be back at eleven o'clock, and it takes an hour to get there. We can go back now if you like, Helen rapped out. Albert apologised, and hoping that something would happen to help her out of her difficulty, she began to represent Morrison's Hotel as being on the whole advantageous to servants. But Helen did not respond. She seems to be getting angrier and angrier, Albert said to herself, and she asked, almost in despair, if the Dodder was pretty all the way down to the sea. And remembering a walk with Joe, Helen answered: There are woods as far as Dartry—the Dartry Dye Works, don't you know them? But I don't think there are any very pretty spots. You know Ring's End, don't you? Albert said she had been there once; and Helen spoke of a large three-masted vessel that she had seen some Sundays ago by the quays. You were there with Joe Mackins, weren't you? Well, what if I was? Only this, Albert answered, that I don't think it is usual for a girl to keep company with two chaps, and I thought— Now, what did you think? Helen said. That you didn't care for me well enough— For what? she asked. You know we've been going out for three months, and it doesn't seem natural to keep talking always, never wanting to put your arm round a girl's waist. I suppose Joe isn't like me, then? Albert asked; and Helen laughed, a scornful little laugh. But, Albert went on, isn't the time for kissing when one is wedded? This is the first time you've said anything about marriage, Helen rapped out. But I thought there had always been an understanding between us, said Albert, and it's only now I can tell you what I have to offer. The words were well chosen. Tell me about it, Helen said, her eyes and voice revealing her cupidity to Albert, who continued all the same to unfold her plans, losing herself in details that bored Helen, whose thoughts returned to the dilemma she was in—to refuse Albert's offer or to break with Joe; and that she should be obliged to do either one or the other was a disappointment to her. All you say about the shop is right enough, but it isn't a very great compliment to a girl. What, to ask her to marry? Albert interjected. Well, no, not if you haven't kissed her first. Don't speak so loud, Albert whispered; I'm sure that couple heard what you said, for they went away laughing. I don't care whether they laughed or cried, Helen answered. You don't want to kiss me, do you? and I don't want to marry a man who isn't in love with me. But I do want to kiss you, and Albert bent down and kissed Helen on both cheeks. Now you can't say I haven't kissed you, can you? You don't call that kissing, do you? Helen asked. But how do you wish me to kiss you, Helen? Well, you are an innocent! she said, and she kissed Albert vindictively. Helen, leave go of me; I'm not used to such kisses. Because you're not in love, Helen replied. In love? Albert repeated. I loved my old nurse very much, but I never wished to kiss her like that. At this Helen exploded with laughter. So you put me in the same class with your old nurse! Well, after that! Come, she said, taking pity upon Albert for a moment, are you or are you not in love with me? I love you deeply, Helen, Albert said. Love? she repeated: the men who have walked out with me were in love with me– In love, Albert repeated after her. I'm sure I love you. I like men to be in love with me, she answered. But that's like an animal, Helen. Whatever put all that muck in your head? I'm going home, she replied, and rose to her feet and started out on the path leading across the darkening fields. You're not angry with me, Helen? Angry? No, I'm not angry with you; you're a fool of a man, that's all. But if you think me a fool of a man, why did you come out this evening to sit under those trees? And why have we been keeping company for the last three months, Albert continued, going out together every week? You didn't always think me a fool of a man, did you? Yes, I did, she answered; and Albert asked Helen for a reason for choosing her company. Oh, you bother me asking reasons for everything, Helen said. But why did you make me love you? Albert asked. Well, if I did, what of it? and as for walking out with you, you won't have to complain of that any more. You don't mean, Helen, that we are never going to walk out again? Yes, I do, she said sullenly. You mean that for the future you'll be walking out with Joe Mackins, Albert lamented. That's my business, she answered. By this time they were by the stile at the end of the field, and in the next field there was a hedge to get through and a wood, and the little path they followed was full of such vivid remembrances that Albert could not believe that she was treading it with Helen for the last time, and besought Helen to take back the words that she would never walk out with her again.

The tram was nearly empty and they sat at the far end, close together, Albert beseeching Helen not to cast her off. If I've been stupid today, Albert pleaded, it's because I'm tired of the work in the hotel; I shall be different when we get to Lisdoonvarna: we both want a change of air; there's nothing like the salt water and the cliffs of Clare to put new spirits into a man. You will be different and I'll be different; everything will be different. Don't say no, Helen; don't say no. I've looked forward to this week in Lisdoonvarna, and Albert urged the expense of the lodgings she had already engaged. We shall have to pay for the lodgings; and there's the new suit of clothes that has just come back from the tailor's; I've looked forward to wearing it, walking with you in the strand, the waves crashing up into cliffs, with green fields among them, I've been told! We shall see the ships passing and wonder whither they are going. I've bought three neck-ties and some new shirts, and what good will these be to me if you'll not come to Lisdoonvarna with me? The lodgings will have to be paid for, a great deal of money, for I said in my letter we shall want two bedrooms. But there need only be one bedroom; but perhaps I shouldn't have spoken like that. Oh, don't talk to me about Lisdoonvarna, Helen answered. I'm not going to Lisdoonvarna with you. But what is to become of the hat I have ordered for you? Albert asked; the hat with the big feather in it; and I've bought stockings and shoes for you. Tell me, what shall I do with these, and with the gloves? Oh, the waste of money and the heart-breaking! What shall I do with the hat? Albert repeated. Helen didn't answer at once. Presently she said: You can leave the hat with me. And the stockings? Albert asked. Yes, you can leave the stockings. And the shoes? Yes, you can leave the shoes too. Yet you won't go to Lisdoonvarna with me? No, she said, I'll not go to Lisdoonvarna with you. But you'll take the presents? It was to please you I said I would take them, because I thought it would be some satisfaction to you to know that they wouldn't be wasted. Not wasted? Albert repeated. You'll wear them when you go out with Joe Mackins. Oh, well, keep your presents. And then the dispute took a different turn, and was continued until they stepped out of the tram at the top of Dawson Street. Albert continued to plead all the way down Dawson Street, and when they were within twenty yards of the hotel, and she saw Helen passing away from her for ever into the arms of Joe Mackins, she begged Helen not to leave her. We cannot part like this, she cried; let us walk up and down the street from Nassau Street to Clare Street, so that we may talk things over and do nothing foolish. You see, Albert began, I had set my heart on driving on an outside car to the Broadstone with you, and catching a train, and the train going into lovely country, arriving at a place we had never seen, with cliffs, and the sunset behind the cliffs. You've told all that before, Helen said, and, she rapped out, I'm not going to Lisdoonvarna with you. And if that is all you had to say to me we might have gone into the hotel. But there's much more, Helen. I haven't told you about the shop yet. Yes, you have told me all there is to tell about the shop; you've been talking about that shop for the last three months. But, Helen, it was only yesterday that I got a letter saying that they had had another offer for the shop, and that they could give me only till Monday morning to close with them; if the lease isn't signed by then we've lost the shop. But do you think, Helen asked, that the shop will be a success? Many shops promise well in the beginning and fade away till they don't get a customer a day. Our shop won't be like that, I know it won't; and Albert began an appraisement of the shop's situation and the custom it commanded in the neighbourhood and the possibility of developing that custom. We shall be able to make a great success of that shop, and people will be coming to see us, and they will be having tea with us in the parlour, and they'll envy us, saying that never have two people had such luck as we have had. And our wedding will be— Will be what? Helen asked. Will be a great wonder. A great wonder indeed, she replied, but I'm not going to wed you, Albert Nobbs, and now I see it's beginning to rain. I can't remain out any longer. You're thinking of your hat; I'll buy another. We may as well say good-bye, she answered, and Albert saw her going towards the doorway. She'll see Joe Mackins before she goes to her bed, and lie dreaming of him; and I shall lie away in my bed, my thoughts flying to and fro the livelong night, zigzagging up and down like bats. And then remembering that if she went into the hotel she might meet Helen and Joe Mackins, she rushed on with a hope in her mind that after a long walk round Dublin she might sleep.

At the corner of Clare Street she met two women strolling after a fare—ten shillings or a sovereign, which? she asked herself—and terrified by the shipwreck of all her hopes, she wished she were one of them. For they at least are women, whereas I am but a perhapser— In the midst of her grief a wish to speak to them took hold of her. But if I speak to them they'll expect me to— All the same her steps quickened, and as she passed the two street-walkers she looked round, and one woman, wishing to attract her attention, said: It was almost a love dream. Almost a love dream? Albert repeated. What are you two women talking about? and the woman next to Albert said: My friend here was telling me of a dream she had last night. A dream, and what was her dream about? Albert asked. Kitty was telling me that she was better than a love dream; now do you think she is, sir? I'll ask Kitty herself, Albert replied, and Kitty answered him: A shade. Only a shade, Albert returned, and as they crossed the street a gallant attached himself to Kitty's companion. Albert and Kitty were left together, and Albert asked her companion to tell her name. My name is Kitty MacCan, the girl replied. It's odd we've never met before, Albert replied, hardly knowing what she was saying. We're not often this way, was the answer. And where do you walk usually—of an evening?

Albert asked. In Grafton Street or down by College Green; sometimes we cross the river. To walk in Sackville Street, Albert interjected; and she tried to lead the woman into a story of her life. But you're not one of them, she said, that think that we should wash clothes in a nunnery for nothing? I'm a waiter in Morrison's Hotel. As soon as the name of Morrison's Hotel passed Albert's lips she began to regret having spoken about herself. But what did it matter now? and the woman didn't seem to have taken heed of the name of the hotel. Is the money good in your hotel? Kitty asked; I've heard that you get as much as half-a-crown for carrying up a cup of tea; and her story dribbled out in remarks, a simple story that Albert tried to listen to, but her attention wandered, and Kitty, who was not unintelligent, began to guess Albert to be in the middle of some great grief. It doesn't matter about me, Albert answered her, and Kitty being a kind girl said to herself: If I can get him to come home with me I'll help him out of his sorrow, if only for a little while. So she continued to try to interest him in herself till they came to Fitzwilliam Place; and it was not till then that Kitty remembered she had only three and sixpence left out of the last money she had received, and that her rent would be due on the morrow. She daren't return home without a gentleman; her landlady would be at her; and the best time of the night was going by talking to a man who seemed like one who would bid her a curt goodnight at the door of his hotel. Where did he say his hotel was? she asked herself; and then, aloud, she said: You're a waiter, aren't you? I've forgotten which hotel you said. Albert didn't answer, and, troubled by her companion's silence, Kitty continued: I'm afraid I'm taking you out of your way. No, you aren't; all ways are the same to me. Well, they aren't to me, she replied. I must get some money tonight. I'll give you some money, Albert said. But won't you come home with me? the girl asked. Albert hesitated, tempted by her company. But if they were to go home together her sex would be discovered. But what did it matter if it were discovered? Albert asked herself, and the temptation came again to go home with this woman, to lie in her arms and tell the story that had been locked up so many years. They could both have a good cry together, and what matter would it be to the woman as long as she got the money she desired. She didn't want a man; it was money she was after, money that meant bread and board to her. She seems a kind, nice girl, Albert said, and she was about to risk the adventure when a man came by whom Kitty knew. Excuse me, he said, and Albert saw them walk away together. I'm sorry, said the woman, returning, but I've just met an old friend; another evening, perhaps. Albert would have liked to put her hand in her pocket and pay the woman with some silver for her company, but she was already half-way back to her friend, who stood waiting for her by the lamp-post. The street-walkers have friends, and when they meet them their troubles are over for the night; but my chances have gone by me; and, checking herself in the midst of the irrelevant question, whether it were better to be casual, as they were, or to have a husband that you could not get rid of, she plunged into her own grief, and walked sobbing through street after street, taking no heed of where she was going.

Why, lord, Mr. Nobbs, whatever has kept you out until this hour? the hall-porter muttered. I'm sorry, she answered, and while stumbling up the stairs she remembered that even a guest was not received very amiably by the hall-porter after two; and for a servant to come in at that time! Her thoughts broke off and she lay too tired to think any more of the hall-porter, of herself, of anything. If she got an hour's sleep it was the most she got that night, and when the time came for her to go to her work she rose indifferently. But her work saved her from thinking, and it was not until the middle of the afternoon, when the luncheon-tables had been cleared, that the desire to see and to speak to Helen could not be put aside; but Helen's face wore an ugly, forbidding look, and Albert returned to the second floor without speaking to her. It was not long after that 34 rang his bell, and Albert hoped to get an order that would send her to the kitchen. Are you going to pass me by without speaking again, Helen? We talked enough last night, Helen retorted; there's nothing more to say, and Joe, in such disorder of dress as behooves a scullion, giggled as he went past, carrying a huge pile of plates. I loved my old nurse, but I never thought of kissing her like that, he said, turning on his heel and so suddenly that some of the plates fell with a great clatter. The ill luck that had befallen him seemed well deserved, and Albert returned upstairs and sat in the passages waiting for the sitting-rooms to ring their bells; and the housemaids, as they came about the head of the stairs with their dusters, wondered how it was that they could not get any intelligible conversation out of the love-stricken waiter. Albert's lovelorn appearance checked their mirth, pity entered their hearts, and they kept back the words: I loved my old nurse, etc. After all, he loves the girl, one said to the other, and a moment after they were joined by another housemaid, who after listening for a while, went away, saying: There's no torment like the love torment; and the three housemaids, Mary, Alice, and

Dorothy, offered Albert their sympathy, trying to lead her into little talks with a view to withdrawing her from the contemplation of her own grief, for women are always moved by a love story. Before long their temper turned against Helen, and they often went by asking themselves why she should have kept company with Albert all these months if she didn't mean to wed him. No wonder the poor man was disappointed. He is destroyed with his grief, said one; look at him, without any more colour in his face than is in my duster. Another said: He doesn't swallow a bit of food. And the third said: I poured out a glass of wine for him that was left over, but he put it away. Isn't love awful? But what can he see in her? another asked, a stumpy, swarthy woman, a little blackthorn bush and as full of prickles; and the three women fell to thinking that Albert would have done better to have chosen one of them. The shop entered into the discussion soon after, and everybody was of opinion that Helen would live to regret her cruelty. The word cruelty did not satisfy; treachery was mentioned, and somebody said that Helen's face was full of treachery. Albert will never recover himself as long as she's here, another remarked. He'll just waste away unless Miss Right comes along. He put all his eggs into one basket, a man said; you see he'd never been known to walk out with a girl before. And what age do you think he is? I put him down at forty-five, and when love takes a man at that age it takes him badly. This is no calf love, the man said, looking into the women's faces, and you'll never be able to mend matters, any of you; and they all declared they didn't wish to, and dispersed in different directions, flicking their dusters and asking themselves if Albert would ever look at another woman.

It was felt generally that he would not have the courage to try again, which was indeed the case, for when it was suggested to Albert that a faint heart never wins a fair lady she answered that her spirit was broken. I shall boil my pot and carry my can, but the spring is broken in me; and it was these words that were remembered and pondered, whereas the joke—I loved my old nurse, etc.—raised no laugh; and the sympathy that Albert felt to be gathering about her cheered her on her way. She was no longer friendless; almost any one of the women in the hotel would have married Albert out of pity for her. But there was no heart in Albert for another adventure; nor any thought in her for anything but her work. She rose every morning and went forth to her work, and was sorry when her work was done, for she had come to dread every interval, knowing that as soon as she sat down to rest the old torment would begin again. Once more she would begin to think that she had nothing more to look forward to; that her life would be but a round of work; a sort of treadmill. She would never see Lisdoonvarna, and the shop with two counters, one at which tobacco, cigarettes and matches were sold, and at the other counter all kinds of sweetstuffs. Like Lisdoonvarna, it had passed away, it had only existed in her mind—a thought, a dream. Yet it had possessed her completely; and the parlour behind the shop that she had furnished and refurnished, hanging a round mirror above the mantelpiece, papering the walls with a pretty colourful paper that she had seen in Wicklow Street and had asked the man to put aside for her. She had hung curtains about the windows in her imagination, and had set two armchairs on either side of the hearth, one in green and one in red velvet, for herself and Helen. The parlour too had passed away like Lisdoonvarna, like the shop, a thought, a dream, no more. There had never been anything in her life but a few dreams, and henceforth there would not even be dreams. It was strange that some people came into the world lucky, and others, for no reason, unlucky; she had been unlucky from her birth; she was a bastard; her parents were grand people whose name she did not know, who paid her nurse a hundred a year to keep her, and who died without making any provision for her. She and her old nurse had to go and live in Temple Lane, and to go out charing every morning; Mr. Congreve had a French mistress, and if it hadn't been for Bessie Lawrence she might have thrown herself in the Thames; she was very near to it that night, and if she had drowned herself all this worry and torment would have been over. She was more resolute in those days than she was now, and would have faced the river, but she shrank from this Dublin river, perhaps because it was not her own river. If one wishes to drown oneself it had better be in one's own country. But why is it a mistake? For a perhapser like herself, all countries were the same; go or stay, it didn't matter. Yes, it did; she stayed in Dublin in the hope that Hubert Page would return to the hotel. Only to Hubert could she confide the misfortune that had befallen her, and she'd like to tell somebody. The three might set up together. A happy family they might make. Two women in men's clothes and one in petticoats. If Hubert were willing. Hubert's wife might not be willing. But she might be dead and Hubert on the look-out for another helpmate. He had never been away so long before; he might return any day. And from the moment that she foresaw herself as Hubert's future wife her life began to expand itself more eagerly than ever in watching for tips, collecting half-crowns, crowns and half-sovereigns. She must at least replace the money that she had spent giving presents to Helen, and as the months went by and the years, she remembered, with increasing bitterness, that she had wasted nearly twenty pounds on Helen, a cruel, heartless girl that had come into her life for three months and had left her for Joe Mackins. She took to counting her money in her room at night. The half-crowns were folded up in brown-paper packets, the half-sovereigns in blue, the rare sovereigns were in pink paper, and all these little packets were hidden away in different corners; some were put in the chimney, some under the carpet. She often thought that these hoards would be safer in the Post Office Bank, but she who has nothing else likes to have her money with her, and a sense of almost happiness awoke in her when she discovered herself to be again as rich as she was before she met Helen. Richer by twenty-five pounds twelve and sixpence, she said, and her eyes roved over the garret floor in search of a plank that might be lifted. One behind the bed was chosen, and henceforth Albert slept securely over her hoard, or lay awake thinking of Hubert, who might return, and to whom she might confide the story of her misadventure; but as Hubert did not return her wish to see him faded, and she began to think that it might be just as well if he stayed away, for, who knows? a wandering fellow like him might easily run out of his money and return to Morrison's Hotel to borrow from her, and she wasn't going to give her money to be spent for the benefit of another woman. The other woman was Hubert's wife. If Hubert came back he might threaten to publish her secret if she didn't give him money to keep it. An ugly thought, of which she was ashamed and which she tried to keep out of her mind. But as time went on a dread of Hubert took possession of her. After all, Hubert knew her secret, and somehow it didn't occur to her that in betraying her secret Hubert would be betraying his own. Albert didn't think as clearly as she used to; and one day she answered Mrs. Baker in a manner that Mrs. Baker did not like. Whilst speaking to Albert the thought crossed Mrs. Baker's mind that it was a long while since they had seen the painter. I cannot think, she said, what has become of Hubert Page; we've not had news of him for a long time; have you heard from him, Albert? Why should you think, ma'am, that I hear from him? I only asked, Mrs. Baker replied, and she heard Albert mumbling something about a wandering fellow, and the tone in which the words were spoken was disrespectful, and Mrs. Baker began to consider Albert; and though a better servant now than he had ever been in some respects, he had developed a fault which she didn't like, a way of hanging round the visitor as he was preparing to leave the hotel that almost amounted to persecution. Worse than that, a rumour had reached her that Albert's service was measured according to the tip he expected to receive. She didn't believe it, but if it were true she would not hesitate to have him out of the hotel in spite of the many years he had spent with them. Another thing: Albert was liked, but not by everybody. The little red-headed boy on the second floor told me, Mrs. Baker said (her thoughts returning to last Sunday, when she had taken the child out to Bray), that he was afraid of Albert, and he confided to me that Albert had tried to pick him up and kiss him. Why can't he leave the child alone? Can't he see the child doesn't like him?

But the Bakers were kind-hearted proprietors, and

could not keep sentiment out of their business, and Albert remained at Morrison's Hotel till she died.

An easy death I hope it was, your honour, for if any poor creature deserved an easy one it was Albert herself. You think so, Alec, meaning that the disappointed man suffers less at parting with this world than the happy one? Maybe you're right. That is as it may be, your honour, he answered, and I told him that Albert awoke one morning hardly able to breathe, and returned to bed and lay there almost speechless till the maid-servant came to make the bed. She ran off again to fetch a cup of tea, and after sipping it Albert said that she felt better. But she never roused completely, and the maid-servant who came up in the evening with a bowl of soup did not press her to try to eat it, for it was plain that Albert could not eat or drink, and it was almost plain that she was dying, but the maid-servant did not like to alarm the hotel and contented herself with saying: He'd better see the doctor tomorrow. She was up betimes in the morning, and on going to Albert's room she found the waiter asleep, breathing heavily. An hour later Albert was dead, and everybody was asking how a man who was in good health on Tuesday could be a corpse on Thursday morning, as if such a thing had never happened before. However often it had happened, it did not seem natural, and it was whispered that Albert might have made away with himself. Some spoke of apoplexy, but apoplexy in a long, thin man is not usual; and when the doctor came down his report that Albert was a woman put all thought of the cause of death out of everybody's mind. Never before or since was Morrison's Hotel agog as it was that morning, everybody asking the other why Albert had chosen to pass herself off as a man, and how she had succeeded in doing this year after year without any one of them suspecting her. She would be getting better wages as a man than as a woman, somebody said, but nobody cared to discuss the wages question; all knew that a man is better paid than a woman. But what Albert would have done with Helen if Helen hadn't gone off with Joe Mackins stirred everybody's imagination. What would have happened on the wedding night? Nothing, of course; but how would she have let on? The men giggled over their glasses, and the women pondered over their cups of tea; the men asked the women and the women asked the men, and the interest in the subject had not quite died down when Hubert Page returned to Morrison's Hotel, in the spring of the year, with her paint pots and brushes. How is Albert Nobbs? was one of her first enquiries, and it fired the train. Albert Nobbs! Don't you know? How should I know? Hubert Page replied. I've only just come back to Dublin. What is there to know? Don't you ever read the papers? Read the papers? Hubert repeated. Then you haven't heard that Albert Nobbs is dead? No, I haven't heard of it. I'm sorry for him, but after all, men die; there's nothing wonderful in that, is there? No; but if you had read the papers you'd have learnt that Albert Nobbs wasn't a man at all. Albert Nobbs was a woman. Albert Nobbs a woman! Hubert replied, putting as much surprise as she could into her voice. So you never heard? And the story began to fall out from different sides, everybody striving to communicate bits to her, until at last she said: If you all speak together, I shall never understand it. Albert Nobbs a woman! A woman as much as you're a man, was the answer, and the story of her courtship of Helen, and Helen's preference for Joe Mackins, and Albert's grief at Helen's treatment of her trickled into a long relation. The biggest deception in the whole world, a scullion cried from his saucepans. Whatever would she have done with Helen if they had married? But the question had been asked so often that it fell flat. So Helen went away with Joe Mackins? Hubert said. Yes; and they don't seem to get on over well together. Serve her right for her unkindness, cried a kitchen-maid. But after all, you wouldn't want her to marry a woman? a scullion answered. Of course not; of course not. The story was taken up by another voice, and the hundreds of pounds that Albert had left behind in many securities were multiplied; nearly a hundred in ready money rolled up in paper, half-crowns, half-sovereigns and sovereigns in his bedroom; his bedroom —her bedroom, I mean; but we are so used to thinking of her as a him that we find it difficult to say her; we're always catching each other up. But what I'm thinking of, said a waiter, is the waste of all that money. A great scoop it was for the Government, eight hundred pounds. The pair were to have bought a shop and lived together, Mr. Page, Annie Watts rapped out, and when the discussion was carried from the kitchen upstairs to the second floor: True for you, said Dorothy, now you mention it, I remember; it's you that should be knowing better than anybody else, Mr. Page, what Albert's sex was like. Didn't you sleep with her? I fell asleep the moment my head was on the pillow, Page answered, for if you remember rightly I was that tired Mrs. Baker hadn't the heart to turn me out of the hotel. I'd been working ten, twelve, fourteen hours a day, and when he took me up to his room I tore off my clothes and fell asleep, and went away in the morning before he was awake. Isn't it wonderful? A woman, Hubert continued, and a minx in the bargain, and an artful minx if ever there was one in the world, and there have been a good many. And now, ladies, I must be about my work. I wonder what Annie Watts was thinking of when she stood looking into my eyes; does she suspect me? Hubert asked herself as she sat on her derrick. And what a piece of bad luck that I shouldn't have found Albert alive when I returned to Dublin.

You see, Alec, this is how it was. Polly, that was Hubert's wife, died six months before Albert; and Hubert had been thinking ever since of going into partnership with Albert. In fact Hubert had been thinking about a shop, like Albert, saying to herself almost every day after the death of her wife: Albert and I might set up together. But it was not until she lay in bed that she fell to thinking the matter out, saying to herself: One of us would have had to give up our job to attend to it. The shop was Albert's idea more than mine, so perhaps she'd have given up waiting, which would not have suited me, for I'm tired of going up these ladders. My head isn't altogether as steady as it used to be; swinging about on a derrick isn't suited to women. So perhaps it's as well that things have fallen out as they have. Hubert turned herself over, but sleep was far from her, and she lay a long time thinking of everything and of nothing in particular, as we all do in our beds, with this thought often uppermost: I wonder what is going to be the end of my life. What new chance do the years hold for me?

And of what would Hubert be thinking, being a married woman? Of what else should she be thinking but of her husband, who might now be a different man from the one she left behind? Fifteen years, she said, makes a great difference in all of us, and perhaps it was the words, fifteen years, that put the children she had left behind her back into her thought. I wouldn't be saying that she hadn't been thinking of them, off and on, in the years gone by, but the thought of them was never such a piercing thought as it was that night. She'd have liked to have jumped out of her bed and run away to them; and perhaps she would have done if she only knew where they were. But she didn't, so she had to keep to her bed; and she lay for an hour or more thinking of them as little children, and wondering what they were like now. Lily was five when she left home. She's a young woman now. Agnes was only two. She is now seventeen, still a girl, Hubert said to herself; but Lily's looking round, thinking of young men, and the other won't be delaying much longer, for young women are much more wide-awake than they used to be in the old days. The rest of my life belongs to them. Their father could have looked after them till now; but now they are thinking of young men he won't be able to cope with them, and maybe he's wanting me too. Bill is forty, and at forty we begin to think of them as we knew them long ago. He must have often thought of me, perhaps oftener than I thought of him; and she was surprised to find that she had forgotten all Bill's ill-usage, and remembered only the good time she had had with him. The rest of my life belongs to him, she said, and to the girls. But how am I to get back to him? how, indeed? . . . Bill may be dead; the children too. But that isn't likely. I must get news of them somehow. The house is there; and lying in the darkness she recalled the pictures on the wall, the chairs that she had sat in, the coverlets on the beds, everything. Bill isn't a wanderer, she said; I'll find him in the same house if he isn't dead. And the children? Did they know anything about her? Had Bill spoken ill of her to them? She didn't think he would do that. But did they want to see her? Well, she could never find that out except by going to see. But how was she going to return home? Pack up her things and go dressed as a man to the house and, meeting Bill on the threshold, say: Don't you know me, Bill? and are you glad to see your mother back, children? No; that wouldn't do. She must return home as a woman, and none of them must know the life she had been living. But what story would she tell him? It would be difficult to tell the story of fifteen years, for fifteen years is a long time, and sooner or later they'd find out she was lying, for they would keep asking her questions.

But sure, said Alec, 'tis an easy story to tell. Well, Alec, what story should she tell them? In these parts, Alec said, a woman who left her husband and returned to him after fifteen years would say she was taken away by the fairies whilst wandering in a wood. Do you think she'd be believed? Why shouldn't she, your honour? A woman that marries another woman, and lives happily with her, isn't a natural woman; there must be something of the fairy in her. But I could see it all happening as you told it, the maid-servants and the serving-men going their own roads, and the only fault I've to find with the story is that you left out some of the best parts. I'd have liked to know what the husband said when she went back to him, and they separated all the years. If he liked her better than he did before, or less. And there is a fine story in the way the mother would be vexed by the two daughters and the husband, and they at her all the time with questions, and she hard set to find answers for them. But mayhap the best bit of all is when Albert began to think that it wouldn't do to have Joe Mackins hanging around, making their home his own, eating and drinking of the best, and when there was a quarrel he'd have a fine threat over them, as good as the Murrigan herself when she makes off of a night to the fair, whirling herself over the people's heads, stirring them up agin each other, making cakes of their skulls. I'm bet, fairly bet, crowed down by the Ballinrobe cock. And now, your honour, you heard the Angelus ringing, and my dinner is on the hob, and I'll be telling you what I think of the story when I come back; but I'm thinking already 'tis the finest that ever came out of Ballinrobe, I am so.

H. G. WELLS

The Magic Shop

One of Wells's most characteristic virtues as a writer was a passionate, fascinated awareness of the drama of the age in which he was living. You may suppose that the same could be said of any good journalist, but this is not so. The awareness of journalists is of a much more limited kind. They see the Present only from the viewpoint of the Present; they know what is news and what isn't, *as of now.* (It is this limitation which makes the day-to-day narrative of most newspapers so irritatingly discontinuous; political trends become crisis-headlines one week and are totally invisible the next.) But Wells, with his nobler kind of excitement and his wider intellectual grasp, tried to understand what the Present was *really* all about, disregarding its temporary celebrities and advertised "historic moments." In order to do this, he tried to look at the Present from the viewpoints of the Past and of the Future. And so it came about that he wrote his magnificent *Outline of History,* and the many science fiction novels and stories by which (much as he would have disliked the fact) he is most usually remembered.

Wells has been rather stupidly praised because he "predicted" television, washing-machines, prefabricated houses, tanks, and other dubious assets of our contemporary culture. But it is an insult to his memory to regard him merely as a high priest of the cult of the gadget. He was never impressed by gadgets themselves; he only valued them symbolically, as the furniture of a coming Utopia. And, actually, he looked toward the Future with violently mixed feelings. His optimism believed that Utopia *could* be established by mankind; his pessimism doubted that it ever *would* be. Nearly all of his science fiction stories end in failure and tragedy.

The greatest of them—*The Time-Machine, The Invisible Man, The Island of Dr. Moreau*—are novelettes, too long to be reprinted here. The secret of Wells's art is that he can make the Future seem an entirely natural phase of evolution from the Present. In fact, it is his vivid sense of the Present which enables him to conjure up the Future so convincingly. He is the most realistic of all fantasts. Even when he is showing us around the Moon, his feet are always, so to speak, planted firmly on the earth.

I first read *The Magic Shop* as a schoolboy, at a time when I myself was an enthusiastic amateur magician. Today, it is still my favorite among Wells's shorter stories. I suppose it can hardly be described as science fiction; and yet—it *almost* persuades us that Magic Shops are only just around the corner, like some new development in electronics. It is frighteningly realistic.

I think I detect satire, also. Haven't we all met that Shopman—superciliously smiling as he displays the latest wonder-appliance to a gaping customer? "This is our Magic Toaster," he tells us, and we nod vaguely. But just what, exactly, does he mean by "magic"? Does he mean what *we* mean? What *do* we mean, anyway? Isn't "magic" simply something that we don't understand and are, deep down, afraid of?

So—if you like symbols—let The Shop represent the modern world of technics, The Shopman the technocrat, The Father the bewildered ordinary citizen. Then The Son, presumably, represents a later generation which will take the machines for granted, without fear, and thus become their master.

As for myself, I confess that, whenever I revisit London, I still get a slight thrill from walking along that part of the street on which, as near as I can calculate, the Magic Shop must be.

I HAD SEEN THE MAGIC SHOP FROM AFAR SEVERAL TIMES; I had passed it once or twice, a shop window of alluring little objects, magic balls, magic hens, wonderful cones, ventriloquist dolls, the material of the basket trick, packs of cards that *looked* all right, and all that sort of thing, but never had I thought of going in until one day, almost without warning, Gip hauled me by my finger right up to the window, and so conducted himself that there was nothing for it but to take him in. I had not thought the place was there, to tell the truth—a modest-sized frontage in Regent Street, between the picture shop and the place where the chicks run about just out of patent incubators,—but there it was sure enough. I had fancied it was down nearer the Circus, or round the corner in Oxford Street, or even in Holborn; always over the way and a little inaccessible it had been, with something of the mirage in its position; but here it was now quite indisputably, and the fat end of Gip's pointing finger made a noise upon the glass.

"If I was rich," said Gip, dabbing a finger at the Disappearing Egg, "I'd buy myself that. And that"—which was The Crying Baby, Very Human—"and that," which was a mystery, and called, so a neat card asserted, "Buy One and Astonish Your Friends."

"Anything," said Gip, "will disappear under one of those cones. I have read about it in a book.

"And there, dadda, is the Vanishing Halfpenny—only they've put it this way up so's we can't see how it's done."

Gip, dear boy, inherits his mother's breeding, and he did not propose to enter the shop or worry in any way; only, you know, quite unconsciously he lugged my finger doorward, and he made his interest clear.

"That," he said, and pointed to the Magic Bottle.

"If you had that?" I said; at which promising inquiry he looked up with a sudden radiance.

"I could show it to Jessie," he said, thoughtful as ever of others.

"It's less than a hundred days to your birthday, Gibbles," I said, and laid my hand on the door-handle.

Gip made no answer, but his grip tightened on my finger, and so we came into the shop.

It was no common shop this; it was a magic shop, and all the prancing precedence Gip would have taken in the matter of mere toys was wanting. He left the burthen of the conversation to me.

It was a little, narrow shop, not very well lit, and the door-bell pinged again with a plaintive note as we closed it behind us. For a moment or so we were alone and could glance about us. There was a tiger in *papier-mâché* on the glass case that covered the low counter—a grave, kind-eyed tiger that waggled his head in a methodical manner; there were several crystal spheres, a china hand holding magic cards, a stock of magic fish-bowls in various sizes, and an immodest magic hat that shamelessly displayed its springs. On the floor were magic mirrors; one to draw you out long and thin, one to swell your head and vanish your legs, and one to make you short and fat like a draught; and while we were laughing at these the shopman, as I suppose, came in.

At any rate, there he was behind the counter—a curious, sallow, dark man, with one ear larger than the other and a chin like the toe-cap of a boot.

"What can we have the pleasure?" he said, spreading his long, magic fingers on the glass case; and so with a start we were aware of him.

"I want," I said, "to buy my little boy a few simple tricks."

"Legerdemain?" he asked. "Mechanical? Domestic?"

"Anything amusing," said I.

"Um!" said the shopman, and scratched his head for a moment as if thinking. Then, quite distinctly, he drew from his head a glass ball. "Something in this way?" he said, and held it out.

The action was unexpected. I had seen the trick done at entertainments endless times before—it's part of the common stock of conjurers—but I had not expected it here. "That's good," I said, with a laugh.

"Isn't it?" said the shopman.

Gip stretched out his disengaged hand to take this object and found merely a blank palm.

"It's in your pocket," said the shopman, and there it was!

"How much will that be?" I asked.

"We make no charge for glass balls," said the shopman politely. "We get them"—he picked one out of his elbow as he spoke—"free." He produced another from the back of his neck, and laid it beside its predecessor on the counter. Gip regarded his glass ball sagely, then directed a look of inquiry at the two on the counter, and finally brought his round-eyed scrutiny to the shopman, who smiled. "You may have those too," said the shopman, "and, if you *don't* mind, one from my mouth. *So!*"

Gip counselled me mutely for a moment, and then in a profound silence put away the four balls, resumed my reassuring finger, and nerved himself for the next event.

"We get all our smaller tricks in that way," the shopman remarked.

I laughed in the manner of one who subscribes to a jest. "Instead of going to the wholesale shop," I said. "Of course, it's cheaper."

"In a way," the shopman said. "Though we pay in the end. But not so heavily—as people suppose. . . . Our larger tricks, and our daily provisions and all the other things we want, we get out of that hat. . . . And you know, sir, if you'll excuse my saying it, there *isn't* a wholesale shop, not for Genuine Magic goods, sir. I don't know if you noticed our inscription—the Genuine Magic shop." He drew a business-card from his cheek and handed it to me. "Genuine," he said, with his finger on the word, and added, "There is absolutely no deception, sir."

He seemed to be carrying out the joke pretty thoroughly, I thought.

He turned to Gip with a smile of remarkable affability. "You, you know, are the Right Sort of Boy."

I was surprised at his knowing that, because, in the

interests of discipline, we keep it rather a secret even at home; but Gip received it in unflinching silence, keeping a steadfast eye on him.

"It's only the Right Sort of Boy gets through that doorway."

And, as if by way of illustration, there came a rattling at the door, and a squeaking little voice could be faintly heard. "Nyar! I *warn* 'a go in there, dadda, I WARN 'a go in there. Ny-a-a-ah!" and then the accents of a downtrodden parent, urging consolations and propitiations. "It's locked, Edward," he said.

"But it isn't," said I.

"It is, sir," said the shopman, "always—for that sort of child," and as he spoke we had a glimpse of the other youngster, a little, white face, pallid from sweet-eating and over-sapid food, and distorted by evil passions, a ruthless little egotist, pawing at the enchanted pane. "It's no good, sir," said the shopman, as I moved, with my natural helpfulness, doorward, and presently the spoilt child was carried off howling.

"How do you manage that?" I said, breathing a little more freely.

"Magic!" said the shopman, with a careless wave of the hand, and behold! sparks of coloured fire flew out of his fingers and vanished into the shadows of the shop.

"You were saying," he said, addressing himself to Gip, "before you came in, that you would like one of our 'Buy One and Astonish your Friends' boxes?"

Gip, after a gallant effort, said "Yes."

"It's in your pocket."

And leaning over the counter—he really had an extraordinarily long body—this amazing person produced the article in the customary conjurer's manner. "Paper," he said, and took a sheet out of the empty hat with the springs; "string," and behold his mouth was a string-box, from which he drew an unending thread, which when he had tied his parcel he bit off—and, it seemed to me, swallowed the ball of string. And then he lit a candle at the nose of one of the ventriloquist's dummies, stuck one of his fingers (which had become sealing-wax red) into the flame, and so sealed the parcel. "Then there was the Disappearing Egg," he remarked, and produced one from within my coat-breast and packed it, and also The Crying Baby, Very Human. I handed each parcel to Gip as it was ready, and he clasped them to his chest.

He said very little, but his eyes were eloquent; the clutch of his arms was eloquent. He was the playground of unspeakable emotions. These, you know, were *real* Magics.

Then, with a start, I discovered something moving about in my hat—something soft and jumpy. I whipped it off, and a ruffled pigeon—no doubt a confederate—dropped out and ran on the counter, and went, I fancy, into a cardboard box behind the *papier-mâché* tiger.

"Tut, tut!" said the shopman, dexterously relieving me of my headdress; "careless bird, and—as I live—nesting!"

He shook my hat, and shook out into his extended hand two or three eggs, a large marble, a watch, about half-a-dozen of the inevitable glass balls, and then crumpled, crinkled paper, more and more and more, talking all the time of the way in which people neglect to brush their hats *inside* as well as out, politely, of course, but with a certain personal application. "All sorts of things accumulate, sir. . . . Not *you,* of course, in particular. . . . Nearly every customer. . . . Astonishing what they carry about with them. . . ." The crumpled paper rose and billowed on the counter more and more and more, until he was nearly hidden from us, until he was altogether hidden, and still his voice went on and on. "We none of us know what the fair semblance of a human being may conceal, sir. Are we all then no better than brushed exteriors, whited sepulchres—"

His voice stopped—exactly like when you hit a neighbour's gramophone with a well-aimed brick, the same instant silence, and the rustle of the paper stopped, and everything was still. . . .

"Have you done with my hat?" I said, after an interval.

There was no answer.

I stared at Gip, and Gip stared at me, and there were our distortions in the magic mirrors, looking very rum, and grave, and quiet. . . .

"I think we'll go now," I said. "Will you tell me how much all this comes to? . . .

"I say," I said, on a rather louder note, "I want the bill; and my hat, please."

It might have been a sniff from behind the paper pile. . . .

"Let's look behind the counter, Gip," I said. "He's making fun of us."

I led Gip round the head-wagging tiger, and what do you think there was behind the counter? No one at all! Only my hat on the floor, and a common conjurer's lop-eared white rabbit lost in meditation, and looking as stupid and crumpled as only a conjurer's rabbit can do. I resumed my hat, and the rabbit lolloped a lollop or so out of my way.

"Dadda!" said Gip, in a guilty whisper.

"What is it, Gip?" said I.

"I *do* like this shop, dadda."

"So should I," I said to myself, "if the counter wouldn't suddenly extend itself to shut one off from the door." But I didn't call Gip's attention to that. "Pussy!" he said, with a hand out to the rabbit as it came lolloping past us; "Pussy, do Gip a magic!" and his eyes followed it as it squeezed through a door I had certainly not remarked a moment before. Then this door opened wider, and the man with one ear larger than the other appeared again. He was smiling still, but his eye met mine with something between amusement and defiance. "You'd like to see our show-room, sir," he said, with an innocent suavity. Gip tugged my finger forward. I glanced at the counter and met the shopman's eye again. I was beginning to think the magic just a little too genuine. "We haven't *very* much time," I said. But somehow we were inside the show-room before I could finish that.

"All goods of the same quality," said the shopman, rubbing his flexible hands together, "and that is the Best. Nothing in the place that isn't genuine Magic, and warranted thoroughly rum. Excuse me, sir!"

I felt him pull at something that clung to my coat-sleeve, and then I saw he held a little, wriggling red demon by the tail—the little creature bit and fought and tried to get at his hand—and in a moment he tossed it carelessly behind a counter. No doubt the thing was only an image of twisted indiarubber, but for the moment—! And his gesture was exactly that of a man who handles some petty biting bit of vermin. I glanced at Gip, but Gip was looking at a magic rocking-horse. I was glad he hadn't seen the thing. "I say," I said, in an undertone, and indicating Gip and the red demon with my eyes, "you haven't many things like *that* about, have you?"

"None of ours! Probably brought it with you," said the shopman—also in an undertone, and with a more dazzling smile than ever. "Astonishing what people *will* carry about with them unawares!" And then to Gip, "Do you see anything you fancy here?"

There were many things that Gip fancied there.

He turned to this astonishing tradesman with mingled confidence and respect. "Is that a Magic Sword?" he said.

"A Magic Toy Sword. It neither bends, breaks, nor cuts the fingers. It renders the bearer invincible in battle against any one under eighteen. Half-a-crown to seven and sixpence, according to size. These panoplies on cards are for juvenile knights-errant and very useful —shield of safety, sandals of swiftness, helmet of invisibility."

"Oh, daddy!" gasped Gip.

I tried to find out what they cost, but the shopman did not heed me. He had got Gip now; he had got him away from my finger; he had embarked upon the exposition of all his confounded stock, and nothing was going to stop him. Presently I saw with a qualm of distrust and something very like jealousy that Gip had hold of this person's finger as usually he has hold of mine. No doubt the fellow was interesting, I thought, and had an interestingly faked lot of stuff, really *good* faked stuff, still—

I wandered after them, saying very little, but keeping an eye on this prestidigital fellow. After all, Gip was enjoying it. And no doubt when the time came to go we should be able to go quite easily.

It was a long, rambling place, that show-room, a gallery broken up by stands and stalls and pillars, with archways leading off to other departments, in which the queerest-looking assistants loafed and stared at one, and with perplexing mirrors and curtains. So perplexing, indeed, were these that I was presently unable to make out the door by which we had come.

The shopman showed Gip magic trains that ran without steam or clockwork, just as you set the signals, and then some very, very valuable boxes of soldiers that all came alive directly you took off the lid and said—. I myself haven't a very quick ear and it was a tongue-twisting sound, but Gip—he has his mother's ear—got it in no time. "Bravo!" said the shopman, putting the men back into the box unceremoniously and handing it to Gip. "Now," said the shopman, and in a moment Gip had made them all alive again.

"You'll take that box?" asked the shopman.

"We'll take that box," said I, "unless you charge its full value. In which case it would need a Trust Magnate—"

"Dear heart! *No!*" and the shopman swept the little men back again, shut the lid, waved the box in the air, and there it was, in brown paper, tied up and—*with Gip's full name and address on the paper!*

The shopman laughed at my amazement.

"This is the genuine magic," he said. "The real thing."

"It's a little too genuine for my taste," I said again.

After that he fell to showing Gip tricks, odd tricks, and still odder the way they were done. He explained them, he turned them inside out, and there was the dear little chap nodding his busy bit of a head in the sagest manner.

I did not attend as well as I might. "Hey, presto!" said the Magic Shopman, and then would come the clear, small "Hey, presto!" of the boy. But I was distracted by other things. It was being borne in upon me just how tremendously rum this place was; it was, so to speak, inundated by a sense of rumness. There was something a little rum about the fixtures even, about the ceiling, about the floor, about the casually distributed chairs. I had a queer feeling that whenever I wasn't looking at them straight they went askew, and moved about, and played a noiseless puss-in-the-corner behind my back. And the cornice had a serpentine design with masks—masks altogether too expressive for proper plaster.

Then abruptly my attention was caught by one of the odd-looking assistants. He was some way off and evidently unaware of my presence—I saw a sort of three-quarter length of him over a pile of toys and through an arch—and, you know, he was leaning against a pillar in an idle sort of way doing the most horrid things with his features! The particular horrid thing he did was with his nose. He did it just as though he was idle and wanted to amuse himself. First of all it was a short, blobby nose, and then suddenly he shot it out like a telescope, and then out it flew and became thinner and thinner until it was like a long, red, flexible whip. Like a thing in a nightmare it was! He flourished it about and flung it forth as a fly-fisher flings his line.

My instant thought was that Gip mustn't see him. I turned about, and there was Gip quite preoccupied with the shopman, and thinking no evil. They were whispering together and looking at me. Gip was standing on a little stool, and the shopman was holding a sort of big drum in his hand.

"Hide and seek, dadda!" cried Gip. "You're He!"

And before I could do anything to prevent it, the shopman had clapped the big drum over him.

I saw what was up directly. "Take that off," I cried, "this instant! You'll frighten the boy. Take it off!"

The shopman with the unequal ears did so without a word, and held the big cylinder towards me to show its emptiness. And the little stool was vacant! In that instant my boy had utterly disappeared? . . .

You know, perhaps, that sinister something that comes like a hand out of the unseen and grips your heart about. You know it takes your common self away and leaves you tense and deliberate, neither slow nor hasty, neither angry nor afraid. So it was with me.

I came up to this grinning shopman and kicked his stool aside.

"Stop this folly!" I said. "Where is my boy?"

"You see," he said, still displaying the drum's interior, "there is no deception—"

I put out my hand to grip him, and he eluded me by a dexterous movement. I snatched again, and he turned from me and pushed open a door to escape. "Stop!" I said, and he laughed, receding. I leapt after him—into utter darkness.

Thud!

"Lor' bless my 'eart! I didn't see you coming, sir!"

I was in Regent Street, and I had collided with a decent-looking working man; and a yard away, perhaps, and looking a little perplexed with himself, was Gip. There was some sort of apology, and then Gip had turned and come to me with a bright little smile, as though for a moment he had missed me.

And he was carrying four parcels in his arm!

He secured immediate possession of my finger.

For the second I was rather at a loss. I stared round to see the door of the magic shop, and, behold, it was not there! There was no door, no shop, nothing, only the common pilaster between the shop where they sell pictures and the window with the chicks! . . .

I did the only thing possible in that mental tumult; I walked straight to the kerbstone and held up my umbrella for a cab.

"'Ansoms," said Gip, in a note of culminating exultation.

I helped him in, recalled my address with an effort, and got in also. Something unusual proclaimed itself in my tail-coat pocket, and I felt and discovered a glass ball. With a petulant expression I flung it into the street.

Gip said nothing.

For a space neither of us spoke.

"Dadda!" said Gip, at last, "that *was* a proper shop!"

I came round with that to the problem of just how the whole thing had seemed to him. He looked completely undamaged—so far, good; he was neither scared nor unhinged, he was simply tremendously satisfied with the afternoon's entertainment, and there in his arms were the four parcels.

Confound it! what could be in them?

"Um!" I said. "Little boys can't go to shops like that every day."

He received this with his usual stoicism, and for a moment I was sorry I was his father and not his mother, and so couldn't suddenly there, *coram publico,* in our hansom, kiss him. After all, I thought, the thing wasn't so very bad.

But it was only when we opened the parcels that I really began to be reassured. Three of them contained boxes of soldiers, quite ordinary lead soldiers, but of so good a quality as to make Gip altogether forget that originally these parcels had been Magic Tricks of the only genuine sort, and the fourth contained a kitten, a little living white kitten, in excellent health and appetite and temper.

I saw this unpacking with a sort of provisional relief. I hung about in the nursery for quite an unconscionable time. . . .

That happened six months ago. And now I am beginning to believe it is all right. The kitten had only the magic natural to all kittens, and the soldiers seem as steady a company as any colonel could desire. And Gip—?

The intelligent parent will understand that I have to go cautiously with Gip. But I went so far as this one day. I said, "How would you like your soldiers to come alive, Gip, and march about by themselves?"

"Mine do," said Gip. "I just have to say a word I know before I open the lid."

"Then they march about alone?"

"Oh, *quite,* dadda. I shouldn't like them if they didn't do that."

I displayed no unbecoming surprise, and since then I have taken occasion to drop in upon him once or twice, unannounced, when the soldiers were about, but so far I have never discovered them performing in anything like a magical manner. . . .

It's so difficult to tell.

There's also a question of finance. I have an incurable habit of paying bills. I have been up and down Regent Street several times, looking for that shop. I am inclined to think, indeed, that in that matter honour is satisfied, and that, since Gip's name and address are known to them, I may very well leave it to these people, whoever they may be, to send in their bill in their own time.

E. M. FORSTER

The Story of the Siren

The theme of this story begins to announce itself already in the first sentence: "Few things have been more beautiful than my notebook on the Deist Controversy as it fell downward through the waters of the Mediterranean." (Deism—to give a rough definition applicable to Forster's meaning here—is a belief that man needs no divine revelation of Life's mysteries but can solve them all by the light of his own reason.) The prosaic notebook, with its cargo of rationalism, becomes mysterious and beautiful when it is immersed in irrational Nature—the water of the Blue Grotto at Capri. And it is rescued by a beautiful young man, the boatman who has rowed the narrator to the Grotto. The boatman is a child of Nature. The narrator is a pupil of academic Reason. When the narrator is asked if he has ever seen the Siren, he answers jokingly, "Often and often"; but the boatman knows at once that he is lying. For the boatman's brother Giuseppe really did see the Siren—and that was no joking matter.

What is the Siren? I don't think it is important to interpret Forster's symbolism exactly. But his general statement seems quite clear: the man who obtains an unusual insight into the nature of things will be unable to fit himself back into the everyday world (just as Giuseppe was unable to fit into his boat) and he is quite likely to be destroyed by the jealous guardians of orthodoxy—those who have a vested interest in keeping the Siren silent and under water. Nevertheless, the search for the Siren will and must go on; by no other means can the world be saved. (Compare this with Lawrence's demand for the reunion of "the mind" with "the blood," as expressed in *The Blind Man.*)

The Story of the Siren is pure Forster, like everything else he has written. He is an author whose personality "comes through" powerfully, even in a single paragraph. It is a personality that seems perennially boyish but not in the least naïve, that is too sincerely warm-hearted to be capable of sentimentalism, that is defiantly and rashly frank but seldom aggressive, that is capable of the subtlest irony but never of spite. It is the personality of the man who wrote:

> "But was the dawn wonderful?" asked Helen. With unforgettable sincerity he replied, "No."

who said of Huysmans' *A Rebours:*

> Was it decadent? Yes, and thank God.

who declared:

> If I had to choose between betraying my country and betraying my friend, I hope I should have the guts to betray my country.

This last quotation is from the essay *What I Believe.* Read that at least, because it will make you either love Forster or hate him; and, if you love him, you will read everything else.

FEW THINGS HAVE BEEN MORE BEAUTIFUL THAN MY notebook on the Deist Controversy as it fell downward through the waters of the Mediterranean. It dived, like a piece of black slate, but opened soon, disclosing leaves of pale green, which quivered into blue. Now it had vanished, now it was a piece of magical india-rubber stretching out to infinity, now it was a book again, but bigger than the book of all knowledge. It grew more fantastic as it reached the bottom, where a puff of sand welcomed it and obscured it from view. But it reappeared, quite sane though a little tremulous, lying decently open on its back, while unseen fingers fidgeted among its leaves.

"It is such pity," said my aunt, "that you will not finish your work in the hotel. Then you would be free to enjoy yourself and this would never have happened."

"Nothing of it but will change into something rich and strange," warbled the chaplain, while his sister said, "Why, it's gone in the water!" As for the boatmen, one of them laughed, while the other, without a word of warning, stood up and began to take his clothes off.

"Holy Moses," cried the Colonel. "Is the fellow mad?"

"Yes, thank him, dear," said my aunt: "that is to say, tell him he is very kind, but perhaps another time."

"All the same I do want my book back," I complained. "It's for my Fellowship Dissertation. There won't be much left of it by another time."

"I have an idea," said some woman or other through her parasol. "Let us leave this child of nature to dive for the book while we go on to the other grotto. We can land him either on this rock or on the ledge inside, and he will be ready when we return."

The idea seemed good; and I improved it by saying I would be left behind too, to lighten the boat. So the two of us were deposited outside the little grotto on a great sunlit rock that guarded the harmonies within. Let us call them blue, though they suggest rather the spirit of what is clean—cleanliness passed from the domestic to the sublime, the cleanliness of all the sea gathered together and radiating light. The Blue Grotto at Capri contains only more blue water, not bluer water. That colour and that spirit are the heritage of every cave in the Mediterranean into which the sun can shine and the sea flow.

As soon as the boat left I realized how imprudent I had been to trust myself on a sloping rock with an unknown Sicilian. With a jerk he became alive, seizing my arm and saying, "Go to the end of the grotto, and I will show you something beautiful."

He made me jump off the rock on to the ledge over a dazzling crack of sea; he drew me away from the light till I was standing on the tiny beach of sand which emerged like powdered turquoise at the farther end. There he left me with his clothes, and returned swiftly to the summit of the entrance rock. For a moment he stood naked in the brilliant sun, looking down at the spot where the book lay. Then he crossed himself, raised his hands above his head, and dived.

If the book was wonderful, the man is past all description. His effect was that of a silver statue, alive beneath the sea, through whom life throbbed in blue and green. Something infinitely happy, infinitely wise—but it was impossible that it should emerge from the depths sunburned and dripping, holding the notebook on the Deist Controversy between its teeth.

A gratuity is generally expected by those who bathe. Whatever I offered, he was sure to want more, and I was disinclined for an argument in a place so beautiful and also so solitary. It was a relief that he should say in conversational tones, "In a place like this one might see the Siren."

I was delighted with him for thus falling into the key of his surroundings. We had been left together in a magic world, apart from all the commonplaces that are called reality, a world of blue whose floor was the sea and whose walls and roof of rock trembled with the sea's reflections. Here only the fantastic would be tolerable, and it was in that spirit I echoed his words, "One might easily see the Siren."

He watched me curiously while he dressed. I was parting the sticky leaves of the notebook as I sat on the sand.

"Ah," he said at last. "You may have read the little book that was printed last year. Who would have thought that our Siren would have given the foreigners pleasure!"

(I read it afterwards. Its account is, not unnaturally, incomplete, in spite of there being a woodcut of the young person, and the words of her song.)

"She comes out of this blue water, doesn't she," I suggested, "and sits on the rock at the entrance, combing her hair."

I wanted to draw him out, for I was interested in his sudden gravity, and there was a suggestion of irony in his last remark that puzzled me.

"Have you ever seen her?" he asked.

"Often and often."

"I, never."

"But you have heard her sing?"

He put on his coat and said impatiently, "How can she sing under the water? Who could? She sometimes tries, but nothing comes from her but great bubbles."

"She should climb on to the rock."

"How can she?" he cried again, quite angry. "The priests have blessed the air, so she cannot breathe it, and blessed the rocks, so that she cannot sit on them. But the sea no man can bless, because it is too big, and always changing. So she lives in the sea."

I was silent.

At this his face took a gentler expression. He looked at me as though something was on his mind, and going out to the entrance rock gazed at the external blue. Then returning into our twilight he said, "As a rule only good people see the Siren."

I made no comment. There was a pause, and he continued. "That is a very strange thing, and the priests do not know how to account for it; for she of course is wicked. Not only those who fast and go to Mass are in danger, but even those who are merely good in daily life. No one in the village had seen her for two generations. I am not surprised. We all cross ourselves before we enter the water, but it is unnecessary. Giuseppe, we thought, was safer than most. We loved him, and many of us he loved: but that is a different thing from being good."

I asked who Giuseppe was.

"That day—I was seventeen and my brother was twenty and a great deal stronger than I was, and it was the year when the visitors, who have brought such prosperity and so many alterations into the village, first began to come. One English lady in particular, of very high birth, came, and has written a book about the place, and it was through her that the Improvement Syndicate was formed, which is about to connect the hotels with the station by a funicular railway."

"Don't tell me about that lady in here," I observed.

"That day we took her and her friends to see the grottoes. As we rowed close under the cliffs I put out my hand, as one does, and caught a little crab, and having pulled off its claws offered it as a curiosity. The ladies groaned, but a gentleman was pleased, and held out money. Being inexperienced, I refused it, saying that his pleasure was sufficient reward! Giuseppe, who was rowing behind, was very angry with me and reached out with his hand and hit me on the side of the mouth, so that a tooth cut my lip, and I bled. I tried to hit him back, but he always was too quick for me, and as I stretched round he kicked me under the armpit, so that for a moment I could not even row. There was a great noise among the ladies, and I heard afterward that they were planning to take me away from my brother and train me as a waiter. That, at all events, never came to pass.

"When we reached the grotto—not here, but a larger one—the gentleman was very anxious that one of us should dive for money, and the ladies consented, as they sometimes do. Giuseppe, who had discovered how much pleasure it gives foreigners to see us in the water, refused to dive for anything but silver, and the gentleman threw in a two-lira piece.

"Just before my brother sprang off he caught sight of me holding my bruise, and crying, for I could not help it. He laughed and said, 'This time, at all events, I shall not see the Siren!' and went into the water without crossing himself. But he saw her."

He broke off and accepted a cigarette. I watched the golden entrance rock and the quivering walls and the magic water through which great bubbles constantly rose.

At last he dropped his hot ash into the ripples and

turned his head away, and said, "He came up without the coin. We pulled him into the boat, and he was so large that he seemed to fill it, and so wet that we could not dress him. I have never seen a man so wet. I and the gentleman rowed back, and we covered Giuseppe with sacking and propped him up in the stern."

"He was drowned, then?" I murmured, supposing that to be the point.

"He was not," he cried angrily. "He saw the Siren. I told you."

I was silenced again.

"We put him to bed, though he was not ill. The doctor came, and took money, and the priest came and spattered him with holy water. But it was no good. He was too big—like a piece of the sea. He kissed the thumb-bones of San Biagio and they never dried till evening."

"What did he look like?" I ventured.

"Like any one who has seen the Siren. If you have seen her 'often and often' how is it you do not know? Unhappy, unhappy because he knew everything. Every living thing made him unhappy because he knew it would die. And all he cared to do was sleep."

I bent over my note-book.

"He did no work, he forgot to eat, he forgot whether he had his clothes on. All the work fell on me, and my sister had to go out to service. We tried to make him into a beggar, but he was too robust to inspire pity, and as for an idiot, he had not the right look in his eyes. He would stand in the street looking at people, and the more he looked at them the more unhappy he became. When a child was born he would cover his face with his hands. If any one was married—he was terrible then, and would frighten them as they came out of church. Who would have believed he would marry himself! I caused that, I. I was reading out of the paper how a girl at Ragusa had 'gone mad through bathing in the sea.' Giuseppe got up, and in a week he and that girl came in.

"He never told me anything, but it seems that he went straight to her house, broke into her room, and carried her off. She was the daughter of a rich mine-owner, so you may imagine our peril. Her father came down, with a clever lawyer, but they could do no more than I. They argued and they threatened, but at last they had to go back and we lost nothing—that is to say, no money. We took Giuseppe and Maria to the church and had them married. Ugh! that wedding! The priest made no jokes afterward, and coming out the children threw stones. . . . I think I would have died to make her happy; but as always happens, one could do nothing."

"Were they unhappy together then?"

"They loved each other, but love is not happiness. We can all get love. Love is nothing. I had two people to work for now, for she was like him in everything—one never knew which of them was speaking. I had to sell our own boat and work under the bad old man you have today. Worst of all, people began to hate us. The children first—everything begins with them—and then the women and last of all the men. For the cause of every misfortune was— You will not betray me?"

I promised good faith, and immediately he burst into the frantic blasphemy of one who has escaped from supervision, cursing the priests, who had ruined his life, he said. "Thus are we tricked!" was his cry, and he stood up and kicked at the azure ripples with his feet, till he had obscured them with a cloud of sand.

I too was moved. The story of Giuseppe, for all its absurdity and superstition, came nearer to reality than anything I had known before. I don't know why, but it filled me with desire to help others—the greatest of all our desires, I suppose, and the most fruitless. The desire soon passed.

"She was about to have a child. That was the end of everything. People said to me, 'When will your charming nephew be born? What a cheerful, attractive child he will be, with such a father and mother!' I kept my face steady and replied, 'I think he may be. Out of sadness shall come gladness'—it is one of our proverbs. And my answer frightened them very much, and they told the priests, who were frightened too. Then the whisper started that the child would be Antichrist. You need not be afraid: he was never born.

"An old witch began to prophesy, and no one stopped her. Giuseppe and the girl, she said, had silent devils, who could do little harm. But the child would always be speaking and laughing and perverting, and last of all he would go into the sea and fetch up the Siren into the air and all the world would see her and hear her sing. As soon as she sang, the Seven Vials would be opened and the Pope would die and Mongibello flame, and the veil of Santa Agata would be burned. Then the boy and the Siren would marry, and together they would rule the world, for ever and ever.

"The whole village was in tumult, and the hotel-keepers became alarmed, for the tourist season was just beginning. They met together and decided that Giuseppe and the girl must be sent inland until the child was born, and they subscribed the money. The night before they were to start there was a full moon and wind from the east, and all along the coast the sea shot up over the cliffs in silver clouds. It is a wonderful sight, and Maria said she must see it once more.

" 'Do not go,' I said. 'I saw the priest go by, and some one with him. And the hotel-keepers do not like you to be seen, and if we displease them also we shall starve.'

" 'I want to go,' she replied. 'The sea is stormy, and I may never feel it again.'

" 'No, he is right,' said Giuseppe. 'Do not go—or let one of us go with you.'

" 'I want to go alone,' she said; and she went alone.

"I tied up their luggage in a piece of cloth, and then I was so unhappy at thinking I should lose them that I went and sat down by my brother and put my arm round his neck, and he put his arm round me, which he had not done for more than a year, and we remained thus I don't remember how long.

"Suddenly the door flew open and moonlight and wind came in together, and a child's voice said laughing, 'They have pushed her over the cliffs into the sea.'

"I stepped to the drawer where I keep my knives.

" 'Sit down again,' said Giuseppe—Giuseppe of all people! 'If she is dead, why should others die too?'

" 'I guess who it is,' I cried, 'and I will kill him.'

"I was almost out of the door, and he tripped me up and, kneeling upon me, took hold of both my hands and sprained my wrists; first my right one, then my left. No one but Giuseppe would have thought of such a thing. It hurt more than you would suppose, and I fainted. When I woke up, he was gone, and I never saw him again."

But Giuseppe disgusted me.

"I told you he was wicked," he said. "No one would have expected him to see the Siren."

"How do you know he did see her?"

"Because he did not see her 'often and often,' but once."

"Why do you love him if he is wicked?"

He laughed for the first time. That was his only reply.

"Is that the end?" I asked.

"I never killed her murderer, for by the time my wrists were well he was in America; and one cannot kill a priest. As for Giuseppe, he went all over the world too, looking for some one else who had seen the Siren—either a man, or, better still, a woman, for then the child might still have been born. At last he came to Liverpool—is the district probable?—and there he began to cough, and spat blood until he died.

"I do not suppose there is any one living now who has seen her. There has seldom been more than one in a generation, and never in my life will there be both a man and a woman from whom that child can be born, who will fetch up the Siren from the sea, and destroy silence, and save the world!"

"Save the world?" I cried. "Did the prophecy end like that?"

He leaned back against the rock, breathing deep. Through all the blue-green reflections I saw him colour. I heard him say: "Silence and loneliness cannot last for ever. It may be a hundred or a thousand years, but the sea lasts longer, and she shall come out of it and sing." I would have asked him more, but at that moment the whole cave darkened, and there rode in through its narrow entrance the returning boat.

RUDYARD KIPLING

Mary Postgate

One usually thinks of Kipling as a writer who deals in adventure and physical action; whose realism is, indeed, somewhat journalistic. Yet, oddly enough, many of his best stories are concerned with the supernatural—*The Mark of the Beast, The Return of Imray, At the End of the Passage, The Wish House, The Gardener* and several more. *The Wish House* is a deeply moving story and I would perhaps have chosen it, if I were not prejudiced against narratives in dialect (with some exceptions—I was forgetting *Huckleberry Finn!*). *The Gardener,* also, is magnificent—these two are among Kipling's last works—and it should be read by everyone who reads *Mary Postgate* because their themes are closely related. But I dislike *The Gardener's* ending. It seems to me merely clever. In any case, the Kipling who wrote the supernatural stories is not the Kipling who was such an important figure in my own early life.

The headmaster of my first boarding-school admired him exceedingly and caused his books to be read aloud to us on Sunday afternoons. Thus they became almost an official part of our curriculum, from which we could learn what Life was really like, what traditions we must respect, what duties we were born to fulfill. In other words, Kipling appeared to me as one of those "old hands" whose delight it has been, in every army and institution since time began, to warn and terrify the young recruits. I was terrified by Kipling's warnings—if Life was as rough as he made it seem, I knew I would never be able to cope with it—but that wasn't the only effect they had on me. I also became aware that the things he approved of—the Empire, the Flag, the Old School Tie and the Stiff Upper Lip—were various aspects of an Enemy whom I, personally, would have to fight, whether I liked it or not, for the rest of my life.

Is it unfair to Kipling to select this terrible and repulsive story? I don't think so. If it reflects an unpleasant side of his personality, it also shows him at the height of his powers. Mary Postgate is described with the economy of a master; it is his triumph that she is both colorless and very much alive, and that we can believe in the fiendish callousness of her behavior to the dying German airman. And how vividly Kipling evokes the awkward eager bustle, the befogged rumor-haunted anxiety of civilians at the beginning of a war! Only one defect prevents this story from being great; Kipling cannot stand outside Mary's hatred of the Germans. Indeed, he shares it—as he makes clear in the mediocre poem which appears next to *Mary Postgate* in the volume called *A Diversity of Creatures:*

It was not suddenly bred,
  It will not swiftly abate,
Through the chill years ahead,
  When Time shall count from the date
  That the English began to hate.

Kipling speaks as if he hoped that the English never *would* stop hating. It is impossible to miss the vindictive note of his approval.

As a corrective to this nonsense, I must tell a true story about the Second World-War in England. The speaker was a farmer's wife in my native village near Manchester, and she was recalling a night during the Manchester Blitz, when a returning Nazi pilot had jumped with a parachute from his damaged plane and landed in one of their fields. "And would you believe it," she said, "when the Police came round, they wanted to take the poor lad away with them and lock him up, before he'd even finished his breakfast!"

OF MISS MARY POSTGATE, LADY MCCAUSLAND WROTE that she was "thoroughly conscientious, tidy, companionable, and ladylike. I am very sorry to part with her, and shall always be interested in her welfare."

Miss Fowler engaged her on this recommendation, and to her surprise, for she had had experience of companions, found that it was true. Miss Fowler was nearer sixty than fifty at the time, but though she needed care she did not exhaust her attendant's vitality. On the contrary, she gave out, stimulatingly and with reminiscences. Her father had been a minor Court official in the days when the Great Exhibition of 1851 had just set its seal on Civilisation made perfect. Some of Miss Fowler's tales, none the less, were not always for the young. Mary was not young, and though her speech was as colourless as her eyes or her hair, she was never shocked. She listened unflinchingly to every one; said at the end, "How interesting!" or "How shocking!" as the case might be, and never again referred to it, for she prided herself on a trained mind, which "did not dwell on these things." She was, too, a treasure at domestic accounts, for which the village tradesmen, with their weekly books, loved her not. Otherwise she had no enemies; provoked no jealousy even among the plainest; neither gossip nor slander had ever been traced to her; she supplied the odd place at the Rector's or the Doctor's table at half an hour's notice; she was a sort of public aunt to very many small children of the village street, whose parents, while accepting everything, would have been swift to resent what they called "patronage"; she served on the Village Nursing Committee as Miss Fowler's nominee when Miss Fowler was crippled by rheumatoid arthritis, and came out of six months' fortnightly meetings equally respected by all the cliques.

And when Fate threw Miss Fowler's nephew, an unlovely orphan of eleven, on Miss Fowler's hands, Mary Postgate stood to her share of the business of education as practised in private and public schools. She checked printed clothes-lists, and unitemised bills of extras; wrote to Head and House masters, matrons, nurses and doctors, and grieved or rejoiced over half-term reports. Young Wyndham Fowler repaid her in his holidays by calling her "Gatepost," "Postey," or "Packthread," by thumping her between her narrow shoulders, or by chasing her bleating, round the garden, her large mouth open, her large nose high in air, at a stiff-necked shamble very like a camel's. Later on he filled the house with clamour, argument, and harangues as to his personal needs, likes and dislikes, and the limitations of "you women," reducing Mary to tears of physical fatigue, or, when he chose to be humorous, of helpless laughter. At crises, which multiplied as he grew older, she was his ambassadress and his interpretress to Miss Fowler, who had no large sympathy with the young; a vote in his interest at the councils on his future; his sewing-woman, strictly accountable for mislaid boots and garments; always his butt and his slave.

And when he decided to become a solicitor, and had entered an office in London; when his greeting had changed from "Hullo, Postey, you old beast," to "Mornin', Packthread," there came a war which, unlike all wars that Mary could remember, did not stay decently outside England and in the newspapers, but intruded on the lives of people whom she knew. As she said to Miss Fowler, it was "most vexatious." It took the Rector's son who was going into business with his elder brother; it took the Colonel's nephew on the eve of fruit-farming in Canada; it took Mrs. Grant's son who, his mother said, was devoted to the ministry; and, very early indeed, it took Wynn Fowler, who announced on a postcard that he had joined the Flying Corps and wanted a cardigan waistcoat.

"He must go, and he must have the waistcoat," said Miss Fowler. So Mary got the proper-sized needles and wool, while Miss Fowler told the men of her establishment—two gardeners and an odd man, aged sixty—that those who could join the Army had better do so. The gardeners left. Cheape, the odd man, stayed on, and was promoted to the gardener's cottage. The cook, scorning to be limited in luxuries, also left, after a spirited scene with Miss Fowler, and took the housemaid with her. Miss Fowler gazetted Nellie, Cheape's seventeen-year-old daughter, to the vacant post; Mrs. Cheape to the rank of cook, with occasional cleaning bouts; and the reduced establishment moved forward smoothly.

Wynn demanded an increase in his allowance. Miss Fowler, who always looked facts in the face, said, "He must have it. The chances are he won't live long to draw it, and if three hundred makes him happy—"

Wynn was grateful, and came over, in his tight-buttoned uniform, to say so. His training centre was not thirty miles away, and his talk was so technical that it had to be explained by charts of the various types of machines. He gave Mary such a chart.

"And you'd better study it, Postey," he said. "You'll be seeing a lot of 'em soon." So Mary studied the chart, but when Wynn next arrived to swell and exalt himself before his womenfolk, she failed badly in cross-examination, and he rated her as in the old days.

"You *look* more or less like a human being," he said in his new Service voice. "You *must* have had a brain at some time in your past. What have you done with it? Where d'you keep it? A sheep would know more than you do, Postey. You're lamentable. You are less use than an empty tin can, you dowey old cassowary."

"I suppose that's how your superior officer talks to *you?*" said Miss Fowler from her chair.

"But Postey doesn't mind," Wynn replied. "Do you, Packthread?"

"Why? Was Wynn saying anything? I shall get this right next time you come," she muttered, and knitted her pale brows again over the diagrams of Taubes, Farmans, and Zeppelins.

In a few weeks the mere land and sea battles which she read to Miss Fowler after breakfast passed her like idle breath. Her heart and her interest were high in the air with Wynn, who had finished "rolling" (whatever that might be) and had gone on from a "taxi" to a machine more or less his own. One morning it circled over their very chimneys, alighted on Vegg's Heath, almost outside the garden gate, and Wynn came in, blue with cold, shouting for food. He and she drew Miss Fowler's bath-chair, as they had often done, along the Heath foot-path to look at the biplane. Mary observed that "it smelt very badly."

"Postey, I believe you think with your nose," said Wynn. "I know you don't with your mind. Now, what type's that?"

"I'll go and get the chart," said Mary.

"You're hopeless! You haven't the mental capacity of a white mouse," he cried, and explained the dials and the sockets for bomb-dropping till it was time to mount and ride the wet clouds once more.

"Ah!" said Mary, as the stinking thing flared upward. "Wait till our Flying Corps gets to work! Wynn says it's much safer than in the trenches."

"I wonder," said Miss Fowler. "Tell Cheape to come and tow me home again."

"It's all downhill. I can do it," said Mary, "if you put the brake on." She laid her lean self against the pushing-bar and home they trundled.

"Now, be careful you aren't heated and catch a chill," said overdressed Miss Fowler.

"Nothing makes me perspire," said Mary. As she bumped the chair under the porch she straightened her long back. The exertion had given her a colour, and the wind had loosened a wisp of hair across her forehead. Miss Fowler glanced at her.

"What do you ever think of, Mary?" she demanded suddenly.

"Oh, Wynn says he wants another three pairs of stockings—as thick as we can make them."

"Yes. But I mean the things that women think about. Here you are, more than forty—"

"Forty-four," said truthful Mary.

"Well?"

"Well?" Mary offered Miss Fowler her shoulder as usual.

"And you've been with me ten years now."

"Let's see," said Mary. "Wynn was eleven when he came. He's twenty now, and I came two years before that. It must be eleven."

"Eleven! And you've never told me anything that matters in all that while. Looking back, it seems to me that *I've* done all the talking."

"I'm afraid I'm not much of a conversationalist. As Wynn says, I haven't the mind. Let me take your hat."

Miss Fowler, moving stiffly from the hip, stamped her rubber-tipped stick on the tiled hall floor. "Mary, aren't you *anything* except a companion? Would you *ever* have been anything except a companion?"

Mary hung up the garden hat on its proper peg. "No," she said after consideration. "I don't imagine I ever should. But I've no imagination, I'm afraid."

She fetched Miss Fowler her eleven-o'clock glass of Contrexéville.

That was the wet December when it rained six inches to the month, and the women went abroad as little as might be. Wynn's flying chariot visited them several times, and for two mornings (he had warned her by postcard) Mary heard the thresh of his propellers at dawn. The second time she ran to the window, and stared at the whitening sky. A little blur passed overhead. She lifted her lean arms towards it.

That evening at six o'clock there came an announcement in an official envelope that Second Lieutenant W. Fowler had been killed during a trial flight. Death was instantaneous. She read it and carried it to Miss Fowler.

"I never expected anything else," said Miss Fowler; "but I'm sorry it happened before he had done anything."

The room was whirling round Mary Postgate, but she found herself quite steady in the midst of it.

"Yes," she said. "It's a great pity he didn't die in action after he had killed somebody."

"He was killed instantly. That's one comfort," Miss Fowler went on.

"But Wynn says the shock of a fall kills a man at once—whatever happens to the tanks," quoted Mary.

The room was coming to rest now. She heard Miss Fowler say impatiently, "But why can't we cry, Mary?" and herself replying, "There's nothing to cry for. He has done his duty as much as Mrs. Grant's son did."

"And when he died, *she* came and cried all the morning," said Miss Fowler. "This only makes me feel tired—terribly tired. Will you help me to bed, please, Mary?—And I think I'd like the hot-water bottle."

So Mary helped her and sat beside, talking of Wynn in his riotous youth.

"I believe," said Miss Fowler suddenly, "that old people and young people slip from under a stroke like this. The middle-aged feel it most."

"I expect that's true," said Mary, rising. "I'm going to put away the things in his room now. Shall we wear mourning?"

"Certainly not," said Miss Fowler. "Except, of course, at the funeral. I can't go. You will. I want you to arrange about his being buried here. What a blessing it didn't happen at Salisbury!"

Every one, from the Authorities of the Flying Corps to the Rector, was most kind and sympathetic. Mary found herself for the moment in a world where bodies were in the habit of being despatched by all sorts of conveyances to all sorts of places. And at the funeral two young men in buttoned-up uniforms stood beside the grave and spoke to her afterwards.

"You're Miss Postgate, aren't you?" said one. "Fowler told me about you. He was a good chap—a first-class fellow—a great loss."

"Great loss!" growled his companion. "We're all awfully sorry."

"How high did he fall from?" Mary whispered.

"Pretty nearly four thousand feet, I should think, didn't he? You were up that day, Monkey?"

"All of that," the other child replied. "My bar made three thousand, and I wasn't as high as him by a lot."

"Then *that's* all right," said Mary. "Thank you very much."

They moved away as Mrs. Grant flung herself weeping on Mary's flat chest, under the lych-gate, and cried, "*I* know how it feels! *I* know how it feels!"

"But both his parents are dead," Mary returned, as she fended her off. "Perhaps they've all met by now," she added vaguely as she escaped towards the coach.

"I've thought of that too," wailed Mrs. Grant; "but then he'll be practically a stranger to them. Quite embarrassing!"

Mary faithfully reported every detail of the ceremony to Miss Fowler, who, when she described Mrs. Grant's outburst, laughed aloud.

"Oh, how Wynn would have enjoyed it! He was always utterly unreliable at funerals. D'you remember—" And they talked of him again, each piecing out the other's gaps. "And now," said Miss Fowler, "we'll pull up the blinds and we'll have a general tidy. That always does us good. Have you seen to Wynn's things?"

"Everything—since he first came," said Mary. "He was never destructive—even with his toys."

They faced that neat room.

"It can't be natural not to cry," Mary said at last. "I'm *so* afraid you'll have a reaction."

"As I told you, we old people slip from under the stroke. It's you I'm afraid for. Have you cried yet?"

"I can't. It only makes me angry with the Germans."

"That's sheer waste of vitality," said Miss Fowler. "We must live till the war's finished." She opened a full wardrobe. "Now, I've been thinking things over. This is my plan. All his civilian clothes can be given away—Belgian refugees, and so on."

Mary nodded. "Boots, collars, and gloves?"

"Yes. We don't need to keep anything except his cap and belt."

"They came back yesterday with his Flying Corps clothes"—Mary pointed to a roll on the little iron bed.

"Ah, but keep his Service things. Some one may be glad of them later. Do you remember his sizes?"

"Five feet eight and a half; thirty-six inches round the chest. But he told me he's just put on an inch and a half. I'll mark it on a label and tie it on his sleeping-bag."

"So that disposes of *that*," said Miss Fowler, tapping the palm of one hand with the ringed third finger of the other. "What waste it all is! We'll get his old school trunk tomorrow and pack his civilian clothes."

"And the rest?" said Mary. "His books and pictures and the games and the toys—and—and the rest?"

"My plan is to burn every single thing," said Miss Fowler. "Then we shall know where they are and no one can handle them afterwards. What do you think?"

"I think that would be much the best," said Mary. "But there's such a lot of them."

"We'll burn them in the destructor," said Miss Fowler.

This was an open-air furnace for the consumption of refuse; a little circular four-foot tower of pierced brick over an iron grating. Miss Fowler had noticed the design in a gardening journal years ago, and had had it built at the bottom of the garden. It suited her tidy soul, for it saved unsightly rubbish-heaps, and the ashes lightened the stiff clay soil.

Mary considered for a moment, saw her way clear, and nodded again. They spent the evening putting away well-remembered civilian suits, underclothes that Mary had marked, and the regiments of very gaudy socks and ties. A second trunk was needed, and, after that, a little packing-case, and it was late next day when Cheape and the local carrier lifted them to the cart. The Rector luckily knew of a friend's son, about five feet eight and a half inches high, to whom a complete Flying Corps outfit would be most acceptable, and sent his gardener's son down with a barrow to take delivery of it. The cap was hung up in Miss Fowler's bedroom, the belt in Miss Postgate's; for, as Miss Fowler said, they had no desire to make tea-party talk of them.

"That disposes of *that,*" said Miss Fowler. "I'll leave the rest to you, Mary. I can't run up and down the garden. You'd better take the big clothes-basket and get Nellie to help you."

"I shall take the wheel-barrow and do it myself," said Mary, and for once in her life closed her mouth.

Miss Fowler, in moments of irritation, had called Mary deadly methodical. She put on her oldest waterproof and gardening-hat and her ever-slipping goloshes, for the weather was on the edge of more rain. She gathered fire-lighters from the kitchen, a half-scuttle of coals, and a faggot of brushwood. These she wheeled in the barrow down the mossed paths to the dank little laurel shrubbery where the destructor stood under the drip of three oaks. She climbed the wire fence into the Rector's glebe just behind, and from his tenant's rick pulled two large armfuls of good hay, which she spread neatly on the fire-bars. Next, journey by journey, passing Miss Fowler's white face at the morning-room window each time, she brought down in the towel-covered clothes-basket, on the wheel-barrow, thumbed and used Hentys, Marryats, Levers, Stevensons, Baroness Orczys, Garvices, schoolbooks, and atlases, unrelated piles of the *Motor Cyclist,* the *Light Car,* and catalogues of Olympia Exhibitions; the remnants of a fleet of sailing-ships from ninepenny cutters to a three-guinea yacht; a prep.-school dressing-gown; bats from three-and-sixpence to twenty-four shillings; cricket and tennis balls; disintegrated steam and clockwork locomotives with their twisted rails; a grey and red tin model of a submarine; a dumb gramophone and cracked records; golf-clubs that had to be broken across the knee, like his walking-sticks, and an assegai; photographs of private and public school cricket and football elevens, and his O.T.C. on the line of march; kodaks, and film-rolls; some pewters, and one real silver cup, for boxing competitions and Junior Hurdles; sheaves of school photographs; Miss Fowler's photograph; her own which he had borne off in fun and (good care she took not to ask!) had never returned; a playbox with a secret drawer; a load of flannels, belts, and jerseys, and a pair of spiked shoes unearthed in the attic; a packet of all the letters that Miss Fowler and she had ever written to him, kept for some absurd reason through all these years; a five-day attempt at a diary; framed pictures of racing motors in full Brooklands career, and load upon load of undistinguishable wreckage of tool-boxes, rabbit-hutches, electric batteries, tin soldiers, fret-saw outfits, and jig-saw puzzles.

Miss Fowler at the window watched her come and go, and said to herself, "Mary's an old woman. I never realised it before."

After lunch she recommended her to rest.

"I'm not in the least tired," said Mary. "I've got it all arranged. I'm going to the village at two o'clock for some paraffin. Nellie hasn't enough, and the walk will do me good."

She made one last quest round the house before she started, and found that she had overlooked nothing. It began to mist as soon as she had skirted Vegg's Heath, where Wynn used to descend—it seemed to her that she could almost hear the beat of his propellers overhead, but there was nothing to see. She hoisted her umbrella and lunged into the blind wet till she had reached the shelter of the empty village. As she came out of Mr. Kidd's shop with a bottle full of paraffin in her string shopping-bag, she met Nurse Eden, the village nurse, and fell into talk with her, as usual, about the village children. They were just parting opposite the "Royal Oak," when a gun, they fancied, was fired immediately behind the house. It was followed by a child's shriek dying into a wail.

"Accident!" said Nurse Eden promptly, and dashed through the empty bar, followed by Mary. They found Mrs. Gerritt, the publican's wife, who could only gasp and point to the yard, where a little cart-lodge was sliding sideways amid a clatter of tiles. Nurse Eden snatched up a sheet drying before the fire, ran out, lifted something from the ground, and flung the sheet round it. The sheet turned scarlet and half her uniform too, as she bore the load into the kitchen. It was little Edna Gerritt, aged nine, whom Mary had known since her perambulator days.

"Am I hurted bad?" Edna asked, and died between Nurse Eden's dripping hands. The sheet fell aside and for an instant, before she could shut her eyes, Mary saw the ripped and shredded body.

"It's a wonder she spoke at all," said Nurse Eden. "What in God's name was it?"

"A bomb," said Mary.

"One o' the Zeppelins?"

"No. An aeroplane. I thought I heard it on the Heath, but I fancied it was one of ours. It must have shut off its engines as it came down. That's why we didn't notice it."

"The filthy pigs!" said Nurse Eden, all white and shaken. "See the pickle I'm in! Go and tell Dr. Hennis, Miss Postgate." Nurse looked at the mother, who had dropped face down on the floor. "She's only in a fit. Turn her over."

Mary heaved Mrs. Gerritt right side up, and hurried off for the doctor. When she told her tale, he asked her to sit down in the surgery till he got her something.

"But I don't need it, I assure you," said she. "I don't

think it would be wise to tell Miss Fowler about it, do you? Her heart is so irritable in this weather."

Dr. Hennis looked at her admiringly as he packed up his bag.

"No. Don't tell anybody till we're sure," he said, and hastened to the "Royal Oak," while Mary went on with the paraffin. The village behind her was as quiet as usual, for the news had not yet spread. She frowned a little to herself, her large nostrils expanded uglily, and from time to time she muttered a phrase which Wynn, who never restrained himself before his womenfolk, had applied to the enemy. "Bloody pagans! They *are* bloody pagans. But," she continued, falling back on the teaching that had made her what she was, "one mustn't let one's mind dwell on these things."

Before she reached the house Dr. Hennis, who was also a special constable, overtook her in his car.

"Oh, Miss Postgate," he said, "I wanted to tell you that that accident at the 'Royal Oak' was due to Gerritt's stable tumbling down. It's been dangerous for a long time. It ought to have been condemned."

"I thought I heard an explosion too," said Mary.

"You might have been misled by the beams snapping. I've been looking at 'em. They were dry-rotted through and through. Of course, as they broke, they would make a noise just like a gun."

"Yes?" said Mary politely.

"Poor little Edna was playing underneath it," he went on, still holding her with his eyes, "and that and the tiles cut her to pieces, you see?"

"I saw it," said Mary, shaking her head. "I heard it too."

"Well, we cannot be sure." Dr. Hennis changed his tone completely. "I know both you and Nurse Eden

(I've been speaking to her) are perfectly trustworthy, and I can rely on you not to say anything—yet at least. It is no good to stir up people unless—"

"Oh, I never do—anyhow," said Mary, and Dr. Hennis went on to the county town.

After all, she told herself, it might, just possibly, have been the collapse of the old stable that had done all those things to poor little Edna. She was sorry she had even hinted at other things, but Nurse Eden was discretion itself. By the time she reached home the affair seemed increasingly remote by its very monstrosity. As she came in, Miss Fowler told her that a couple of aeroplanes had passed half an hour ago.

"I thought I heard them," she replied, "I'm going down to the garden now. I've got the paraffin."

"Yes, but—what *have* you got on your boots? They're soaking wet. Change them at once."

Not only did Mary obey but she wrapped the boots in a newspaper, and put them into the string bag with the bottle. So, armed with the longest kitchen poker, she left.

"It's raining again," was Miss Fowler's last word, "but—I know you won't be happy till that's disposed of."

"It won't take long. I've got everything down there, and I've put the lid on the destructor to keep the wet out."

The shrubbery was filling with twilight by the time she had completed her arrangements and sprinkled the sacrificial oil. As she lit the match that would burn her heart to ashes, she heard a groan or a grunt behind the dense Portugal laurels.

"Cheape?" she called impatiently, but Cheape, with his ancient lumbago, in his comfortable cottage would be the last man to profane the sanctuary. "Sheep," she concluded, and threw in the fusee. The pyre went up in a roar, and the immediate flame hastened night around her.

"How Wynn would have loved this!" she thought, stepping back from the blaze.

By its light she saw, half hidden behind a laurel not five paces away, a bareheaded man sitting very stiffly at the foot of one of the oaks. A broken branch lay across his lap—one booted leg protruding from beneath it. His head moved ceaselessly from side to side, but his body was as still as the tree's trunk. He was dressed—she moved sideways to look more closely—in a uniform something like Wynn's, with a flap buttoned across the chest. For an instant, she had some idea that it might be one of the young flying men she had met at the funeral. But their heads were dark and glossy. This man's was as pale as a baby's, and so closely cropped that she could see the disgusting pinky skin beneath. His lips moved.

"What do you say?" Mary moved towards him and stooped.

"Laty! Laty! Laty!" he muttered, while his hands picked at the dead wet leaves. There was no doubt as to his nationality. It made her so angry that she strode back to the destructor, though it was still too hot to use the poker there. Wynn's books seemed to be catching well. She looked up at the oak behind the man; several of the light upper and two or three rotten lower branches had broken and scattered their rubbish on the shubbery path. On the lowest fork a helmet with dependent strings, showed like a bird's-nest in the light of a long-tongued flame. Evidently this person had fallen through the tree. Wynn had told her that it was quite possible for people to fall out of aeroplanes. Wynn told her too, that trees were useful things to break an aviator's fall, but in this case the aviator must have been broken or he would have moved from his queer position. He seemed helpless except for his horrible rolling head. On the other hand, she could see a pistol case at his belt—and Mary loathed pistols. Months ago, after reading certain Belgian reports together, she and Miss Fowler had had dealings with one—a huge revolver with flat-nosed bullets, which latter, Wynn said, were forbidden by the rules of war to be used against civilised enemies. "They're good enough for us," Miss Fowler had replied. "Show Mary how it works." And Wynn, laughing at the mere possibility of any such need, had led the craven, winking Mary into the Rector's disused quarry, and had shown her how to fire the terrible machine. It lay now in the top-left-hand drawer of her toilet-table—a memento not included in the burning. Wynn would be pleased to see how she was not afraid.

She slipped up to the house to get it. When she came through the rain, the eyes in the head were alive with expectation. The mouth even tried to smile. But at sight of the revolver its corners went down just like Edna Gerritt's. A tear trickled from one eye, and the head rolled from shoulder to shoulder as though trying to point out something.

"Cassée. Tout cassée," it whimpered.

"What do you say?" said Mary disgustedly, keeping well to one side, though only the head moved.

"Cassée," it repeated. "Che me rends. Le médicin! Toctor!"

"Nein!" said she, bringing all her small German to bear with the big pistol. "Ich haben der todt Kinder gesehn."

The head was still. Mary's hand dropped. She had been careful to keep her finger off the trigger for fear of accidents. After a few moments' waiting, she returned to the destructor, where the flames were falling, and churned up Wynn's charring books with the poker. Again the head groaned for the doctor.

"Stop that!" said Mary, and stamped her foot. "Stop that, you bloody pagan!"

The words came quite smoothly and naturally. They were Wynn's own words, and Wynn was a gentleman who for no consideration on earth would have torn little Edna into those vividly coloured strips and strings. But this thing hunched under the oak-tree had done that thing. It was no question of reading horrors out of newspapers to Miss Fowler. Mary had seen it with her own eyes on the "Royal Oak" kitchen table. She must not allow her mind to dwell upon it. Now Wynn was dead, and everything connected with him was lumping and rustling and tinkling under her busy poker into red black dust and grey leaves of ash. The thing beneath the oak would die too. Mary had seen death more than once. She came of a family that had a knack of dying under, as she told Miss Fowler, "most distressing circumstances." She would stay where she was till she was entirely satisfied that It was dead—dead as dear papa in the late 'eighties; aunt Mary in 'eighty-nine; mamma in 'ninety-one; cousin Dick in 'ninety-five; Lady McCausland's housemaid in 'ninety-nine; Lady McCausland's sister in nineteen hundred and one; Wynn buried five days ago; and Edna Gerritt still waiting for decent earth to hide her. As she thought—her underlip caught up by one faded canine, brows knit and nostrils wide—she wielded the poker with lunges that jarred the grating at the bottom, and careful scrapes round the brick-work above. She looked at her wrist-watch. It was getting on to half-past four, and the rain was coming down in earnest. Tea would be at five. If It did not die before that time, she would be soaked and would have to change. Meantime, and this occupied her, Wynn's things were burning well in spite of the hissing wet, though now and again a bookback with a quite distinguishable title would be heaved up out of the mass. The exercise of stoking had given her a glow which seemed to reach to the marrow of her bones. She hummed—Mary never had a voice—to herself. She had never believed in all those advanced views—though Miss Fowler herself leaned a little that way—of woman's work in the world; but now she saw there was much to be said for them. This, for instance, was *her* work—work which no man, least of all Dr. Hennis, would ever have done. A man, at such a crisis, would be what Wynn called a "sportsman"; would leave everything to fetch help, and would certainly bring It into the house. Now a woman's business was to make a happy home for—for a husband and children. Failing these—it was not a thing one should allow one's mind to dwell upon—but—

"Stop it!" Mary cried once more across the shadows. "Nein, I tell you! Ich haben der todt Kinder gesehn."

But it was a fact. A woman who had missed these things could still be useful—more useful than a man in certain respects. She thumped like a pavior through the settling ashes at the secret thrill of it. The rain was damping the fire, but she could feel—it was too dark to see—that her work was done. There was a dull red glow at the bottom of the destructor, not enough to char the wooden lid if she slipped it half over against the driving wet. This arranged, she leaned on the poker and waited, while an increasing rapture laid hold on her.

She ceased to think. She gave herself up to feel. Her long pleasure was broken by a sound that she had waited for in agony several times in her life. She leaned forward and listened, smiling. There could be no mistake. She closed her eyes and drank it in. Once it ceased abruptly.

"Go on," she murmured, half aloud. "That isn't the end."

Then the end came very distinctly in a lull between two rain-gusts. Mary Postgate drew her breath short between her teeth and shivered from head to foot. "*That's* all right," said she contentedly, and went up to the house, where she scandalised the whole routine by taking a luxurious hot bath before tea, and came down looking, as Miss Fowler said when she saw her lying all relaxed on the other sofa, "quite handsome!"

D. H. LAWRENCE

The Blind Man

Even while Lawrence was still alive—he died in 1930 —you often heard him spoken of as a "genius." I have begun to doubt whether this vague, intimidating word should ever be applied to anybody, but I think I know what people meant when they used it to describe Lawrence. They meant that he is the kind of writer who somehow or other creates powerful effects while breaking all the literary rules. (Theodore Dreiser, too, has this quality.) Certainly, Lawrence is often careless, rambling and repetitive. He writes, as it were, by touch rather than by thought; his greatest gift is his understanding of physical contact and its implications. He is wonderfully able to convey what art critics call the "tactile values" of men, animals, vegetables and inanimate objects, and in this he resembles a sculptor or a painter. It is not too much, I think, to say that he revolutionized the art of description, by bringing to it a new degree of subjective intimacy. That is, he relates everything in his scene to the subjective "I," the observer—so that we get the illusion of being right inside this observer and of seeing through his eyes and feeling through his nerves. For example, Lawrence's description of the Taos ranch-house in *St. Mawr*—surely one of the finest passages of its kind ever written—shows us how an entire landscape is transformed by the awe, admiration, fear and hatred of a New England woman who cannot come to terms with the spirit of the Western wilderness.

Lawrence frequently expressed a burning contempt for those who failed to enter into the "dark" (this was a favorite adjective of his: it meant, approximately, "intuitive") "stream of the blood"—who failed, in other words, to realize the power and the glory of their own instinctive, animal nature. Such mean spirits—condemned as being too mental, too cerebral, as having their sex "in the head" only—are his villains or perhaps one should say his victims. In this story, we see the humiliation of Bertie Reid, in being proved unworthy of the friendship of Isabel's blind husband, Maurice. Bertie is terrified and recoils in disgust when Maurice tries to initiate him into the fellowship of tactile relations by making him put his fingers on Maurice's eye-sockets, which are disfigured by the war wound that has blinded him. How tremendous is Lawrence's description of the blinded man: "He looked so strong-blooded and healthy, and, at the same time, cancelled"!

It should be noted, however, that Lawrence did *not* take sides with "the blood" against "the mind," as some critics have suggested. His protest was against our puritanical rejection of "the blood" as something dirty and unmentionable, and against the consequent division of our human nature. Isabel is aware of this division and she fights desperately against it. She wants to share her life between Maurice her husband and Bertie her friend, knowing that both have much to give her. But this, she finds, is impossible because she cannot bring "blood" and "mind"—as typified by Maurice and Bertie—together.

I have already recommended one book of literary criticism, by Chesterton. I must now recommend another, by Lawrence; equally funny and exciting in its different way, and with a title just as formidable—*Studies in Classic American Literature.*

ISABEL PERVIN WAS LISTENING FOR TWO SOUNDS—FOR THE sound of wheels on the drive outside and for the noise of her husband's footsteps in the hall. Her dearest and oldest friend, a man who seemed almost indispensable to her living, would drive up in the rainy dusk of the closing November day. The trap had gone to fetch him from the station. And her husband, who had been blinded in Flanders, and who had a disfiguring mark on his brow, would be coming in from the outhouses.

He had been home for a year now. He was totally blind. Yet they had been very happy. The Grange was Maurice's own place. The back was a farmstead, and the Wernhams, who occupied the rear premises, acted as farmers. Isabel lived with her husband in the handsome rooms in front. She and he had been almost entirely alone together since he was wounded. They talked and sang and read together in a wonderful and unspeakable intimacy. Then she reviewed books for a Scottish newspaper, carrying on her old interest, and he occupied himself a good deal with the farm. Sightless, he could still discuss everything with Wernham, and he could also do a good deal of work about the place—menial work, it is true, but it gave him satisfaction. He milked the cows, carried in the pails, turned the separator, attended to the pigs and horses. Life was still very full and strangely serene for the blind man, peaceful with the almost incomprehensible peace of immediate contact in darkness. With his wife he had a whole world, rich and real and invisible.

They were newly and remotely happy. He did not even regret the loss of his sight in these times of dark, palpable joy. A certain exultance swelled his soul.

But as time wore on, sometimes the rich glamour would leave them. Sometimes, after months of this intensity, a sense of burden overcame Isabel, a weariness, a terrible *ennui,* in that silent house approached between a colonnade of tall-shafted pines. Then she felt she would go mad, for she could not bear it. And sometimes he had devastating fits of depression, which seemed to lay waste his whole being. It was worse than depression—a black misery, when his own life was a torture to him, and when his presence was unbearable to his wife. The dread went down to the roots of her soul as these black days recurred. In a kind of panic she tried to wrap herself up still further in her husband. She forced the old spontaneous cheerfulness and joy to continue. But the effort it cost her was almost too much. She knew she could not keep it up. She felt she would scream with the strain, and would give anything, anything, to escape. She longed to possess her husband utterly; it gave her inordinate joy to have him entirely to herself. And yet, when again he was gone in a black and massive misery, she could not bear him, she could not bear herself; she wished she could be snatched away off the earth altogether, anything rather than live at this cost.

Dazed, she schemed for a way out. She invited friends, she tried to give him some further connection with the outer world. But it was no good. After all their joy and suffering, after their dark, great year of blindness and solitude and unspeakable nearness, other people seemed to them both shallow, rattling, rather impertinent. Shallow prattle seemed presumptuous. He became impatient and irritated, she was wearied. And so they lapsed into their solitude again. For they preferred it.

But now, in a few weeks' time, her second baby would be born. The first had died, an infant, when her husband first went out to France. She looked with joy and relief to the coming of the second. It would be her salvation. But also she felt some anxiety. She was thirty years old, her husband was a year younger. They both wanted the child very much. Yet she could not help feeling afraid. She had her husband on her hands, a terrible joy to her, and a terrifying burden. The child would occupy her love and attention. And then, what of Maurice? What would he do? If only she could feel that he, too, would be at peace and happy when the child came! She did so want to luxuriate in a rich, physical satisfaction of maternity. But the man, what would he do? How could she provide for him, how avert those shattering black moods of his, which destroyed them both?

She sighed with fear. But at this time Bertie Reid wrote to Isabel. He was her old friend, a second or third cousin, a Scotchman, as she was a Scotchwoman. They had been brought up near to one another, and all her life he had been her friend, like a brother, but better than her own brothers. She loved him—though not in the marrying sense. There was a sort of kinship between them, an affinity. They understood one another instinctively. But Isabel would never have thought of marrying Bertie. It would have seemed like marrying in her own family.

Bertie was a barrister and a man of letters, a Scotchman of the intellectual type, quick, ironical, sentimental, and on his knees before the woman he adored but did not want to marry. Maurice Pervin was different. He came of a good old country family—the Grange was not a very great distance from Oxford. He was passionate, sensitive, perhaps over-sensitive, wincing—a big fellow with heavy limbs and a forehead that flushed painfully. For his mind was slow, as if drugged by the strong provincial blood that beat in his veins. He was very sensitive to his own mental slowness, his feelings being quick and acute. So that he was just the opposite to Bertie, whose mind was much quicker than his emotions, which were not so very fine.

From the first the two men did not like each other. Isabel felt that they *ought* to get on together. But they did not. She felt that if only each could have the clue to the other there would be such a rare understanding between them. It did not come off, however. Bertie adopted a slightly ironical attitude, very offensive to Maurice, who returned the Scotch irony with English resentment, a resentment which deepened sometimes into stupid hatred.

This was a little puzzling to Isabel. However, she accepted it in the course of things. Men were made freakish and unreasonable. Therefore, when Maurice was going out to France for the second time, she felt that, for her husband's sake, she must discontinue her friendship with Bertie. She wrote to the barrister to this effect. Bertram Reid simply replied that in this, as in all other matters, he must obey her wishes, if these were indeed her wishes.

For nearly two years nothing had passed between the two friends. Isabel rather gloried in the fact; she had no compunction. She had one great article of faith, which was, that husband and wife should be so important to one another, that the rest of the world simply did not count. She and Maurice were husband and wife. They loved one another. They would have children. Then let everybody and everything else fade into insignificance outside this connubial felicity. She professed herself quite happy and ready to receive Maurice's friends. She was happy and ready: the happy wife, the ready woman in possession. Without knowing why, the friends retired abashed, and came no more. Maurice, of course, took as much satisfaction in this connubial absorption as Isabel did.

He shared in Isabel's literary activities, she cultivated a real interest in agriculture and cattle-raising. For she, being at heart perhaps an emotional enthusiast, always cultivated the practical side of life and prided herself on her mastery of practical affairs. Thus the husband and wife had spent the five years of their married life. The last had been one of blindness and unspeakable intimacy. And now Isabel felt a great indifference coming over her, a sort of lethargy. She wanted to be allowed to bear her child in peace, to nod by the fire and drift vaguely, physically, from day to day. Maurice was like an ominous thunder-cloud. She had to keep waking up to remember him.

When a little note came from Bertie, asking if he were to put up a tombstone to their dead friendship, and speaking of the real pain he felt on account of her husband's loss of sight, she felt a pang, a fluttering agitation of re-awakening. And she read the letter to Maurice.

"Ask him to come down," he said.

"Ask Bertie to come here!" she re-echoed.

"Yes—if he wants to."

Isabel paused for a few moments.

"I know he wants to—he'd only be too glad," she replied. "But what about you, Maurice? How would you like it?"

"I should like it."

"Well—in that case— But I thought you didn't care for him—"

"Oh, I don't know. I might think differently of him now," the blind man replied. It was rather abstruse to Isabel.

"Well, dear," she said, "if you're quite sure—"

"I'm sure enough. Let him come," said Maurice.

So Bertie was coming, coming this evening, in the November rain and darkness. Isabel was agitated, racked with her old restlessness and indecision. She had always suffered from this pain of doubt, just an agonizing sense of uncertainty. It had begun to pass off, in the lethargy of maternity. Now it returned, and she resented it. She struggled as usual to maintain her calm, composed, friendly bearing, a sort of mask she wore over all her body.

A woman had lighted a tall lamp beside the table and spread the cloth. The long dining-room was dim, with its elegant but rather severe pieces of old furniture. Only the round table glowed softly under the light. It had a rich, beautiful effect. The white cloth glistened and dropped its heavy, pointed lace corners almost to the carpet, the china was old and handsome, creamy-yellow, with a blotched pattern of harsh red and deep blue, the cups large and bell-shaped, the teapot gallant. Isabel looked at it with superficial appreciation.

Her nerves were hurting her. She looked automatically again at the high, uncurtained windows. In the last dusk she could just perceive outside a huge fir-tree swaying its boughs: it was as if she thought it rather than saw it. The rain came flying on the window panes. Ah, why had she no peace? These two men, why did they tear at her? Why did they not come—why was there this suspense?

She sat in a lassitude that was really suspense and irritation. Maurice, at least, might come in—there was nothing to keep him out. She rose to her feet. Catching sight of her reflection in a mirror, she glanced at herself with a slight smile of recognition, as if she were an old friend to herself. Her face was oval and calm, her nose a little arched. Her neck made a beautiful line down to her shoulder. With hair knotted loosely behind, she had something of a warm, maternal look. Thinking this of herself, she arched her eyebrows and her rather heavy eyelids, with a little flicker of a smile, and for a moment her grey eyes looked amused and wicked, a little sardonic, out of her transfigured Madonna face.

Then, resuming her air of womanly patience—she was really fatally self-determined—she went with a little jerk towards the door. Her eyes were slightly reddened.

She passed down the wide hall and through a door at the end. Then she was in the farm premises. The scent of dairy, and of farm-kitchen, and of farm-yard and of leather almost overcame her: but particularly the scent of dairy. They had been scalding out the pans. The flagged passage in front of her was dark, puddled, and wet. Light came out from the open kitchen door. She went forward and stood in the doorway. The farm-people were at tea, seated at a little distance from her, round a long, narrow table, in the centre of which stood a white lamp. Ruddy faces, ruddy hands holding food, red mouths working, heads bent over the tea-cups: men, land-girls, boys: it was tea-time, feeding-time. Some faces caught sight of her. Mrs. Wernham, going round behind the chairs with a large black teapot, halting slightly in her walk, was not aware of her for a moment. Then she turned suddenly.

"Oh, is it Madam!" she exclaimed. "Come in, then, come in! We're at tea." And she dragged forward a chair.

"No, I won't come in," said Isabel. "I'm afraid I interrupt your meal."

"No—no—not likely, Madam, not likely."

"Hasn't Mr. Pervin come in, do you know?"

"I'm sure I couldn't say! Missed him, have you, Madam?"

"No, I only wanted him to come in," laughed Isabel, as if shyly.

"Wanted him, did ye? Get up, boy—get up, now—"

Mrs. Wernham knocked one of the boys on the shoulder. He began to scrape to his feet, chewing largely.

"I believe he's in top stable," said another face from the table.

"Ah! No, don't get up. I'm going myself," said Isabel.

"Don't you go out of a dirty night like this. Let the lad go. Get along wi' ye, boy," said Mrs. Wernham.

"No, no," said Isabel, with a decision that was always obeyed. "Go on with your tea, Tom. I'd like to go across to the stable, Mrs. Wernham."

"Did ever you hear tell!" exclaimed the woman.

"Isn't the trap late?" asked Isabel.

"Why, no," said Mrs. Wernham, peering into the distance at the tall, dim clock. "No, Madam—we can give it another quarter or twenty minutes yet, good—yes, every bit of a quarter."

"Ah! It seems late when darkness falls so early," said Isabel.

"It do, that it do. Bother the days, that they draw

in so," answered Mrs. Wernham. "Proper miserable!"

"They are," said Isabel, withdrawing.

She pulled on her overshoes, wrapped a large tartan shawl around her, put on a man's felt hat, and ventured out along the causeways of the first yard. It was very dark. The wind was roaring in the great elms behind the outhouses. When she came to the second yard the darkness seemed deeper. She was unsure of her footing. She wished she had brought a lantern. Rain blew against her. Half she liked it, half she felt unwilling to battle.

She reached at last the just visible door of the stable. There was no sign of a light anywhere. Opening the upper half, she looked in: into a simple well of darkness. The smell of horses, and ammonia, and of warmth was startling to her, in that full night. She listened with all her ears but could hear nothing save the night, and the stirring of a horse.

"Maurice!" she called, softly and musically, though she was afraid. "Maurice—are you there?"

Nothing came from the darkness. She knew the rain and wind blew in upon the horses, the hot animal life. Feeling it wrong, she entered the stable and drew the lower half of the door shut, holding the upper part close. She did not stir, because she was aware of the presence of the dark hind-quarters of the horses, though she could not see them, and she was afraid. Something wild stirred in her heart.

She listened intensely. Then she heard a small noise in the distance—far away, it seemed—the chink of a pan, and a man's voice speaking a brief word. It would be Maurice, in the other part of the stable. She stood motionless, waiting for him to come through the partition door. The horses were so terrifyingly near to her, in the invisible.

The loud jarring of the inner door-latch made her start; the door was opened. She could hear and feel her husband entering and invisibly passing among the horses near to her, darkness as they were, actively intermingled. The rather low sound of his voice as he spoke to the horses came velvety to her nerves. How near he was, and how invisible! The darkness seemed to be in a strange swirl of violent life, just upon her. She turned giddy.

Her presence of mind made her call, quietly and musically:

"Maurice! Maurice—dea-ar!"

"Yes," he answered. "Isabel?"

She saw nothing, and the sound of his voice seemed to touch her.

"Hello!" she answered cheerfully, straining her eyes to see him. He was still busy, attending to the horses near her, but she saw only darkness. It made her almost desperate.

"Won't you come in, dear?" she said.

"Yes, I'm coming. Just half a minute. *Stand over—now!* Trap's not come, has it?"

"Not yet," said Isabel.

His voice was pleasant and ordinary, but it had a slight suggestion of the stable to her. She wished he would come away. Whilst he was so utterly invisible, she was afraid of him.

"How's the time?" he asked.

"Not yet six," she replied. She disliked to answer into the dark. Presently he came very near to her, and she retreated out of doors.

"The weather blows in here," he said, coming steadily forward, feeling for the doors. She shrank away. At last she could dimly see him.

"Bertie won't have much of a drive," he said, as he closed the doors.

"He won't indeed!" said Isabel calmly, watching the dark shape at the door.

"Give me your arm, dear," she said.

She pressed his arm close to her, as she went. But she longed to see him, to look at him. She was nervous. He walked erect, with face rather lifted, but with a curious tentative movement of his powerful, muscular legs. She could feel the clever, careful, strong contact of his feet with the earth, as she balanced against him. For a moment he was a tower of darkness to her, as if he rose out of the earth.

In the house-passage he wavered and went cautiously, with a curious look of silence about him as he felt for the bench. Then he sat down heavily. He was a man with rather sloping shoulders, but with heavy limbs, powerful legs that seemed to know the earth. His head was small, usually carried high and light. As he bent down to unfasten his gaiters and boots he did not look blind. His hair was brown and crisp, his hands were large, reddish, intelligent, the veins stood out in the wrists; and his thighs and knees seemed massive. When he stood up his face and neck were surcharged with blood, the veins stood out on his temples. She did not look at his blindness.

Isabel was always glad when they had passed through the dividing door into their own regions of repose and beauty. She was a little afraid of him, out there in the animal grossness of the back. His bearing also changed, as he smelt the familiar indefinable odour that pervaded his wife's surroundings, a delicate, refined scent, very faintly spicy. Perhaps it came from the potpourri bowls.

He stood at the foot of the stairs, arrested, listening.

She watched him, and her heart sickened. He seemed to be listening to fate.

"He's not here yet," he said. "I'll go up and change."

"Maurice," she said, "you're not wishing he wouldn't come, are you?"

"I couldn't quite say," he answered. "I feel myself rather on the qui vive."

"I can see you are," she answered. And she reached up and kissed his cheek. She saw his mouth relax into a slow smile.

"What are you laughing at?" she said roguishly.

"You consoling me," he answered.

"Nay," she answered. "Why should I console you? You know we love each other—you know *how* married we are! What does anything else matter?"

"Nothing at all, my dear."

He felt for her face and touched it, smiling.

"*You're* all right, aren't you?" he asked anxiously.

"I'm wonderfully all right, love," she answered. "It's you I am a little troubled about, at times."

"Why me?" he said, touching her cheeks delicately with the tips of his fingers. The touch had an almost hypnotizing effect on her.

He went away upstairs. She saw him mount into the darkness, unseeing and unchanging. He did not know that the lamps on the upper corridor were unlighted. He went on into the darkness with unchanging step. She heard him in the bath-room.

Pervin moved about almost unconsciously in his familiar surroundings, dark though everything was. He seemed to know the presence of objects before he touched them. It was a pleasure to him to rock thus through a world of things, carried on the flood in a sort of blood-prescience. He did not think much or trouble much. So long as he kept this sheer immediacy of blood-contact with the substantial world he was happy, he wanted no intervention of visual consciousness. In this state there was a certain rich positivity, bordering sometimes on rapture. Life seemed to move in him like a tide lapping, lapping, and advancing, enveloping all things darkly. It was a pleasure to stretch forth the hand and meet the unseen object, clasp it, and possess it in pure contact. He did not try to remember, to visualize. He did not want to. The new way of consciousness substituted itself in him.

The rich suffusion of this state generally kept him happy, reaching its culmination in the consuming passion for his wife. But at times the flow would seem to be checked and thrown back. Then it would beat inside him like a tangled sea, and he was tortured in the shattered chaos of his own blood. He grew to dread this arrest, this throw-back, this chaos inside himself, when he seemed merely at the mercy of his own powerful and conflicting elements. How to get some measure of control or surety, this was the question. And when the question rose maddening in him, he would clench his fists as if he would *compel* the whole universe to submit to him. But it was in vain. He could not even compel himself.

Tonight, however, he was still serene, though little tremors of unreasonable exasperation ran through him. He had to handle the razor very carefully, as he shaved, for it was not at one with him, he was afraid of it. His hearing also was too much sharpened. He heard the woman lighting the lamps on the corridor, and attending to the fire in the visitors' room. And then, as he went to his room, he heard the trap arrive. Then came Isabel's voice, lifted and calling, like a bell ringing:

"Is it you, Bertie? Have you come?"

And a man's voice answered out of the wind:

"Hello, Isabel! There you are."

"Have you had a miserable drive? I'm so sorry we couldn't send a closed carriage. I can't see you at all, you know."

"I'm coming. No, I liked the drive—it was like Perthshire. Well, how are you? You're looking fit as ever, as far as I can see."

"Oh, yes," said Isabel. "I'm wonderfully well. How are you? Rather thin, I think—"

"Worked to death—everybody's old cry. But I'm all right, Ciss. How's Pervin?—isn't he here?"

"Oh, yes, he's upstairs changing. Yes, he's awfully well. Take off your wet things; I'll send them to be dried."

"And how are you both, in spirits? He doesn't fret?"

"No—no, not at all. No, on the contrary, really. We've been wonderfully happy, incredibly. It's more than I can understand—so wonderful: the nearness, and the peace—"

"Ah! Well, that's awfully good news—"

They moved away. Pervin heard no more. But a childish sense of desolation had come over him, as he heard their brisk voices. He seemed shut out—like a child that is left out. He was aimless and excluded, he did not know what to do with himself. The helpless desolation came over him. He fumbled nervously as he dressed himself, in a state almost of childishness. He disliked the Scotch accent in Bertie's speech, and the slight response it found on Isabel's tongue. He disliked the slight purr of complacency in the Scottish speech. He disliked intensely the glib way in which Isabel spoke of their happiness and nearness. It made him recoil. He was fretful and beside himself like a child, he had almost a childish nostalgia to be included in the life circle. And at the same time he was a man, dark and powerful and infuriated by his own weakness. By some fatal flaw, he could not be by himself, he had to depend on the support of another. And this very dependence enraged him. He hated Bertie Reid, and at the same time he knew the hatred was nonsense, he knew it was the outcome of his own weakness.

He went downstairs. Isabel was alone in the dining-room. She watched him enter, head erect, his feet tentative. He looked so strong-blooded and healthy and, at the same time, cancelled. Cancelled—that was the word that flew across her mind. Perhaps it was his scar suggested it.

"You heard Bertie come, Maurice?" she said.

"Yes—isn't he here?"

"He's in his room. He looks very thin and worn."

"I suppose he works himself to death."

A woman came in with a tray—and after a few minutes Bertie came down. He was a little dark man, with a very big forehead, thin, wispy hair, and sad, large eyes. His expression was inordinately sad—almost funny. He had odd, short legs.

Isabel watched him hesitate under the door, and glance nervously at her husband. Pervin heard him and turned.

"Here you are, now," said Isabel. "Come, let us eat."

Bertie went across to Maurice.

"How are you, Pervin?" he said, as he advanced.

The blind man stuck his hand out into space, and Bertie took it.

"Very fit. Glad you've come," said Maurice.

Isabel glanced at them, and glanced away, as if she

could not bear to see them.

"Come," she said. "Come to table. Aren't you both awfully hungry? I am, tremendously."

"I'm afraid you waited for me," said Bertie, as they sat down.

Maurice had a curious monolithic way of sitting in a chair, erect and distant. Isabel's heart always beat when she caught sight of him thus.

"No," she replied to Bertie. "We're very little later than usual. We're having a sort of high tea, not dinner. Do you mind? It gives us such a nice long evening, uninterrupted."

"I like it," said Bertie.

Maurice was feeling, with curious little movements, almost like a cat kneading her bed, for his plate, his knife and fork, his napkin. He was getting the whole geography of his cover into his consciousness. He sat erect and inscrutable, remote-seeming. Bertie watched the static figure of the blind man, the delicate tactile discernment of the large, ruddy hands, and the curious mindless silence of the brow, above the scar. With difficulty he looked away, and without knowing what he did, picked up a little crystal bowl of violets from the table, and held them to his nose.

"They are sweet-scented," he said. "Where do they come from?"

"From the garden—under the windows," said Isabel.

"So late in the year—and so fragrant! Do you remember the violets under Aunt Bell's south wall?"

The two friends looked at each other and exchanged a smile, Isabel's eyes lighting up.

"Don't I?" she replied. "*Wasn't* she queer!"

"A curious old girl," laughed Bertie. "There's a streak of freakishness in the family, Isabel."

"Ah—but not in you and me, Bertie," said Isabel. "Give them to Maurice, will you?" she added, as Bertie was putting down the flowers. "Have you smelled the violets, dear? Do!—they are so scented."

Maurice held out his hand, and Bertie placed the tiny bowl against his large, warm-looking fingers. Maurice's hand closed over the thin white fingers of the barrister. Bertie carefully extricated himself. Then the two watched the blind man smelling the violets. He bent his head and seemed to be thinking. Isabel waited.

"Aren't they sweet, Maurice?" she said at last, anxiously.

"Very," he said. And he held out the bowl. Bertie took it. Both he and Isabel were a little afraid, and deeply disturbed.

The meal continued. Isabel and Bertie chatted spasmodically. The blind man was silent. He touched his food repeatedly, with quick, delicate touches of his knife-point, then cut irregular bits. He could not bear to be helped. Both Isabel and Bertie suffered: Isabel wondered why. She did not suffer when she was alone with Maurice. Bertie made her conscious of a strangeness.

After the meal the three drew their chairs to the fire, and sat down to talk. The decanters were put on a table near at hand. Isabel knocked the logs on the fire, and clouds of brilliant sparks went up the chimney. Bertie noticed a slight weariness in her bearing.

"You will be glad when your child comes now, Isabel?" he said.

She looked up to him with a quick wan smile.

"Yes, I shall be glad," she answered. "It begins to seem long. Yes, I shall be very glad. So will you, Maurice, won't you?" she added.

"Yes, I shall," replied her husband.

"We are both looking forward so much to having it," she said.

"Yes, of course," said Bertie.

He was a bachelor, three or four years older than Isabel. He lived in beautiful rooms overlooking the river, guarded by a faithful Scottish man-servant. And he had his friends among the fair sex—not lovers, friends. So long as he could avoid any danger of courtship or marriage, he adored a few good women with constant and unfailing homage, and he was chivalrously fond of quite a number. But if they seemed to encroach on him, he withdrew and detested them.

Isabel knew him very well, knew his beautiful constancy, and kindness, also his incurable weakness, which made him unable ever to enter into close contact of any sort. He was ashamed of himself because he could not marry, could not approach women physically. He wanted to do so. But he could not. At the centre of him he was afraid, helplessly and even brutally afraid. He had given up hope, had ceased to expect any more that he could escape his own weakness. Hence he was a brilliant and successful barrister, also a *littérateur* of high repute, a rich man, and a great social success. At the centre he felt himself neuter, nothing.

Isabel knew him well. She despised him even while she admired him. She looked at his sad face, his little short legs, and felt contempt of him. She looked at his dark grey eyes, with their uncanny, almost childlike, intuition, and she loved him. He understood amazingly—but she had no fear of his understanding. As a man she patronized him.

And she turned to the impassive, silent figure of her husband. He sat leaning back, with folded arms, and face a little uptilted. His knees were straight and massive. She sighed, picked up the poker, and again began to prod the fire, to rouse the clouds of soft brilliant sparks.

"Isabel tells me," Bertie began suddenly, "that you have not suffered unbearably from the loss of sight."

Maurice straightened himself to attend but kept his arms folded.

"No," he said, "not unbearably. Now and again one struggles against it, you know. But there are compensations."

"They say it is much worse to be stone deaf," said Isabel.

"I believe it is," said Bertie. "Are there compensations?" he added, to Maurice.

"Yes. You cease to bother about a great many things." Again Maurice stretched his figure, stretched the strong muscles of his back, and leaned backwards, with uplifted face.

"And that is a relief," said Bertie. "But what is there in place of the bothering? What replaces the activity?"

There was a pause. At length the blind man replied, as out of a negligent, unattentive thinking:

"Oh, I don't know. There's a good deal when you're not active."

"Is there?" said Bertie. "What, exactly? It always seems to me that when there is no thought and no action, there is nothing."

Again Maurice was slow in replying.

"There is something," he replied. "I couldn't tell you what it is."

And the talk lapsed once more, Isabel and Bertie chatting gossip and reminiscence, the blind man silent.

At length Maurice rose restlessly, a big obtrusive figure. He felt tight and hampered. He wanted to go away.

"Do you mind," he said, "if I go and speak to Wernham?"

"No—go along, dear," said Isabel.

And he went out. A silence came over the two friends. At length Bertie said:

"Nevertheless, it is a great deprivation, Cissie."

"It is, Bertie. I know it is."

"Something lacking all the time," said Bertie.

"Yes, I know. And yet—and yet—Maurice is right. There is something else, something *there,* which you never knew was there, and which you can't express."

"What is there?" asked Bertie.

"I don't know—it's awfully hard to define it—but something strong and immediate. There's something strange in Maurice's presence—indefinable—but I couldn't do without it. I agree that it seems to put one's mind to sleep. But when we're alone I miss nothing; it seems awfully rich, almost splendid, you know."

"I'm afraid I don't follow," said Bertie.

They talked desultorily. The wind blew loudly outside, rain chattered on the window-panes, making a sharp drum-sound because of the closed, mellow-golden shutters inside. The logs burned slowly, with hot, almost invisible small flames. Bertie seemed uneasy, there were dark circles round his eyes. Isabel, rich with her approaching maternity, leaned looking into the fire. Her hair curled in odd, loose strands, very pleasing to the man. But she had a curious feeling of old woe in her heart, old, timeless night-woe.

"I suppose we're all deficient somewhere," said Bertie.

"I suppose so," said Isabel wearily.

"Damned, sooner or later."

"I don't know," she said, rousing herself. "I feel quite

all right, you know. The child coming seems to make me indifferent to everything, just placid. I can't feel that there's anything to trouble about, you know."

"A good thing, I should say," he replied slowly.

"Well, there it is. I suppose it's just Nature. If only I felt I needn't trouble about Maurice, I should be perfectly content—"

"But you feel you must trouble about him?"

"Well—I don't know—" She even resented this much effort.

The night passed slowly. Isabel looked at the clock. "I say," she said. "It's nearly ten o'clock. Where can Maurice be? I'm sure they're all in bed at the back. Excuse me a moment."

She went out, returning almost immediately.

"It's all shut up and in darkness," she said. "I wonder where he is. He must have gone out to the farm—"

Bertie looked at her.

"I suppose he'll come in," he said.

"I suppose so," she said. "But it's unusual for him to be out now."

"Would you like me to go out and see?"

"Well—if you wouldn't mind. I'd go, but—" She did not want to make the physical effort.

Bertie put on an old overcoat and took a lantern. He went out from the side door. He shrank from the wet and roaring night. Such weather had a nervous effect on him: too much moisture everywhere made him feel almost imbecile. Unwilling, he went through it all. A dog barked violently at him. He peered in all the buildings. At last, as he opened the upper door of a sort of intermediate barn, he heard a grinding noise, and looking in, holding up his lantern, saw Maurice, in his shirt-sleeves, standing listening, holding the handle of a turnip-pulper. He had been pulping sweet roots, a pile of which lay dimly heaped in a corner behind him.

"That you, Wernham?" said Maurice, listening.

"No, it's me," said Bertie.

A large, half-wild grey cat was rubbing at Maurice's leg. The blind man stooped to rub its sides. Bertie watched the scene, then unconsciously entered and shut the door behind him. He was in a high sort of barn-place, from which, right and left, ran off the corridors in front of the stalled cattle. He watched the slow, stooping motion of the other man, as he caressed the great cat.

Maurice straightened himself.

"You came to look for me?" he said.

"Isabel was a little uneasy," said Bertie.

"I'll come in. I like messing about doing these jobs."

The cat had reared her sinister, feline length against his leg, clawing at his thigh affectionately. He lifted her claws out of his flesh.

"I hope I'm not in your way at all at the Grange here," said Bertie, rather shy and stiff.

"My way? No, not a bit. I'm glad Isabel has somebody to talk to. I'm afraid it's I who am in the way. I know I'm not very lively company. Isabel's all right, don't you think? She's not unhappy, is she?"

"I don't think so."

"What does she say?"

"She says she's very content—only a little troubled about you."

"Why me?"

"Perhaps afraid that you might brood," said Bertie, cautiously.

"She needn't be afraid of that." He continued to caress the flattened grey head of the cat with his fingers. "What I am a bit afraid of," he resumed, "is that she'll find me a dead weight, always alone with me down here."

"I don't think you need think that," said Bertie, though this was what he feared himself.

"I don't know," said Maurice. "Sometimes I feel it isn't fair that she's saddled with me." Then he dropped his voice curiously. "I say," he asked, secretly struggling, "is my face much disfigured? Do you mind telling me?"

"There is the scar," said Bertie, wondering. "Yes, it is a disfigurement. But more pitiable than shocking."

"A pretty bad scar, though," said Maurice.

"Oh, yes."

There was a pause.

"Sometimes I feel I am horrible," said Maurice, in a low voice, talking as if to himself. And Bertie actually felt a quiver of horror.

"That's nonsense," he said.

Maurice again straightened himself, leaving the cat.

"There's no telling," he said. Then again, in an odd tone, he added: "I don't really know you, do I?"

"Probably not," said Bertie.

"Do you mind if I touch you?"

The lawyer shrank away instinctively. And yet, out of very philanthropy, he said, in a small voice: "Not at all."

But he suffered as the blind man stretched out a strong, naked hand to him. Maurice accidentally knocked off Bertie's hat.

"I thought you were taller," he said, starting. Then he laid his hand on Bertie Reid's head, closing the dome of the skull in a soft, firm grasp, gathering it, as it were; then, shifting his grasp and softly closing again, with a fine, close pressure, till he had covered the skull and the face of the smaller man, tracing the brows, and touching the full, closed eyes, touching the small nose and the nostrils, the rough, short moustache, the mouth, the rather strong chin. The hand of the blind man grasped the shoulder, the arm, the hand of the other man. He seemed to take him, in the soft, travelling grasp.

"You seem young," he said quietly, at last.

The lawyer stood almost annihilated, unable to answer.

"Your head seems tender, as if you were young," Maurice repeated. "So do your hands. Touch my eyes, will you?—touch my scar."

Now Bertie quivered with revulsion. Yet he was under the power of the blind man, as if hypnotized. He lifted his hand, and laid the fingers on the scar, on the scarred eyes. Maurice suddenly covered them with his own hand, pressed the fingers of the other man upon his disfigured eye-sockets, trembling in every fibre, and rocking slightly, slowly, from side to side. He remained thus for a minute or more, whilst Bertie stood as if in a swoon, unconscious, imprisoned.

Then suddenly Maurice removed the hand of the other man from his brow, and stood holding it in his own.

"Oh, my God," he said, "we shall know each other now, shan't we? We shall know each other now."

Bertie could not answer. He gazed mute and terror-struck, overcome by his own weakness. He knew he could not answer. He had an unreasonable fear, lest the other man should suddenly destroy him. Whereas Maurice was actually filled with hot, poignant love, the passion of friendship. Perhaps it was this very passion of friendship which Bertie shrank from most.

"We're all right together now, aren't we?" said Maurice. "It's all right now, as long as we live, so far as we're concerned?"

"Yes," said Bertie, trying by any means to escape.

Maurice stood with head lifted, as if listening. The new delicate fulfilment of mortal friendship had come as a revelation and surprise to him, something exquisite and unhoped-for. He seemed to be listening to hear if it were real.

Then he turned for his coat.

"Come," he said, "we'll go to Isabel."

Bertie took the lantern and opened the door. The cat disappeared. The two men went in silence along the causeways. Isabel, as they came, thought their footsteps sounded strange. She looked up pathetically and anxiously for their entrance. There seemed a curious elation about Maurice. Bertie was haggard, with sunken eyes.

"What is it?" she asked.

"We've become friends," said Maurice, standing with his feet apart, like a strange colossus.

"Friends!" re-echoed Isabel. And she looked again at Bertie. He met her eyes with a furtive, haggard look; his eyes were as if glazed with misery.

"I'm so glad," she said, in sheer perplexity.

"Yes," said Maurice.

He was indeed so glad. Isabel took his hand with both hers, and held it fast.

"You'll be happier now, dear," she said.

But she was watching Bertie. She knew that he had one desire—to escape from this intimacy, this friendship, which had been thrust upon him. He could not bear it that he had been touched by the blind man, his insane reserve broken in. He was like a mollusc whose shell is broken.

KATHERINE MANSFIELD

Marriage a la Mode

Katherine Mansfield had published one book before the outbreak of the first World-War, but her period of wide recognition did not begin until *Bliss* appeared in 1920. *The Garden Party* (a collection which includes this story) followed in 1922. Less than a year later, Mansfield died of tuberculosis at the age of thirty-three. A good half of her writings—a Journal, Letters and two more volumes of stories—was published posthumously; the more important half in some respects, for it revealed the personality of Mansfield herself—and it is as a personality, quite apart from her stories, that many readers have come to admire and love her. I myself felt a strong personal love for her at one time in my life, and it seems a little strange to me, even now, that we never actually met. She was so very much one of my circle of friends.

Although my love has weakened, I still feel great admiration for some of Mansfield's stories and great respect for the integrity of her struggle as an artist. Though she often failed, she really did try her hardest all of the time—which is more than you can say of most of us. She notes disgustedly in her Journal: "I look at the mountains, I try to pray and I think of something *clever.*" "Cleverness" seems to have been at the bottom of Mansfield's psychological problems: in her, the mature, sophisticated woman was at war with the child. As a girl, she revolted against the provincialism of New Zealand, where she had been born, and longed for the brilliance of bohemian London. But London, when she came to know it, disappointed her; and she began to make a cult of her New Zealand childhood, imagining it as a paradise and repressing all contradictory memories. The resulting conflict often spoiled her work, as might well be expected. She is no longer a child but she tries to write with a child's consciousness. Then the mature woman looks over her shoulder, reaches forward impatiently, snatches the pen—and suddenly the sentences become embarrassingly contrived, neat and shiny and false.

The childhood stories contain many passages of truly magical insight but, for the reasons I have tried to indicate above, they are apt to be patchy. A story like *Marriage à la Mode* seems to me, on the other hand, entirely successful—perhaps just because it is about sophisticated adults and deals frankly with Mansfield's own problem. You couldn't have gone to a London studio-party in the twenties without hearing someone talk exactly like Moira Morrison and her disciple Isabel. I used often to hear such talk myself, and it made me grind my teeth in disgust. Now, I find it delightfully nostalgic. Yet the story of William and Isabel and the failure of their marriage isn't merely *à la Mode;* it belongs to no special period. Basically, it is often retold in American divorce-courts today.

ON HIS WAY TO THE STATION WILLIAM REMEMBERED WITH a fresh pang of disappointment that he was taking nothing down to the kiddies. Poor little chaps! It was hard lines on them. Their first words always were as they ran to greet him, "What have you got for me, daddy?" and he had nothing. He would have to buy them some sweets at the station. But that was what he had done for the past four Saturdays; their faces had fallen last time when they saw the same old boxes produced again.

And Paddy had said, "I had red ribbing on mine *bee*-fore!"

And Johnny had said, "It's always pink on mine, I hate pink."

But what was William to do? The affair wasn't so easily settled. In the old days, of course, he would have taken a taxi off to a decent toyshop and chosen them something in five minutes. But nowadays they had Russian toys, French toys, Serbian toys—toys from God knows where. It was over a year since Isabel had scrapped the old donkeys and engines and so on because they were so "dreadfully sentimental" and "so appallingly bad for the babies' sense of form."

"It's so important," the new Isabel had explained, "that they should like the right things from the very beginning. It saves so much time later on. Really, if the poor pets have to spend their infant years staring at these horrors, one can imagine them growing up and asking to be taken to the Royal Academy."

And she spoke as though a visit to the Royal Academy was certain immediate death to any one . . . .

"Well, I don't know," said William slowly. "When I was their age I used to go to bed hugging an old towel with a knot in it."

The new Isabel looked at him, her eyes narrowed, her lips apart.

"*Dear* William! I'm sure you did!" She laughed in the new way.

Sweets it would have to be, however, thought William gloomily, fishing in his pocket for change for the taxi-man. And he saw the kiddies handing the boxes round—they were awfully generous little chaps—while Isabel's precious friends didn't hesitate to help themselves. . . .

What about fruit? William hovered before a stall just inside the station. What about a melon each? Would they have to share that, too? Or a pineapple for Pad, and a melon for Johnny? Isabel's friends could hardly go sneaking up to the nursery at the children's meal-times. All the same, as he bought the melon William had a horrible vision of one of Isabel's young poets lapping up a slice, for some reason, behind the nursery door.

With his two very awkward parcels he strode off to his train. The platform was crowded, the train was in. Doors banged open and shut. There came such a loud hissing from the engine that people looked dazed as they scurried to and fro. William made straight for a first-class smoker, stowed away his suit-case and parcels, and taking a huge wad of papers out of his inner pocket, he flung down in the corner and began to read.

"Our client moreover is positive. . . . We are inclined to reconsider . . . in the event of—" Ah, that was better. William pressed back his flattened hair and stretched his legs across the carriage floor. The familiar dull gnawing in his breast quietened down. "With regard to our decision—" He took out a blue pencil and scored a paragraph slowly.

Two men came in, stepped across him, and made for the farther corner. A young fellow swung his golf clubs into the rack and sat down opposite. The train gave a gentle lurch, they were off. William glanced up and saw the hot, bright station slipping away. A red-faced girl raced along by the carriages, there was something strained and almost desperate in the way she waved and called. "Hysterical!" thought William dully. Then a greasy, black-faced workman at the end of the platform grinned at the passing train. And William thought, "A filthy life!" and went back to his papers.

When he looked up again there were fields, and beasts standing for shelter under the dark trees. A wide river, with naked children splashing in the shallows, glided into sight and was gone again. The sky shone pale, and one bird drifted high like a dark fleck in a jewel.

"We have examined our client's correspondence files. . . ." The last sentence he had read echoed in his mind. "We have examined . . ." William hung on to that sentence, but it was no good; it snapped in the middle, and the fields, the sky, the sailing bird, the water, all said, "Isabel." The same thing happened every Saturday afternoon. When he was on his way to meet Isabel there began those countless imaginary meetings. She was at the station, standing just a little apart from everybody else; she was sitting in the open taxi outside; she was at the garden gate; walking across the parched grass; at the door, or just inside the hall.

And her clear, light voice said, "'It's William," or "Hillo, William!" or "So William has come!" He touched her cool hand, her cool cheek.

The exquisite freshness of Isabel! When he had been

a little boy, it was his delight to run into the garden after a shower of rain and shake the rosebush over him. Isabel was that rosebush, petal-soft, sparkling and cool. And he was still that little boy. But there was no running into the garden now, no laughing and shaking. The dull, persistent gnawing in his breast started again. He drew up his legs, tossed the papers aside, and shut his eyes.

"What is it, Isabel? What is it?" he said tenderly. They were in their bedroom in the new house. Isabel sat on a painted stool before the dressing-table that was strewn with little black and green boxes.

"What is what, William?" And she bent forward, and her fine light hair fell over her cheeks.

"Ah, you know!" He stood in the middle of the strange room and he felt a stranger. At that Isabel wheeled round quickly and faced him.

"Oh, William!" she cried imploringly, and she held up the hair-brush: "Please! Please don't be so dreadfully stuffy and—tragic. You're always saying or looking or hinting that I've changed. Just because I've got to know really congenial people, and go about more, and am frightfully keen on—on everything, you behave as though I'd—" Isabel tossed back her hair and laughed—"killed our love or something. It's so awfully absurd"—she bit her lip—"and it's so maddening, William. Even this new house and the servants you grudge me."

"Isabel!"

"Yes, yes, it's true in a way," said Isabel quickly. "You think they are another bad sign. Oh, I know you do. I feel it," she said softly, "every time you come up the stairs. But we couldn't have gone on living in that other poky little hole, William. Be practical, at least! Why, there wasn't enough room for the babies even."

No, it was true. Every morning when he came back from chambers it was to find the babies with Isabel in the back drawing-room. They were having rides on the leopard skin thrown over the sofa back, or they were playing shops with Isabel's desk for a counter, or Pad was sitting on the hearthrug rowing away for dear life with a little brass fire shovel, while Johnny shot at pirates with the tongs. Every evening they each had a pick-a-back up the narrow stairs to their fat old Nanny.

Yes, he supposed it was a poky little house. A little white house with blue curtains and a windowbox of petunias. William met their friends at the door with "Seen our petunias? Pretty terrific for London, don't you think?"

But the imbecile thing, the absolutely extraordinary thing was that he hadn't the slightest idea that Isabel wasn't as happy as he. God, what blindness! He hadn't the remotest notion in those days that she really hated that inconvenient little house, that she thought the fat Nanny was ruining the babies, that she was desperately lonely, pining for new people and new music and pictures and so on. If they hadn't gone to that studio party at Moira Morrison's—if Moira Morrison hadn't said as they were leaving, "I'm going to rescue your wife, selfish man. She's like an exquisite little Titania"—if Isabel hadn't gone with Moira to Paris—if—if . . .

The train stopped at another station. Bettingford. Good heavens! They'd be there in ten minutes. William stuffed the papers back into his pockets; the young man opposite had long since disappeared. Now the other two got out. The late afternoon sun shone on women in cotton frocks and little sunburnt, barefoot children. It blazed on a silky yellow flower with coarse leaves which sprawled over a bank of rock. The air ruffling through the window smelled of the sea. Had Isabel the same crowd with her this week-end, wondered William?

And he remembered the holidays they used to have, the four of them, with a little farm girl, Rose, to look after the babies. Isabel wore a jersey and her hair in a plait; she looked about fourteen. Lord! how his nose used to peel! And the amount they ate, and the amount they slept in that immense feather bed with their feet locked together. . . . William couldn't help a grim smile as he thought of Isabel's horror if she knew the full extent of his sentimentality.

"Hillo, William!" She was at the station after all, standing just as he had imagined, apart from the others, and—William's heart leapt—she was alone.

"Hallo, Isabel!" William stared. He thought she looked so beautiful that he had to say something, "You look very cool."

"Do I?" said Isabel. "I don't feel very cool. Come along, your horrid old train is late. The taxi's outside." She put her hand lightly on his arm as they passed the ticket collector. "We've all come to meet you," she said. "But we've left Bobby Kane at the sweet shop, to be called for."

"Oh!" said William. It was all he could say for the moment.

There in the glare waited the taxi, with Bill Hunt and Dennis Green sprawling on one side, their hats tilted over their faces, while on the other, Moira Morrison, in a bonnet like a huge strawberry, jumped up and down.

"No ice! No ice! No ice!" she shouted gaily.

And Dennis chimed in from under his hat. "*Only* to be had from the fishmonger's."

And Bill Hunt, emerging, added, "With *whole* fish in it."

"Oh, what a bore!" wailed Isabel. And she explained to William how they had been chasing round the town for ice while she waited for him. "Simply everything is running down the steep cliffs into the sea, beginning with the butter."

"We shall have to anoint ourselves with the butter," said Dennis. "May thy head, William, lack not ointment."

"Look here," said William, "how are we going to sit? I'd better get up by the driver."

"No, Bobby Kane's by the driver," said Isabel. "You're to sit between Moira and me." The taxi started. "What have you got in those mysterious parcels?"

"De-cap-it-ated heads!" said Bill Hunt, shuddering beneath his hat.

"Oh, fruit!" Isabel sounded very pleased. "Wise William! A melon and a pineapple. How too nice!"

"No, wait a bit," said William, smiling. But he really was anxious. "I brought them down for the kiddies."

"Oh, my dear!" Isabel laughed, and slipped her hand through his arm. "They'd be rolling in agonies if they were to eat them. No"—she patted his hand—"you must bring them something next time. I refuse to part with my pineapple."

"Cruel Isabel! Do let me smell it!" said Moira. She flung her arms across William appealingly. "Oh!" The strawberry bonnet fell forward: she sounded quite faint.

"A Lady in Love with a Pineapple," said Dennis, as the taxi drew up before a little shop with a striped blind. Out came Bobby Kane, his arms full of little packets.

"I do hope they'll be good. I've chosen them because of the colours. There are some round things which really look too divine. And just look at this nougat," he cried ecstatically, "just look at it! It's a perfect little ballet."

But at that moment the shopman appeared. "Oh, I forgot. They're none of them paid for," said Bobby, looking frightened. Isabel gave the shopman a note, and Bobby was radiant again. "Hallo, William! I'm sitting by the driver." And bareheaded, all in white, with his sleeves rolled up to the shoulders, he leapt into his place. "Avanti!" he cried. . . .

After tea the others went off to bathe, while William stayed and made his peace with the kiddies. But Johnny and Paddy were asleep, the rose-red glow had paled, bats were flying, and still the bathers had not returned. As William wandered downstairs, the maid crossed the hall carrying a lamp. He followed her into the sitting-room. It was a long room, coloured yellow. On the wall opposite William some one had painted a young man, over life-size, with very wobbly legs, offering a wide-eyed daisy to a young woman who had one very short arm and one very long, thin one. Over the chairs and sofa there hung strips of black material, covered with big splashes like broken eggs, and everywhere one looked there seemed to be an ash-tray full of cigarette ends. William sat down in one of the arm-chairs. Nowadays, when one felt with one hand down the sides, it wasn't to come upon a sheep with three legs or a cow that had lost one horn, or a very fat dove out of the Noah's Ark. One fished up yet another little paper-covered book of smudged-looking poems. . . . He thought of the wad of papers in his pocket, but he was too hungry and tired to read. The door was open;

sounds came from the kitchen. The servants were talking as if they were alone in the house. Suddenly there came a loud screech of laughter and an equally loud "Sh!" They had remembered him. William got up and went through the French windows into the garden, and as he stood there in the shadow he heard the bathers coming up the sandy road; their voices rang through the quiet.

"I think it's up to Moira to use her little arts and wiles."

A tragic moan from Moira.

"We ought to have a gramophone for the week-ends that played 'The Maid of the Mountains.' "

"Oh no! Oh no!" cried Isabel's voice. "That's not fair to William. Be nice to him, my children! He's only staying until tomorrow evening."

"Leave him to me," cried Bobby Kane. "I'm awfully good at looking after people."

The gate swung open and shut. William moved on the terrace; they had seen him. "Hallo, William!" And Bobby Kane, flapping his towel, began to leap and pirouette on the parched lawn. "Pity you didn't come, William. The water was divine. And we all went to a little pub afterwards and had sloe gin."

The others had reached the house. "I say, Isabel," called Bobby, "would you like me to wear my Nijinsky dress tonight?"

"No," said Isabel, "nobody's going to dress. We're all starving. William's starving, too. Come along, *mes amis,* let's begin with sardines."

"I've found the sardines," said Moira, and she ran into the hall, holding a box high in the air.

"A Lady with a Box of Sardines," said Dennis gravely.

"Well, William, and how's London?" asked Bill Hunt, drawing the cork out of a bottle of whisky.

"Oh, London's not much changed," answered William.

"Good old London," said Bobby, very hearty, spearing a sardine.

But a moment later William was forgotten. Moira Morrison began wondering what colour one's legs really were under water.

"Mine are the palest, palest mushroom colour."

Bill and Dennis ate enormously. And Isabel filled glasses, and changed plates, and found matches, smiling blissfully. At one moment she said, "I do wish, Bill, you'd paint it."

"Paint what?" said Bill loudly, stuffing his mouth with bread.

"Us," said Isabel, "round the table. It would be so fascinating in twenty years' time."

Bill screwed up his eyes and chewed. "Light's wrong," he said rudely, "far too much yellow"; and went on eating. And that seemed to charm Isabel, too.

But after supper they were all so tired they could do nothing but yawn until it was late enough to go to bed. . . .

It was not until William was waiting for his taxi the next afternoon that he found himself alone with Isabel. When he brought his suit-case down into the hall, Isabel left the others and went over to him. She stooped down and picked up the suit-case. "What a weight!" she said, and she gave a little awkward laugh. "Let me carry it! To the gate."

"No, why should you?" said William. "Of course, not. Give it to me."

"Oh, please do let me," said Isabel. "I want to,

really." They walked together silently. William felt there was nothing to say now.

"There," said Isabel triumphantly, setting the suitcase down, and she looked anxiously along the sandy road. "I hardly seem to have seen you this time," she said breathlessly. "It's so short, isn't it? I feel you've only just come. Next time–" The taxi came into sight. "I hope they look after you properly in London. I'm so sorry the babies have been out all day, but Miss Neil had arranged it. They'll hate missing you. Poor William, going back to London." The taxi turned. "Goodbye!" She gave him a little hurried kiss; she was gone.

Fields, trees, hedges streamed by. They shook through the empty, blind-looking little town, ground up the steep pull to the station.

The train was in. William made straight for a first-class smoker, flung back into the corner, but this time he let the papers alone. He folded his arms against the dull, persistent gnawing, and began in his mind to write a letter to Isabel.

The post was late as usual. They sat outside the house in long chairs under coloured parasols. Only Bobby Kane lay on the turf at Isabel's feet. It was dull, stifling; the day drooped like a flag.

"Do you think there will be Mondays in Heaven?" asked Bobby childishly.

And Dennis murmured, "Heaven will be one long Monday."

But Isabel couldn't help wondering what had happened to the salmon they had for supper last night. She had meant to have fish mayonnaise for lunch and now . . .

Moira was asleep. Sleeping was her latest discovery.

"It's *so* wonderful. One simply shuts one's eyes, that's all. It's *so* delicious."

When the old ruddy postman came beating along the sandy road on his tricycle one felt the handle-bars ought to have been oars.

Bill Hunt put down his book. "Letters," he said complacently, and they all waited. But, heartless postman—O malignant world! There was only one, a fat one for Isabel. Not even a paper.

"And mine's only from William," said Isabel mournfully.

"From William—already?"

"He's sending you back your marriage lines as a gentle reminder."

"Does everybody have marriage lines? I thought they were only for servants."

"Pages and pages! Look at her! A Lady reading a Letter," said Dennis.

My darling, precious Isabel. Pages and pages there were. As Isabel read on her feeling of astonishment changed to a stifled feeling. What on earth had induced William . . . ? How extraordinary it was. . . . What could have made him . . . ? She felt confused, more and more excited, even frightened. It was just like William. Was it? It was absurd, of course, it must be absurd, ridiculous. "Ha, ha, ha! Oh dear!" What was she to do? Isabel flung back in her chair and laughed till she couldn't stop laughing.

"Do, do tell us," said the others. "You must tell us."

"I'm longing to," gurgled Isabel. She sat up, gathered the letter, and waved it at them. "Gather round," she said. "Listen, it's too marvellous. A love-letter!"

"A love-letter! But how divine!" *Darling, precious*

Isabel. But she had hardly begun before their laughter interrupted her.

"Go on, Isabel, it's perfect."

"It's the most marvellous find."

"Oh, do go on, Isabel!"

God forbid, my darling, that I should be a drag on your happiness.

"Oh! oh! oh!"

"Sh! sh! sh!"

And Isabel went on. When she reached the end they were hysterical: Bobby rolled on the turf and almost sobbed.

"You must let me have it just as it is, entire, for my new book," said Dennis firmly. "I shall give it a whole chapter."

"Oh, Isabel," moaned Moira, "that wonderful bit about holding you in his arms!"

"I always thought those letters in divorce cases were made up. But they pale before this."

"Let me hold it. Let me read it, mine own self," said Bobby Kane.

But, to their surprise, Isabel crushed the letter in her hand. She was laughing no longer. She glanced quickly at them all; she looked exhausted. "No, not just now. Not just now," she stammered.

And before they could recover she had run into the house, through the hall, up the stairs into her bedroom. Down she sat on the side of the bed. "How vile, odious, abominable, vulgar," muttered Isabel. She pressed her eyes with her knuckles and rocked to and fro. And again she saw them, but not four, more like forty, laughing, sneering, jeering, stretching out their hands while she read them William's letter. Oh, what a loathsome thing to have done. How could she have done it! *God forbid, my darling, that I should be a drag on your happiness.* William! Isabel pressed her face into the pillow. But she felt that even the grave bedroom knew her for what she was, shallow, tinkling, vain. . . .

Presently from the garden below there came voices.

"Isabel, we're all going for a bathe. Do come!"

"Come, thou wife of William!"

"Call her once before you go, call once yet!"

Isabel sat up. Now was the moment, now she must decide. Would she go with them, or stay here and write to William. Which, which should it be? "I must make up my mind." Oh, but how could there be any question? Of course she would stay here and write.

"Titania!" piped Moira.

"Isa-bel?"

No, it was too difficult. "I'll—I'll go with them, and write to William later. Some other time. Later. Not now. But I shall *certainly* write," thought Isabel hurriedly.

And, laughing in the new way, she ran down the stairs.

ETHEL COLBURN MAYNE

The Man of the House

More than three miles to the west of the so-called West End of London, on the far boundary of Kensington, is the "long, perfectly straight Street" (Holland Road) which is described in this story. Ethel Mayne herself lived there during the 'twenties. Not far away was the "Carlington Road" of Compton Mackenzie's novel *Sinister Street;* but that was already West Kensington—not so much a district as an excuse for not admitting that you lived in Hammersmith, which was then thought to be vulgar. At the wrong, non-Mayne end of Holland Road was Shepherd's Bush; if anything, even vulgarer. I go into these sociological details because *The Man of the House* is about people on the insecure frontier of gentility; a characteristically Irish theme.

Ethel Mayne came to London from Ireland in the 'nineties. Her first publications (under a pseudonym) were in volumes of *The Yellow Book* for '95 and '96; daintily breathless tales spiced with bits of French and with words put between quotation marks to indicate some exquisite shade of meaning utterly beyond the reach of the barbarous English tongue. She became skilled at writing the fashionable, neo-Jamesian kind of dialogue that resembled championship tennis: the two participants exchanging shots of impossibly far-fetched allusion and oblique repartee throughout a rally of half a dozen pages. There is scarcely a trace of such affectations in the story I have chosen, for it is the work of a maturer Ethel Mayne, the wise and understanding lady I myself knew, whose delicacy of perception had become fortified by a robust and sometimes quite unladylike Irish wit. I suppose its action is set in the early 'twenties, but I can find only one reference—to the fashion of wearing "amusingly unbecoming" tortoiseshell glasses—which seems to indicate the period. In any case, I would put it next to Katherine Mansfield's story, for the sake of contrast. Of the two writers, Mayne seems to me to be the more practically minded. I never feel I quite know how Mansfield's characters support themselves, unless they are married women. But I believe unquestioningly in the jobs which are held down by Mayne's three spinsters; I even believe that they get paid for them. And then there is the death of the cat; Mansfield, I suspect, would have made it macabre, fantastic, almost a scene from a ballet. The anecdote itself *is* fantastic, but Mayne handles it so honestly that I overlook this aspect of it and find it simply very touching. I am not saying any of this to belittle Mansfield. I only want to suggest that Mayne can stand up to a distinguished comparison.

In addition to her stories and novels, Ethel Mayne wrote a good deal of biography; her books on Byron and on Lady Noel Byron are still regarded as standard works. She was also an excellent translator. She died in 1941, from the aftereffects of injuries received in one of the air-raids of the London Blitz.

WHEN OLD DR. MOUNT DIED, AND IN A FEW MONTHS MRS. Mount, the three Miss Mounts left Nottingham for London. Their father had advised them to do this when they became "whole orphans," as he said; there would be better opportunities in London. He meant opportunities in their professions. Melicent, the eldest, was a maternity nurse; Thomasine a masseuse; Constance a dispenser. Dr. Mount had insisted that his daughters should learn a trade—not that they would need to live by it, for each would have a little money. But he held that in another sense all men and women needed an occupation to "live by"; and he had made up his mind that none of the girls would marry. He said to Mrs. Mount that Thomasine and Constance talked too much, and Melicent not enough.

"So, either way, men can't get to know them. If Melicent could speak at all—" He mused a moment. "That young Brierly. . . . But he's as dumb as she is, and if possible a little shyer. Affinity may go too far," said Dr. Mount.

Mrs. Mount was "dumb," like Melicent; but Dr. Mount declared she wasn't shy, so he had got to know her. She had never got to know *him*, but that did not matter; one was enough, he said. She looked up when he mentioned "that young Brierly."

"Yes," said Dr. Mount. "He brought her lilies-of-the-valley the other day, and now she has a bunch of artificial ones in her best hat. Didn't you notice? *I* did."

By the time Dr. Mount died Mr. Brierly had married a girl whom he had got to know, through her talking enough and not too much. Melicent was maternity nurse to their two babies, for Mrs. Brierly had no idea that there had ever been the little interlude, and was determined to engage her both times. The Brierlys had no more babies, but Melicent went on seeing a great deal of them and of "her" children.

While they were quite young, the three Miss Mounts had not been glad to learn their trades. They said it was a shame, or Thomasine and Constance did; Melicent said nothing. But as they grew older Thomasine and Constance became interested, and declared that after all it *was* a blessing not to be old maids.

Melicent, who sometimes of course did speak, said once: "Aren't we old maids?"

Thomasine and Constance both cried that indeed they weren't. You weren't old maids when you were business-women.

"At all events," said Constance, "no one *says* you are."

But Thomasine, who was most like their father, saw a little deeper. "That's not it; you really aren't. Old maids are failures; we aren't failures."

"Oh, I see," said Melicent.

They took their house in London in a long, perfectly straight street which at their end preserved a flavour of gentility. The houses in their block had no bay-windows, porticoes, nor red-brick trimmings; they were reticent, not tall for London, with nice first-floor balconies and hall-doors that well repaid attention from the housemaids. Three shallow steps led up to the hall-doors; the areas weren't abysses.

They settled down with Nana, their old nurse, and a new youthful "general." Melicent and Thomasine worked up their connections; Constance found a post at once. They were not young, but neither were they old; their little incomes, added to their earnings, gave them ease of mind in money-matters. Very fond of one another, and successes now at their three trades, each brought into the common stock an ever-changing interest which sometimes quite developed—Melicent's particularly. She entered more familiarly the lives of those for whom she worked than Thomasine or Constance could; but all had anecdotes to make diversion for the others and for Nana.

Nana had her meals with them; they sat together in the evenings. Irene, the new importation, wasn't jealous. She would have thought it awful to be mewed up after dinner in the drawing-room; as for meals, she much preferred hers in the kitchen, where she could eat as she liked and read the story in the *Daily Mirror* while she ate. Every one, in short, was happy, occupied, and sensible.

But there had to be a folly somewhere, and for the Miss Mounts and Nana that was Timothy the cat. He, like Nana, was a bit of the old home; they'd had him thirteen years. He was black, not handsome, of no special breed, although he had a plumy tail. The tail was Orientalism enough for them. "At all events," said Constance, "he can't swallow his fur." He was uncannily clever; he knew every word you said about him; "in another tick he'd speak to you," said Thomasine.

Like all cats, he did precisely as he pleased to the top limit of his powers. The Miss Mounts and Nana asked for nothing better. To claim anything from Timothy would be to make him less than cat. If he wanted to catch mice, he would; they never shut him in the coal-cellar, or withheld his meals to make him hungry. They bought fish for him three times a week; a saucer of milk stood always full in dining-room and kitchen; he drank tea too, and thin bread-and-butter was as much for him as them.

Timothy repaid their devotion. He showed no favouritism; perhaps, they said, he turned a little more to Nana in his illnesses, and the depression of the mating seasons when he saw the real males (for Timothy, as a kitten, had been "attended to") crouch moaning on the garden wall, or leap, still moaning, on the females who allured them. The Miss Mounts were clear-eyed in these matters, and they noticed that he did, at such times, turn to Nana—she was always there for him, and they were not. She did not boast; she couldn't but be proud, yet would have been as proud, they knew, in quite another way, if he had taken his poor puzzled head and body to *their* laps, for Nana loved the three Miss Mounts with all her heart.

Melicent said once, in May, that if she had realised she wouldn't have permitted the early attention to Timothy. That was natural, the other two said; Melicent's profession led her to think more than they did about "That." The only thing that puzzled them was how she hadn't realised—for when Timothy was a kitten, she was already a maternity nurse. They asked her, and she didn't answer for a moment; then she said: "Well, I'm the eldest."

Next day she observed, when feeding Timothy at dinner time, that he had never had his chance. "However, we can make it up to *him,* in some ways."

Thomasine and Constance didn't understand. They say that she was nervous, as she always was in May; but even Constance, who was noted for outspokenness, did not ask her what she meant. She never liked to be asked that; she found it difficult enough to say what she did say.

Constance, like Thomasine, talked enormously—Thomasine the faster, but Constance the more lengthily. Nothing stopped her, except her own giggle. She would break off to giggle, but went on again before the other could break in. Thomasine had learnt to speak at the same time, and let the giggle do what it could for her; occasionally Constance noticed, and did stop.

Constance was the youngest, but the plainest. She was low on the ground, like a dachshund; pale, and wore rimless glasses. The blue eyes behind the glasses were well-set and honest. A cousin, whom they didn't like, said Connie's eyes were honest, all for nothing. It was silly—how could eyes or anything be honest all for nothing? but it wounded Constance. "Call her clever! *That* isn't clever, at all events," said Constance and took off her glasses, wiping them with the silk handkerchief she kept expressly for the purpose. The cousin had said too, when Constance first adopted them, that of all futile vanities she thought that rimless glasses were the chief.

"Smart women wear tortoiseshell rims, as dark as possible. Then the glasses are *amusingly* unbecoming. Isn't it clever?"

"All very well for them!" cried Thomasine. "Other people can't afford tortoiseshell."

"Celluloid or horn looks just the same," the cousin said.

"The fashion will soon die, then—always does when cheap imitations begin," retorted Thomasine, who knew quite as much about smart women as the cousin could; and indeed the cousin laughed and said that Thomasine was right. "But I detest the rimless things!"

It was afterwards that she said that about Connie's eyes. Of course it wasn't clever, Melicent agreed. She said so in her timid manner, looking very nice in her grey cloak with the white bonnet, for she had come back from a case, and met the cousin on the doorstep.

"You look like a nun," the cousin cried, "with your great melancholy eyes and your clear brows. *Mille-Saintes!*"

They hated that joke of the cousin's, who declared that "Melicent" came from the French, when the Miss Mounts all knew—for a very learned friend of Dr. Mount's had told them—that it was straight from the Greek, and meant as sweet as honey.

Melicent had come in smiling; the cousin pretended to be fond of her and she *was* as sweet as honey, and liked every one who liked her. But when Constance told her she looked angry, and that comforted poor Constance, who said Melicent was like still waters: "you run deep, I mean." Constance didn't mind being plain, if she *was* plain; she knew she spoke freely enough herself, but it was always kind, at all events, sobbed Constance.

The Mounts indeed were kind. They would lend their telephone to neighbours, and ring for neighbours' cats who mewed at the hall-doors. Once, on a moonlit night, Constance came downstairs when she had taken off her skirt and blouse, and was in her dressing-jacket and flannel petticoat, with her hair plaited. She heard a mew outside, and opened the hall-door. Their right-hand neighbour's cat was wanting to get in, so she rang. Before she could escape, the door was opened by a gentleman in evening-dress.

"Wasn't it awful?" said Constance, who slipped into Thomasine's room to tell her. "When I remembered I was in my flannel petticoat and my red dressing-jacket, and my hair tied with a bit of boot-lace—!"

She giggled, and Thomasine said: *"Boot-lace!* Oh, my goodness!"

"I couldn't find a ribbon," Constance said. "At all events, he mayn't have noticed. I only remembered afterwards, the moon was so bright. He thanked me very much, and said 'Come in, puss.' I suppose he didn't know their cat's name is Girlie. Of course he might have thought Girlie would sound queer when I was there alone, if any one had been passing."

She giggled again, but Thomasine was too sleepy to take advantage. Besides, she felt angry with Constance. That soiled red jacket and a *flannel* petticoat (why had she taken off her moirette one?) and boot-lace in her hair! It was to be hoped he wouldn't recognise her if he saw her in the daytime.

Thomasine was very nearly good-looking. Her back was quite good-looking. Men who saw her passing quickly, sometimes looked again. She had pretty feet and ankles, and she dressed them well; her clothes sat smartly. Her face—a pointed oval with great breadth between the eyes—was like a leaf, now withered. Thomasine *had* to dress, for she massaged so many fashionable women. From them she picked up hints; they talked to their maids, or frocks and hats would arrive and be unpacked, and Thomasine in this way saw the first-fruits of the "Paris openings"—that was what you said. Her stories were the most exciting of the stock; there were Ladies So-and-So in them, often.

Nana always went to bed soon after dinner, and the Miss Mounts read or sewed. Thomasine and Constance liked the sewing best, for they could talk; but when Melicent was tired, as she sometimes was, they got their books. Timothy sat on anybody's lap, and whoever had him took him down to the garden the last thing, and waited for him. He came in soon, having no temptation to stay out. Sometimes, though, he cried as he came in. When Thomasine or Constance took him down, she told the others when he cried. Melicent, they thought, did not. He must have done it with her too, but she said nothing, for some reason. He slept in her room; he could have slept in anybody's, but Melicent had a sofa —he liked that.

They called him the man of the house, and said the hat in the hall-rack was his. Thomasine often apologised to him at breakfast for reading the paper first, but pointed out that she would have no other chance till evening while he had the whole day to himself. Timothy listened, blinking his yellow eyes and smiling. He would put out a paw and pat the paper, as if to say he understood and Thomasine might have it.

She was the social favourite. Everything combined for that—profession, clothes, looks, "quickness": her speciality was quickness. She knew what everybody meant, except sometimes the cousin. Even she could not explain the thing the cousin said to Melicent about her grey-and-white uniform. "So Puritan; and child-beds are so Pagan!"

You expected coarseness from the cousin; but what could she mean by Pagan? The children were always christened. Melicent said so, and the cousin laughed and kissed her. "Oh, *isn't* it Mille-Saintes?" she cried; and Thomasine herself confessed that she was puzzled.

One summer, Thomasine had a delightful invitation for her holiday. Some old friends who had gone to Cornwall asked her there. None of the Miss Mounts had been to Cornwall, which was a nice part, they knew; and the old friends were dear, so Thomasine accepted.

She looked well when she went off, in a check coat and a small, dashing hat, and shoes and stockings that surpassed all earlier ones. As she got into the taxi a man passed, and turned to look again. Melicent and Constance, on the steps with Nana and Timothy, thought that she must know him; Constance ran out and asked her, in a whisper. But she said she never had laid eyes on him before. She was blushing a little. "At all events he'll know you again," said Constance, and Thomasine said "Nonsense!"

She drove off then, alert and gay; Timothy kissed a paw to her, and she to him.

Constance soon departed, leaving Melicent at home, for she was out of work. Timothy was with her, in a heavenly mood, rubbing his head, stretching his paws: "Quite a flirtation," said Constance on the steps, more loudly than she should have, but she *was* a madcap sometimes.

She came home that evening to find Melicent in great anxiety. Not about Thomasine, who had wired and had a comfortable journey; but about Timothy. He wouldn't eat, he wouldn't even drink his milk. The one thing he would touch was water. Like most cats, he never cared for water if you poured it out for him; he'd only take it from the bedroom jugs. Melicent had gone into her room and found him trying, but the jug was nearly empty. So she filled it in the bathroom: "He waited all the time, the clever little man!" Then he had drunk till she thought he would never stop; but not a morsel had he eaten.

He lay on Nana's lap. His ears and nose were hot; his eyes looked heavy. "We must have the vet.," said Constance, and she telephoned that instant. But they had to dine before the vet. arrived.

He said that there was nothing much the matter; he would send some pills. "You know how to give them?" It would be queer, said Constance, if she didn't; at all events, she worked at a chemist's.

"He'll be all right," the vet. said, hurrying off. Late as it was, he was going into the country about a horse.

"A horse, of course!" said Constance. "They care about nothing but horses. *I* don't believe they understand cats; at all events, they never do them any good."

The pills came, and she gave Timothy the two ordained. He would sleep in Melicent's room as usual, and if Melicent was going to sit up with him, so would Constance.

Nana was crying. "You mustn't cry," they said. "He'll be himself tomorrow."

"No, he won't," said Nana. "And Miss Thomasine at the Land's End—indeed they may well say it!"

"We'll wire in the morning, if he isn't better," Constance said. "It's a shame it should have happened, when she's only just gone. But we must let her know, at all events, or else she'd never forgive us, if anything happened."

Timothy got worse in the night; they all assembled in Melicent's room, except Irene. In the morning Constance went out, first thing, and wired to Thomasine: "Timothy very ill. Will wire again during day." She telephoned to her chemist to say she couldn't come, because their cat was ill.

The vet. came again, and said that Timothy was dying.

"Last night you said there was nothing the matter!" Constance cried.

"Cats are deceptive," he answered. "The pills did him no harm, you know."

"They didn't do him any good, at all events," said Constance.

Melicent said nothing, but looked like a ghost. Nana said she always knew it. They sat in Melicent's room; they hadn't dared to move him. Irene did the room out gently; she was a good girl.

Timothy lay on the sofa, his head between his outstretched paws. His coat had lost its gloss; his eyes were so dilated now that when you saw them, you might think that he was well—they were so bright. But his little heart . . . his little heart was scarcely beating; he moaned pitifully now and then; he didn't seem to know them. Constance was to give him two more pills; they'd ease his going, the vet. had said. She did it beautifully, but when it was done, she cried a moment. Timothy had moaned when she disturbed him. "I *had* to, little man," she whispered. "Do you think I would if I could help it?" and she pressed his head against her breast; but Nana said: "I wouldn't do that, Miss Constance; he wants all the air he can get"; so they dared only stroke him very softly.

They sat up there till lunch-time; then went one by one to lunch, and then sat there again, just waiting.

About four o'clock he stretched a little, opening his eyes. They weren't bright now, but glazed and wild. He turned them upon Nana. All were kneeling close, but it was Nana that he looked at.

"Little man," she said, and smiled at him; but then she cried: "For God's sake, love, be done with it! Oh, I can't bear his eyes."

Melicent and Constance would have liked to cover their eyes too, for Timothy's were so beseeching and so terrified that they could hardly bear them either. But Melicent said: "He'd feel deserted. *You* do, Constance, if you like"; but Constance said she'd do what she could, at all events. So they knelt, smiling through their tears at Timothy, but now Timothy was gazing at the door as if he wanted to run away from them, and from something else—he even raised himself a little. But he was too weak; he fell back, gazing still and uttered a faint growl, as when he saw a dog.

"May I never again see a dumb creature die!" sobbed Nana. "I'd sooner watch a dozen men and women."

She moaned as Timothy had moaned at first; but Timothy had done with moaning. There was nothing but a feeble panting now; then once more the eyes closed—he stretched a paw forth blindly.

Melicent took it in both hands and kissed it. She couldn't see him any more, her tears were gathering so thick—the little paw that seemed to beg for love to help him through. . . . "Thank God!" said Nana's voice in a few moments; and Melicent knew then that he was dead. She trembled; Constance clasped her hand, and Nana put her arm about them both.

Not long afterwards came Thomasine's wire. She would be with them about seven.

"I *knew* she'd come!" Constance exclaimed. "If only she had been in time!"

But Nana said: "Indeed, I'm thankful one of us was spared it."

Melicent went out of the dining-room where they were having tea—the first meal without him. She came back with him in her arms—quite calm at first, but then she broke down dreadfully. None of them had ever seen her cry like that. Constance and Nana took the little body from her arms, and laid it on the table. His black coat was rough and stiff; the white evening-waistcoat he had kept so beautifully looked all poor and soiled.

Their tears fell upon the staring coat; they tried to smoothe it, but it wouldn't smoothe. The cold roughness made them think of rabbits and hares in shops; none of them could ever eat a hare or rabbit.

"Ought we to let her see him?" Constance whispered.

Nana said, "Leave him to me."

They hid their faces.

"Now go out, the two of you, and take a breath of air," continued Nana. "Leave the little love to me."

"You'd never have the strength," said Constance.

"Strength? What strength?" cried Nana.

"It'll be a job, the soil's so stiff."

Nana had a queer look in her eyes, but only said: "Come back in half an hour and see." She pushed them gently out and shut the door.

They went to their own rooms; not out. In half an hour they came back to the dining-room. Nana was there, and on the table still was Timothy. But now there was a white cloth on the table—the best afternoon one, with the Irish crochet border. Timothy was laid on it, his head just raised against a pillow. He was on his side, his front paws lightly crossed, his back limbs turned a little, so that he was not at full length. The plumy tail showed beautifully, the coat no longer stared; it glimmered sleek and dark, and the white waistcoat was like snow. You might have thought he was alive.

"Doesn't he look lovely?" Nana said. "I thought my nice macassar oil would do it. But it was a job."

She seemed consoled by her success, for she was smiling.

"Yes, he looks lovely, Nana," Melicent and Constance said; but into both their minds had crept a fear.

He looked just as if he were alive, and Thomasine might think he was.

"I know!" cried Constance, and she hurried out.

Melicent looked after her, then followed eagerly. Nana soon went too, for she must wash her hands. She looked back from the door and said: "I won't be long, my love."

About seven Thomasine arrived. She looked as trim as yesterday, but that she couldn't help, and her white face was anxious. They shook their heads in answer; then got the taxi away quickly, and drew her to the dining-room. She understood at once, for now a white silk scarf of Constance's was tied in a big bow about his neck, and in his front paws lay a little bunch of artificial lilies-of-the-valley, fastened with white satin ribbon; and Thomasine knelt down and hid her face upon the corner of the table.

She couldn't speak for a long time, though she soon raised her head and looked at him. At last she said: "How beautiful he looks!"—and she got up and kissed his head between the ears. They led her away then, and she took off her things and came to dinner, which was in the drawing-room. Irene had made "Nana's pudding," of her own accord, while Nana had been busy. It was not a good attempt, but very nice of her to think of it, they all said kindly.

After dinner—not till then, they had agreed—they told Thomasine about his sudden illness; and on the way to bed, they went into the dining-room again.

"We'll leave a bead of gas for him," said Melicent. "I know cats see in darkness, but—*he* can't."

She covered up her face again, but did not cry this time.

"Yes, a nice bead, at all events," said Constance with

a glance at Thomasine and Nana, who both nodded. Melicent would miss him worse than they, at night.

"That ribbon shows up very handsome on his coat," said Nana.

"And the lilies look so sweet," said Thomasine. "Where did you find them?"

Constance turned to Melicent, but Melicent still had her hands over her face.

"Well, come to bed, my dears," said Nana then.

They looked back from the door. By the faint light they saw the gleam of the white cloth and ribbons, and his waistcoat and the lilies.

"Long ago," said Thomasine, "in Egypt, people used to worship cats."

"At all events," said Constance, on the stairs, "we made him happy."

Melicent, who was in front, turned quickly round. She looked as if she meant to speak, but she turned back again and went into her room without a word, and shut the door.

ROBERT GRAVES

The Shout

Robert Graves stands impressively, cantankerously, comically, nobly apart from his contemporaries. You can't even classify him as the leader of his own school. He hasn't one. Indeed, it may be said that he draws his great strength from wrestling single-handed with the brutish mob.

Certainly he is a major poet. Probably he is the best living historical novelist (*I, Claudius; Claudius the God,* etc.). His anthropological studies (such as *The White Goddess*) combine careful scholarship with brilliant guesswork. He has written an exhaustive encyclopedia of Greek myths, a handbook for writers called *The Reader Over Your Shoulder* (which haunts me with its warnings as I write these lines) and an autobiography, *Goodbye to All That,* which contains an unforgettable account of trench life in World-War One.

The Shout is also, indirectly, a product of Graves's war experience. He says of it that it was written in 1926, when "I was still living on the neurasthenic verge of nightmare," and that "Richard in the story is a surrogate for myself." It is easy enough to believe that a work of such frightening power must have come up out of very dark depths. One does not write like that just for entertainment. As Dante puts it:

> To describe the Bottom of the Universe is not a task which one undertakes for sport; nor is it for a tongue that cries "mama" and "papa."

It is far more difficult to tell a story of terror—that which excites dread and awe—than a story of horror—that which merely causes alarm, loathing and disgust. (Horror is always aware of its cause; terror never is. That is precisely what makes terror terrifying.) There is some horror in *Mary Postgate.* There is some terror in *The Invisible Man, The Magic Shop* and *The Story of the Siren.* But *The Shout* is sheer terror from beginning to end.

It is also partly about Cricket, and this alone would warrant its inclusion in a book of English stories. Better still, it is about Cricket at a lunatic asylum—which is how the National Game often appeared to me, who had difficulty in taking it sanely and seriously.

WHEN WE ARRIVED WITH OUR BAGS AT THE ASYLUM cricket ground, the chief medical officer, whom I had met at the house where I was staying, came up to shake hands. I told him that I was only scoring for the Lampton team today (I had broken a finger the week before, keeping wicket on a bumpy pitch). He said: "Oh, then you'll have an interesting companion."

"The other scoresman?" I asked.

"Crossley is the most intelligent man in the asylum," answered the doctor, "a wide reader, a first-class chess-player, and so on. He seems to have travelled all over the world. He's been sent here for delusions. His most serious delusion is that he's a murderer, and his story is that he killed two men and a woman at Sydney, Australia. The other delusion, which is more humorous, is that his soul is split in pieces—whatever that means. He edits our monthly magazine, he stage manages our Christmas theatricals, and he gave a most original conjuring performance the other day. You'll like him."

He introduced me. Crossley, a big man of forty or fifty, had a queer, not unpleasant, face. But I felt a little uncomfortable, sitting next to him in the scoring box, his black-whiskered hands so close to mine. I had no fear of physical violence, only the sense of being in the presence of a man of unusual force, even perhaps, it somehow came to me, of occult powers.

It was hot in the scoring box in spite of the wide window. "Thunderstorm weather," said Crossley, who spoke in what country people call a "college voice," though I could not identify the college. "Thunderstorm weather makes us patients behave even more irregularly than usual."

I asked whether any patients were playing.

"Two of them, this first wicket partnership. The tall one, B. C. Brown, played for Hants three years ago, and the other is a good club player. Pat Slingsby usually turns out for us too—the Australian fast bowler, you know—but we are dropping him today. In weather like this he is apt to bowl at the batsman's head. He is not insane in the usual sense, merely magnificently ill-tempered. The doctors can do nothing with him. He wants shooting, really." Crossley began talking about the doctor. "A good-hearted fellow and, for a mental-hospital physician, technically well advanced. He actually studies morbid psychology and is fairly well-read, up to about the day before yesterday. I have a good deal of fun with him. He reads neither German nor French, so I keep a stage or two ahead in psychological fashions; he has to wait for the English translations. I invent significant dreams for him to interpret; I find he likes me to put in snakes and apple pies, so I usually do. He is convinced that my mental trouble is due to the good old 'antipaternal fixation'—I wish it were as simple as that."

Then Crossley asked me whether I could score and listen to a story at the same time. I said that I could. It was slow cricket.

"My story is true," he said, "every word of it. Or, when I say that my story is 'true,' I mean at least that I am telling it in a new way. It is always the same story, but I sometimes vary the climax and even recast the characters. Variation keeps it fresh and therefore true. If I were always to use the same formula, it would soon drag and become false. I am interested in keeping it alive, and it is a true story, every word of it. I know the people in it personally. They are Lampton people."

We decided that I should keep score of the runs and extras and that he should keep the bowling analysis, and at the fall of every wicket we should copy from each other. This made story-telling possible.

Richard awoke one morning saying to Rachel: "But what an unusual dream."

"Tell me, my dear," she said, "and hurry, because I want to tell you mine."

"I was having a conversation," he said, "with a person (or persons, because he changed his appearance so often) of great intelligence, and I can clearly remember the argument. Yet this is the first time I have ever been able to remember any argument that came to me in sleep. Usually my dreams are so different from waking that I can only describe them if I say: 'It it as though I were living and thinking as a tree, or a bell, or middle C, or a five-pound note; as though I had never been human.' Life there is sometimes rich for me and sometimes poor, but I repeat, in every case so different, that if I were to say: 'I had a conversation,' or 'I was in love,' or 'I heard music,' or 'I was angry,' it would be as far from the fact as if I tried to explain a problem of philosophy, as Rabelais's Panurge did to Thaumast, merely by grimacing with my eyes and lips."

"It is much the same with me," she said. "I think that when I am asleep I become, perhaps, a stone with all the natural appetites and convictions of a stone. 'Senseless as a stone' is a proverb, but there may be more sense in a stone, more sensibility, more sensitivity, more sentiment, more sensibleness, than in many men and women. And no less sensuality," she added thoughtfully.

It was Sunday morning, so that they could lie in bed, their arms about each other, without troubling about the time; and they were childless, so breakfast could wait. He told her that in his dream he was walking in the sand hills with this person or persons, who said to him: "These sand hills are a part neither of the sea before us nor of the grass links behind us, and are not related to the mountains beyond the links. They are of themselves. A man walking on the sand hills soon knows this by the tang in the air, and if he were to refrain from eating and drinking, from sleeping and speaking, from thinking and desiring, he could continue among them for ever without change. There is no life and no death in the sand hills. Anything might happen in the sand hills."

Rachel said that this was nonsense, and asked: "But what was the argument? Hurry up!"

He said it was about the whereabouts of the soul, but that now she had put it out of his head by hurrying him. All that he remembered was that the man was first a Japanese, then an Italian, and finally a kangaroo.

In return she eagerly told her dream, gabbling over the words. "I was walking in the sand hills; there were rabbits there, too; how does that tally with what he said of life and death? I saw the man and you walking arm in arm towards me, and I ran from you both and I noticed that he had a black silk handkerchief; he ran after me and my shoe buckle came off and I could not wait to pick it up. I left it lying, and he stooped and put it into his pocket."

"How do you know that it was the same man?" he asked.

"Because," she said, laughing, "he had a black face and wore a blue coat like that picture of Captain Cook. And because it was in the sand hills."

He said, kissing her neck: "We not only live together and talk together and sleep together, but it seems we now even dream together."

So they laughed.

Then he got up and brought her breakfast.

At about half past eleven, she said: "Go out now for a walk, my dear, and bring home something for me to think about: and be back in time for dinner at one o'clock."

It was a hot morning in the middle of May, and he went out through the wood and struck the coast road, which after half a mile led into Lampton.

("Do you know Lampton well?" asked Crossley. "No," I said, "I am only here for the holidays, staying with friends.")

He went a hundred yards along the coast road, but then turned off and went across the links: thinking of Rachel and watching the blue butterflies and looking at the heath roses and thyme, and thinking of her again, and how strange it was that they could be so near to each other; and then taking a pinch of gorse flower and smelling it, and considering the smell and thinking, "If she should die, what would become of me?" and taking a slate from the low wall and skimming it across the pond and thinking, "I am a clumsy fellow to be her husband"; and walking towards the sand hills, and then edging away again, perhaps half in fear of meeting the person of their dream, and at last making a half circle towards the old church beyond Lampton, at the foot of the mountain.

The morning service was over and the people were out by the cromlechs behind the church, walking in twos and threes, as the custom was, on the smooth turf. The squire was talking in a loud voice about King Charles, the Martyr: "A great man, a very great man, but betrayed by those he loved best," and the doctor was arguing about organ music with the rector. There was a group of children playing ball. "Throw it here, Elsie. No, to me, Elsie, Elsie, Elsie." Then the rector appeared and pocketed the ball and said that it was Sunday; they should have remembered. When he was gone they made faces after him.

Presently a stranger came up and asked permission to sit down beside Richard; they began to talk. The stranger had been to the church service and wished to discuss the sermon. The text had been the immortality of the soul: the last of a series of sermons that had begun at Easter. He said that he could not grant the preacher's premiss that *the soul is continually resident in the body*. Why should this be so? What duty did the soul perform in the daily routine task of the body? The soul was neither the brain, nor the lungs, nor the stomach, nor the heart, nor the mind, nor the imagination. Surely it was a thing apart? Was it not indeed less likely to be resident in the body than outside the body? He had no proof one way or the other, but he would say: Birth and death are so odd a mystery that the principle of life may well lie outside the body which is the visible evidence of living. "We cannot," he said, "even tell to a nicety what are the moments of birth and death. Why, in Japan, where I have travelled, they reckon a man to be already one year old when he is born; and lately in Italy a dead man—but come and walk on the sand hills and let me tell you my conclusions. I find it easier to talk when I am walking."

Richard was frightened to hear this, and to see the man wipe his forehead with a black silk handkerchief. He stuttered out something. At this moment the children, who had crept up behind the cromlech, suddenly, at an agreed signal, shouted loud in the ears of the two men; and stood laughing. The stranger was startled into anger; he opened his mouth as if he were about to curse them, and bared his teeth to the gums. Three of the children screamed and ran off. But the one whom they called Elsie fell down in her fright and lay sobbing. The doctor, who was near, tried to comfort her. "He has a face like a devil," they heard the child say.

The stranger smiled good-naturedly: "And a devil I was not so very long ago. That was in Northern Australia, where I lived with the black fellows for twenty years. 'Devil' is the nearest English word for the position that they gave me in their tribe; and they also gave me an eighteenth-century British naval uniform to wear as my ceremonial dress. Come and walk with me in the sand hills and let me tell you the whole story. I have a passion for walking in the sand hills: that is why I came to this town . . . My name is Charles."

Richard said: "Thank you, but I must hurry home to my dinner."

"Nonsense," said Charles, "dinner can wait. Or, if you wish, I can come to dinner with you. By the way, I have had nothing to eat since Friday. I am without money."

Richard felt uneasy. He was afraid of Charles, and did not wish to bring him home to dinner because of the dream and the sand hills and the handkerchief: yet on the other hand the man was intelligent and quiet and decently dressed and had eaten nothing since Friday; if Rachel knew that he had refused him a meal, she would renew her taunts. When Rachel was out of sorts, her favourite complaint was that he was overcareful about money; though when she was at peace with him, she owned that he was the most generous man she knew, and that she did not mean what she said; when she was angry with him again, out came the taunt of stinginess: "Tenpence-halfpenny," she would say, "tenpence-halfpenny and threepence of that in stamps"; his ears would burn and he would want to hit her. So he said now: "By all means come along to dinner, but that little girl is still sobbing for fear of you. You ought to do something about it."

Charles beckoned her to him and said a single soft word; it was an Australian magic word, he afterwards told Richard, meaning *Milk:* immediately Elsie was comforted and came to sit on Charles' knee and played with the buttons of his waistcoat for awhile until Charles sent her away.

"You have strange powers, Mr. Charles," Richard said.

Charles answered: "I am fond of children, but the shout startled me; I am pleased that I did not do what, for a moment, I was tempted to do."

"What was that?" asked Richard.

"I might have shouted myself," said Charles.

"Why," said Richard, "they would have liked that better. It would have been a great game for them. They probably expected it of you."

"If I had shouted," said Charles, "my shout would have either killed them outright or sent them mad. Probably it would have killed them, for they were standing close."

Richard smiled a little foolishly. He did not know whether or not he was expected to laugh, for Charles spoke so gravely and carefully. So he said: "Indeed, what sort of shout would that be? Let me hear you shout."

"It is not only children who would be hurt by my shout," Charles said. "Men can be sent raving mad by it; the strongest, even, would be flung to the ground. It is a magic shout that I learned from the chief devil of the Northern Territory. I took eighteen years to perfect it, and yet I have used it, in all, no more than five times."

Richard was so confused in his mind with the dream and the handkerchief and the word spoken to Elsie that he did not know what to say, so he muttered: "I'll give you fifty pounds now to clear the cromlechs with a shout."

"I see that you do not believe me," Charles said. "Perhaps you have never before heard of the terror shout?"

Richard considered and said: "Well, I have read of the hero shout which the ancient Irish warriors used, that would drive armies backwards; and did not Hector, the Trojan, have a terrible shout? And there were sudden shouts in the woods of Greece. They were ascribed to the god Pan and would infect men with a madness of fear; from this legend indeed the word 'panic' has come into the English language. And I remember another shout in the *Mabinogion,* in the story of Lludd and Llevelys. It was a shriek that was heard on every May Eve and went through all hearts and so scared them that the men lost their hue and their strength and the women their children, and the youths and maidens their senses, and the animals and trees, the earth and the waters were left barren. But it was caused by a dragon."

"It must have been a British magician of the dragon clan," said Charles. "I belonged to the Kangaroos. Yes, that tallies. The effect is not exactly given, but near enough."

They reached the house at one o'clock, and Rachel was at the door, the dinner ready. "Rachel," said Richard, "here is Mr. Charles to dinner; Mr. Charles is a great traveller."

Rachel passed her hand over her eyes as if to dispel a cloud, but it may have been the sudden sunlight. Charles took her hand and kissed it, which surprised her. Rachel was graceful, small, with eyes unusually blue for the blackness of her hair, delicate in her movements, and with a voice rather low-pitched; she had a freakish sense of humour.

("You would like Rachel," said Crossley, "she visits me here sometimes.")

Of Charles it would be difficult to say one thing or another: he was of middle age, and tall; his hair grey; his face never still for a moment; his eyes large and bright, sometimes yellow, sometimes brown, sometimes grey; his voice changed its tone and accent with the subject; his hands were brown and hairy at the back, his nails well cared for. Of Richard it is enough to say that he was a musician, not a strong man but a lucky one. Luck was his strength.

After dinner Charles and Richard washed the dishes together, and Richard suddenly asked Charles if he would let him hear the shout: for he thought that he could not have peace of mind until he had heard it. So horrible a thing was, surely, worse to think about than to hear: for now he believed in the shout.

Charles stopped washing up; mop in hand. "As you wish," said he, "but I have warned you what a shout it is. And if I shout it must be in a lonely place where nobody else can hear; and I shall not shout in the second degree, the degree which kills certainly, but in the first, which terrifies only, and when you want me to stop put your hands to your ears."

"Agreed," said Richard.

"I have never yet shouted to satisfy an idle curiosity," said Charles, "but only when in danger of my life from enemies, black or white, and once when I was alone in the desert without food or drink. Then I was forced to shout, for food."

Richard thought: "Well at least I am a lucky man, and my luck will be good enough even for this."

"I am not afraid," he told Charles.

"We will walk out on the sand hills tomorrow early," Charles said, "when nobody is stirring; and I will shout. You say you are not afraid."

But Richard was very much afraid, and what made his fear worse was that somehow he could not talk to Rachel and tell her of it: he knew that if he told her she would either forbid him to go or she would come with him. If she forbade him to go, the fear of the shout and the sense of cowardice would hang over him ever afterwards; but if she came with him, either the shout would be nothing and she would have a new taunt for his credulity and Charles would laugh with her, or if it were something, she might well be driven mad. So he said nothing.

Charles was invited to sleep at the cottage for the night, and they stayed up late talking.

Rachel told Richard when they were in bed that she liked Charles and that he certainly was a man who had seen many things, though a fool and a big baby. Then Rachel talked a great deal of nonsense, for she had had two glasses of wine, which she seldom drank, and she said: "Oh, my dearest, I forgot to tell you. When I put on my buckled shoes this morning while you were away I found a buckle missing. I must have noticed that it was lost before I went to sleep last night and yet not fixed the loss firmly in my mind, so that it came out as a discovery in my dream; but I have a feeling, in fact I am certain, that Mr. Charles has that buckle in his pocket; and I am sure that he is the man whom we met in our dream. But I don't care, not I."

Richard grew more and more afraid, and he dared not tell of the black silk handkerchief, or of Charles' invitations to him to walk in the sand hills. And what was worse, Charles had used only a white handkerchief while he was in the house, so that he could not be sure whether he had seen it after all. Turning his head away, he said lamely: "Well, Charles knows a lot of things. I am going for a walk with him early tomorrow if you don't mind; an early walk is what I need."

"Oh, I'll come too," she said.

Richard could not think how to refuse her; he knew that he had made a mistake in telling her of the walk. But he said: "Charles will be very glad. At six o'clock then."

At six o'clock he got up, but Rachel after the wine was too sleepy to come with them. She kissed him goodbye and off he went with Charles.

Richard had had a bad night. In his dreams nothing was in human terms, but confused and fearful, and he had felt himself more distant from Rachel than he had ever felt since their marriage, and the fear of the shout was gnawing at him. He was also hungry and cold. There was a stiff wind blowing towards the sea from the mountains and a few splashes of rain. Charles spoke hardly a word, but chewed a stalk of grass and walked fast.

Richard felt giddy, and said to Charles: "Wait a moment, I have a stitch in my side." So they stopped, and Richard asked, gasping: "What sort of shout is it? Is it loud, or shrill? How is it produced? How can it madden a man?"

Charles was silent, so Richard went on with a foolish smile: "Sound, though, is a curious thing. I remember once, when I was at Cambridge, that a King's College man had his turn of reading the evening lesson. He had not spoken ten words before there was a groaning and ringing and creaking, and pieces of wood and dust fell from the roof; for his voice was exactly attuned to that of the building, so that he had to stop, else the roof might have fallen; as you can break a wine glass by playing its note on a violin."

Charles consented to answer: "My shout is not a matter of tone or vibration but something not to be explained. It is a shout of pure evil, and there is no fixed place for it on the scale. It may take any note. It is pure terror, and if it were not for a certain intention of mine, which I need not tell you, I would not shout for you."

Richard had a great gift of fear, and this new account of the shout disturbed him more and more; he wished himself at home in bed, and Charles two continents away. But he was fascinated. They were crossing the links now and going through the bent grass that pricked through his stockings and soaked them.

Now they were on the bare sand hills. From the highest of them Charles looked about him; he could see the beach stretched out for two miles and more. There was no one in sight. Then Richard saw Charles take something out of his pocket and begin carelessly to juggle with it as he stood, tossing it from finger tip to finger tip and spinning it up with finger and thumb to catch it on the back of his hand. It was Rachel's buckle.

Richard's breath came in gasps, his heart beat violently and he nearly vomited. He was shivering with cold, and yet sweating. Soon they came to an open place among the sand hills near the sea. There was a raised bank with sea holly growing on it and a little sickly grass; stones were strewn all around, brought there, it seemed, by the sea years before. Though the place was behind the first rampart of sand hills, there was a gap in the line through which a high tide might have broken, and the winds that continually swept through the gap kept them uncovered of sand. Richard had his hands in his trouser pockets for warmth and was nervously twisting a soft piece of wax around his right forefinger—a candle end that was in his pocket from the night before when he had gone downstairs to lock the door.

"Are you ready?" asked Charles.

Richard nodded.

A gull dipped over the crest of the sand hills and rose again screaming when it saw them. "Stand by the sea holly," said Richard, with a dry mouth, "and I'll be here among the stones, not too near. When I raise my hand, shout! When I put my fingers to my ears, stop at once."

So Charles walked twenty steps towards the holly. Richard saw his broad back and the black silk handkerchief sticking from his pocket. He remembered the dream, and the shoe buckle and Elsie's fear. His resolution broke: he hurriedly pulled the piece of wax in two, and sealed his ears. Charles did not see him.

He turned, and Richard gave the signal with his hand.

Charles leaned forward oddly, his chin thrust out, his teeth bared, and never before had Richard seen such a look of fear on a man's face. He had not been prepared for that. Charles' face, that was usually soft and changing, uncertain as a cloud, now hardened to a rough stone mask, dead white at first, and then flushing outwards from the cheek bones red and redder, and at last as black, as if he were about to choke. His mouth then slowly opened to the full, and Richard fell on his face, his hands to his ears, in a faint.

When he came to himself he was lying alone among the stones. He sat up, wondering numbly whether he had been there long. He felt very weak and sick, with a chill on his heart that was worse than the chill of his body. He could not think. He put his hand down to lift himself up and it rested on a stone, a larger one than most of the others. He picked it up and felt its surface, absently. His mind wandered. He began to think about shoemaking, a trade of which he had known nothing, but now every trick was familiar to him. "I must be a shoemaker," he said aloud.

Then he corrected himself: "No, I am a musician. Am I going mad?" He threw the stone from him; it struck against another and bounced off.

He asked himself: "Now why did I say that I was a shoemaker? It seemed a moment ago that I knew all there was to be known about shoemaking and now I know nothing at all about it. I must get home to Rachel. Why did I ever come out?"

Then he saw Charles on a sand hill a hundred yards away, gazing out to sea. He remembered his fear and made sure that the wax was in his ears: he stumbled to his feet. He saw a flurry on the sand and there was a rabbit lying on its side, twitching in a convulsion. As Richard moved towards it, the flurry ended: the rabbit was dead. Richard crept behind a sand hill out of Charles' sight and then struck homeward, running awkwardly in the soft sand. He had not gone twenty paces before he came upon the gull. It was standing stupidly on the sand and did not rise at his approach, but fell over dead.

How Richard reached home he did not know, but there he was opening the back door and crawling upstairs on his hands and knees. He unsealed his ears.

Rachel was sitting up in bed, pale and trembling. "Thank God you're back," she said; "I have had a nightmare, the worst of all my life. It was frightful. I was in my dream, in the deepest dream of all, like the one of which I told you. I was like a stone, and I was aware of you near me; you were you, quite plain, though I was a stone, and you were in great fear and I could do nothing to help you, and you were waiting for something and the terrible thing did not happen to you, but it happened to me. I can't tell you what it was, but it was as though all my nerves cried out in pain at once, and I was pierced through and through with a beam of some intense evil light and twisted inside out. I woke up and my heart was beating so fast that I had to gasp for breath. Do you think I had a heart attack and my heart missed a beat? They say it feels like that. Where have you been, dearest? Where is Mr. Charles?"

Richard sat on the bed and held her hand. "I have had a bad experience too," he said. "I was out with Charles by the sea and as he went ahead to climb on the highest sand hill I felt very faint and fell down among a patch of stones, and when I came to myself I was in a desperate sweat of fear and had to hurry home. So I came back running alone. It happened perhaps half an hour ago," he said.

He did not tell her more. He asked, could he come back to bed and would she get breakfast? That was a thing she had not done all the years they were married.

"I am as ill as you," said she. It was understood between them always that when Rachel was ill, Richard must be well.

"You are not," said he, and fainted again.

She helped him to bed ungraciously and dressed herself and went slowly downstairs. A smell of coffee and bacon rose to meet her and there was Charles, who had lit the fire, putting two breakfasts on a tray. She was so relieved at not having to get breakfast and so confused by her experience that she thanked him and called him a darling, and he kissed her hand gravely and pressed it. He had made the breakfast exactly to her liking: the coffee was strong and the eggs fried on both sides.

Rachel fell in love with Charles. She had often fallen in love with men before and since her marriage, but it was her habit to tell Richard when this happened, as he agreed to tell her when it happened to him: so that the suffocation of passion was given a vent and there was no jealousy, for she used to say (and he had the liberty of saying): "Yes, I am in *love* with so-and-so, but I only *love* you."

That was as far as it had ever gone. But this was different. Somehow, she did not know why, she could not own to being in love with Charles: for she no longer loved Richard. She hated him for being ill, and said that he was lazy, and a sham. So about noon he got up, but went groaning around the bedroom until she sent him back to bed to groan.

Charles helped her with the housework, doing all the cooking, but he did not go up to see Richard, since he had not been asked to do so. Rachel was ashamed, and apologized to Charles for Richard's rudeness in running away from him. But Charles said mildly that he took it as no insult; he had felt queer himself that morning; it was as though something evil was astir in the air as they reached the sand hills. She told him that she too had had the same queer feeling.

Later she found all Lampton talking of it. The doctor maintained that it was an earth tremor, but the country people said that it had been the Devil passing by. He had come to fetch the black soul of Solomon Jones, the gamekeeper, found dead that morning in his cottage by the sand hills.

When Richard could go downstairs and walk about a little without groaning, Rachel sent him to the cobbler's to get a new buckle for her shoe. She came with him to the bottom of the garden. The path ran beside a steep bank. Richard looked ill and groaned slightly as he walked, so Rachel, half in anger, half in fun, pushed him down the bank, where he fell sprawling among the nettles and old iron. Then she ran back into the house laughing loudly.

Richard sighed, tried to share the joke against himself with Rachel—but she had gone—heaved himself up, picked the shoes from among the nettles, and after awhile walked slowly up the bank, out of the gate, and down the lane in the unaccustomed glare of the sun.

When he reached the cobbler's he sat down heavily. The cobbler was glad to talk to him. "You are looking bad," said the cobbler.

Richard said: "Yes, on Friday morning I had a bit of a turn; I am only now recovering from it."

"Good God," burst out the cobbler, "if you had a bit of a turn, what did I not have? It was as if someone handled me raw, without my skin. It was as if someone seized my very soul and juggled with it, as you might juggle with a stone, and hurled me away. I shall never forget last Friday morning."

A strange notion came to Richard that it was the cobbler's soul which he had handled in the form of a stone. "It may be," he thought, "that the souls of every man and woman and child in Lampton are lying there." But he said nothing about this, asked for a buckle, and went home.

Rachel was ready with a kiss and a joke; he might have kept silent, for his silence always made Rachel ashamed. "But," he thought, "why make her ashamed? From shame she goes to self-justification and picks a quarrel over something else and it's ten times worse. I'll be cheerful and accept the joke."

He was unhappy. And Charles was established in the house: gentle-voiced, hard-working, and continually taking Richard's part against Rachel's scoffing. This was galling, because Rachel did not resent it.

("The next part of the story," said Crossley, "is the comic relief, an account of how Richard went again to the sand hills, to the heap of stones, and identified the souls of the doctor and rector—the doctor's because it was shaped like a whiskey bottle and the rector's because it was as black as original sin—and how he proved to himself that the notion was not fanciful. But I will skip that and come to the point where Rachel two days later suddenly became affectionate and loved Richard she said, more than ever before.")

The reason was that Charles had gone away, nobody knows where, and had relaxed the buckle magic for the time, because he was confident that he could renew it on his return. So in a day or two Richard was well again and everything was as it had been, until one afternoon the door opened, and there stood Charles.

He entered without a word of greeting and hung his hat upon a peg. He sat down by the fire and asked: "When is supper ready?"

Richard looked at Rachel, his eyebrows raised, but Rachel seemed fascinated by the man.

She answered: "Eight o'clock," in her low voice, and stooping down, drew off Charles' muddy boots and found him a pair of Richard's slippers.

Charles said: "Good. It is now seven o'clock. In another hour, supper. At nine o'clock the boy will bring the evening paper. At ten o'clock, Rachel, you and I sleep together."

Richard thought that Charles must have gone suddenly mad. But Rachel answered quietly: "Why, of course, my dear." Then she turned viciously to Richard: "And you run away, little man!" she said, and slapped his cheek with all her strength.

Richard stood puzzled, nursing his cheek. Since he could not believe that Rachel and Charles had both gone mad together, he must be mad himself. At all events, Rachel knew her mind, and they had a secret compact that if either of them ever wished to break the marriage promise, the other should not stand in the way. They had made this compact because they wished to feel themselves bound by love rather than by ceremony. So he said as calmly as he could: "Very well, Rachel. I shall leave you two together."

Charles flung a boot at him, saying: "If you put your nose inside the door between now and breakfast time, I'll shout the ears off your head."

Richard went out this time not afraid, but cold inside and quite clear-headed. He went through the gate, down the lane, and across the links. It wanted three hours yet until sunset. He joked with the boys playing stump cricket on the school field. He skipped stones. He thought of Rachel and tears started to his eyes. Then he sang to comfort himself. "Oh, I'm certainly mad," he said, "and what in the world has happened to my luck?"

At last he came to the stones. "Now," he said, "I shall find my soul in this heap and I shall crack it into a hundred pieces with this hammer"—he had picked up the hammer in the coal shed as he came out.

Then he began looking for his soul. Now, one may recognize the soul of another man or woman, but one can never recognize one's own. Richard could not find his. But by chance he came upon Rachel's soul and recognized it (a slim green stone with glints of quartz in it) because she was estranged from him at the time. Against it lay another stone, an ugly misshapen flint of a mottled brown. He swore: "I'll destroy this. It must be the soul of Charles."

He kissed the soul of Rachel; it was like kissing her lips. Then he took the soul of Charles and poised his hammer. "I'll knock you into fifty fragments!"

He paused. Richard had scruples. He knew that Rachel loved Charles better than himself, and he was bound to respect the compact. A third stone (his own, it must be) was lying the other side of Charles' stone; it was of smooth grey granite, about the size of a cricket ball. He said to himself: "I will break my own soul in pieces and that will be the end of me." The world grew black, his eyes ceased to focus, and he all but fainted. But he recovered himself, and with a great cry brought down the coal hammer crack, and crack again, on the grey stone.

It split in four pieces, exuding a smell like gunpowder: and when Richard found that he was still alive and whole, he began to laugh and laugh. Oh, he was mad, quite mad! He flung the hammer away, lay down exhausted, and fell asleep.

He awoke as the sun was just setting. He went home

in confusion, thinking: "This is a very bad dream and Rachel will help me out of it."

When he came to the edge of the town he found a group of men talking excitedly under a lamppost. One said: "About eight o'clock it happened, didn't it?" The other said: "Yes." A third said: "Ay, mad as a hatter. 'Touch me,' he says, 'and I'll shout. I'll shout you into a fit, the whole blasted police force of you. I'll shout you mad.' And the inspector says: 'Now, Crossley, put your hands up, we've got you cornered at last.' 'One last chance,' says he. 'Go and leave me or I'll shout you stiff and dead.' "

Richard had stopped to listen. "And what happened to Crossley then?" he said. "And what did the woman say?"

" 'For Christ's sake,' she said to the inspector, 'go away or he'll kill you.' "

"And did he shout?"

"He didn't shout. He screwed up his face for a moment and drew in his breath. A'mighty, I've never seen such a ghastly looking face in my life. I had to take three or four brandies afterwards. And the inspector he drops the revolver and it goes off; but nobody hit. Then suddenly a change comes over this man Crossley. He claps his hands to his side and again to his heart, and his face goes smooth and dead again. Then he begins to laugh and dance and cut capers. And the woman stares and can't believe her eyes and the police lead him off. If he was mad before, he was just harmless dotty now; and they had no trouble with him. He's been taken off in the ambulance to the Royal West County Asylum."

So Richard went home to Rachel and told her everything and she told him everything, though there was not much to tell. She had not fallen in love with Charles, she said; she was only teasing Richard and she had never said anything or heard Charles say anything in the least like what he told her; it was part of his dream. She loved him always and only him, for all his faults; which she went through—his stinginess, his talkativeness, his untidiness. Charles and she had eaten a quiet supper, and she did think it had been bad of Richard to rush off without a word of explanation and stay away for three hours like that. Charles might have murdered her. He did start pulling her about a bit, in fun, wanting her to dance with him, and then the knock came on the door, and the inspector shouted: "Walter Charles Crossley, in the name of the King, I arrest you for the murder of George Grant, Harry Grant, and Ada Coleman at Sydney, Australia." Then Charles had gone absolutely mad. He had pulled out a shoe buckle and said to it: "Hold her for me." And then he had told the police to go away or he'd shout them dead. After that he made a dreadful face at them and went to pieces altogether. "He was rather a nice man; I liked his face so much and feel so sorry for him."

"Did you like that story?" asked Crossley.

"Yes," said I, busy scoring, "a Milesian tale of the best. Lucius Apuleius, I congratulate you."

Crossley turned to me with a troubled face and hands clenched trembling. "Every word of it is true," he said. "Crossley's soul was cracked in four pieces and I'm a madman. Oh, I don't blame Richard and Rachel. They are a pleasant, loving pair of fools and I've never wished them harm; they often visit me here. In any case, now that my soul lies broken in pieces, my powers are gone. Only one thing remains to me," he said, "and that is the shout."

I had been so busy scoring and listening to the story at the same time that I had not noticed the immense bank of black cloud that swam up until it spread across the sun and darkened the whole sky. Warm drops of rain fell: a flash of lightning dazzled us and with it came a smashing clap of thunder.

In a moment all was confusion. Down came a drenching rain, the cricketers dashed for cover, the lunatics began to scream, bellow, and fight. One tall young man, the same B. C. Brown who had once played for Hants, pulled all his clothes off and ran about stark naked. Outside the scoring box an old man with a beard began to pray to the thunder: "Bah! Bah! Bah!"

Crossley's eyes twitched proudly. "Yes," said he, pointing to the sky, "that's the sort of shout it is; that's the effect it has; but I can do better than that." Then his face fell suddenly and became childishly unhappy and anxious. "Oh dear God," he said, "he'll shout at me again, Crossley will. He'll freeze my marrow."

The rain was rattling on the tin roof so that I could hardly hear him. Another flash, another clap of thunder even louder than the first. "But that's only the second degree," he shouted in my ear; "it's the first that kills."

"Oh," he said. "Don't you understand?" He smiled foolishly. "I'm Richard now, and Crossley will kill me."

The naked man was running about brandishing a cricket stump in either hand and screaming: an ugly sight. "Bah! Bah! Bah!" prayed the old man, the rain spouting down his back from his uptilted hat.

"Nonsense," said I, "be a man, remember you're Crossley. You're a match for a dozen Richards. You played a game and lost, because Richard had the luck; but you still have the shout."

I was feeling rather mad myself. Then the Asylum doctor rushed into the scoring box, his flannels streaming wet, still wearing pads and batting gloves, his glasses gone; he had heard our voices raised, and tore Crossley's hands from mine. "To your dormitory at once, Crossley!" he ordered.

"I'll not go," said Crossley, proud again, "you miserable Snake and Apple Pie Man!"

The doctor seized him by his coat and tried to hustle him out.

Crossley flung him off, his eyes blazing with madness. "Get out," he said, "and leave me alone here or I'll shout. Do you hear? I'll shout. I'll kill the whole damn lot of you. I'll shout the Asylum down. I'll wither the grass. I'll shout." His face was distorted in terror. A red spot appeared on either cheek bone and spread over his face.

I put my fingers to my ears and ran out of the scoring box. I had run perhaps twenty yards, when an indescribable pang of fire spun me about and left me dazed and numbed. I escaped death somehow; I suppose that I am lucky, like the Richard of the story. But the lightning struck Crossley and the doctor dead.

Crossley's body was found rigid, the doctor's was crouched in a corner, his hands to his ears. Nobody could understand this because death had been instantaneous, and the doctor was not a man to stop his ears against thunder.

It makes a rather unsatisfactory end to the story to say that Rachel and Richard were the friends with whom I was staying—Crossley had described them most accurately—but that when I told them that a man called

Charles Crossley had been struck at the same time as their friend the doctor, they seemed to take Crossley's death casually by comparison with his. Richard looked blank; Rachel said: "Crossley? I think that was the man who called himself the Australian Illusionist and gave that wonderful conjuring show the other day. He had practically no apparatus but a black silk handkerchief. I liked his face so much. Oh, and Richard didn't like it at all."

"No, I couldn't stand the way he looked at you all the time," Richard said.

W. SOMERSET MAUGHAM

The Book-Bag

There must be many thousands of readers who have wished themselves, as I often have, at Maugham's side on board some small slow freighter, as it steams up a tropical river or into the harbor of a Pacific island. On the jetty, the Maugham characters are waiting: the cynical District Commissioner with the secret sorrow, the prim adulterous Married Lady, the handsome curly-haired callow Secretary, the drunken Doctor. They invite you to stay with them, they offer you honorary membership of their club, they are delighted to welcome you—for, now that you have arrived, their drama can begin.

There is a passage in Flaubert's novel *Sentimental Education:* "He traveled. He knew the melancholy of the steamboat; the cold awakening in the tent; the tedium of scenery and ruins; the bitterness of interrupted friendship." These words might well have been written about Maugham; for, oddly enough, his great charm as a traveling-companion is his boredom—or perhaps I should say his *air* of boredom, since, if he were really so bored, he would hardly make the effort of telling us his stories. Exotic place-names drop from his lips with the weariness of utter familiarity. About one character he says, "he was glad to settle down quietly at Apia for twelve months at least"; and you would think, from Maugham's tone, that he was speaking of some particularly dreary London suburb. Like Kipling, Maugham is an "old hand." He knows the ropes. He can tell you what to expect from any given situation. His information is pessimistic enough and yet, unlike Kipling's, it is strangely reassuring.

I have chosen *The Book-Bag* for several reasons other than the fact that it is less well known than it deserves to be. I like its leisurely, autobiographical opening which introduces us to Maugham himself and thereby greatly strengthens the credibility of the whole story. I admire it for its extraordinary narrative tact. I don't mean that I think reticence is *necessarily* a virtue; but you cannot help admiring such a classic demonstration of how to handle a "shocking" subject–incest–in an absolutely inoffensive manner, yet without sacrificing any of the shock. Notice how the nature of the situation is conveyed entirely by the violence of the reaction to it, not by any description of the situation itself. In other words–*because* Olive cares sufficiently to commit suicide when her brother Tim gets married, we know that she and her brother must have been lovers. Maugham does not need to elaborate; there is no other possible explanation.

I find the end of the story deeply moving in its quietness. It beautifully illustrates a quality in Maugham's writing which I have already mentioned –the quality of giving reassurance. When we are introduced to Mark Featherstone and Tim, the woman they have both loved has been dead for many years. Tim's wife has long since left him and gone back to England. (Ironically enough, she–the injured party–is the only unsympathetic character in this story.) The two men meet occasionally at the club and play cards, never speaking of the past. And that is how Life is, Maugham seems to say—one survives somehow, and it is, after all, not quite as bad as one might have expected.

To borrow one of those double negatives of which the Master is so fond—I am not disinclined to agree with him.

SOME PEOPLE READ FOR INSTRUCTION, WHICH IS PRAISE-worthy, and some for pleasure, which is innocent, but not a few read from habit, and I suppose that this is neither innocent nor praiseworthy. Of that lamentable company am I. Conversation after a time bores me, games tire me and my own thoughts, which we are told are the unfailing resource of a sensible man, have a tendency to run dry. Then I fly to my book as the opium-smoker to his pipe. I would sooner read the catalogue of the Army and Navy Stores or Bradshaw's Guide than nothing at all, and indeed I have spent many delightful hours over both these works. At one time I never went out without a second-hand bookseller's list in my pocket. I know no reading more fruity. Of course to read in this way is as reprehensible as doping, and I never cease to wonder at the impertinence of great readers who, because they are such, look down on the illiterate. From the standpoint of what eternity is it better to have read a thousand books than to have ploughed a million furrows? Let us admit that reading with us is just a drug that we cannot do without—who of this band does not know the restlessness that attacks him when he has been severed from reading too long, the apprehension and irritability, and the sigh of relief which the sight of a printed page extracts from him?—and so let us be no more vainglorious than the poor slaves of the hypodermic needle or the pint-pot.

And like the dope-fiend who cannot move from place to place without taking with him a plentiful supply of his deadly balm I never venture far without a sufficiency of reading matter. Books are so necessary to me that when in a railway train I have become aware that fellow-travellers have come away without a single one I have been seized with a veritable dismay. But when I am starting on a long journey the problem is formidable. I have learnt my lesson. Once, imprisoned by illness for three months in a hill-town in Java, I came to the end of all the books I had brought with me, and knowing no Dutch was obliged to buy the school-books from which intelligent Javanese, I suppose, acquired knowledge of French and German. So I read again after five and twenty years the frigid plays of Goethe, the fables of La Fontaine and the tragedies of the tender and exact Racine. I have the greatest admiration for Racine, but I admit that to read his plays one after the other requires a certain effort in a person who is suffering from colitis. Since then I have made a point of travelling with the largest sack made for carrying soiled linen and filling it to the brim with books to suit every possible occasion and every mood. It weighs a ton and strong porters reel under its weight. Customhouse officials look at it askance, but recoil from it with consternation when I give them my word that it contains nothing but books. Its inconvenience is that the particular work I suddenly hanker to read is always at the bottom and it is impossible for me to get it without emptying the book-bag's entire contents upon the floor. Except for this, however, I should perhaps never have heard the singular history of Olive Hardy.

I was wandering about Malaya, staying here and there, a week or two if there was a rest-house or a hotel, and a day or so if I was obliged to inflict myself on a planter or a District Officer whose hospitality I had no wish to abuse; and at the moment I happened to be at Penang. It is a pleasant little town, with a hotel that has always seemed to me very agreeable, but the stranger finds little to do there and time hung a trifle heavily on my hands. One morning I received a letter from a man I knew only by name. This was Mark Featherstone. He was Acting Resident, in the absence on leave of the Resident, at a place called Tenggarah. There was a sultan there and it appeared that a water festival of some sort was to take place which Featherstone thought would interest me. He said that he would be glad if I would come and stay with him for a few days. I wired to tell him that I should be delighted and next day took the train to Tenggarah. Featherstone met me at the station. He was a man of about thirty-five, I should think, tall and handsome, with fine eyes and a strong, stern face. He had a wiry black moustache and bushy eyebrows. He looked more like a soldier than a government official. He was very smart in white ducks, with a white topi, and he wore his clothes with elegance. He was a little shy, which seemed odd in a strapping fellow of resolute mien, but I surmised that this was only because he was unused to the society of that strange fish, a writer, and I hoped in a little to put him at his ease.

"My boys'll look after your barang," he said. "We'll go down to the club. Give them your keys and they'll unpack before we get back."

I told him that I had a good deal of luggage and thought it better to leave everything at the station but what I particularly wanted. He would not hear of it.

"It doesn't matter a bit. It'll be safer at my house. It's always better to have one's barang with one."

"All right."

I gave my keys and the ticket for my trunk and my book-bag to a Chinese boy who stood at my host's elbow. Outside the station a car was waiting for us and we stepped in.

"Do you play bridge?" asked Featherstone.

"I do."

"I thought most writers didn't."

"They don't," I said. "It's generally considered among authors a sign of deficient intelligence to play cards."

The club was a bungalow, pleasing but unpretentious; it had a large reading-room, a billiard-room with one table, and a small card-room. When we arrived it was empty but for one or two persons reading the English weeklies, and we walked through to the tennis courts where a couple of sets were being played. A number of people were sitting on the verandah, looking on, smoking and sipping long drinks. I was introduced to one or two of them. But the light was failing and soon the players could hardly see the ball. Featherstone asked one of the men I had been introduced to if he would like a rubber. He said he would. Featherstone looked about for a fourth. He caught sight of a man sitting a little by himself, paused for a second, and went up to him. The two exchanged a few words and then came towards us. We strolled in to the card-room. We had a very nice game. I did not pay much attention to the two men who made up the four. They stood me drinks, and I, a temporary member of the club, returned the compliment. The drinks were very small, quarter whiskies, and in the two hours we played each of us was able to show his openhandedness without an excessive consumption of alcohol. When the advancing hour suggested that the next rubber must be the last we changed from whisky to gin pahits. The rubber came to an end. Featherstone called for the book and the winnings and losings of each one of us were set down. One of the men got up.

"Well, I must be going," he said.

"Going back to the Estate?" asked Featherstone.

"Yes," he nodded. He turned to me. "Shall you be here tomorrow?"

"I hope so."

He went out of the room.

"I'll collect my mem and get along home to dinner," said the other.

"We might be going too," said Featherstone.

"I'm ready whenever you are," I replied.

We got into the car and drove to his house. It was a longish drive. In the darkness I could see nothing much, but presently I realised that we were going up a rather steep hill. We reached the Residency.

It had been an evening like any other, pleasant, but not at all exciting, and I had spent I don't know how many just like it. I did not expect it to leave any sort of impression on me.

Featherstone led me into his sitting-room. It looked comfortable, but it was a trifle ordinary. It had large basket arm-chairs covered with cretonne and on the walls were a great many framed photographs; the tables were littered with papers, magazines and official reports, with pipes, yellow tins of straight-cut cigarettes and pink tins of tobacco. In a row of shelves were untidily stacked a good many books, their bindings stained with damp and the ravages of white ants. Featherstone showed me my room and left me with the words:

"Shall you be ready for a gin pahit in ten minutes?"

"Easily," I said.

I had a bath and changed and went downstairs. Featherstone, ready before me, mixed our drink as he heard me clatter down the wooden staircase. We dined. We talked. The festival which I had been invited to see was the next day but one, but Featherstone told me he had arranged for me before that to be received by the Sultan.

"He's a jolly old boy," he said. "And the palace is a sight for sore eyes."

After dinner we talked a little more, Featherstone put on the gramophone, and we looked at the latest illustrated papers that had arrived from England. Then we went to bed. Featherstone came to my room to see that I had everything I wanted.

"I suppose you haven't any books with you," he said. "I haven't got a thing to read."

"Books?" I cried.

I pointed to my book-bag. It stood upright, bulging oddly, so that it looked like a humpbacked gnome somewhat the worse for liquor.

"Have you got books in there? I thought that was your dirty linen or a camp-bed or something. Is there anything you can lend me?"

"Look for yourself."

Featherstone's boys had unlocked the bag, but quailing before the sight that then discovered itself had done no more. I knew from long experience how to unpack it. I threw it over on its side, seized its leather bottom and, walking backwards, dragged the sack away from its contents. A river of books poured on to the floor. A look of stupefaction came upon Featherstone's face.

"You don't mean to say you travel with as many books as that? By George, what a snip."

He bent down and turning them over rapidly looked at the titles. There were books of all kinds. Volumes of verse, novels, philosophical works, critical studies (they say books about books are profitless, but they certainly make very pleasant reading), biographies, history; there were books to read when you were ill and books to read when your brain, all alert, craved for something to grapple with, there were books that you had always wanted to read, but in the hurry of life at home had never found time to, there were books to read at sea when you were meandering through narrow waters on a tramp steamer, and there were books for bad weather when your whole cabin creaked and you had to wedge yourself in your bunk in order not to fall out; there were books chosen solely for their length, which you took with you when on some expedition you had to travel light, and there were books you could read when you could read nothing else. Finally Featherstone picked out a life of Byron that had recently appeared.

"Hullo, what's this?" he said. "I read a review of it some time ago."

"I believe it's very good," I replied. "I haven't read it yet."

"May I take it? It'll do me for tonight at all events."

"Of course. Take anything you like."

"No, that's enough. Well, good-night. Breakfast at eight-thirty."

When I came down next morning the head boy told me that Featherstone, who had been at work since six, would be in shortly. While I waited for him I glanced at his shelves.

"I see you've got a grand library of books on bridge," I remarked as we sat down to breakfast.

"Yes, I get every one that comes out. I'm very keen on it."

"That fellow we were playing with yesterday plays a good game."

"Which? Hardy?"

"I don't know. Not the one who said he was going to collect his wife. The other."

"Yes, that was Hardy. That was why I asked him to play. He doesn't come to the club very often."

"I hope he will tonight."

"I wouldn't bank on it. He has an estate about thirty miles away. It's a longish ride to come just for a rubber of bridge."

"Is he married?"

"No. Well, yes. But his wife is in England."

"It must be awfully lonely for those men who live by themselves on those estates," I said.

"Oh, he's not so badly off as some. I don't think he much cares about seeing people. I think he'd be just as lonely in London."

There was something in the way Featherstone spoke that struck me as a little strange. His voice had what I can only describe as a shuttered tone. He seemed suddenly to have moved away from me. It was as though one were passing along a street at night and paused for a second to look in at a lighted window that showed a comfortable room and suddenly an invisible hand pulled down a blind. His eyes, which habitually met those of the person he was talking to with frankness, now avoided mine and I had a notion that it was not only my fancy that read in his face an expression of pain. It was drawn for a moment as it might be by a twinge of neuralgia. I could not think of anything to say and Featherstone did not speak. I was conscious that his thoughts, withdrawn from me and what we were about, were turned upon a subject unknown to me. Presently he gave a little sigh, very slight, but unmistakable, and seemed with a deliberate effort to pull himself together.

"I'm going down to the office immediately after breakfast," he said. "What are you going to do with yourself?"

"Oh, don't bother about me. I shall slack around. I'll stroll down and look at the town."

"There's not much to see."

"All the better. I'm fed up with sights."

I found that Featherstone's verandah gave me sufficient entertainment for the morning. It had one of the most enchanting views I had seen in the F.M.S. The Residency was built on the top of a hill and the garden was large and well-cared for. Great trees gave it almost the look of an English park. It had vast lawns and there Tamils, black and emaciated, were scything with deliberate and beautiful gestures. Beyond and below, the jungle grew thickly to the bank of a broad, winding and swiftly flowing river, and on the other side of this, as far as the eye could reach, stretched the wooded hills of Tenggarah. The contrast between the trim lawns, so strangely English, and the savage growth of the jungle beyond pleasantly titillated the fancy. I sat and read and smoked. It is my business to be curious about people and I asked myself how the peace of this scene, charged nevertheless with a tremulous and dark significance, affected Featherstone who lived with it. He knew it under every aspect: at dawn when the mist rising from the river shrouded it with a ghostly pall; in the splendour of noon; and at last when the shadowy gloaming crept softly out of the jungle, like an army making its way with caution in unknown country, and presently enveloped the green lawns and the great flowering trees and the flaunting cassias in the silent night. I wondered whether, unbeknownst to him, the tender and yet strangely sinister aspect of the scene, acting on his nerves and his loneliness, imbued him with some mystical quality so that the life he led, the life of the capable administrator, the sportsman and the good fellow, on occasion seemed to him not quite real. I smiled at my own fancies, for certainly the conversation we had had the night before had not indicated in him any stirrings of the soul. I had thought him quite nice. He had been at Oxford and was a member of a good London club. He seemed to attach a good deal of importance to social things. He was a gentleman and slightly conscious of the fact that he belonged to a better class than most of the Englishmen his life brought him in contact with. I gathered from the various silver pots that adorned his dining-room that he excelled in games. He played tennis and billiards. When he went on leave he hunted and, anxious to keep his weight down, he dieted carefully. He talked a good deal of what he would do when he retired. He hankered after the life of a country gentleman. A little house in Leicestershire, a couple of hunters and neighbours to play bridge with. He would have his pension and he had a little money of his own. But meanwhile he worked hard and did his work, if not brilliantly, certainly with competence. I have no doubt that he was looked upon by his superiors as a reliable officer. He was cut upon a pattern that I knew too well to find very interesting. He was like a novel that is careful, honest and efficient, yet a little ordinary, so that you seem to have read it all before, and you turn the pages listlessly knowing that it will never afford you a surprise or move you to excitement.

But human beings are incalculable and he is a fool who tells himself that he knows what a man is capable of.

In the afternoon Featherstone took me to see the Sultan. We were received by one of his sons, a shy, smiling youth who acted as his A.D.C. He was dressed in a neat blue suit, but round his waist he wore a sarong, white flowers on a yellow ground, on his head a red fez, and on his feet knobby American shoes. The palace, built in the Moorish style, was like a very big doll's house and it was painted bright yellow, which is the royal colour. We were led into a spacious room, furnished with the sort of furniture you would find in an English lodging-house at the seaside, but the chairs were covered with yellow silk. On the floor was a Brussels carpet and on the walls photographs in very grand gilt frames of the Sultan at various state functions. In a cabinet was a large collection of all kinds of fruit done entirely in crochet work. The Sultan came in with several attendants. He was a man of fifty, perhaps, short and stout, dressed in trousers and tunic of a large white and yellow check; round his middle he wore a very beautiful yellow sarong and on his head a white fez. He had large, handsome, friendly eyes. He gave us coffee to drink, sweet cakes to eat and cheroots to smoke. Conversation was not difficult, for he was affable, and he told me that he had never been to a theatre or played cards, for he was very religious, and he had four wives and twenty-four children. The only bar to the happiness of his life seemed to be that common decency obliged him to divide his time equally between his four wives. He said that an hour with one was a month and with another five minutes. I remarked that Professor Einstein—or was it Bergson?—had made similar observations upon time and indeed on this question had given the world much to ponder over. Presently we took our leave and the Sultan presented me with some beautiful white Malaccas.

In the evening we went to the club. One of the men we had played with the day before got up from his chair as we entered.

"Ready for a rubber?" he said.

"Where's our fourth?" I asked.

"Oh, there are several fellows here who'll be glad to play."

"What about that man we played with yesterday?" I had forgotten his name.

"Hardy? He's not here."

"It's not worth while waiting for him," said Featherstone. "He very seldom comes to the club. I was surprised to see him last night."

I did not know why I had the impression that behind the very ordinary words of these two men there was an odd sense of embarrassment. Hardy had made no impression on me and I did not even remember what he looked like. He was just a fourth at the bridge table. I had a feeling that they had something against him. It was no business of mine and I was quite content to play with a man who at that moment joined us. We certainly had a more cheerful game than before. A good deal of chaff passed from one side of the table to the other. We played less serious bridge. We laughed. I wondered if it was only that they were less shy of the stranger who had happened in upon them or if the presence of Hardy had caused in the other two a certain constraint. At half-past eight we broke up and Featherstone and I went back to dine at his house.

After dinner we lounged in arm-chairs and smoked cheroots. For some reason our conversation did not flow easily. I tried topic after topic, but could not get Featherstone to interest himself in any of them. I began to think that in the last twenty-four hours he had said all he had to say. I fell somewhat discouraged into silence. It prolonged itself and again, I did not know why, I had a faint sensation that it was charged with a significance that escaped me. I felt slightly uncomfortable. I had that queer feeling that one sometimes has when sitting in an empty room that one is not by oneself. Presently I was conscious that Featherstone was steadily looking at me. I was sitting by a lamp, but he was in shadow so that the play of his features was hidden from me. But he had very large brilliant eyes and in the half darkness they seemed to shine dimly. They were like new boot-buttons that caught a reflected light. I wondered why he looked at me like that. I gave him a glance and catching his eyes insistently fixed upon me faintly smiled.

"Interesting book that one you lent me last night," he said suddenly, and I could not help thinking his voice did not sound quite natural. The words issued from his lips as though they were pushed from behind.

"Oh, the Life of Byron?" I said breezily. "Have you read it already?"

"A good deal of it. I read till three."

"I've heard it's very well done. I'm not sure that Byron interests me so much as all that. There was so much in him that was so frightfully second-rate. It makes one rather uncomfortable."

"What do you think is the real truth of that story about him and his sister?"

"Augusta Leigh? I don't know very much about it. I've never read Astarte."

"Do you think they were really in love with one another?"

"I suppose so. Isn't it generally believed that she was the only woman he ever genuinely loved?"

"Can you understand it?"

"I can't really. It doesn't particularly shock me. It just seems to me very unnatural. Perhaps 'unnatural' isn't the right word. It's incomprehensible to me. I can't throw myself into the state of feeling in which such a thing seems possible. You know, that's how a writer gets to know the people he writes about, by standing himself in their shoes and feeling with their hearts."

I knew I did not make myself very clear, but I was trying to describe a sensation, an action of the subconscious, which from experience was perfectly familiar to me, but which no words I knew could precisely indicate. I went on.

"Of course she was only his half-sister, but just as habit kills love I should have thought habit would prevent its arising. When two persons have known one another all their lives and lived together in close contact I can't imagine how or why that sudden spark should flash that results in love. The probabilities are that they would be joined by mutual affection and I don't know anything that is more contrary to love than affection."

I could just see in the dimness the outline of a smile flicker for a moment on my host's heavy, and it seemed to me then, somewhat saturnine face.

"You only believe in love at first sight?"

"Well, I suppose I do, but with the proviso that people may have met twenty times before seeing one another. 'Seeing' has an active side and a passive one. Most people we run across mean so little to us that we never bestir ourselves to look at them. We just suffer the impression they make on us."

"Oh, but one's often heard of couples who've known one another for years and it's never occurred to one they cared two straws for each other and suddenly they go and get married. How do you explain that?"

"Well, if you're going to bully me into being logical and consistent, I should suggest that their love is of a different kind. After all, passion isn't the only reason for marriage. It may not even be the best one. Two people may marry because they're lonely or because they're good friends or for convenience' sake. Though I said that affection was the greatest enemy of love, I would never deny that it's a very good substitute. I'm not sure that a marriage founded on it isn't the happiest."

"What did you think of Tim Hardy?"

I was a little surprised at the sudden question, which seemed to have nothing to do with the subject of our conversation.

"I didn't think of him very much. He seemed quite nice. Why?"

"Did he seem to you just like everybody else?"

"Yes. Is there anything peculiar about him? If you'd told me that I'd have paid more attention to him."

"He's very quiet, isn't he? I suppose no one who knew nothing about him would give him a second thought."

I tried to remember what he looked like. The only thing that had struck me when we were playing cards was that he had fine hands. It passed idly through my mind that they were not the sort of hands I should have expected a planter to have. But why a planter should have different hands from anybody else I did not trouble to ask myself. His were somewhat large, but very well formed, with peculiarly long fingers, and the nails were of an admirable shape. They were virile and yet oddly sensitive hands. I noticed this and thought no more about it. But if you are a writer, instinct and the habit of years enable you to store up impressions that you are not aware of. Sometimes of course they do not correspond with the facts and a woman for example may remain in your subconsciousness as a dark, massive and ox-eyed creature when she is indeed rather small and of a nondescript colouring. But that is of no consequence. The impression may very well be more exact than the sober truth. And now, seeking to call up from the depths of me a picture of this man I had a feeling of some ambiguity. He was cleanshaven and his face, oval but not thin, seemed strangely pale under the tan of long exposure to the tropical sun. His features were vague. I did not know whether I remembered it or only imagined now that his rounded chin gave one the impression of a certain weakness. He had thick brown hair, just turning grey, and a long wisp fell down constantly over his forehead. He pushed it back with a gesture that had become habitual. His brown eyes were rather large and gentle, but perhaps a little sad; they had a melting softness which, I could imagine, might be very appealing.

After a pause Featherstone continued:

"It's rather strange that I should run across Tim Hardy here after all these years. But that's the way of the F.M.S. People move about and you find yourself in the same place as a man you'd known years before in another part of the country. I first knew Tim when he had an estate near Sibuku. Have you ever been there?"

"No. Where is it?"

"Oh, it's up north. Towards Siam. It wouldn't be worth your while to go. It's just like every other place in the F.M.S. But it was rather nice. It had a very jolly little club and there were some quite decent people. There was the schoolmaster and the head of the police, the doctor, the padre and the government engineer. The usual lot, you know. A few planters. Three or four women. I was A.D.O. It was one of my first jobs. Tim Hardy had an estate about twenty-five miles away. He lived there with his sister. They had a bit of money of their own and he'd bought the place. Rubber was pretty good then and he wasn't doing at all badly. We rather cottoned on to one another. Of course it's a toss-up with planters. Some of them are very good fellows, but they're not exactly . . ." he sought for a word or a phrase that did not sound snobbish. "Well, they're not the sort of people you'd be likely to meet at home. Tim and Olive were of one's own class, if you understand what I mean."

"Olive was the sister?"

"Yes. They'd had a rather unfortunate past. Their parents had separated when they were quite small, seven or eight, and the mother had taken Olive and the father had kept Tim. Tim went to Clifton, they were West Country people, and only came home for the holidays. His father was a retired naval man who lived at Fowey. But Olive went with her mother to Italy. She was educated in Florence; she spoke Italian perfectly and French too. For all those years Tim and Olive never saw one another once, but they used to write to one another regularly. They'd been very much attached when they were children. As far as I could understand, life when their people were living together had been rather stormy with all sorts of scenes and upsets, you know the sort of thing that happens when two people who are married don't get on together, and that had thrown them on their own resources. They were left a good deal to themselves. Then Mrs. Hardy died and Olive came home to England and went back to her father. She was eighteen then and Tim was seventeen. A year later the war broke out. Tim joined up and his father, who was over fifty, got some job at Portsmouth. I take it he had been a hard liver and a heavy drinker. He broke down before the end of the war and died after a lingering illness. They don't seem to have had any relations. They were the last of a rather old family; they had a fine old house in Dorsetshire that had belonged to them for a good many generations, but they had never been able to afford to live in it and it was always let. I remember seeing photographs of it. It was very much a gentleman's house, of grey stone and rather stately, with a coat of arms carved over the front door and mullioned windows. Their great ambition was to make enough money to be able to live in it. They used to talk about it a lot. They never spoke as though either of them would marry, but always as though it were a settled thing that they would remain together. It was rather funny considering how young they were."

"How old were they then?" I asked.

"Well, I suppose he was twenty-five or twenty-six and she was a year older. They were awfully kind to me when I first went up to Sibuku. They took a fancy to me at once. You see, we had more in common than most of the people there. I think they were glad of my company. They weren't particularly popular."

"Why not?" I asked.

"They were rather reserved and you couldn't help seeing that they liked their own society better than other people's. I don't know if you've noticed it, but that always seems to put people's backs up. They resent it somehow if they have a feeling that you can get along very well without them."

"It's tiresome, isn't it?" I said.

"It was rather a grievance to the other planters that Tim was his own master and had private means. They had to put up with an old Ford to get about in, but Tim had a real car. Tim and Olive were very nice when they came to the club and they played in the tennis tournaments and all that sort of thing, but you had an impression that they were always glad to get away again. They'd dine out with people and make themselves very pleasant, but it was pretty obvious that they'd just as soon have stayed at home. If you had any sense you couldn't blame them. I don't know if you've been much to planters' houses. They're a bit dreary. A lot of gimcrack furniture and silver ornaments and tiger skins. And the food's uneatable. But the Hardys had made their bungalow rather nice. There was nothing very grand in it; it was just easy and homelike and comfortable. Their living-room was like a drawing-room in an English country house. You felt that their things meant something to them and that they had had them a long time. It was a very jolly house to stay at. The bungalow was in the middle of the estate, but it was on the brow of a little hill and you looked right over the rubber trees to the sea in the distance. Olive took a lot of trouble with her garden and it was really topping. I never saw such a show of cannas. I used to go there for week-ends. It was only about half an hour's drive to the sea and we'd take our lunch with us and bathe and sail. Tim kept a small boat there. Those days were grand. I never knew one could enjoy oneself so much. It's a beautiful bit of coast and it was really extraordinarily romantic. Then in the evenings we'd play patience and chess or turn on the gramophone. The cooking was damned good too. It was a change from what one generally got. Olive had taught their cook to make all sorts of Italian dishes and we used to have great wallops of macaroni and risotto and gnocchi and things like that. I couldn't help envying them their life, it was so jolly and peaceful, and when they talked of what they'd do when they went back to England for good I used to tell them they'd always regret what they'd left.

" 'We've been very happy here,' " said Olive.

"She had a way of looking at Tim, with a slow, sidelong glance from under her long eyelashes, that was rather engaging.

"In their own house they were quite different from what they were when they went out. They were so easy and cordial. Everybody admitted that and I'm bound to say that people enjoyed going there. They often asked people over. They had the gift of making you feel at home. It was a very happy house, if you know what I mean. Of course no one could help seeing how attached they were to one another. And whatever people said about their being standoffish and self-centered, they were bound to be rather touched by the affection they had for one another. People said they couldn't have been more united if they were married, and when you saw how some couples got on you couldn't help thinking they made most marriages look rather like a washout. They seemed to think the same things at the same time. They had little private jokes that made them laugh like children. They were so charming with one another, so gay and happy, that really to stay with them was, well, a spiritual refreshment. I don't know what else you could call it. When you left them, after a couple of days at the bungalow, you felt that you'd absorbed some of their peace and their sober gaiety. It was as though your soul had been sluiced with cool clear water. You felt strangely purified."

It was singular to hear Featherstone talking in this exalted strain. He looked so spruce in his smart white coat, technically known as a bum-freezer, his moustache was so trim, his thick curly hair so carefully brushed, that his high-flown language made me a trifle uncomfortable. But I realised that he was trying to express in his clumsy way a very sincerely felt emotion.

"What was Olive Hardy like?" I asked.

"I'll show you. I've got quite a lot of snapshots."

He got up from his chair and going to a shelf brought me a large album. It was the usual thing, indifferent photographs of people in groups and unflattering likenesses of single figures. They were in bathing dress or in shorts or tennis things, generally with their faces all screwed up because the sun blinded them, or puckered by the distortion of laughter. I recognised Hardy, not much changed after ten years, with his wisp of hair hanging across his forehead. I remembered him better now that I saw the snapshots. In them he looked nice and fresh and young. He had an alertness of expression that was attractive and that I certainly had not noticed when I saw him. In his eyes was a sort of eagerness for life that danced and sparkled through the fading print. I glanced at the photographs of his sister. Her bathing dress showed that she had a good figure, well-developed, but slender; and her legs were long and slim.

"They look rather alike," I said.

"Yes, although she was a year older they might have been twins, they were so much alike. They both had the same oval face and that pale skin without any colour in the cheeks, and they both had those soft brown eyes, very liquid and appealing, so that you felt whatever they did you could never be angry with them. And they both had a sort of careless elegance that made them look charming whatever they wore and however untidy they were. He's lost that now, I suppose, but he certainly had it when I first knew him. They always rather reminded me of the brother and sister in Twelfth Night. You know whom I mean."

"Viola and Sebastian."

"They never seemed to belong quite to the present. There was something Elizabethan about them. I don't think it was only because I was very young then that I couldn't help feeling they were strangely romantic somehow. I could see them living in Illyria."

I gave one of the snapshots another glance.

"The girl looks as though she had a good deal more character than her brother," I remarked.

"She had. I don't know if you'd have called Olive beautiful, but she was awfully attractive. There was something poetic in her, a sort of lyrical quality as it were, that coloured her movements, her acts and everything about her. It seemed to exalt her above common cares. There was something so candid in her expression, so courageous and independent in her bearing, that—oh, I don't know, it made mere beauty just flat and dull."

"You speak as if you'd been in love with her," I interrupted.

"Of course I was. I should have thought you'd guessed that at once. I was frightfully in love with her."

"Was it love at first sight?" I smiled.

"Yes, I think it was, but I didn't know it for a month

or so. When it suddenly struck me that what I felt for her—I don't know how to explain it, it was a sort of shattering turmoil that affected every bit of me—that that was love, I knew I'd felt it all along. It was not only her looks, though they were awfully alluring, the smoothness of her pale skin and the way her hair fell over her forehead and the grave sweetness of her brown eyes, it was more than that; you had a sensation of well-being when you were with her, as though you could relax and be quite natural and needn't pretend to be anything you weren't. You felt she was incapable of meanness. It was impossible to think of her as envious of other people or catty. She seemed to have a natural generosity of soul. One could be silent with her for an hour at a time and yet feel that one had had a good time."

"A rare gift," I said.

"She was a wonderful companion. If you made a suggestion to do something she was always glad to fall in with it. She was the least exacting girl I ever knew. You could throw her over at the last minute and however disappointed she was it made no difference. Next time you saw her she was just as cordial and serene as ever."

"Why didn't you marry her?"

Featherstone's cheroot had gone out. He threw the stub away and deliberately lit another. He did not answer for a while. It may seem strange to persons who live in a highly civilised state that he should confide these intimate things to a stranger; it did not seem strange to me. I was used to it. People who live so desperately alone, in the remote places of the earth, find it a relief to tell someone whom in all probability they will never meet again the story that has burdened perhaps for years their waking thoughts and their dreams at night. And I have an inkling that the fact of your being a writer attracts their confidence. They feel that what they tell you will excite your interest in an impersonal way that makes it easier for them to discharge their souls. Besides, as we all know from our own experience, it is never unpleasant to talk about oneself.

"Why didn't you marry her?" I had asked him.

"I wanted to badly enough," Featherstone answered at length. "But I hesitated to ask her. Although she was always so nice to me and so easy to get on with, and we were such good friends, I always felt that there was something a little mysterious in her. Although she was so simple, so frank and natural, you never quite got over the feeling of an inner kernel of aloofness, as if deep in her heart she guarded, not a secret, but a sort of privacy of the soul that not a living person would ever be allowed to know. I don't know if I make myself clear."

"I think so."

"I put it down to her upbringing. They never talked of their mother, but somehow I got the impression that she was one of those neurotic, emotional women who wreck their own happiness and are a pest to everyone connected with them. I had a suspicion that she'd led rather a hectic life in Florence and it struck me that Olive owed her beautiful serenity to a disciplined effort of her own will and that her aloofness was a sort of citadel she'd built to protect herself from the knowledge of all sorts of shameful things. But of course that aloofness was awfully captivating. It was strangely exciting to think that if she loved you, and you were married to her, you would at last pierce right into the hidden heart of that mystery; and you felt that if you could share that with her it would be as it were a consummation of all you'd ever desired in your life. Heaven wouldn't be in it. You know, I felt about it just like Bluebeard's wife about the forbidden chamber in the castle. Every room was open to me, but I should never rest till I had gone into that last one that was locked against me."

My eye was caught by a chik-chak, a little brown house lizard with a large head, high up on the wall. It is a friendly little beast and it is good to see it in a house. It watched a fly. It was quite still. On a sudden it made a dart and then as the fly flew away fell back with a sort of jerk into a strange immobility.

"And there was another thing that made me hesitate. I couldn't bear the thought that if I proposed to her and she refused me she wouldn't let me come to the bungalow in the same old way. I should have hated that, I enjoyed going there so awfully. It made me so happy to be with her. But you know, sometimes one can't help oneself. I did ask her at last, but it was almost by accident. One evening, after dinner, when we were sitting on the verandah by ourselves, I took her hand. She withdrew it at once.

" 'Why did you do that?' I asked her.

" 'I don't very much like being touched,' she said. She turned her head a little and smiled. 'Are you hurt? You mustn't mind, it's just a funny feeling I have. I can't help it.'

" 'I wonder if it's ever occurred to you that I'm frightfully fond of you,' I said.

"I expect I was terribly awkward about it, but I'd never proposed to anyone before." Featherstone gave a little sound that was not quite a chuckle and not quite a sigh. "For the matter of that, I've never proposed to anyone since. She didn't say anything for a minute. Then she said:

" 'I'm very glad, but I don't think I want you to be anything more than that.'

" 'Why not?' I asked.

" 'I could never leave Tim.'

" 'But supposing he marries?'

" 'He never will.'

"I'd gone so far then that I thought I'd better go on. But my throat was so dry that I could hardly speak. I was shaking with nervousness.

" 'I'm frightfully in love with you, Olive. I want to marry you more than anything in the world.'

"She put her hand very gently on my arm. It was like a flower falling to the ground.

" 'No, dear, I can't,' she said.

"I was silent. It was difficult for me to say what I wanted to. I'm naturally rather shy. She was a girl. I couldn't very well tell her that it wasn't quite the same thing living with a husband and living with a brother. She was normal and healthy; she must want to have babies; it wasn't reasonable to starve her natural instincts. It was such a waste of her youth. But it was she who spoke first.

" 'Don't let's talk about this any more,' she said. 'D'you mind? It did strike me once or twice that perhaps you cared for me. Tim noticed it. I was sorry because I was afraid it would break up our friendship. I don't want it to do that, Mark. We do get on so well together, the three of us, and we have such jolly times. I don't know what we should do without you now.'

" 'I thought of that too,' I said.

" 'D'you think it need?' she asked me.

" 'My dear, I don't want it to,' I said. 'You must know how much I love coming here. I've never been so happy anywhere before!'

" 'You're not angry with me?'

" 'Why should I be? It's not your fault. It only means that you're not in love with me. If you were you wouldn't care a hang about Tim.'

" 'You are rather sweet,' she said.

"She put her arm round my neck and kissed me lightly on the cheek. I had a notion that in her mind it settled our relation. She adopted me as a second brother.

"A few weeks later Tim went back to England. The tenant of their house in Dorset was leaving and though there was another in the offing, he thought he ought to be on the spot to conduct negotiations. And he wanted some new machinery for the estate. He thought he'd get it at the same time. He didn't expect to be gone more than three months and Olive made up her mind not to go. She knew hardly anyone in England, and it was practically a foreign country to her, she didn't mind being left alone, and she wanted to look after the estate. Of course they could have put a manager in charge, but that wasn't the same thing. Rubber was falling and in case of accidents it was just as well that one or other of them should be there. I promised Tim I'd look after her and if she wanted me she could always call me up. My proposal hadn't changed anything. We carried on as though nothing had happened. I don't know whether she'd told Tim. He made no sign that he knew. Of course I loved her as much as ever, but I kept it to myself. I have a good deal of self-control, you know. I had a sort of feeling I hadn't a chance. I hoped eventually my love would change into something else and we could just be wonderful friends. It's funny, it never has, you know. I suppose I was hit too badly ever to get quite over it.

"She went down to Penang to see Tim off and when

she came back I met her at the station and drove her home. I couldn't very well stay at the bungalow while Tim was away, but I went over every Sunday and had tiffin and we'd go down to the sea and have a bathe. People tried to be kind to her and asked her to stay with them, but she wouldn't. She seldom left the estate. She had plenty to do. She read a lot. She was never bored. She seemed quite happy in her own company, and when she had visitors it was only from a sense of duty. She didn't want them to think her ungracious. But it was an effort and she told me she heaved a sigh of relief when she saw the last of them and could again enjoy without disturbance the peaceful loneliness of the bungalow. She was a very curious girl. It was strange that at her age she should be so indifferent to parties and the other small gaieties the station afforded. Spiritually, if you know what I mean, she was entirely self-supporting. I don't know how people found out that I was in love with her; I thought I'd never given myself away in anything, but I had hints here and there that they knew. I gathered they thought Olive hadn't gone home with her brother on my account. One woman, a Mrs. Sergison, the policeman's wife, actually asked me when they were going to be able to congratulate me. Of course I pretended I didn't know what she was talking about, but it didn't go down very well. I couldn't help being amused. I meant so little to Olive in that way that I really believe she'd entirely forgotten that I'd asked her to marry me. I can't say she was unkind to me, I don't think she could have been unkind to anyone; but she treated me with just the casualness with which a sister might treat a younger brother. She was two or three years older than I. She was always terribly glad to see me, but it never occurred to her to put herself out for me, she was almost amazingly intimate with me; but unconsciously, you know, as you might be with a person you'd known so well all your life that you never thought of putting on frills with him. I might not have been a man at all, but an old coat that she wore all the time because it was easy and comfortable and she didn't mind what she did in it. I should have been crazy not to see that she was a thousand miles away from loving me.

"Then one day, three or four weeks before Tim was due back, when I went to the bungalow I saw she'd been crying. I was startled. She was always so composed. I'd never seen her upset over anything.

" 'Hullo, what's the matter?' I said.

" 'Nothing.'

" 'Come off it, darling,' I said. 'What have you been crying about?'

"She tried to smile."

" 'I wish you hadn't got such sharp eyes,' she said. 'I think I'm being silly. I've just had a cable from Tim to say he's postponed his sailing.'

" 'Oh, my dear, I am sorry,' I said. 'You must be awfully disappointed.'

" 'I've been counting the days. I want him back so badly.'

" 'Does he say why he's postponing?' I asked.

" 'No, he says he's writing. I'll show you the cable.'

"I saw that she was very nervous. Her slow quiet eyes were filled with apprehension and there was a little frown of anxiety between her brows. She went into her bedroom and in a moment came back with the cable. I felt that she was watching me anxiously as I read. So far as I remember it ran: *Darling, I cannot sail on the seventh after all. Please forgive me. Am writing fully. Fondest love. Tim.*

" 'Well, perhaps the machinery he wanted isn't ready and he can't bring himself to sail without it,' I said.

" 'What could it matter if it came by a later ship? Anyhow, it'll be hung up at Penang.'

" 'It may be something about the house.'

" 'If it is why doesn't he say so? He must know how frightfully anxious I am.'

" 'It wouldn't occur to him,' I said. 'After all, when you're away you don't realise that the people you've left behind don't know something that you take as a matter of course.'

"She smiled again, but now more happily.

" 'I daresay you're right. In point of fact Tim is a little like that. He's always been rather slack and casual. I daresay I've been making a mountain out of a molehill. I must just wait patiently for his letter.'

"Olive was a girl with a lot of self-control and I saw her by an effort of will pull herself together. The little line between her eyebrows vanished and she was once more her serene, smiling and kindly self. She was always gentle: that day she had a mildness so heavenly that it was shattering. But for the rest of the time I could see that she kept her restlessness in check only by the deliberate exercise of her common sense. It was as though she had a foreboding of ill. I was with her the day before the mail was due. Her anxiety was all the more pitiful to see because she took such pains to hide it. I was always busy on mail day, but I promised to go up to the estate later on and hear the news. I was just thinking of starting when Hardy's seis came along in the car with a message from the amah asking me to go at once to her mistress. The amah was a decent, elderly woman to whom I had given a dollar or two and said that if anything went wrong on the estate she was to let me know at once. I jumped into my car. When I arrived I found the amah waiting for me on the steps.

" 'A letter came this morning,' she said.

"I interrupted her. I ran up the steps. The sitting-room was empty.

" 'Olive,' I called.

"I went into the passage and suddenly I heard a sound that froze my heart. The amah had followed me and now she opened the door to Olive's room. The sound I had heard was the sound of Olive crying. I went in. She was lying on her bed, on her face, and her sobs shook her from head to foot. I put my hand on her shoulder.

" 'Olive, what is it?' I asked.

" 'Who's that?' she cried. She sprang to her feet suddenly, as though she were scared out of her wits. And then: 'Oh, it's you,' she said. She stood in front of me, with her head thrown back and her eyes closed, and the tears streamed from them. It was dreadful. 'Tim's married,' she gasped, and her face screwed up in a sort of grimace of pain.

"I must admit that for one moment I had a thrill of exultation, it was like a little electric shock tingling through my heart; it struck me that now I had a chance, she might be willing to marry me; I know it was terribly selfish of me; you see, the news had taken me by surprise; but it was only for a moment, after that I was melted by her awful distress and the only thing I felt was deep sorrow because she was unhappy. I put my arm round her waist.

" 'Oh, my dear, I'm so sorry,' I said. 'Don't stay here. Come into the sitting-room and sit down and we'll talk about it. Let me give you something to drink.'

"She let me lead her into the next room and we sat

down on the sofa. I told the amah to fetch the whisky and syphon and I mixed her a good strong stengah and made her drink a little. I took her in my arms and rested her head on my shoulder. She let me do what I liked with her. The great tears streamed down her poor face.

" 'How could he?' she moaned. 'How could he?'

" 'My darling,' I said, 'it was bound to happen sooner or later. He's a young man. How could you expect him never to marry? It's only natural.'

" 'No, no, no,' she gasped.

"Tight-clenched in her hand I saw that she had a letter and I guessed that it was Tim's.

" 'What does he say?' I asked.

"She gave a frightened movement and clutched the letter to her heart as though she thought I would take it from her.

" 'He says he couldn't help himself. He says he had to. What does it mean?'

" 'Well, you know, in his way he's just as attractive as you are. He has so much charm. I suppose he just fell madly in love with some girl and she with him.'

" 'He's so weak,' she moaned.

" 'Are they coming out?' I asked.

" 'They sailed yesterday. He says it won't make any difference. He's insane. How *can* I stay here?'

"She began to cry hysterically. It was torture to see that girl, usually so calm, utterly shattered by her emotion. I had always felt that her lovely serenity masked a capacity for deep feeling. But the abandon of her distress simply broke me up. I held her in my arms and kissed her, her eyes and her wet cheek and her hair. I don't think she knew what I was doing. I was hardly conscious of it myself. I was so deeply moved.

" 'What shall I do?' she wailed.

" 'Why won't you marry me?' I said.

"She tried to withdraw herself from me, but I wouldn't let her go.

" 'After all, it would be a way out,' I said.

" 'How can I marry you?' she moaned. 'I'm years older than you are.'

" 'Oh, what nonsense, two or three. What do I care?'

" 'No, no.'

" 'Why not?' I said.

" 'I don't love you,' she said.

" 'What does that matter? I love you.'

"I don't know what I said. I told her that I'd try to make her happy. I said I'd never ask anything from her but what she was prepared to give me. I talked and talked. I tried to make her see reason. I felt that she didn't want to stay there, in the same place as Tim, and I told her that I'd be moved soon to some other district. I thought that might tempt her. She couldn't deny that we'd always got on awfully well together. After a time she did seem to grow a little quieter. I had a feeling that she was listening to me. I had even a sort of feeling that she knew that she was lying in my arms and that it comforted her. I made her drink a drop more whisky. I gave her a cigarette. At last I thought I might be just mildly facetious.

" 'You know, I'm not a bad sort really,' I said. 'You might do worse.'

" 'You don't know me,' she said. 'You know nothing whatever about me.'

" 'I'm capable of learning,' I said.

"She smiled a little.

" 'You're awfully kind, Mark,' she said.

" 'Say yes, Olive,' I begged.

"She gave a deep sigh. For a long time she stared at

the ground. But she did not move and I felt the softness of her body in my arms. I waited. I was frightfully nervous and the minutes seemed endless.

" 'All right,' she said at last, as though she were not conscious that any time had passed between my prayer and her answer.

"I was so moved that I had nothing to say. But when I wanted to kiss her lips, she turned her face away, and wouldn't let me. I wanted us to be married at once, but she was quite firm that she wouldn't. She insisted on waiting till Tim came back. You know how sometimes you see so clearly in people's thoughts that you're more certain of them than if they'd spoken them; I saw that she couldn't quite believe that what Tim had written was true and that she had a sort of miserable hope that it was all a mistake and he wasn't married after all. It gave me a pang, but I loved her so much, I just bore it. I was willing to bear anything. I adored her. She wouldn't even let me tell anyone that we were engaged. She made me promise not to say a word till Tim's return. She said she couldn't bear the thought of the congratulations and all that. She wouldn't even let me make any announcement of Tim's marriage. She was obstinate about it. I had a notion that she felt if the fact were spread about it gave it a certainty that she didn't want it to have.

"But the matter was taken out of her hands. News travels mysteriously in the East. I don't know what Olive had said in the amah's hearing when first she received the news of Tim's marriage; anyhow, the Hardys' seis told the Sergisons' and Mrs. Sergison attacked me the next time I went into the club.

" 'I hear Tim Hardy's married,' she said.

" 'Oh?' I answered, unwilling to commit myself.

"She smiled at my blank face, and told me that her amah having told her the rumour she had rung up Olive and asked her if it was true. Olive's answer had been rather odd. She had not exactly confirmed it, but said that she had received a letter from Tim telling her he was married.

" 'She's a strange girl,' said Mrs. Sergison. 'When I asked her for details she said she had none to give and when I said: "Aren't you thrilled?" she didn't answer.'

" 'Olive's devoted to Tim, Mrs. Sergison,' I said. 'His marriage has naturally been a shock to her. She knows nothing about Tim's wife. She's nervous about her.'

" 'And when are you two going to be married?' she asked me abruptly.

" 'What an embarrassing question!' I said, trying to laugh it off.

"She looked at me shrewdly.

" 'Will you give me your word of honour that you're not engaged to her?'

"I didn't like to tell her a deliberate lie, nor to ask her to mind her own business, and I'd promised Olive faithfully that I would say nothing till Tim got back. I hedged.

" 'Mrs. Sergison,' I said, 'when there's anything to tell I promise that you'll be the first person to hear it. All I can say to you now is that I do want to marry Olive more than anything in the world.'

" 'I'm very glad that Tim's married,' she answered. 'And I hope she'll marry you very soon. It was a morbid and unhealthy life that they led up there, those two, they kept far too much to themselves and they were far too much absorbed in one another.'

"I saw Olive practically every day. I felt that she didn't want me to make love to her, and I contented myself with kissing her when I came and when I went. She was very nice to me, kindly and thoughtful; I knew she was glad to see me and sorry when it was time for me to go. Ordinarily, she was apt to fall into silence, but during this time she talked more than I had ever heard her talk before. But never of the future and never of Tim and his wife. She told me a lot about her life in Florence with her mother. She had led a strange lonely life, mostly with servants and governesses, while her mother, I suspected, engaged in one affair after another with vague Italian counts and Russian princes. I guessed that by the time she was fourteen there wasn't much she didn't know. It was natural for her to be quite unconventional: in the only world she knew till she was eighteen conventions weren't mentioned because they didn't exist. Gradually, Olive seemed to regain her serenity and I should have thought that she was beginning to accustom herself to the thought of Tim's marriage if it hadn't been that I couldn't but notice how pale and tired she looked. I made up my mind that the moment he arrived I'd press her to marry me at once. I could get short leave whenever I asked for it, and by the time that was up I thought I could manage a transfer to some other post. What she wanted was change of air and fresh scenes.

"We knew, of course, within a day when Tim's ship would reach Penang, but it was a question whether she'd get in soon enough for him to catch the train and I wrote to the P. & O. agent asking him to telegraph as soon as he had definite news. When I got the wire and took it up to Olive I found that she'd just received one from Tim. The ship had docked early and he was arriving next day. The train was supposed to get in at eight o'clock in the morning, but it was liable to be anything from one to six hours late, and I bore with me an invitation from Mrs. Sergison asking Olive to come back with me to stay the night with her so that she would be on the spot and need not go to the station till the news came through that the train was coming.

"I was immensely relieved. I thought that when the blow at last fell Olive wouldn't feel it so much. She had worked herself up into such a state that I couldn't help thinking that she must have a reaction now. She might take a fancy to her sister-in-law. There was no reason why they shouldn't all three get on very well together. To my surprise Olive said she wasn't coming down to the station to meet them.

" 'They'll be awfully disappointed,' I said.

" 'I'd rather wait here,' she answered. She smiled a little. 'Don't argue with me, Mark, I've quite made up my mind.'

" 'I've ordered breakfast in my house,' I said.

" 'That's all right. You meet them and take them to your house and give them breakfast, and then they can come along here afterwards. Of course I'll send the car down.'

" 'I don't suppose they'll want to breakfast if you're not there,' I said.

" 'Oh, I'm sure they will. If the train gets in on time they wouldn't have thought of breakfasting before it arrived and they'll be hungry. They won't want to take this long drive without anything to eat.'

"I was puzzled. She had been looking forward so intensely to Tim's coming, it seemed strange that she should want to wait all by herself while the rest of us were having a jolly breakfast. I suppose she was nervous and wanted to delay as long as possible meeting the strange woman who had come to take her place. It seemed unreasonable. I couldn't see that an hour sooner or an hour later could make any difference, but I knew women were funny, and anyhow I felt Olive wasn't in the mood for me to press it.

" 'Telephone when you're starting so that I shall know when to expect you,' she said.

" 'All right,' I said, 'but you know I shan't be able to come with them. It's my day for going to Lahad.'

"This was a town that I had to go to once a week to take cases. It was a good way off and one had to ferry across a river, which took some time, so that I never got back till late. There were a few Europeans there and a club. I generally had to go on there for a bit to be sociable and see that things were getting along all right.

" 'Besides,' I added, 'with Tim bringing his wife home for the first time I don't suppose he'll want me about. But if you'd like to ask me to dinner I'll be glad to come to that.'

"Olive smiled.

" 'I don't think it'll be my place to issue any more invitations, will it?' she said. 'You must ask the bride.'

"She said this so lightly that my heart leaped. I had a feeling that at last she had made up her mind to accept the altered circumstances and, what was more, was accepting them with cheerfulness. She asked me to stay to dinner. Generally I left about eight and dined at home. She was very sweet, almost tender, and I was happier than I'd been for weeks. I had never been more desperately in love with her. I had a couple of gin pahits and I think I was in rather good form at dinner. I know I made her laugh. I felt that at last she was casting away the load of misery that had oppressed her. That was why I didn't let myself be very much disturbed by what happened at the end.

" 'Don't you think it's about time you were leaving a presumably maiden lady?' she said.

"She spoke in a manner that was so quietly gay that I answered without hesitation:

" 'Oh, my dear, if you think you've got a shred of reputation left you deceive yourself. You're surely not under the impression that the ladies of Sibuku don't know that I've been coming to see you every day for a month. The general feeling is that if we're not married it's high time we were. Don't you think it would be just as well if I broke it to them that we're engaged?'

" 'Oh, Mark, you mustn't take our engagement very seriously,' she said.

"I laughed.

" 'How else do you expect me to take it? It is serious.'

"She shook her head a little.

" 'No. I was upset and hysterical that day. You were being very sweet to me. I said yes because I was too miserable to say no. But now I've had time to collect myself. Don't think me unkind. I made a mistake. I've been very much to blame. You must forgive me.'

" 'Oh, darling, you're talking nonsense. You've got nothing against me.'

"She looked at me steadily. She was quite calm. She had even a little smile at the back of her eyes.

" 'I can't marry you. I can't marry anyone. It was absurd of me ever to think I could.'

"I didn't answer at once. She was in a queer state and I thought it better not to insist.

" 'I suppose I can't drag you to the altar by main force,' I said.

"I held out my hand and she gave me hers. I put my arm round her, and she made no attempt to withdraw. She suffered me to kiss her as usual on her cheek.

"Next morning I met the train. For once in a way it was punctual. Tim waved to me as his carriage passed the place where I was standing, and by the time I had walked up he had already jumped out and was handing down his wife. He grasped my hand warmly.

" 'Where's Olive?' he said, with a glance along the platform. 'This is Sally.'

"I shook hands with her and at the same time explained why Olive was not there.

" 'It was frightfully early, wasn't it?' said Mrs. Hardy.

"I told them that the plan was for them to come and have a bit of breakfast at my house and then drive home.

" 'I'd love a bath,' said Mrs. Hardy.

" 'You shall have one,' I said.

"She was really an extremely pretty little thing, very fair, with enormous blue eyes and a lovely little straight nose. Her skin, all milk and roses, was exquisite. A little of the chorus girl type, of course, and you may happen to think that rather namby-pamby, but in that style she was enchanting. We drove to my house, they both had a bath and Tim a shave; I just had two minutes alone with him. He asked me how Olive had taken his marriage. I told him she'd been upset.

" 'I was afraid so,' he said, frowning a little. He gave a short sigh. 'I couldn't do anything else.'

"I didn't understand what he meant. At that moment Mrs. Hardy joined us and slipped her arm through her husband's. He took her hand in his and gently pressed it. He gave her a look that had in it something pleased and humorously affectionate, as though he didn't take her quite seriously, but enjoyed his sense of proprietorship and was proud of her beauty. She really was lovely. She was not at all shy, she asked me to call her Sally before we'd known one another ten minutes, and she was quick in the uptake. Of course, just then she was excited at arriving. She'd never been East and everything thrilled her. It was quite obvious that she was head over heels in love with Tim. Her eyes never left him and she hung on his words. We had a jolly breakfast and then we parted. They got into their car to go home and I into mine to go to Lahad. I promised to go straight to the estate from there and in point of fact it was out of my way to pass by my house. I took a change with me. I didn't see why Olive shouldn't like Sally very much, she was frank and gay, and ingenuous; she was extremely young, she couldn't have been more than nineteen, and her wonderful prettiness couldn't fail to appeal to Olive. I was just as glad to have had a reasonable excuse to leave the three of them by themselves for the day, but as I started out from Lahad I had a notion that by the time I arrived they would all be pleased to see me. I drove up to the bungalow and blew my horn two or three times, expecting someone to appear. Not a soul. The place was in total darkness. I was surprised. It was absolutely silent. I couldn't make it out. They must be in. Very odd, I thought. I waited a moment, then got out of the car and walked up the steps. At the top of them I stumbled over something. I swore and bent down to see what it was; it had felt like a body. There was a cry and I saw it was the amah. She shrank back cowering as I touched her and broke into loud wails.

" 'What the hell's the matter?' I cried, and then I felt a hand on my arm and heard a voice. Tuan, Tuan. I turned and in the darkness recognised Tim's head boy. He began to speak in little frightened gasps. I listened to him with horror. What he told me was unspeakable.

I pushed him aside and rushed into the house. The sitting-room was dark. I turned on the light. The first thing I saw was Sally huddled up in an arm-chair. She was startled by my sudden appearance and cried out. I could hardly speak. I asked her if it was true. When she told me it was I felt the room suddenly going round and round me. I had to sit down. As the car that bore Tim and Sally drove up the road that led to the house and Tim sounded the Klaxon to announce their arrival and the boys and the amah ran out to greet them there was the sound of a shot. They ran to Olive's room and found her lying in front of the looking-glass in a pool of blood. She had shot herself with Tim's revolver.

" 'Is she dead?' I said.

" 'No, they sent for the doctor, and he took her to the hospital.'

"I hardly knew what I was doing. I didn't even trouble to tell Sally where I was going. I got up and staggered to the door. I got into the car and told my seis to drive like hell to the hospital. I rushed in. I asked where she was. They tried to bar my way, but I pushed them aside. I knew where the private rooms were. Someone clung to my arm, but I shook him off. I vaguely understood that the doctor had given instructions that no one was to go into the room. I didn't care about that. There was an orderly at the door; he put out his arm to prevent me from passing. I swore at him and told him to get out of my way. I suppose I made a row, I was beside myself; the door was opened and the doctor came out.

" 'Who's making all this noise?' he said. 'Oh, it's you. What do you want?'

" 'Is she dead?' I asked.

" 'No. But she's unconscious. She never regained consciousness. It's only a matter of an hour or two.'

" 'I want to see her.'

" 'You can't.'

" 'I'm engaged to her.'

" 'You?' he cried, and even at that moment I was aware that he looked at me strangely. 'That's all the more reason.'

"I didn't know what he meant. I was stupid with horror.

" 'Surely you can do something to save her,' I cried.

"He shook his head.

" 'If you saw her you wouldn't wish it,' he said.

"I stared at him aghast. In the silence I heard a man's convulsive sobbing.

" 'Who's that?' I asked.

" 'Her brother.'

"Then I felt a hand on my arm. I looked round and saw it was Mrs. Sergison.

" 'My poor boy,' she said. 'I'm so sorry for you.'

" 'What on earth made her do it?' I groaned.

" 'Come away, my dear,' said Mrs. Sergison. 'You can do no good here.'

" 'No, I must stay,' I said.

" 'Well, go and sit in my room,' said the doctor.

"I was so broken that I let Mrs. Sergison take me by the arm and lead me into the doctor's private room. She made me sit down. I couldn't bring myself to realise that it was true. I thought it was a horrible nightmare from which I must awake. I don't know how long we sat there. Three hours. Four hours. At last the doctor came in.

" 'It's all over,' he said.

"Then I couldn't help myself, I began to cry. I didn't

care what they thought of me. I was so frightfully unhappy.

"We buried her next day.

"Mrs. Sergison came back to my house and sat with me for a while. She wanted me to go to the club with her. I hadn't the heart. She was very kind, but I was glad when she left me by myself. I tried to read, but the words meant nothing to me. I felt dead inside. My boy came in and turned on the lights. My head was aching like mad. Then he came back and said that a lady wished to see me. I asked who it was. He wasn't quite sure, but he thought it must be the new wife of the tuan at Putatan. I couldn't imagine what she wanted. I got up and went to the door. He was right. It was Sally. I asked her to come in. I noticed that she was deathly white. I felt sorry for her. It was a frightful experience for a girl of that age and for a bride a miserable homecoming. She sat down. She was very nervous. I tried to put her at her ease by saying conventional things. She made me very uncomfortable because she stared at me with those enormous blue eyes of hers, and they were simply ghastly with horror. She interrupted me suddenly.

" 'You're the only person here I know,' she said. 'I had to come to you. I want you to get me away from here.'

"I was dumbfounded.

" 'What *do* you mean?' I said.

" 'I don't want you to ask me any questions. I just want you to get me away. At once. I want to go back to England!'

" 'But you can't leave Tim like that just now,' I said. 'My dear, you must pull yourself together. I know it's been awful for you. But think of Tim. I mean, he'll be miserable. If you have any love for him the least you can do is to try and make him a little less unhappy.'

" 'Oh, you don't know,' she cried. 'I can't tell you. It's too horrible. I beseech you to help me. If there's a train tonight let me get on it. If I can only get to Penang I can get a ship. I can't stay in this place another night. I shall go mad.'

"I was absolutely bewildered.

" 'Does Tim know?' I asked her.

" 'I haven't seen Tim since last night. I'll never see him again. I'd rather die.'

"I wanted to gain a little time.

" 'But how can you go without your things? Have you got any luggage?'

" 'What does that matter?' she cried impatiently. 'I've got what I want for the journey.'

" 'Have you any money?'

" 'Enough. Is there a train tonight?'

" 'Yes,' I said. 'It's due just after midnight.'

" 'Thank God. Will you arrange everything? Can I stay here till then?'

" 'You're putting me in a frightful position,' I said. 'I don't know what to do for the best. You know, it's an awfully serious step you're taking.'

" 'If you knew everything you'd know it was the only possible thing to do.'

" 'It'll create an awful scandal here. I don't know what people'll say. Have you thought of the effect on Tim?' I was worried and unhappy. 'God knows I don't want to interfere in what isn't my business. But if you want me to help you I ought to know enough to feel justified in doing so. You must tell me what's happened.'

" 'I can't. I can only tell you that I know everything.'

"She hid her face with her hands and shuddered. Then she gave herself a shake as though she were recoiling from some frightful sight.

" 'He had no right to marry me. It was monstrous.'

"And as she spoke her voice rose shrill and piercing. I was afraid she was going to have an attack of hysterics. Her pretty doll-like face was terrified and her eyes stared as though she could never close them again.

" 'Don't you love him any more?' I asked.

" 'After that?'

" 'What will you do if I refuse to help you?' I said.

" 'I suppose there's a clergyman here or a doctor. You can't refuse to take me to one of them.'

" 'How did you get here?'

" 'The head boy drove me. He got a car from somewhere.'

" 'Does Tim know you've gone?'

" 'I left a letter for him.'

" 'He'll know you're here.'

" 'He won't try to stop me. I promise you that. He daren't. For God's sake don't you try either. I tell you I shall go mad if I stay here another night.'

"I sighed. After all she was of an age to decide for herself."

I, the writer of this, hadn't spoken for a long time.

"Did you know what she meant?" I asked Featherstone.

He gave me a long, haggard look.

"There was only one thing she could mean. It was unspeakable. Yes, I knew all right. It explained everything. Poor Olive. Poor sweet. I suppose it was unreasonable of me, at that moment I only felt a horror of that little pretty fair-haired thing with her terrified eyes. I hated her. I didn't say anything for a while.

Then I told her I'd do as she wished. She didn't even say thank you. I think she knew what I felt about her. When it was dinner time I made her eat something and then she asked me if there was a room she could go and lie down in till it was time to go to the station. I showed her into my spare room and left her. I sat in the sitting-room and waited. My God, I don't think the time has ever passed so slowly for me. I thought twelve would never strike. I rang up the station and was told the train wouldn't be in till nearly two. At midnight she came back to the sitting-room and we sat there for an hour and a half. We had nothing to say to one another and we didn't speak. Then I took her to the station and put her on the train."

"Was there an awful scandal?"

Featherstone frowned.

"I don't know. I applied for short leave. After that I was moved to another post. I heard that Tim had sold his estate and bought another. But I didn't know where. It was a shock to me at first when I found him here."

Featherstone, getting up, went over to a table and mixed himself a whisky and soda. In the silence that fell now I heard the monotonous chorus of the croaking frogs. And suddenly the bird that is known as the fever-bird, perched in a tree close to the house, began to call. First, three notes in a descending, chromatic scale, then five, then four. The varying notes of the scale succeeded one another with maddening persistence. One was compelled to listen and to count them, and because one did not know how many there would be it tortured one's nerves.

"Blast that bird," said Featherstone. "That means no sleep for me tonight."

V. S. PRITCHETT

Sense of Humour

V. S. Pritchett was born in 1900. A biographical note on him (in the second [1936] volume of John Lehmann's *New Writing*, to which he had contributed this story) says, with intriguing brevity: "He first earned his living in the leather and photography businesses. He then went to France where he sold feathers and theatre tickets." Pritchett has published several novels and short stories; and today he is one of the best known English literary critics.

I have chosen *Sense of Humour* because it so vividly evokes for me the atmosphere of middle-class provincial England—as it was in the 'thirties and as I believe it still is, essentially, at the present time. A couple of clues—the place-names and a reference to a moor—hint to me that the scene is set in Yorkshire; but it could be anywhere in the Midlands. And there are, alas, few corners of the entire island still immune from that disease of quaintness which creates Olde Tea Shoppes and substitutes K's for hard C's—as in the "Kounty Garage" which Pritchett mentions.

In the traveling-salesman who narrates this story, you can recognize a type that seems almost more American than English. One may argue, however, that this type first emerged in England, as an offspring of the Industrial Revolution, and that its shrewd spirit of enterprise impelled many of its members to emigrate to the States and reproduce themselves there. It is not a pleasant type, especially when we see it in action to get what it wants—blandly displaying its smug, cynical opportunism. Pritchett shows how the fittest survive and inherit the earth, aided by a "sense of humor" and a sly shameless know-how which relentlessly drives the weaker opponent to the wall with a wisecrack. Colin, the loser, has no sense of humor, no glamour, no prudence in money matters—only the negative virtue of not being utterly corrupt. Ineffectual in death as in life, he tags along behind Arthur and his girl. But this precious pair—unlike the relatively naïve Macbeths—are not in the least afraid of the ghost of their victim. Indeed, with a sentimentality that marks the true monsters, they adopt it as one of the family.

Next to *Mary Postgate,* this is easily the most shocking story in my book.

IT STARTED ONE SATURDAY. I WAS WORKING NEW GROUND and I decided I'd stay at the hotel the weekend and put in an appearance at church.

"All alone?" asked the girl at the cash desk.

It had been raining since ten o'clock.

"Mr. Good has gone," she said. "And Mr. Straker. He usually stays with us. But he's gone."

"That's where they make their mistake," I said. "They think they know everything because they've been on the road all their lives."

"You're a stranger here, aren't you?" she said.

"I am," I said. "And so are you."

"How do you know that?"

"Obvious," I said. "Way you speak."

"Let's have a light," she said.

"So's I can see you," I said.

That was how it started. The rain was pouring down on the glass roof of the office.

She'd a cup of tea steaming on the register. I said I'd have one, too. What's it going to be and I'll tell them, she said, but I said just a cup of tea.

"I'm T.T.," I said. "Too many soakers on the road as it is."

I was staying there the weekend so as to be sharp on the job on Monday morning. What's more it pays in these small towns to turn up at church on Sundays, Presbyterians in the morning, Methodists in the evening. Say "Good morning" and "Good evening" to them. "Ah!" they say. "Churchgoer! Pleased to see that! T.T., too." Makes them have a second look at your lines in the morning. "Did you like our service, Mr.—er—er?" "Humphrey's my name." "Mr. Humphrey." See? It pays.

"Come into the office, Mr. Humphrey," she said, bringing me a cup. "Listen to that rain."

I went inside.

"Sugar?" she said.

"Three," I said. We settled to a very pleasant chat. She told me all about herself, and we got on next to families.

"My father was on the railway," she said.

" 'The engine gave a squeal,' " I said. " 'The driver took out his pocket-knife and scraped him off the wheel.' "

"That's it," she said. "And what is your father's business? You said he had a business."

"Undertaker," I said.

"Undertaker?" she said.

"Why not?" I said. "Good business. Seasonable like everything else. High-class undertaker," I said.

She was looking at me all the time wondering what to say, and suddenly she went into fits of laughter.

"Undertaker," she said, covering her face with her hands and went on laughing.

"Here," I said, "what's up?"

"Undertaker!" She laughed and laughed. Struck me as being a pretty thin joke.

"Don't mind me," she said. "I'm Irish."

"Oh, I see," I said. "That's it, is it? Got a sense of humour."

Then the bell rang and a woman called out "Muriel! Muriel!" and there was a motor bike making a row at the front door.

"All right," the girl called out. "Excuse me a moment, Mr. Humphrey," she said. "Don't think me rude. That's my boy friend. He wants the bird turning up like this."

She went out, but there was her boy friend looking over the window ledge into the office. He had come in. He had a cape on, soaked with rain, and the rain was in beads in his hair. It was fair hair. It stood up on end. He'd been economizing on the brilliantine. He didn't wear a hat. He gave me a look and I gave him a look. I didn't like the look of him. And he didn't like the look of me. A smell of oil and petrol and rain and mackintosh came off him. He had a big mouth with thick lips. They were very red. I recognized him at once as the son of the man who ran the Kounty

Garage. I saw this chap when I put my car away. The firm's car. Locked up, because of the samples. Took me ten minutes to ram the idea into his head. He looked as though he'd never heard of samples. Slow—you know the way they are in the provinces. Slow on the job.

"Oh, Colin," says she. "What do you want?"

"Nothing," the chap said. "I came in to see you."

"To see me?"

"Just to see you."

"You came in this morning."

"That's right," he said. He went red. "You was busy," he said.

"Well, I'm busy now," she said.

He bit his tongue and licked his big lips over and took a look at me. Then he started grinning.

"I got the new bike, Muriel," he said. "I've got it outside. It's just come down from the works," he said.

"The laddie wants you to look at his bike," I said. So she went out and had a look at it.

When she came back she had got rid of him.

"Listen to that rain," she said. "Lord, I'm fed up with this line," she said.

"What line?" I said. "The hotel line?"

"Yes," she said. "I'm fed right up to the back teeth with it."

"And you've got good teeth," I said.

"There's not the class of person there used to be in it," she said. "All our family have got good teeth."

"Not the class?"

"I've been in it five years and there's not the same class at all. You never meet any fellows."

"Well," said I, "if they're like that half-wit at the garage, they're nothing to be stuck on. And you've met me."

I said it to her like that.

"Oh," says she. "It isn't as bad as that yet."

It was cold in the office. She used to sit all day in her overcoat. She was a smart girl with a big friendly chin and a second one coming, and her forehead and nose were covered with freckles. She had copper-coloured hair too. She got her shoes through the trade from Duke's traveller and her clothes, too, off the Hollenborough mantle man. I told her I could do her better stockings than the ones she'd got on. She got a good reduction on everything. Twenty-five or thirty-three and a third. She had her expenses cut right back. I took her to the pictures that night in the car. I made Colin get the car out for me.

"That boy wanted me to go on the back of his bike. On a night like this," she said.

"Oh," she said, when we got to the pictures. "Two shillings's too much. Let's go into the one-and-sixes at the side and we can nip across into the two-shillings when the lights go down."

"Fancy your father being an undertaker," she said in the middle of the show. And she started laughing as she had laughed before.

She had her head screwed on all right. She said:

"Some girls have no pride once the lights go down."

Every time I went to that town I took a box of something. Samples, mostly, they didn't cost me anything.

"Don't thank me," I said. "Thank the firm."

Every time I took her out I pulled the blinds in the back seat of the car to hide the samples. That chap Colin used to give us oil and petrol. He used to give me a funny look. Fishy sort of small eyes he'd got. Always looking miserable. Then we would go off. Sunday was her free day. Not that driving's any holiday for me. And, of course, the firm paid. She used to take me down to see her family for the day. Start in the morning, and taking it you had dinner and tea there, a day's outing cost us nothing. Her father was something on the railway, retired. He had a long stocking, somewhere, but her sister, the one that was married, had had her share already.

He had a tumour after his wife died and they just played upon the old man's feelings. It wasn't right. She wouldn't go near her sister and I don't blame her, taking the money like that. Just played upon the old man's feelings.

Every time I was up there Colin used to come in looking for her.

"Oh, Colin," I used to say. "Done my car yet?" He knew where he got off with me.

"No, now, I can't, Colin. I tell you I'm going out with Mr. Humphrey," she used to say to him. I heard her.

"He keeps on badgering me," she said to me.

"You leave him to me," I said.

"No, he's all right," she said.

"You let me know if there's any trouble with Colin," I said. "Seems to be a harum-scarum sort of half-wit to me," I said.

"And he spends every penny he makes," she said.

Well, we know that sort of thing is all right while it lasts, I told her, but the trouble is that it doesn't last.

We were always meeting Colin on the road. I took no notice of it first of all and then I grew suspicious and awkward at always meeting him. He had a new motor bicycle. It was an Indian, a scarlet thing that he used to fly over the moor with, flat out. Muriel and I used to go out over the moor to Ingley Wood in the firm's Morris—I had a customer out that way.

"May as well do a bit of business while you're about it," I said.

"About what?" she said.

"Ah ha!" I said. "That's what Colin wants to know," I said.

Sure enough, coming back we'd hear him popping and backfiring close behind us, and I put out my hand to stop him and keep him following us, biting our dirt.

"I see his little game," I said. "Following us."

So I saw to it that he did follow. We could hear him banging away behind us, and the traffic is thick on the Ingley road in the afternoon.

"Oh, let him pass," Muriel said. "I can't stand those dirty things banging in my ears."

I waved him on and past he flew with his scarf flying out, blazing red into the traffic. "We're doing fifty-eight ourselves," she said, leaning across to look.

"Powerful buses those," I said. "Any fool can do it if he's got the power. Watch me step on it."

But we did not catch Colin. Half an hour later he passed us coming back. Cut right in between us and a lorry—I had to brake hard. I damn nearly killed him. His ears were red with the wind. He didn't wear a hat. I got after him as soon as I could, but I couldn't touch him.

Nearly every weekend I was in that town seeing my girl, that fellow was hanging around. He came into the bar on Saturday nights, he poked his head into the office on Sunday mornings. It was a sure bet that if we went out in the car he would pass us on the road. Every time we would hear that scarlet thing roar by like a horse-stinger. It didn't matter where we were. He passed us on the main road, he met us down the side roads. There was a little cliff under oak trees at May Ponds, she said, where the view was pretty. And there, soon after we got there, was Colin on the other side of the water, watching us. Once we found him sitting on his bike, just as though he were waiting for us.

"You been here in a car?" I said.

"No, motor bike," she said, and blushed. "Cars can't follow in these tracks."

She knew a lot of places in that country. Some of the roads weren't roads at all and were bad for tires and I didn't want the firm's car scratched by bushes, but you would have thought Colin could read what was in her mind. For nine times out of ten he was there. It got on my nerves. It was a red, roaring, powerful thing and he opened it full out.

"I'm going to speak to Colin," I said. "I won't have him annoying you."

"He's not annoying me," she said. "I've got a sense of humour."

"Here, Colin," I said one evening when I put the car away. "What's the idea?"

He was taking off his overalls. He pretended he did not know what I was talking about. He had a way of rolling his eyeballs, as if they had got wet and loose in his head, while he was speaking to me, and you never knew if it was sweat or oil on his face. It was always pale, with high colour on his cheeks and very red lips.

"Miss MacFarlane doesn't like being followed," I said.

He dropped his jaw and gaped at me. I could not tell whether he was being very surprised or very sly. I used to call him "Marbles" because when he spoke he seemed to have a lot of marbles in his mouth.

Then he said he never went to the places we went to, except by accident. He wasn't following us, he said, but we were following him. We never let him alone, he said. Everywhere he went, he said, we were there. Take last Saturday, he said, we were following him for miles down the by-pass, he said. "But you passed us first and then sat down in front," I said. "I went to Ingley Wood," he said. "And you followed me there." No, we didn't, I said, Miss MacFarlane decided to go there.

He said he did not want to complain, but fair was fair. "I suppose you know," he said, "that you have taken my girl off me. Well, you can leave *me* alone, can't you?"

"Here," I said. "One minute! Not so fast! You said I've taken Miss MacFarlane from you. Well, she was never your girl. She only knew you in a friendly way."

"She was my girl," was all he said.

He was pouring oil into my engine. He had some cotton wool in one hand and the can in the other. He wiped up the green oil that had overflowed, screwed on the cap, pulled down the bonnet, and whistled to himself.

I went back to Muriel and told her what Colin had said.

"I don't like trouble," I said.

"Don't you worry," she said. "I had to have someone to go to all these places with before you came. Couldn't stick in here all day Sunday."

"Ah," I said. "That's it, is it? You've been to all these places with him?"

"Yes," she said. "And he keeps on going to them. He's sloppy about me."

"Good God," I said. "Sentimental memories."

I felt sorry for that fellow. He knew it was hopeless, but he loved her. I suppose he couldn't help himself. Well, it takes all sorts to make a world, as my old mother used to say. If we were all alike it wouldn't do. Some men can't save money. It just runs through their fingers. He couldn't save money, so he lost her. I suppose all he thought of was love.

I could have been friends with that fellow. As it was, I put a lot of business his way. I didn't want him to get the wrong idea about me. We're all human after all.

We didn't have any more trouble with Colin after this until bank holiday. I was going to take her down to see my family. The old man's getting a bit past it now and has given up living over the shop. He's living out on the Barnum Road, beyond the tram stop. We were going down in the firm's car, as per usual, but something went wrong with the mag and Colin had not got it right for the holiday. I was wild about this. What's the use of a garage who can't do a rush job for the holidays! What's the use of being an old customer if they're going to let you down! I went for Colin bald-headed.

"You knew I wanted it," I said. "It's no use trying to put me off with a tale about the stuff not coming down from the works. I've heard that one before."

I told him he'd got to let me have another car, because he'd let me down. I told him I wouldn't pay his account. I said I'd take my business away from him. But there wasn't a car to be had in the town because of the holiday. I could have knocked the fellow down. After the way I'd sent business to him.

Then I saw through his little game. He knew Muriel and I were going to my people and he had done this to stop it. The moment I saw this I let him know that it would take more than him to stop me doing what I wanted.

I said: "Right. I shall take the amount of Miss MacFarlane's train fare and my own from the account at the end of the month."

I said: "You may run a garage, but you don't run the railway service."

I was damned angry going by train. I felt quite lost on the railway after having a car. It was crowded with trippers too. It was slow—stopping at all the stations. The people come in, they tread all over your feet, they make you squeeze up till you're crammed against the window, and the women stick out their elbows and fidget. And then the expense! a return for two runs you into just over a couple of quid. I could have murdered Colin.

We got there at last. We walked up from the tram stop. Mother was at the window and let us in.

"This is Miss MacFarlane," I said.

And mother said: "Oh, pleased to meet you. We've heard a lot about you.

"Oh," Mother said to me, giving me a kiss, "are you tired? You haven't had your tea, have you? Sit down. Have this chair, dear. It's more comfortable."

"Well, my boy," my father said.

"Want a wash," my father said. "We've got a washbasin downstairs," he said. "I used not to mind about washing upstairs before. Now I couldn't do without it. Funny how your ideas change as you get older."

"How's business?" he said.

"Mustn't grumble," I said. "How's yours?"

"You knew," he said, "we took off the horses: except

for one or two of the older families we have got motors now."

But he'd told me that the last time I was there. I'd been at him for years about motor hearses.

"You've forgotten I used to drive them," I said.

"Bless me, so you did," he said.

He took me up to my room. He showed me everything he had done to the house. "Your mother likes it," he said. "The traffic's company for her. You know what your mother is for company."

Then he gives me a funny look.

"Who's the girl?" he says.

My mother came in then and said: "She's pretty, Arthur."

"Of course she's pretty," I said. "She's Irish."

"Oh," said the old man. "Irish! Got a sense of humour, eh?"

"She wouldn't be marrying me if she hadn't," I said. And then I gave *them* a look.

"Marrying her, did you say?" exclaimed my father.

"Any objection?" I said.

"Now, Ernest dear," said my mother. "Leave the boy alone. Come down while I pop the kettle on."

She was terribly excited.

"Miss MacFarlane," the old man said.

"No sugar, thank you, Mrs. Humphrey. I beg your pardon, Mr. Humphrey?"

"The Glen Hotel at Swansea, I don't suppose you know that?" my father said. "I wondered if you did, being in the catering line."

"It doesn't follow she knows every hotel," my mother said.

"Forty years ago," the old man said. "I was staying at the Glen in Swansea and the head waiter—"

"Oh no, not that one. I'm sure Miss MacFarlane doesn't want to hear that one," my mother said.

"How's business with you, Mr. Humphrey?" said Muriel. "We passed a large cemetery near the station."

"Dad's Ledger," I said.

"The whole business has changed so that you wouldn't know it, in my lifetime," said my father. "Silver fittings have gone clean out. Everyone wants simplicity nowadays. Restraint. Dignity," my father said.

"Prices did it," my father said.

"The war," he said.

"You couldn't get the wood," he said.

"Take ordinary mahogany, just an ordinary piece of mahogany. Or teak," he said. "Take teak. Or walnut."

"You can certainly see the world go by in this room," I said to my mother.

"It never stops," she said.

Now it was all bicycles over the new concrete road from the gun factory. Then traction engines and cars. They came up over the hill where the A.A. man stands and choked up round the tram stop. It was mostly holiday traffic. Everything with a wheel on it was out.

"On this stretch," my father told me, "they get three accidents a week." There was an ambulance station at the crossroads.

We had hardly finished talking about this—in fact, the old man was still saying that something ought to be done—when the telephone rang.

"Name of MacFarlane?" the voice said on the wire.

"No. Humphrey," my father said. "There is a Miss MacFarlane here."

"There's a man named Colin Mitchell lying seriously injured in an accident at the Cottage Hospital, gave me the name of MacFarlane as his nearest relative."

That was the Police. On to it at once. That fellow Colin had followed us down by road.

Cry, I never heard a girl cry as Muriel cried when we came back from the hospital. He had died in the ambulance. Cutting in, the old game he used to play on me. Clean off the saddle and under the Birmingham bus. The blood was everywhere, they said. People were still looking at it when we went by. Head on. What a mess! Don't let's talk about it.

She wanted to see him, but they said "No." There wasn't anything recognizable to see. She put her arms round my neck and cried: "Colin, Colin," as if I were Colin, and clung to me. I was feeling sick myself. I held her tight and I kissed her and I thought: "Holiday ruined.

"Damn fool man," I thought. "Poor devil," I thought.

"I knew he'd do something like this."

"There, there," I said to her. "Don't think about Colin." Didn't she love me, I said, and not Colin? Hadn't she got me? She said, yes, she had. And she loved me. But, "Oh, Colin! Oh, Colin!" she cried. "And Colin's mother," she cried. "Oh, it's terrible." She cried and cried.

We put her to bed and I sat with her, and my mother kept coming in.

"Leave her to me," I said. "I understand her."

Before they went to bed they both came in and looked at her. She lay sobbing with her head in the pillow.

I could quite understand her being upset. Colin was a decent fellow. He was always doing things for her. He mended her electric lamp and he riveted the stem of a wineglass so that you couldn't see the break. He used to make things for her. He was very good with his hands.

She lay on her side with her face burning and feverish with misery and crying, scalded by the salt, and her lips shrivelled up. I put my arm under her neck and I stroked her forehead. She groaned. Sometimes she shivered and sometimes she clung to me, crying: "Oh, Colin! Colin!"

My arm ached with the cramp and I had a crick in my back, sitting in the awkward way I was on the bed. It was late. There was nothing to do but to ache and sit watching her and thinking. It is funny the way your mind drifts. When I was kissing her and watching her I was thinking out who I'd show our new Autumn range to first. Her hand held my wrist tight, and when I kissed her I got her tears on my lips. They burned and stung. Her neck and shoulders were soft and I could feel her breath hot out of her nostrils on the back of my hand. Ever noticed how hot a woman's breath gets when she's crying? I drew out my hand and lay down beside her and "Oh, Colin, Colin," she sobbed, turning over and clinging to me. And so I lay there, listening to the traffic, staring at the ceiling, and shivering whenever the picture of Colin shooting right off that damned red thing into the bus came into my mind—until I did not hear the traffic any more, or see the ceiling any more, or think any more, but a change happened—I don't know when. This Colin thing seemed to have knocked the bottom out of everything and I had a funny feeling we were going down and down and down in a lift. And the further we went, the hotter and softer she got. Perhaps it was when I found with my hands that she had very big breasts. But it was like being on the mail steamer and feeling engines start under your feet, thumping louder and louder. You can feel it in every vein of your body. Her mouth opened and her tears dried. Her breath came through her open mouth and her voice was blind and husky. Colin, Colin, Colin, she said, and her fingers were hooked into me. I got out and turned the key in the door.

In the morning I left her sleeping. It did not matter to me what my father might have heard in the night, but still I wondered. She would hardly let me touch her before that. I told her I was sorry, but she shut me up. I was afraid of her. I was afraid of mentioning Colin. I wanted to go out of the house there and then and tell someone everything. Did she love Colin all the time? Did she think I was Colin? And every time I thought of that poor devil covered over with a white sheet in the hospital mortuary, a kind of picture of her and me under the sheets with love came into my mind. I couldn't separate the two things. Just as though it had all come from Colin.

I'd rather not talk any more about that. I never talked to Muriel about it. I waited for her to say something, but she didn't. She didn't say a word.

The next day was a bad day. It was grey and hot and the air smelled of oil fumes from the road. There's always a mess to clear up when things like this happen. I had to see to it. I had the job of ringing up the boy's mother. But I got round that, thank God, by ringing up the garage and getting them to go round and see the old lady. My father is useless when things are like this. I was the whole morning on the phone: to the hospital, the police, the coroner—and he stood fussing beside me, jerking up and down like a fat indiarubber ball.

I found my mother washing up at the sink and she said: "That poor boy's mother! I can't stop thinking of her."

Then my father comes in and says—just as though I was a customer: "Of course if Mrs. Mitchell desires it we can have the remains of the deceased conveyed to his house by one of our new specially sprung motor hearses and can, if necessary, make all the funeral arrangements."

I could have hit him because Muriel came into the room when he was saying this. But she stood there as if nothing had happened.

"It's the least we can do for poor Mrs. Mitchell," she said. There were small creases of shadow under her eyes, which shone with a soft strong light I had never seen before. She walked as if she were really still in that room with me, asleep. God, I loved that girl! God, I wanted to get all this over, this damned Colin business that had come right into the middle of everything like this, and I wanted to get married right away. I wanted to be alone with her. That's what Colin did for me.

"Yes," I said. "We must do the right thing by Colin."

"We are sometimes asked for long-distance estimates," my father said.

"It will be a little something," my mother said.

"Dad and I will talk it over," I said.

"Come into the office," my father said. "It occurred to me that it would be nice to do the right thing by this friend of yours."

We talked it over. We went into the cost of it. There was the return journey to reckon. We worked it out that it would come no dearer to old Mrs. Mitchell than if she took the train and buried the boy here. That is to say, my father said, if I drove it.

"It would look nice," my father said. "Saves money and it would look a bit friendly," my father said. "You've done it before."

"Well," I said. "I suppose I can get a refund on my return ticket from the railway."

But it was not as simple as it looked, because Muriel wanted to come. She wanted to drive back with me and the hearse. My mother was very worried about this. It might upset Muriel, she thought. Father thought it might not look nice to see a young girl sitting by the coffin of a grown man.

"It must be dignified," my father said. "You see, if she was there, it might look as though she were just doing it for the ride—like these young women on bakers' vans."

My father took me out into the hall to tell me this because he did not want her to hear. But she would not have it. She wanted to come back with Colin.

"Colin loved me. It is my duty to him," she said. "Besides," she said, suddenly, in her full open voice—it had seemed to be closed and carved and broken and small—"I've never been in a hearse before."

"And it will save her fare too," I said to my father.

That night I went again to her room. She was awake. I said I was sorry to disturb her, but I would go at once only I wanted to see if she was all right. She said, in the closed voice again, that she was all right.

"Are you sure?" I said.

She did not answer. I was worried. I went over to the bed.

"What is the matter? Tell me what is the matter," I said.

For a long time she was silent. I held her hand, I stroked her head. She was lying stiff in the bed. She would not answer. I dropped my hand to her small white shoulder. She stirred and drew up her legs and half turned and said, "I was thinking of Colin. Where is he?" she asked.

"They've brought him round. He's lying downstairs."

"In the front room?"

"Yes, ready for the morning. Now be a sensible girl and go back by train."

"No, no," she said. "I want to go with Colin. Poor Colin. He loved me and I didn't love him." And she drew my hands down to her breasts.

"Colin loved me," she whispered.

"Not like this," I whispered.

It was a warm grey morning like all the others when we took Colin back. They had fixed the coffin in before Muriel came out. She came down wearing the bright blue hat she had got off Dormer's millinery man and she kissed my mother and father good-bye. They were very sorry for her. "Look after her, Arthur," my mother said. Muriel got in beside me without a glance behind her at the coffin. I started the engine. They smiled at us. My father raised his hat, but whether it was to Muriel and me or to Colin, or to the three of us, I do not know. He was not, you see, wearing his top hat. I'll say this for the old boy, thirty years in the trade have taught him tact.

After leaving my father's house you have to go down to the tram terminus before you get on the by-pass. There was always one or two drivers, conductors, or inspectors there, doing up their tickets, or changing over the trolley arms. When we passed I saw two of them drop their jaws, stick their pencils in their ears, and raise their hats. I was so surprised by this that I nearly raised mine in acknowledgment, forgetting that we had the coffin behind. I had not driven one of my father's hearses for years.

Hearses are funny things to drive. They are well-sprung, smooth-running cars, with quiet engines, and, if you are used to driving a smaller car, before you know where you are, you are speeding. You know you ought to go slow, say twenty-five to thirty maximum, and it's hard to keep it down. You can return empty at seventy if you like. It's like driving a fire engine. Go fast out and come back slow—only the other way round. Open out in the country, but slow down past houses. That's what it means. My father was very particular about this.

Muriel and I didn't speak very much at first. We sat listening to the engine and the occasional jerk of the coffin behind when we went over a pot-hole. We passed the place where poor Colin—but I didn't say anything to Muriel, and she, if she noticed—which I doubt—did not say anything to me. We went through Cox Hill, Wammering, and Yodley Mount, flat country, don't care for it myself. "There's a wonderful lot of building going on," Muriel said at last.

"You won't know these places in five years," I said.

But my mind kept drifting away from the road and the green fields and the dullness, and back to Colin—five days before, he had come down this way. I expected to see that Indian coming flying straight out of every corner. But it was all bent and bust up properly now. I saw the damned thing.

He had been up to his old game, following us, and that had put the end to following. But not quite; he was following us now, behind us in the coffin. Then my mind drifted off that and I thought of those nights at my parents' house, and Muriel. You never know what a woman is going to be like. I thought, too, that it had put my calculations out. I mean, supposing she had a baby. You see I had reckoned on waiting eighteen months or so. I would have eight hundred then. But if we had to get married at once, we should have to cut right down. Then I kept thinking it was funny her saying "Colin!" like that in the night; it was funny it made her feel that way with me, and how it made me feel when she called me Colin. I'd never thought of her in that way, in what you might call the "Colin" way.

I looked at her and she looked at me and she smiled but still we did not say very much, but the smiles kept coming to both of us. The light-railway bridge at Dootheby took me by surprise and I thought the coffin gave a jump as we took it.

"Colin's still watching us," I nearly said.

There were tears in her eyes.

"What was the matter with Colin?" I said. "Nice chap, I thought. Why didn't you marry him?"

"Yes," she said. "He was a nice boy. But he'd no sense of humour.

"And I wanted to get out of that town," she said.

"I'm not going to stay there, at that hotel," she said.

"I want to get away," she said. "I've had enough."

She had a way of getting angry with the air, like that. "You've got to take me away," she said. We were passing slowly into Muster, there was a tram ahead and people thick on the narrow pavements, dodging out into the road. But when we got into the Market Square, where they were standing around, they saw the coffin. They began to raise their hats. Suddenly she laughed. "It's like being the King and Queen," she said.

"They're raising their hats," she said.

"Not all of them," I said.

She squeezed my hand and I had to keep her from jumping about like a child on the seat as we went through.

"There they go."

"Boys always do," I said.

"And another.

"Let's see what the policeman does."

She started to laugh, but I shut her up. "Keep your sense of humour to yourself," I said.

Through all those towns that run into one another as you might say, we caught it. We went through, as she said, like royalty. So many years since I drove a hearse, I'd forgotten what it was like.

I was proud of her. I was proud of Colin, and I was proud of myself. And after what had happened, I mean on the last two nights, it was like a wedding. And although we knew it was for Colin, it was for us too, because Colin was with both of us. It was like this all the way.

"Look at that man there. Why doesn't he raise his hat? People ought to show respect for the dead," she said.

WILLIAM PLOMER

The Child of Queen Victoria

William Plomer's autobiography, *Double Lives,* begins:

> It was in 1903 (when men were at last beginning to fly, though in contraptions more like birdcages than birds) that I first, to use an old phrase, saw the light. It was dazzling, for the scene of this event was, of all places, the Northern Transvaal; but since nobody, if a cat happens to have kittens in an oven, regards them as biscuits, I should be no more justified in pretending to be a South African than in declaring myself a Bantu. Yet the African sun warmed my young bones, and to Africa I must always partly belong, though my parents, of whom I was the first child, were in fact very English.

Plomer goes on to tell us how he was sent to school in England and how he returned to Africa immediately afer the first World-War. In 1922 he went into business with his parents at a trading post in Zululand. This must have been the setting he used for *The Child of Queen Victoria,* though the story obviously isn't autobiographical in most other respects.

Modern English literature includes some masterly studies of the relation between imperialism's heirs and its victims—a relation which becomes increasingly complex with the passing of the generations. The heir is often an amiably confused creature of bad conscience and good intentions; sometimes he is an outspoken enemy of the system which has placed him in this guilty position. But, even so, he can't decline all responsibility for it, since he has inherited the fruits of its crimes and, to some extent, benefited from them. Nor is the victim himself usually quite innocent; for he has probably accepted his inherited servitude while reserving the right to resent it silently and use every kind of dishonesty in his dealings with the oppressor. He dares not resist, but he refuses to forgive.

E. M. Forster's *A Passage to India* is generally agreed to be the classic novel in this field; and I think immediately of two later ones, George Orwell's *Burmese Days* and Alan Paton's *Cry, the Beloved Country*. Plomer's story most resembles Forster's, in the exactness of its observation and in the restraint that is put upon its strong inner emotion. And the frustrated love-affair between Frant and Seraphina is reminiscent of the frustrated friendship between Forster's Fielding and Dr. Aziz.

This story is relatively early Plomer. His mature talent has produced verses of a fiendish humor, delighting some and disgusting others. (If you think your stomach is strong, try *The Flying Bum: 1944*, which describes a vegetarian birthday dinner during an air raid, and its loathsome last course.) Among his many works, I most admire *Museum Pieces* (1952). This could, I suppose, be described as a "light" novel. It is certainly very amusing. But it also contains passages of a compassionate irony which move me as much as anything in Flaubert, and in somewhat the same way.

1

A Ford car, rattling its way up a rough road in Lembuland in the most brilliant sunshine, carried two very different people—a hard-bitten colonial of Scotch descent, a trader, MacGavin by name, nearer thirty than forty, with a sour red face, and a young Englishman called Frant who had just left school. It was really very awkward. They did not know what to say to each other. MacGavin thought his passenger was despising him simply for being what he was, and Frant, feeling foolish and useless in contrast with this sunburnt, capable man, made a painful effort to be hearty, and looked inquiringly at the country. The road wound in and out, climbing through grassy hills, with patches of virgin forest here and there, especially in the hollows. There were outcrops of rock, and small tilled fields of red earth, and any number of beehive-shaped huts perched here and there in twos and threes. And there were always natives in sight, with herds of bony cattle and ragged goats. It did not need a specially acute eye to see that the landscape, though picturesque, was overcrowded, and that the whites, coveting the lowlands for sugarcane, had gradually squeezed the natives up into these heights which were poor in soil, coarse in pasturage, and too full of ups and downs to afford space for any proper attempts at cultivation. Frant looked at the natives, naturally, with some curiosity. He wondered what they were like when you got to know them, and then he wondered if he couldn't say something suitable to MacGavin about them. At last he said:

"It seems a pity that the natives haven't got a higher standard of living, then there would be so much more money to be made out of them."

MacGavin looked at him with the savage expression sometimes to be seen on the faces of the ignorant when confronted with what seems to them a new and difficult and rather mad idea.

"The black bastards!" he exclaimed. "There's bloody little to be made out of *them,* as you'll pretty soon find out."

And he violently changed gear. As the car began to strain its way up a steep hill, Frant, vibrating by his side, was glad that the noise of the engine destroyed what would have been a painful silence.

Sons of the "new poor," young wasters, retrenched civil servants or Indian Army officers, and other mostly misguided wretches, they went to settle overseas—one even heard of suicides, because not everybody is tough enough to stand an absolute change of environment, or frightful isolation in some magnificent landscape. And Frant, lured by advertisements, driven by enterprise, encouraged by supposedly responsible persons, went out like them, only fresh from a public school.

His incipient relationship with MacGavin was not made easier by the practical basis on which it rested, for Frant came to him neither as a partner, nor as a servant, nor as a guest, nor had he paid one penny by way of premium. A committee in London had picked out MacGavin's name as that of a person who had declared himself willing to give a young Englishman free board and lodging and two or three years' training in the art of trading with the Lembus in exchange for nothing but that young stranger's "services." MacGavin was in some ways a practical man, and the chance of obtaining a responsible white servant who need be paid no wages seemed to him a good one. Frant had been brought up to be eager to oblige. And that was how they started.

Frant was young—so young that, bumping adventurously along into the heart of Lembuland, he could not help thinking of his former schoolfellows and of how they would have envied him if they could have seen him at that moment. A fatal eagerness possessed him. He was flying in the face of the world, as the young are apt to do, with the finest of ambitions. For some of us when young it does not seem so important that we should be successful in a wordly sense and at once enjoy money and comfort, as that we should try and become our true selves. We want to blossom out and fulfil our real natures. The process is complex, and is obviously conditioned by our approaches to the work we mean to do or have to do in life, by the way our heredity and upbringing make us react to our environment, and especially by our relations with other people. In the long run this affair of becoming a grown-up person, a real person (for that is what it amounts to) is, for most of us, an affair of the heart. We hear a great deal about sex nowadays; it is possible to overestimate its importance, because there are always people who pay it little attention or who apparently manage, like Sir Isaac Newton, to get along, without giving it a thought. But Frant came of a susceptible family. He arrived in Lembuland with a pretty appetite for life, and little knew what he was letting himself in for.

2

The trading station at Madumbi occupied the top of a slope a little back from the road, or track rather, and consisted of two main buildings, the store and the house, about fifty yards apart, and a number of ramshackle outhouses. In front, there had been some attempt at a garden—not much of an attempt, for cows and chickens always roamed about in it, and it was now and then invaded by monkeys. At the back, there was some rough grazing land and a patch of forest that went with the place. The buildings themselves were made of corrugated iron, painted khaki and lined with deal boards, looking out, curiously hideous, on the land which sloped away from them on all sides with streams, and clumps of trees, and grassy spaces like a well-planned park. But Mr. and Mrs. MacGavin, in settling at Madumbi, had been little influenced by the scenery.

The store itself was lighted only by two small windows and the open door, and as you came in from the strong sunlight it was at first difficult to get your bearings. The place was so crowded with goods that it looked like a cave crowded with all sorts of plunder. Your head bumping against a suspended trek-chain or storm-lantern, you looked up and saw that the ceiling was almost entirely hidden in festoons of kettles and baskets, hanks of Berlin wool, enormous bouquets of handkerchiefs of all sizes and colours, bunches of tunics and trousers interspersed with camisoles, frying-pans, wreaths of artificial forget-me-nots, hatchets and matchets, necklaces and ploughshares. As for the shelves, they were entirely crammed with different kinds of goods, for the production of which a hundred factories had smoked and roared in four continents. All kinds of shoddy clothing and showy piece-goods, brittle ironmongery and chinaware, the most worthless patent medicines, the gaudiest cheap jewellery, the coarsest groceries, bibles, needles, pipes, celluloid collars, soup tureens, hair-oil, notebooks, biscuits and lace curtains rose in tiers and patterns on every side. Certain shelves were full of refuse left over from the war—grey cotton socks made in Chicago for American recruits who had never enlisted, khaki tunics and breeches, puttees, Balaclava helmets and so forth, all ugly and serviceable, made and carried by machinery to contribute to a scene of universal murder, produced in too great quantities, by contract instead of by necessity or impulse, and at last deposited here, so that a profit might be made out of the pleasure these things, by their novelty, gave to the blacks. The whole world seemed to have conspired to make a profit on this lonely Lambu hilltop.

Two doors at the back of the store itself gave access to two other rooms. One was large, and was used for storing reserves of bulky goods—sacks of salt, sugar and grain; ironware; boxes of sweets and soap; besides a profusion of bunches of Swazi tobacco leaves, at least two feet long, their fragrance preserved by an occasional sprinkling with water. It was the custom to give away a leaf or two of tobacco to each adult shopper, and to the young a handful of the cheapest sweets, their virulent pinks and greens and acid chemical flavours promising a quick decay to strong white teeth. The other and smaller room was used as an office, and contained a table, a chair, a safe, and a great accumulation of MacGavin's papers. The window, which received the afternoon sun, would not open, and was always buzzing with flies and hornets in various stages of fatigue.

A flea-bitten dog was usually asleep on a pile of unpaid bills in the corner, while the ink, from standing so much in the sun, was always evaporating, so that when one had occasion to write one had to use a pencil.

But all that was only the background. The space before the counter was often thronged with Lembus of all ages and both sexes. The noise was overpowering. They would all be talking at once, some laughing, some arguing, some gossiping, some bargaining, while all the time a peculiarly strident gramophone was playing records of Caruso and Clara Butt. Sometimes an old black woman, nearly blind and nearly naked, her last peppercorns of hair grizzled to a pepper-and-salt colour, and her dry old dugs so long that she could comfortably tuck the ends of them into her belt, might be seen listening to it, with her head on one side, for the first time, uttering occasional exclamations of incredulity *("Abantu! Inkosi yami! Maye babo!")* and slapping her scrawny thighs, as she demanded whether the voice was the voice of a spirit.

In another part of the room the only vacant space on the wall was occupied by a pier-glass, before which a group of very fat girls were fond of comparing their charms, to the accompaniment of shrieks of delight. Their main wish was to observe the reflection of their bottoms, partly out of pure curiosity and partly with a view to interesting the men present. Standing among the older customers there were always some children, patiently awaiting their turn to be served with threepennyworths of this and that. Some brought eggs or wild fruit to trade, which they carried in small bowl-shaped baskets on their heads. One might have a fowl under her arm, and a little boy of seven would perhaps bring an enormous scarlet lily, complete with leaves and root.

To say that all this was strange to Frant would be an understatement. It was a new world. Into this exotic atmosphere he was plunged; this was where he had to work; this was what he had to learn. What is called adaptability is little more than freshness and keenness and readiness to learn, and Frant, who had been brought up to obey, made himself completely and at first willingly subservient to MacGavin's instructions. He didn't like MacGavin, and it was plain that he never would do so, but it was also plain that MacGavin knew his business, and Frant's presence at Madumbi was, in theory, a business matter. So he rose early and retired late, working hours that no trade union would approve at a job that needed endless patience and good humour, with diligence and imagination as well. He struggled with a strange language, did accounts, avoided cheating or being cheated (he had been brought up to be honest) and toiled morning, noon and night, without haste, without rest, never for a moment questioning what he conceived to be his duty. And MacGavin, finding that he had to do with an honest and docile and responsible person, confided to his wife that the plan was succeeding beyond his hopes. Very soon, he felt, he would be able to leave Frant in entire charge of the proceedings, while he himself attended to other money-making operations out of doors. Mrs. MacGavin was pleased too, because she found she was less often required to help in the store, and could spend more time in the house. Though God knows the store was the pleasanter building of the two.

On his very first afternoon Frant had been given tea on the veranda of the house, in order to afford Mrs.

MacGavin an early chance of sizing him up, but after that his tea was always sent over to the store. Apart from that he had meals in the house, and he slept in it, and spent part of his Sunday leisure in it as well. There were only four rooms. Frant's own room, nine feet by seven, was oppressively hot, was never properly cleaned, and had a disagreeable smell. The living-room, not large in itself, was so crammed with furniture that one person could with difficulty turn round in it, whereas three people were supposed to eat and sleep and rest in it, quite in addition to the fact that, the house lacking either hall or passage, it had to serve as both. Thus the pattern on the linoleum was in places quite worn away, and behind the front door was a rack bulging with hats, coats and mackintoshes, which gave off a greenish odour of stale sweat, cheap rubber and mildew. The middle of the room was occupied by a large table covered with a khaki mohair table-cloth with bobbles round the edges, and in the middle of that stood a large oil-lamp with a shade of crinkly pink paper. A sideboard held a load of worthless ornaments, and on the walls faded wedding-groups in bamboo Oxford frames alternated with dusty paper fans, cuckoo clocks and fretwork brackets supporting electro-plated vases containing dusty everlasting flowers in process of perishing from dry-rot. With difficulty it was possible to make one's way to a small bookcase which stood beneath a reproduction of a problem picture, showing a woman in evening dress in the fashion of 1907 kneeling on the floor before a man in a dinner-jacket, the whole suffused in a red glow from a very hot-looking fire in the background, and called "The Confession." Among the books were several by Marie Corelli, a brochure on the diseases of cattle, and a girlish album of

Mrs. MacGavin's, in which her friends had written or attempted to draw personal tributes and pleasantries. Had this album been a little more vulgar, it might have been almost a curiosity, but the commonness of colonial schoolgirls in the second decade of this century has scarcely even a period interest. It must be admitted, however, that one contributor had written the following very appropriate wisecrack:

Roses are red and violets blue,
Pickles are sour and so are you.

"Fond of reading?" MacGavin, in an expansive moment, once asked Frant. "No time myself."

"Yes and no," said Frant, who was trying to make up for his education and had a copy of *The Brothers Karamazov* in his bedroom. "It depends."

On the table in that front room there was nearly always a fly-haunted still-life consisting of a teapot and some dirty cups, for Mrs. MacGavin drank very strong tea seven times daily, a habit which no doubt accounted partly for the state of her complexion. But all day long and most evenings the double doors on to the veranda were open, and there was the view. As the trading station was on the top of a hill and partly surrounded with groves of mimosa trees, the outlook was very fine. Beyond the trees, it could be seen that every depression in the landscape had its rivulet and patch of forest, and that in every sheltered and elevated place there was a kraal of beehive-shaped huts with small fields of grain and roots; cattle were grazing here and there; and in the distance rose range upon range of blue mountains. At first sight it seemed, like so many African landscapes, a happy mixture of pastoral and the magnificent, but those who lived under its influence came to feel gradually a mingled sense of uneasiness and sorrow, so that what at first seemed grand became indifferent or menacing, what at first seemed peaceful was felt to be brooding, and stillness and quietness seemed to be an accumulation of repressed and troubled forces, like the thunderclouds that often hung over the horizon of an afternoon. Those sunny hills seemed to be possessed by a spirit that nursed a grievance.

3

Frant's approach to the natives was complicated by his character and education, which in some ways helped and in some ways hindered him. As a polite person, he treated them with good-humoured consideration which they were quite unused to receiving from the whites, but then the whites in Lembuland are an unusually discouraging lot—the way they behave to one another is proof of that. A natural quick sympathy and warmth in his character immediately attracted the natives, who are uncannily quick at character, but at the same time they found a certain reserve in him. It was not that he stood on his dignity with them, but simply that he was a little too conscientious. There were certain vague ideas about the white man's prestige and so on which made him rather careful in his behaviour. He imagined that if he let himself go at all he might in some way damage MacGavin's standing and do harm to the trade, and of course MacGavin, in teaching him the trade, was careful to try and instil various principles about treating the natives firmly. And to MacGavin's credit it may be added that he insisted on the natives being treated as fairly as possible, though this was a matter of business rather than principle with him. And after all, there was no need to tell Frant to be fair—it was clear that though a trifle priggish, he was no swindler. This priggishness of his was easy to account for. It was partly in his nature, but also he had been brought up with certain rigid English ideas about being a gentleman, playing the game, and all that sort of thing, and until now he had had no reason to doubt that they were right. The effect of being abruptly transferred to a completely new environment; of being cut off from those familiar companions and surroundings which had enabled his principles to be taken for granted; and of associating with Mr. and Mrs. MacGavin, was not to make him doubt those principles but to convince him that they were right. And to be all by oneself and to think oneself right is really rather fatal, especially if one naturally tends to be both straightforward and severe. Already he would receive some of the opinions of MacGavin and his wife in a silence that was even stronger in its effect than the quiet and smiling "Oh, I'm afraid I can't quite agree with you" which he often had to use in conversation with them.

"He always thinks he's right," MacGavin remarked to his wife, "but it doesn't matter about that. What's more important is that the niggers like him. There's a slight improvement in the takings this month, and I shouldn't be surprised if it's partly due to him. He does what he's told for the most part, and I shouldn't be surprised if he turns out a good salesman when he knows the lingo a bit better."

The Lembu language presents no great difficulties, and it is surprising what good use one can make of a language as soon as one has a small working vocabulary and a few colloquial turns of phrase. Frant enjoyed speaking it, because it is one of those Bantu languages which, to be spoken well, have to be spoken with gusto, and it can be both sonorous and elegant. His progress in the language naturally made his work more easy and pleasant, but it had other effects—it drew him closer into sympathy with the Lembus, and showed him how little they liked the whites. In fact, he began to realize that the remains of the white man's prestige, in Lembuland at least, rested mainly on fear—fear of the white man's money, his mechanical genius and his ruthless and largely joyless energy—and not on love or respect. And since he himself had very little money, no mechanical genius and a certain joyful vitality, he felt that there must be something rather "un-white" about himself. This discovery acted directly upon his pride—it made him resolve to treat the natives with as much kindness and dignity as were consonant with his odd position (the ruling race behind the counter!), as if to show that there were still white men who knew how to behave humanely. This made him think himself better than MacGavin and the few other whites with whom he came in touch, and shut him up in a small cell of his own (as it were) closely barred with high principles.

He did not pretend to himself that the Lembus were paragons of virtue. The very fact that as customers in a shop they had a certain right to order the shopkeepers about, added to the fact that these shopkeepers were nominally their "superiors," was a temptation to some of the natives to be tiresome, cheeky or even insolent, and that was one reason why a great deal of persevering good temper was needed in dealing with them. By the time they had convinced themselves that Frant was both patient and cheerful he had already begun to get a good name amongst them. They were used to MacGavin, whom they thought of as a beast, but a just beast, and finding Frant just without being a beast, and youthful and personable as well, they undoubtedly began to come to Madumbi in greater numbers.

At first he had been much struck by the extreme suspiciousness and diffidence of the customers. They never entered the place with that air of cheerful confidence which, in the dreams of good shopkeepers, is found on every customer's face. On the contrary, they always seemed to come in expecting the worst. Many an old, wild woman, skirted in skins, smeared with fat and ochre, hung with charms, a bladder or an antelope's horn suspended at her neck, her hair dressed high and stuck with bone ornaments, a snuff-box at her waist, perhaps having about her too a couple of pounds, every penny of which she meant to spend, would pause in the doorway with a roving eye and an expression of extreme disillusionment and contempt, as though she found herself there unwillingly and by chance. After some time she would perhaps help herself to a cupful of water from a tank that stood at the door, and would then sit down in the shade and take a lot of snuff with immense deliberation, the expression on her face seeming to say, "Well, here I am, and I don't give a damn for anybody. I haven't lived all these years for nothing. Experience has taught me to expect the worst of every situation and every person, particularly if he or she happens to be white. If I condescend to do any shopping here, I mean to see everything, and to have exactly what I want or nothing at all. Don't think you can swindle me, because you can't. However, I shall proceed on the assumption that you mean to try, that all your goods are damaged, that you're a cunning profiteer, and that you think I'm a fool." And when at last she deigned to enter the store, she would proceed accordingly.

But it was not only old women who were so much on their guard. Many and many a customer would show the same symptoms of a deep and cynical mistrust, walking in as if they were threading their way among mantraps all carefully set for them. Even children would show plainly how they had been forewarned, repeating innocently the last parental injunctions, and carefully counting their change from sixpence. And all this was not due to MacGavin but to the reputation which the white overlords of Lembuland had managed, in the course of two or three decades, to build up for themselves.

If for Frant this unpleasant relationship between the two races was one of his earliest and most enduring impressions, even stronger was that of the immediate physical presence of the Lembus. So many more or less naked bodies of men and women, coloured a warm brown, smooth-skinned and mostly graceful, with white teeth, straight backs and easy manners, do not leave one, when one is young and susceptible and unfamiliar with them, exactly indifferent.

"Don't worry about the stink," MacGavin had said. "You'll get used to it."

Stink? The whites always say that the blacks have a bad smell. Well, there at Madumbi was a confined space usually tightly packed with natives, but although the weather was hot and the air sometimes scarcely moving, it could not have been said that the smell was much more than strange, though to Frant it was heady, like the very smell of life itself, and excited him with a promise of joys not yet tasted. The wholesome smell of an out-of-door race cannot in any case seem unpleasant, except to diseased nerves, and the lightly clad or unclad bodies of the Lembus are continually exposed to sun, air and water, while they are almost as vegetarian as their flocks and herds. If some of the old women were a little inclined to accumulate several layers of ochre and fat all over them by way of skin treatment, they were quite amusing enough in their manners and conversation, and had quite enough natural style, to make up for it. At Madumbi there was a far more oppressive smell than that of the natives, and that was the combined aroma of the dressing that stiffened the calicoes of Osaka and Manchester into a dishonest stoutness, and, to speak figuratively, of the sand in the sugar.

4

In places like Madumbi, time seems more of a thief and enemy than in crowded cities or even in circles where the months are frittered away in useless leisure. In that part of Lembuland the changing of the seasons is less marked than in the highlands, and at Madumbi life was a packed routine; work began at half-past five or six in the morning; fatigue often precluded thought; and the tired eyes, turning towards clock or calendar, would close in sleep. Sometimes all sense of chronological sequence was lost; sometimes it seemed almost as if time were going backwards; and now and again Frant would realize with a shock how many weeks or months had slipped by since this or that trifling break in his existence. But he was not discontented, for he was interested in his work, not so much for its own sake as for the close contact with some of the realities of human nature into which it brought him.

There were certain things which he could never sell without a smile. Now and then a young Lembu would come in and say rather furtively, *"Amafuta wemvubu akona na?"* That is to say, "Have you got any hippopotamus fat?" Whereupon Frant used to go to the small showcase in which the medicines were kept, and produce a small bottle with a label bearing a Lembu inscription, and underneath, in very small letters, PEDERSEN'S GENUINE HIPPO FAT. This commodity looked like ordinary lard, probably was ordinary lard, was put up by a Norwegian chemist in Dunnsport, and sold for a shilling a bottle. It was used for a love philtre, and helped the manufacturer to maintain his son at a theological seminary in Oslo. But other "lines" were more lucrative than hippo fat. Love philtres, after all, were usually only required by the young and romantically inclined, whereas PEDERSEN'S BLUE WONDERS, as another Lembu inscription testified, were indispensable to both young and old. Certainly they were always in demand. Pills as large as peas and the colour of gun-metal, they were not merely an infallible, but a powerful aphrodisiac. When MacGavin happened to be asked for either of these medicines, he would never sell them without a clumsy pleasantry, a habit which had resulted in a falling-off of the sales of the hippo fat, for the younger natives, though their morals, according to some standards, were not above reproach, had their finer feelings. However, his misplaced humour did not much affect the demand for Blue Wonders, which were usually bought by customers of a coarser fibre. Mrs. MacGavin herself came to lend a hand in the store when business was brisk, and it would sometimes happen that she would be called upon to serve a customer with these things, which she would do with the grimmest face in the world—her expression might well have suggested a subject for an allegorical picture, "Avarice overcoming Chastity." But still, out of all the hotchpotch that the store contained, there was one kind of goods which she would neither buy nor sell. The male natives of those parts were in the habit of using a peculiar kind of *cache-sexe* made of the leaves of the wild banana. At Madumbi these were made, in assorted sizes, by an old vagabond of a native who sold them to MacGavin at wholesale prices. When he came to the store it was always at some odd time, when there was nobody else about, either on a very hot afternoon or just after the store had been locked up, or at dawn, or when the moon was rising. If he saw MacGavin, the business was soon settled. If he encountered Mrs. MacGavin, he would wave his bundle of unmentionables right under her nose, saluting her with his free hand and uttering all sorts of high-flown and wholly ironical compliments before crying the virtues of his wares. Nothing annoyed her more, as he very well knew. She always told him rudely to wait for her husband. If it was Frant he chanced to find, he would say with real politeness, *"Sa' ubona, umtwana ka Kwini Victoli!"* Greeting, child of Queen Victoria! This became shortened later to "Child of the Queen" and at last simply to "Child." The very first time he had seen Frant he had said, "Ah, I can see you're a real Englishman from *over there,"* and since England suggested Queen Victoria to him more than anything else it was not hard to account for the complimentary title. The old man, to whom Frant always gave an extra large leaf or two of tobacco, was also fond of saying that the *amaBhunu,* the Boers, were "no good," which was partly his real opinion and meant partly as a piece of indirect flattery, though as Frant had not had anything to do with any Dutch people it was not particularly effectual.

"How can you allow that dirty old swine to call you 'child'!" exclaimed MacGavin.

"Why, he's old enough to be my grandfather!" Frant retorted.

Frant's point of view seemed so fantastic to MacGavin that he laughed a short, harsh laugh.

"My advice is, don't stand any cheek from any nigger," he said.

"He isn't cheeky to *me,*" said Frant. "Only friendly."

And with an irritable grunt from MacGavin the conversation was closed. It seemed extraordinary how full of prejudice the trader was. He was fond of generalizations about the natives which were not even remotely true, such as that they were incapable of gratitude (as if they had such a lot to be grateful for!) and he seemed to have a fixed idea that every black is determined to try and score off every white, under any conditions whatsoever. And when, as occasionally happened, a native addressed him politely in English, it made him so furious that he was no longer master of himself—it seemed to him a suggested assumption of equality between the races!

The MacGavins were amazed at Frant's continued progress, and if they welcomed his popularity with the natives as being good for trade, they resented a little that a stranger and a *rooinek*[1] should be able to beat them at their own game. As to what went on in his

[1]"Red neck." Dutch nickname for Englishman.

mind, they knew and cared nothing. They neither knew nor cared that neither work nor fatigue could prevent him from feeling at times an overwhelming loneliness and an intolerable hunger for experiences which his youth, the climate and the glorious suggestiveness of his surroundings did everything to sharpen, while its satisfaction was firmly forbidden by circumstances—or so it seemed to Frant. Already esteemed by the natives, he valued their good opinion of him too much to take chances with it, and in the background of his thoughts, in spite of the MacGavins, or perhaps because of them, there still presided that tyrannical spectre, the "white man's prestige." What it is to be an ex-prefect of an English public school!

5

It was bound to happen that sooner or later his attention would become centred in some individual out of the hundreds he had to do with in the course of a week. One drowsy afternoon, when he was alone behind the counter and there was nobody in the store but a couple of gossips and a child, a young woman came in rather shyly and stood near the door, hesitating to speak. He couldn't see her very well because of the bright sunshine behind her, but he asked her what she wanted and she made a small purchase.

"Do you remember me?" she asked suddenly in a very quiet voice, looking at him gravely while she spoke.

He was surprised. He didn't remember ever having seen her before, but not wishing to offend her, he said in a slightly ironical tone of voice:

"Oh, when I've once seen people, *just once,* I never forget them."

"Well!" she exclaimed, and uttered a little peal of laughter, partly because she was surprised at his ready answer and amused at his white man's accent; partly because, as a Lembu, she could appreciate irony; and partly because it made her happy that he should talk to her. But as soon as she had uttered that little laugh she grew shamefaced and cast down her eyes with the incomparable grace of a young woman with whom modesty is natural, and not a mere device of coquetry. There was more sadness than usual in her expression, because she had at once understood that he did not remember her, and no woman likes to be forgotten by any young man. She had moved now, and the diffused radiance reflected from the sunburnt hilltop outside shone full upon her through the open door. Her hair was dressed in a cylinder on the crown of her head, stained with red ochre, and stuck with a long bone pin at the broad end of which was a minute incised design; she wore no ornament but a flat necklace of very small blue beads and a few thin bangles and anklets of silver and copper wire. She was dressed in a single piece of dark red stuff which was supported by her pointed young breasts and fastened under the arms—it fell in straight, classical folds almost to her feet, and at the sides it did not quite join but revealed a little her soft flanks. From bearing weights on her head from early childhood she carried herself very erect; she was slender, and an awareness of her graceful nubility gave every movement the value of nature perfectly controlled by art. The fineness of her appearance may have been due to some remote Arab strain in her blood, for though unmistakably negroid, her features were in no sense exaggerated. Her nose, for example, though the nostrils were broad, was very slightly aquiline; her skin was unusually light in tone;

and the modelling of her cheeks and temples could only be described as delicate. Her mouth was good-humoured, her eyes were lustrous, and though one side of her face was marked with a long scar, this only drew closer attention to its beauty.

"You don't come here very often, do you?" said Frant, leaning on the counter, partly because he did not want their conversation to be overheard by anybody else, and partly because he felt somehow weak in the legs. He was in the grip of an unaccustomed shyness, he felt unsure of himself, and so excited that his heart was beating very quickly.

"No," she said, avoiding his eyes. "I don't live very near."

"Where do you live?"

"Down there—down in the valley," she said, extending an exquisite arm and looking out through the open doorway with a vague and dreamy air. He noticed the light colour of the insides of her hands. "Near the river," she said.

"That's not very far away," he said.

"You've been there, then?" she said. "You know the place?"

"No, but I don't think it's very far."

"The hill is long and steep," she said.

Frant suddenly remembered two lines of verse—

> Does the road wind uphill all the way?
> Yes, to the very end.

"I don't know your name," he said.

She looked at him quickly and uttered an exclamation of surprise.

"What's the matter?" he said.

"Why do you want to know my name?" she asked anxiously, for the use of names is important in witchcraft.

"I'm just asking. I just want to know it."

"My name is Seraphina," she said, with a mixture of modesty and seductiveness.

"What?"

"Seraphina."

"How on earth did you get a name like that? It's not a Lembu name! You're not a Christian, are you?"

She laughed, as though the idea of her being a Christian was absolutely ridiculous—which indeed it was.

"No!" she said. "A missionary gave it to me when I was a child. He made magic water on my head and said that Christ wanted me to be called Seraphina."

This time Frant laughed.

"Christ chose well," he said. "But none of your family are Christians, are they?"

"No, it just happened like that."

He laughed again.

"You don't know my name," he said.

"Yes, I do," she said, and pronounced it "Front," and they both laughed.

Just then some noisy customers arrived, and he had to leave her. Suddenly bold, he said:

"Good-bye, go in peace. Please come again. I like talking with you."

He couldn't possibly have dared to speak so directly of his feelings in English, but somehow in Lembu it was easier. Besides, he was stirred as he had never been stirred before.

"Good-bye," she said, smiling. "Stay in peace."

She turned to go, and looked like some virgin in an archaic frieze saying farewell to the world. As for Frant, his hands were trembling, and there was a wild gladness in his heart.

6

His tortures now began in earnest. His dreams and waking thoughts were haunted by the image of the black girl, tantalizing and yet infinitely remote. As his desire for her increased, so did its fulfilment seem to recede. He knew little or nothing of her; he knew little enough of her language and nothing at all of her situation in life. He had been so busy learning to make a profit out of the natives that he had had little chance of learning much about their customs, the way they lived and thought. Supposing, he said to himself, for the sake of argument, this girl were to become my mistress? First of all, is it possible? I am certain that to some extent she reciprocates my feelings, but to what extent? What would she expect of me? What would her family think of her? How would the affair be possible in any case? How am I to communicate with her? And then the MacGavins—presumably his success in his trading depends to some extent on the fact that he is not one of these white men who get mixed up with the natives; and if I were to become the lover of Seraphina, should I not damage his livelihood, besides ruining my own? Whatever happened, everybody would know about it, of course. And how could we live together? Are we to meet furtively in the forest? And have I the right to take this black girl? How can I pretend to myself that I love her? Is it not simply that I want to sleep with her, to touch, kiss, embrace and caress her? He found no answers to his questions, but the very fact that he could ask them was significant. His loneliness and his difficulties had taught him one of the very things that his education had been evolved to prevent—the habit of introspection. He was being Hamletized by circumstances.

Of the numerous forms of anguish which Providence has designed for her creatures few can be more intense than the state of mind and body of a man who is young, sensual by nature and sexually repressed; and who, instead of yielding to the voluptuous provocations of his surroundings, tries to exorcize them with the public-school spirit. When he might well have acted with boldness, he found himself filled with doubts, scruples and equivocations, in addition to the ordinary fears of a lover. And he had nobody to turn to, there was nobody who would say to him what so much needed to be said, "Well, go ahead and have the woman. You will have your pleasure and she will have hers, and you will both be a bit the wiser and possibly the happier for the experience. You will treat her with consideration, because it is your nature to be considerate. You are in no danger of 'going native,' because you aren't the sort of person who goes native. And as for worrying about the MacGavins, do you imagine they worry at all about you, or are likely to do so as long as you rake in the bawbees for them? Be a man! *Carpe diem,* etc." Lacking such an adviser, Frant continued to torment himself.

Each day he got up with Seraphina in his thoughts. Day followed day, and Seraphina did not appear. Round the trading station, meanwhile, Africa unrolled her splendours and her cruelties. The seasons did not assert themselves overmuch. One waited for the rains to stop, or one suddenly noticed buds among thorns. One was aware, all too aware, of the spring, the season of trouble, when more people die, in all countries, than at any other time of the year. The sap was troubled, and the heart with it. All the mimosa trees at Madumbi broke into pollenous clouds of blossom, creaming in a light wind against the cobalt morning sky. Glossy toucans with scarlet bills nested in them, swooping among the boughs, and uttering the most touching mating-cries. Fireflies went through their luminous rites under a coral-tree; crested hoopoes, the colour of cinnamon, pursued their fitful flight across the clear green of dawn; on long, sultry afternoons a group of turkey-bustards, as grave as senators, would plod grumbling across some grassy plateau, looking carefully for the snakes which they could kill at a blow; raindrops pattered down on leaves as large as tables, magenta-veined; and on dry, tranquil afternoons, when the days were still short and some solitary voice was singing far away, an aromatic smell of burning sweet-grass sometimes drifted through the air, the clear light, and the music, and the odour all playing together on the nerves, and inducing an emotion inexpressibly painful and delicious.

When he was free, Frant could not bear to stay near the house: but in roaming about, which became his habit, he was none the less a prisoner. Fettered by scruples and afflicted with a kind of moral impotence, he wandered in a lovely world from which he was barred almost as effectually as if he were literally in a steel cage on wheels. His troubled eyes turned to the natural scenes around him but found no rest in them, and his repression might just have gone on increasing in morbidity had not a number of unexpected things happened.

Now the arrival of Frant at Madumbi had put a check on certain of MacGavin's habits. At one time, when the Scotchman was alone in the store, in the afternoons for instance, when the weather was hot or wet and business slack, or when his wife was busy in the house, he had not been disinclined for a little amusement at the expense of some of the coarser Lembu girls who came to deal with him. Joking with them in order to try and convert their apprehensive titters into abandoned fits of giggling, he had sometimes gone so far as to pinch their breasts and slap their behinds in order to win their confidence. The bolder ones had quickly taken advantage of his susceptibilities in order to try and get something for nothing, and pointing to this or that, had copied the horseleech's daughters and cried, "Give, give!" When MacGavin so far overcame his sense of commercial fitness as to give them a string of beads or a damaged jews' harp, they immediately asked for more, determined to lose nothing for the want of asking. He would then refuse, but they would not go away, leaning on the counter and repeating their requests over and over again in a whining voice until he began to fear that his wife might come in. Whereupon he would suddenly fly into a raging temper. Purple in the face and trembling with anger, he would hammer on the counter with his fists and utter violent threats and abuse, and if that did not frighten the young women away he would hustle them out. One or two in particular loved to provoke him to the utmost, and then fly screaming with laughter down the road, their large naked breasts wobbling and flapping and tears running out of their eyes. But he had grown tired of these scenes, and even before Frant's arrival had abstained from inducing them. With the arrival of Frant he determined to behave himself, at least in Frant's presence, as he wanted the young man to concentrate on business and not begin his stay by getting obsessed with black women. But now that he had found Frant what he would have called "steady," he was about to revert to his old habits, and it cannot be said that his wife, that freckled virago, with her ever-increasing indigestion and her less and less amiable moods, acted exactly as a strong deterrent.

But the first time Frant saw MacGavin behaving familiarly with a gross fat girl it gave him a shock—not because he was prudish by nature, but because it was something he was not used to, and the discovery that MacGavin did not always practise what he preached seemed likely to modify his own behaviour. The thought immediately occurred to him that MacGavin might abuse the modesty of Seraphina, and the idea that the trader's bloodshot and slightly protuberant eye might focus itself upon her natural elegance produced in him a most violent reaction. He said nothing. After MacGavin's wench had departed he came up to Frant and said:

"You'll excuse my saying so, Frant, but don't you feel you want a woman sometimes?"

The effect of this remark upon the young man was extraordinary.

"I do," he answered at once in a quiet voice, "but not a black one."

And he launched into a flood of abuse! He said that he would rather do anything than touch a black woman; he said that they were dirty, that they stank, that they were no better than animals; he said that the blacks and whites were in his opinion races apart, and that on no account should they mix in any way; he said that white men ought to be respected by black ones, and that that could only be possible if they treated them as inferiors, absolute inferiors. He grew white with passion and the heat of his denunciation. His words almost choked him.

MacGavin was astonished beyond measure. He did not know whether to take it all as an attack on himself, or whether Frant had not gone a little out of his mind.

"Well, you do surprise me," he said, in what was meant to be a sarcastic tone of voice. "You've always given me the impression of being a bit too fond of the niggers, and treating them a bit too much as if they were really human beings."

"I get a bit sick of the sight of them at times," said Frant in a much quieter voice, not in the least meaning and indeed hardly knowing what he said. Then he turned away, and the incident was closed, except that MacGavin confided to his wife that he thought Frant was getting a bit restless, and perhaps needed a change or a holiday.

"He can surely wait till Christmas," she said in an aggrieved whisper, for the walls of the house were thin. "We could take him away with us then for a couple of days. But if you ask me, he's unsociable and disagreeable by nature."

"Don't forget that the takings showed another increase last month," said MacGavin.

"That's just why I don't want him to go away now," she said.

It was a brilliant moonlight night, as quiet as the grave, and in his little room Frant was asking himself what on earth could have made him say a whole lot of things he did not mean, what on earth had made him lose control of himself. He felt he had come to the end of everything, that he could not bear this impossible kind of life any longer, and would have to go away. His head was hot, he could not sleep, and he rolled uneasily on his bed. Suddenly, somewhere in a tree, a galago began to scream. Its screams filled the naked air and the heavy silence, the African silence; scream after scream, like prophecies of endless and unthinkable supernatural horrors, uttered by a furred and furtive little creature, hidden large-eyed among moon-drenched branches. Frant got up from his bed and drew back the curtains on a world chalk-white like the face of a clown or pierrot, silent and heartless, and with a sense of terror, of madness almost, let them fall back again.

And the next day Seraphina appeared.

7

There she stood, balancing on her head a light bundle tied with grass. Her arms hung by her side, and when she turned her head authority and resignation, patience and sensibility were in the movement.

> Nowhere but here did ever meet
> Sweetness so sad, sadness so sweet.

Before the coming of the white man the Lembus lived under a system of strict discipline and formality, which did not, however, fail to allow various channels for the various passions of the Lembu heart. It was a system which recognized that some of life's best rewards are best appreciated by those who have not been able to win them too easily. In those days they were all warriors under a mad military autocrat, who believed that too easy an access to heterosexual pleasures might impair the morale and efficiency of his regiments; he trammelled them with a hundred taboos and would not allow them to marry young, while adultery was punished by pushing the guilty parties over separate cliffs of no small height. As for the girls and women, they had a most clearly prescribed course of life, and each stage in their development was made to conform to strict rules. The later relaxation of tribal ethics, for which the white man offered little substitute but calico drawers and hymns A. and M., rapidly weakened the fibre of the race. But it still happened that there were members of it who managed to live lives not wholly devoid of order and dignity, there were still families "of the old school" who from the force of heredity or a kind of good breeding managed to do homage to the ghosts of the beliefs of their forefathers. And such a family was Seraphina's. Both its ancient pride and its present obscurity had gone to the making of her features, and its vigour and vitality as well.

They were alone together in the space before the counter.

"Greeting, Seraphina."

"Greeting, my white-man."

Frant could hardly speak, he was so agitated. His heart seemed to fill the whole of his breast with its leaping, and he could scarcely recognize the sound of his own voice as he asked:

"Why have you been so long returning?"

"Do I know?" she said. "Perhaps I was afraid."

She had reason to be afraid—of gossip, of her family, of herself, of Frant, of consequences. With an unhurried movement she took down the bundle from her head and laid it on the floor without bending her knees.

Then she untied the grass ropes that held it together and began to open it.

"A snakeskin!" said Frant.

It was a broad snakeskin, and crackled stiffly as it was unrolled. She put her foot on the tail to hold it down while Frant unrolled it. Fully opened, it was at least fifteen feet long, and a great part of it was quite two feet in width. It was the skin of a python, and there were two large rents in the middle of the back as if a spear had killed it. It was not often that the natives traded such things.

"How much are you asking for it?" said Frant in a caressing voice most unsuitable for a commercial transaction.

"I am not selling it," said Seraphina without looking at him. "I am giving it."

"Giving it! To me?"

"To you."

"I thank you very much indeed," he said. In Lembu the same word means to thank and to praise.

There was a pause, then he said:

"Where did it come from? Who killed it?"

"I was hoeing in a maize-field near the river, and it disturbed me. Besides, two of the children were with me. So I killed it."

"You killed it? What with?"

"With my hoe."

When he had got over his astonishment he said, his face shining with admiration:

"But you mustn't give it to me. I must give you some money for it."

"I don't want money," she said, and looked at him with troubled, almost angry eyes.

"I thank you very much," he said again, with the

humility and the pride of a lover, and hardly knowing what he was doing he caught hold of her and kissed her on the mouth.

She uttered a cry of surprise and sprang away from him. She simply did not understand him, and was afraid. Natives do not make love as we do. She laughed, just a trifle hysterically.

"What are you doing?" she said.

"What's the matter?" said Frant, approaching again. "I won't hurt you."

"How do I know?" she said.

And he would have answered "Because I love you" (which would have been so hard to say in English and was so easy in Lembu) had they not just at that moment been interrupted.

"Come again soon," Frant said hurriedly. "I want to see you."

And he stooped down and rolled up his snakeskin. When he had finished she was gone.

In the evening he nailed up the skin on the walls of his bedroom. It was so long that it took up the whole of two sides. And very late, before putting out his light, he lay in bed looking at it. Like a banner it hung there to celebrate the intensity of his happiness; it hung like a trophy—the skin of the dragon of his misery, killed by Seraphina as she hoed her father's field of maize.

The next day at noon Mrs. MacGavin said:

"Oh, Mr. Frant, that skin in your room—it gave me such a nasty turn when I went in there this morning!"

"Isn't it a beauty? You don't mind my putting it up, I suppose?"

"Oh, *I* don't mind," she said, "though I couldn't bear to have such a thing over *my* bed. If there's one thing

I can't stand it's snakes, alive or dead."

It was nearly Christmas time and the MacGavins told Frant they thought a holiday would do him good, and that they would take him with them to the nearest town. The trading station would be closed for three days, and would be quite safe in the care of the servants. They were extremely surprised when he refused—not because he wanted to help to guard their property, but because the nearest town, of which he had had a few glimpses, did not attract him, and because he had other plans in mind. He felt no inclination to attend the gymkhana or the dance at which, in an atmosphere of false bonhomie and commonplace revelry, the white inhabitants tried annually to forget for a time all about the white man's burden. The MacGavins thought him almost mad for refusing.

"Whatever will you do with yourself?" they said.

"I shall be quite happy," he said.

They felt that something was amiss.

"What, are you 'going native' or something?" cried MacGavin. "You need a change, you know."

He always did his work well, and on account of his natural air of independence they both respected and feared him a little. They gave up trying to argue with him and murmured to each other instead. Then on Christmas Eve the Ford car, newly washed, went rattling away, leaving behind it a cloud of blue smoke and a stink, both of which soon vanished. After the MacGavins had gone Frant felt greatly relieved. It was such a blessing to be free to see and hear what was going on round him instead of being haunted by those harsh stupid voices, that sour red face and that pasty drab one, which had already got on his nerves. Unlike most white men alone in native territories, he had neither a gun nor alcohol in his possession. He did not feel the want of them. For the first time in his life he was to spend Christmas by himself. There would be no exchange of presents; no heavy meals; no forced gaiety; no stuck-up relations. His time, for once, was his own.

8

On Christmas morning he stood on the veranda and stretched his arms, filled with a delicious sense of anticipation. Then he felt in his pocket for a cigarette, and failing to find one took a key and went to fetch a packet from the store. The atmosphere in that building, so closely shuttered at holiday times, was more than oppressive. It was a brilliant morning, and the heat of the sun on the corrugated-iron roof made the interior like an oven. He found some cigarettes, and paused a moment in the doorway to look round at the place where his days were spent. He shuddered slightly, then went out, locking the door behind him. Enjoying his cigarette, and the sun, and the shade, and the peacefulness of not having to look at *those* faces, of not having to listen to *those* voices, he took a path which led through a deserted garden, on the site of the first settlement at Madumbi, towards the forest. In the old garden the foundations of the earlier house remained, but the whole place was now a tangle of vegetation. The hardier growths had survived, and some still withstood the wildings that struggled to oust them. Thickets of ragged junipers and berberis made a forbidding fence which few ever sought to penetrate, and indeed the natives thought the place haunted. Snake apples, those cruel trees, with every bud a barb, and every fruit an ugly bulb filled with dry and poisonous powder, extended their angry foliage over crumbling brickwork. Rankly growing mimosas split with their coarse-grained roots what had once been a path, and month by month in the summer raised their smooth bark and feathery foliage perceptibly higher into the air. A solitary yucca, survivor of several, had produced a single spire thickly hung with white bells, which the mountain wind shook together as if they were made of paper. Tendrils of Christ-thorn put out here and there a few sticky scarlet flowers, and passion flowers hung in unexpected places, in the grass or high up among the junipers, together with the oval, dented granadillas into which they too would change.

Leaving the garden, Frant followed the path to the forest. Then, forcing his way through the undergrowth, parting lianas and monkey-ropes, breaking cobwebs so thick that their breaking was audible, being scratched by thorns, sinking up to the ankles in leaf-mould, he reached a glade he had been to before in times of unhappiness. In the middle of the glade there was a shallow stream of very clear water gliding over sand, and it was sheltered by the vast indigenous trees from the heat of the day.

Here, as he had done before, he threw himself on the breast of earth, surrendering himself to the trees, the water and the quietness. He lay on his back and looked up through half-closed eyes at the topmost branches, watching the fall of a leaf, hearing the call of a bird, the lapse of water, and the thin cries of insects. Under his hand lay a skeleton leaf, over his head a few epiphytic orchids lolled their greenish mouths open over the ancient, rotting bough that gave them life, and at times the wind brought a hint of the perfume of a hidden syringa or laurustinus. A clump of clivia lilies were blooming in deep shadow—they were living and dying in secret, without argument, and untroubled by eyes and voices. A humming-bird appeared from nowhere, and poising itself on the wing before every open flower, whirred there like a moth, gleamed like a jewel, darting its thin curved beak, as sharp as a needle, into each for honey. Nature is inevitable—this stone lies on that one, because it must; fronds uncurl from the hairy trunk of a tree-fern; each new growth and decay seems spontaneous and impersonal; there is a kind of harmony of conflict, and it may have been some sense of that harmony that brought Frant to a decision he might, had he not been so solitary, have taken long before. He was roused. He would act boldly. He would give up caution, discretion, doubt, hesitation, he would forget all about the MacGavins, the trade, the future, he would give up all fear of gossip, of crisis, of reputation, he would break through the bars of his prison. He would go that very day down into the valley and visit the home of Seraphina. He would behave with candour, he would be open in his dealings. He had proved in commerce that he was "a white man"; he would now be bold, and prove it in love.

Such was his resolution, but the enterprise was not entirely successful. He set out early in the afternoon, carrying a camera, and a stick in case he should meet snakes. He walked as fast as if he were in a more temperate climate, and felt the heat. The first part of the journey took him across an undulating plateau, through country much like that immediately round Madumbi. But after about an hour he came to the top of a hill which marked the end of an escarpment ("The hill is long and steep," Seraphina had said) and he began to follow a downward path winding among rocks and thorn trees. This brought him out on to a platform or small tableland and before him lay suddenly open an immense view. Directly below lay the valley of the Umgazi river, where Seraphina lived, and he sat down under a bean tree to rest and to gaze at the scene.

Somebody was coming up the hill. It was a young man. He was a typical Lembu, naked except for a fur codpiece and some bead ornaments, upright, slender and vigorous. He came striding along, singing joyfully as he went, glistening with oil and sweat, his movements full of natural pride. He was holding a tiny shield, a stick and a knobkerrie in one hand, and in the other a large black cotton Brummagem umbrella, to shelter himself from the sun. When he saw Frant he looked surprised and then saluted him with a large and cheerful gesture. Frant knew him by sight and responded cordially.

"What are you doing here?" said the young man. "Are you out on holiday?"

"Yes," said Frant, "I am just out on holiday."

"Why aren't you riding?"

"I have no horse."

"But white men don't walk!"

"I like walking."

The native expressed surprise.

"Is that a camera?" he said.

"Yes, it's a camera."

"Will you take my picture?"

"All right. Go and stand over there. But you must close your umbrella."

"What, must I close my umbrella?"

So Frant stood under the bean tree with his feet among the open pods and little black-and-scarlet beans that had fallen from it, and took a photograph of the native, who stood smiling and glistening in the sun.

"Do you know me?" said the young man.

"Yes," said Frant.

"Do you know Seraphina?"

Frant was startled.

"Yes," he said, unable to conceal his surprise.

"She is my sister."

"What! You're her brother?"

"Yes."

"Fancy that!"

"Seraphina likes you," said her brother. But, thought Frant, is he really her brother? The natives used such terms somewhat loosely. Was this perhaps a rival trying to warn him off? He put the thought out of his mind, for the native was so friendly. "Seraphina likes you," he said. But in Lembu the same word means to like and to love, so perhaps he meant "Seraphina loves you."

"I like Seraphina," said Frant.

"It is not good," said the native, "when a white man likes a black girl."

There was no condemnation in his tone, no threat, no high moral purpose. He smiled as he spoke what he no doubt regarded as a self-obvious truism.

"Why?" said Frant.

"Do I know? It is so."

Frant wanted to say "Would you be angry if your sister married a white man?" but he had no wish to suggest any such thing. And it seemed too crude to say "Would you be angry if your sister slept with a white man?" So he said:

"We are all people."

"Yes, we are all people, but we are different."

"I like natives," said Frant.

"I know you do. But you live in Lembuland, and there are no white people near here for you to like."

This was really unanswerable.

"There are Mr. MacGavin and his wife," said Frant.

Seraphina's brother (if he was Seraphina's brother) laughed.

"Nobody likes *them!*" he said.

"What is your name?" said Frant.

"Me? Umlilwana."

"And where do you live?"

"Down there," said Umlilwana, pointing to the valley.

The river Umgazi, which seemed to consist mostly of a broad bed of stones, with only a small stream of water in the middle, curved in a gigantic S-shaped bend just below where they stood. And on some slightly raised ground in one of the curves of the S were a group of grass domes, which were huts, and a cattle kraal made of thorn trees and brushwood, and a few patches of maize and millet and sweet potatoes. And that was the home of Seraphina. It looked the most peaceful place in the world.

"Will you take me there?" said Frant.

"Take you there! What would you do there?"

"I want to see your home. I want to see Seraphina."

"Seraphina is not there."

"Not there! Where is she?"

"She has gone on a journey to the mountains for several days with our mother and father to see our cousins. There's nobody down there but an old woman and some children."

"Oh," said Frant, and was silent a moment. "I am sorry," he said then. "I wanted to see Seraphina."

And suddenly everything seemed utterly remote. The view was like a view in a dream. Seraphina (*could* that be her name?) seemed only an idea and her cousins like characters in a myth. And even the friendly smiling Umlilwana seemed utterly strange and unapproachable.

"Yes, I am sorry," Frant repeated in a dull voice. "But I should like some day to visit your home and take photographs of Seraphina—and of all your family."

Umlilwana was a little suspicious of this, but he said Frant would be welcome.

"Will you do something for me?" said Frant. "Will you come and tell me when Seraphina returns? Tell Seraphina I want to see her. Tell her I want to see her again."

"All right," said Umlilwana in English and with great affability. It was about all the English he knew.

"Umlilwana, you are my friend."

"All right, will you give me some cigarettes?"

Frant smiled, and gave him all he had. Umlilwana was loud in thanks.

Some children could be seen playing near Seraphina's kraal. They looked as small as ants. The distant mountains looked infinitely blue and remote, with the shadows of a few light clouds patterning their peaks. There was nothing to do but to return to Madumbi.

9

Frant returned to Madumbi. So, a couple of days later, did the MacGavins, both with a touch of righteous indignation at Frant's oddness in not having gone with them, and Mrs. MacGavin with more than a touch of dyspepsia. Life then resumed its usual course. But things were not quite the same. First of all, Frant was in a far more cheerful frame of mind. Not only had he begun to act with some initiative, not only had he seen Seraphina's home and made friends with her brother, but he had told somebody of his love for her. As soon as she returned he meant to bring matters to a head, even though he and she were "different." And if her continued absence was a great trial to his patience, he got up every morning in hopes of a visit and news from Umlilwana in the course of the day. But day followed day, and Umlilwana did not appear. Frant played with the idea of sending him a message, but as it would have to be a verbal one, he thought it more prudent not to do so. And when he once ventured to inquire about Umlilwana, and to ask if he were really Seraphina's brother, the people he spoke to said they had never heard of either of them. And at night he lay naked and sweating on his bed, tortured continually with the image of Seraphina, remembering her gestures, her "sadness so sweet," and the touch of her flesh.

"Frant should have gone away with us," MacGavin remarked to his wife. "He's quite liverish now at times."

"This weather's enough to make anybody liverish," said she. "I always did say that January was the worst month of the year. It's bilious weather. But it's not his liver, if you ask me, it's his nerves."

January was certainly a bad month at Madumbi, and that year it was more trying than ever. There had been no rain for weeks, and things were beginning to look parched. The heat was dry and intense. And then, day after day, clouds would collect in the morning and accumulate in the afternoon, thunder was occasionally heard and once even a few drops of rain fell in the dust, as if a few devils had spat from a great height. Every morning seemed to promise a thunderstorm, and one began to imagine how the earth would smell after rain, and how cool the air would be, and how the flying ants would come out in the twilight, but every evening the clouds dispersed and left a hot moon to glare down on the veld, or the glittering arrogance of the stars. And every morning Frant said to himself, "Umlilwana will come, or Seraphina herself," but every evening he found himself alone again, exhausted and restless. Even the natives, in their anxiety about their crops, were beginning to get on one another's nerves. The air seemed charged with electricity, it seemed to brace one's very muscles against a shock which was not forthcoming, and to leave them at once taut and tired. Even MacGavin took to glancing often at the sky, at the great cumulus clouds that hung in it all the afternoon, and he would say, "It'll be serious if something doesn't happen soon."

It was like waiting for an earthquake, a revolution, the day of judgment almost. There was an awful mixture of certainty that something was going to happen, and of uncertainty as to when it would happen. "We only want a storm to clear the air," Mrs. MacGavin repeated every day until Frant almost felt that he could murder her. The sweat ran down inside his shirt, his overheated blood inflamed his overstrained imagination, he found it more and more difficult to sleep and eat. Trade grew slack, because few could endure to climb up the slopes to Madumbi, and when the store was empty it was far less tolerable than when it was full. The morning sun beat down on the corrugated iron and the interior grew so hot that it failed to cool down during the night. Strange stories came in—that some grass had caught fire simply from the heat of the sun shining through an empty bottle, and several huts had been burnt in consequence; that a young crocodile had come right up one of the little tributaries of the Umgazi and had been found less than a mile from Madumbi itself, an occurrence never before known; and that a native woman had been arrested for killing a new-born baby with six fingers on one hand, in the belief that this deformity was keeping the rain away. Where was Umlilwana? Where was Seraphina? "I will wait till next Sunday," said Frant to himself, "and if neither of them has come by then I shall go down to the kraal itself on the pretext of wanting to take photographs." But he did not have to wait till Sunday, for the weather broke.

The worst day of all was the fourteenth of the month.

"Well, this is the worst we've had yet," said Mrs. MacGavin at supper time.

"You've said that for the last four days," observed her husband.

All the doors and windows were wide open. The sky was completely overcast and nothing was stirring but the moths and other insects which flew in from the garden and bumped against the paper lampshade, or against the glass which covered "The Confession," or fell into the soup, the powder from their wings mingling with the film of grease which already covered that liquid. The rays of lamplight lay on the creepers of the veranda itself and on the path, but beyond them was utter silence and hot, heavy darkness.

"Hark! Was that thunder?" said Mrs. MacGavin.

"You always say that at supper time," remarked her husband.

"It *was* thunder," she said, her head on one side,

as she pushed a stray wisp of hair out of her eye.

Yes, it *was* thunder. They all heard it. Low, continuous thunder.

"That's up in the mountains," said MacGavin. "It's a bad sign if it begins up there. If there *is* a storm, it'll probably miss us altogether . . . Ah, did you see the lightning? Yes, that's where it is. I bet it's pouring up there already. And I don't like a dry storm. It's much more dangerous. More likely to strike the trees."

Frant's heart was beating loud and fast as if in anticipation of some personal, not a meteorological event. He walked alone to the bottom of the garden and stood there watching the play of lightning in the distance, but it did not seem much more than on previous nights. He came in and tried to read a paper, lighted several cigarettes in succession, throwing one or two away half-smoked, paced up and down in the garden, glancing up at the darkness, and then retired to his room where he lay on his bed without undressing. His hands were clenched, the nails dug into the palms, and he was conscious of little but the beating of his heart. He couldn't hear the MacGavins talking anywhere, or any natives, and had lost all sense of the time. He put out his light, and like a convict without a crime, in a prison that was not locked, for a sentence of indeterminate duration, he just lay there sweating.

At last he got up and went to the window. The moon was out again. It was almost full, and stood high in the sky, flooding the landscape with light. To the south, vast banks of cloud were ranged above the forest, and among them, now and then, a worm of lightning played, followed by a distant roll of thunder. Not a leaf seemed to be stirring, when he noticed that a light breeze was rising and feathering the tops of the distant trees. Very soon the tops of the mimosas near the house bowed, lightly swaying towards the moon, and a tremor ran through the grass as if an invisible hand had stroked it. The wind rose, the clouds towered and toppled upwards, the moon was caught in a web of flying mist, the thunder grew louder, and the flashes of lightning more frequent. A greenish light seemed to emanate from the moon, and as the sky grew more heavily loaded, the forest, by contrast, appeared more ethereal, the heavy boscage and the trunks of the huge indigenous trees appearing in great detail, all dry and luminous and lurid, the foliage beginning to churn and writhe slowly on the topmost boughs. The tenseness of the atmosphere, the expectancy of nature, and the way in which the whole landscape, the very buildings and their shadows, seemed to take part in the great symphony of the impending storm, combined to produce an effect so dramatic as to seem almost supernatural.

The rolling of the thunder was now continuous. All the mountain country was overhung with the incessant play of sheet-lightning, as if a curtain of fire, continually agitated by unseen forces, hung over half the world. The wind began to howl round the house, leaves and twigs to fly from the trees, a pile of timber was blown over, and the moon was half hidden in a swirl of clouds. Chains and forks of lightning, steely-blue and sulphurous red, larger and brighter and more frequent than Frant had ever seen, lighted everything with a continuous, shaken glare. Thunder pealed almost overhead, phalanxes of cloud advanced like avenging armies, the house shook, the windows rattled, and he put his hand to his burning and throbbing head. His pulses raced, sweat poured down his face and body, and he felt as if his veins would burst. Suddenly he caught sight of a white horse, which had broken loose from heaven knows where, and was careering madly, its mane and tail flying, its halter trailing, along the slope of the nearest hill. It seemed a creature of fire as it tossed its head, swerved at sudden obstacles, and galloped up to the ridge. There for a moment it stood, quivering with fear and exertion in the quivering glare of the lightning, and then, made splendid by freedom, disappeared from view.

"I can't stay in the house an instant longer!" Frant said aloud to himself, and taking up an electric torch, he stepped out into the garden. A strong refreshing breeze was blowing, but not a drop of rain had fallen. "It looks as though MacGavin was right—the storm seems to have missed us altogether . . ." He wondered what on earth he had brought the torch for, since the lightning was quivering incessantly, like a network of luminous nerves.

"Is that you, Frant?"

It was MacGavin calling from the house.

"Yes. I can't sleep. I'm going for a walk. It's much fresher out now."

"A walk! At this time! Don't go far. It's risky. And if it *should* come on to rain . . ."

"I'll be all right, thanks. Good night."

He disappeared from view, and instinctively found himself taking the path he had taken on Christmas Day. He was frightened of the night, of losing his way, of the storm. He had at first no thought of going far, but when he paused to try and calculate how far he had already come he was almost as afraid to turn back as to go on, so he went on. He had got an idea that he must get to the bean tree, and he kept telling himself that it was not really very far. The wind was behind him now, and its freshness gave him energy. The glare and racket of the storm grew no less—it now seemed to be everywhere except immediately overhead. He hurried on, stumbling now and again, for the path was in places rough and narrow. He saw lights once or twice but did not meet a soul. And back at Madumbi MacGavin had grown anxious about him.

Before he came to the escarpment there was a loud detonation just overhead, and it began to rain. He had come too far now to turn back, so he hurried on, vaguely imagining that he would ask for shelter at Seraphina's. Near the top of the hill he realized that the worst of the weather was in front of him. The lightning revealed a thick grey veil of rain beyond the valley, and he could hear a tremendous steady downpour in the distance. The nearer he got to the top the louder the tumult grew, and he thought, "The river must be a lot fuller by now than when I last saw it." He was going downhill at last, but not so fast as he wanted, for it was raining pretty hard now and the paths were getting slippery. A feeling of terror seized him. He felt that he would never get down to the valley, that the storm would beat him, that it was no good thinking of turning back.

There was no doubt as to what he could hear now. The river must be in flood. And he suddenly thought, would the kraal be safe? Hardly . . . He was running now, to reach the bean tree. He was soaked to the skin, and his feet kept slipping. He missed the way twice and found it again, and then, waiting for the lightning to show him where he was, he found he was only a few yards from the tree.

And just at that moment, exactly as before, he saw a man coming towards him. Only this time the man was running. And this time it was not Umlilwana he saw. And this time he was terrified.

The man didn't see Frant until he almost ran into him, and he was too frightened.

"Au!" cried a familiar voice. *"Umtwana ka Kwini!* Child of the Queen! What are you doing here? Where are you going? Child! My child! Have you *seen?* Look, look!"

He dragged Frant over the slippery rocks to the very edge of the tableland.

"Look!" he cried.

A prolonged flash of lightning lit up the whole valley with a tremulous, pale violet glare like the light of some hellish arc-lamp, and in a few seconds Frant had understood. Gone was the S-shaped bend, gone were the grassy domes, the kraal and little fields! There was nothing where they had been but a gigantic swirl of greyish water, in which trunks of trees could be seen travelling, spinning and half raising themselves above the surface like animate things.

"Seraphina!" cried Frant. "Do you know Seraphina?"

He had caught hold of the little old man, who was shivering with fear and cold and seemed the only reality left in the world.

"Seraphina!" cried Frant. "Do you know her? Did she came back? Was she at home?"

"She was at home for two weeks, *umtwana,"* said the old man, shaking like a leaf. "The cattle are drowned!" he cried in the voice of Job and of Lear. "The houses, the people—all are drowned!"

"Drowned?" cried Frant, shining his torch full in the old man's face. "Why? Why are they drowned?"

"The water came like a wall, my child," said the old man, and the torchlight made the raindrops running down his face look as if it was covered with tears. He was shivering violently from top to toe, and his old tunic clung to his skin.

"Umlilwana," said Frant. "Was Umlilwana her brother?"

"Umlilwana?" said the old man. "Umlilwana wasn't her brother! She was going to marry Umlilwana."

In the lightning-glare he saw Frant's face.

"All is finished!" he cried, putting out a black and bony claw, as if to defend himself from some unknown danger. In Lembu the same word means to be finished or to be destroyed. "Are you bewitched?"

Yes, all was finished, all was destroyed. Already the rolling of the thunder was increasing in volume, but the roar of the flood seemed to grow louder, and the rain was coming down like whips of ice and steel. It was like the coming of the deluge itself. It was like the end of the world.

Something in Frant urged him to leave the old man and run down the hill and plunge into those maddened waters and lose himself, but something stronger told him that he must return to Madumbi, to the store, to the MacGavins, to the making of a livelihood, to the fashioning of a way of life, to a roll of undeveloped negatives, and to a python skin nailed to a wall like a banner, with two large holes in it cut by a girl with a hoe.

"I must go back!" he said to the old man, and gripped his shoulder for an instant. Then he made off in the direction of Madumbi, flashing the torch on the path. The old man called after him to take care, but he was at once out of earshot in the downpour. After he had stumbled a short way one spasmodic sob escaped from him, and he began to run.